It's Not You It's Him

SOPHIE RANALD

Published by Bookouture in 2019

An imprint of Storyfire Ltd.
Carmelite House
50 Victoria Embankment
London EC4Y 0DZ

www.bookouture.com

ISBN: 978-1-78681-930-7
eBook ISBN: 978-1-78681-929-1

BOOKS BY SOPHIE RANALD

Sorry Not Sorry

It's Not
You
It's
Him

For my dearest aunt Carmel, with so much love

Chapter One

New Year's Eve. If you ask me, it needs to take a long, hard look at itself. I mean, seriously. It has to be the most overrated night of the year, right? Worse even than Valentine's Day. Actually, maybe not – I'd be lying if I said I was feeling much enthusiasm for Valentine's Day either. But at least that was several weeks away – what felt like an eternity in the future. First of all, I had to get through a night of enforced jollity, bucketloads of prosecco and talk of new beginnings.

I didn't want new beginnings. I wanted my old beginning back.

But still, I'd accepted the invitation to see the New Year in quietly, having a nice chilled-out party with my housemates Charlotte and Adam and some of Charlotte's friends. It had seemed like a good idea at the time, because it would be only a matter of days until my boyfriend Renzo got back from spending the Christmas break with his family in Rome, and we could pick up our six-month-old relationship and move it on to the next level.

Things had been going so well: we'd been spending most weekends together, and I'd been staying over at his flat a couple of nights every week, too. When we weren't together, he texted and called and told me he missed me. I was quite sure that if we'd been together just a couple of months longer, he'd have invited me to spend Christmas with his family, and I'd have got to meet the sisters and nieces and nephews he talked about with so much affection. As it was, I'd felt sure that we were ready to make our relationship official – whatever that meant. He might even ask me to move in with him, I'd thought in my soppier moments, imagining myself waking up next to him every morning, cooking us dinner every evening (not that I was much of a cook) and even ironing his shirts for him (this is not as 1950s housewife as it sounds – although I know it makes me sound like a freak – I love ironing).

But things tend not to work out the way you plan.

Just ten days before, I'd been the happiest I've ever been. Now, I was probably the most miserable.

I kept replaying *that* evening in my mind, like a particularly annoying ad on the telly, except I couldn't fast-forward past it or get up and make a cup of tea or go for a wee.

When I closed my eyes to go to sleep at night and as soon as I opened them in the morning, and at random moments in between, there it was, playing on a loop in my brain, every detail perfect. I could see myself in my sparkling red dress, surrounded by Renzo's colleagues at their end-of-year party, except the rest of them might as well not even have been there, because my focus was all on him, pinpoint-sharp. I could see his face, a couple of inches above my own even though I'm tall and I was wearing five-inch heels. I could see the tenderness in his hazel eyes, and smell the cologne he was wearing, clean and leathery like the inside of an expensive car. I could feel his arms around me as we danced, the whole length of his body pressed against mine, the muscles in his back and shoulders moving smoothly under my hands.

Renzo, who made me feel like all my Christmases had come at once, all my dreams come true. Tall, dark, handsome, successful Renzo, who gave me butterflies in my stomach and made me weak at the knees. Renzo, who would've been every cliché of the perfect boyfriend if he hadn't been real, and mine. Until he wasn't…

I could hear his voice as he said the words I'd been longing to hear, and feel the whisper of his breath on my cheek.

'Tansy,' he said. 'I think I'm in love with you.'

And I could remember, vividly, the second of hesitation, the make-or-break moment, the opportunity to not fuck it all up beyond repair, before I replied, 'I love you too. But there's something I need to tell you.'

After that, the video stops playing. The ad break is over. Time to return to the main event. I don't know whether it's because it was all so horrible, so chaotic and confusing, that I just can't properly remember what I said to him and what he said back. Or it might be that it's so raw and brutal that I've locked it away in a place deep in my mind where I'll never go.

But I know the outcome. I told him the truth that had been gnawing at me from inside since the day we met, casting a shadow over my happiness – and then he dumped me. Hard and spectacularly, in front of everyone. Like tearing my heart out from under the scarlet sequins, chucking it across the room and stomping on it.

And it was all my fault.

Now, what had been both the worst and the best year of my life was almost over. I was surrounded by Charlotte's friends and the detritus of crisps and dips, pizza boxes and prosecco bottles, and the memory played through my mind again and again, and only the first chimes of Big Ben ringing in the New Year jerked me out of it.

Everyone was hugging and kissing and clinking glasses. Even Adam, usually paralysed with shyness around people he didn't know well, was smiling, and he squeezed my shoulder and asked if I was okay.

'I'm fine,' I said. I'd been saying that a lot, but it didn't make it true. 'Happy New Year! It's going to be a good one for you, I just know it.'

That exact moment, when the chimes are over, the toasts drunk, the old year officially seen on its way, is probably the most depressing part of a depressing evening. It's also a tipping point: do you do the sensible thing and go to bed, quitting while you're ahead? Or do you fill your glass and press on, wringing every last drop of fun out of a night that's not got much to spare?

Charlotte's friends were a pretty sensible bunch, and they opted for something in between. We all slumped on the sofas by the telly, watching the crowds on the Embankment by the River Thames and the last blaze of the fireworks display. Someone opened another bottle of bubbly. Someone else found what was left of the pizza in the kitchen and dumped the boxes on the coffee table.

'So,' Charlotte's friend Maddy said, 'New Year's resolutions. Come on, what's everyone going to achieve this year? It's a massive one for you, Charlotte.'

'I know, right?' Charlotte gazed up adoringly at Xander, her new boyfriend, and he gazed adoringly back at her. The two of them were so loved-up and happy, it was almost impossible not to smile when you looked at them. They'd only got together a couple of weeks before, on the same night Renzo dumped me, in fact, in a particularly cruel twist of fate.

'We need to get our travel plans nailed down,' Xander said. 'And then we're going to see the world.'

'And then when we get back, I suppose I'll need to find another job,' Charlotte replied, ever practical. She'd already made me and Adam promise to keep her room empty for two months, while she paid the rent, just in case she decided she couldn't stand travelling and had to come back home.

'I'm going to lose a stone if it kills me,' said one of Charlotte's other friends, and there was a chorus of, 'Oh, no, you don't need to, you look amazing.'

'I'm hoping to put on weight,' Maddy said. 'A couple of stone, to be exact. And then lose it again.'

Everyone looked blank, and then Charlotte said, 'Oh my God, you're going to try for a baby!'

I took a huge swig of my drink. I know it makes me the worst person in the world, but how hard is it to be happy for other people when your whole life has crumbled and you can't see a way to put it back together? I looked at Maddy's husband's arm around her shoulders, and Xander and Charlotte's intertwined fingers, and felt like I was bleeding inside.

'Well, I lost eleven stone the week before Christmas,' said another of the women. 'In the form of that useless, commitment-phobic waste of space William. So my New Year's resolution is to get out there and have fun. Tinder, here I come! Tansy, we could maybe do it together? Compare notes and stuff?'

I replied, 'Thanks, that's really sweet of you. But I've already made my New Year's resolution. I'm going to get Renzo back.'

There was a sudden pause in the conversation. Everyone looked at me. The expressions on their faces were all the same – a kind of pitying disbelief.

I splashed more prosecco into my glass, watching as the bubbles whooshed up to the top and spilled over, like the time I put Fairy Liquid in the washing machine because I'd run out of Persil.

'I've got it,' Adam said, mopping up the mess with a wad of kitchen roll.

I took another big gulp of fizz and passed the bottle on to Charlotte, even though it was almost empty. Maddy's husband fetched another from the fridge and topped up everyone's glasses.

'Look, Tansy,' Charlotte said, 'I know this has been grim for you. Renzo treated you appallingly. I work with the guy – and I blame myself for you two getting together in the first place. I've known him longer than you and I know what he's like. He's hot, he's generous and he can be really kind. But he can also be a bit of a shit and, to be honest, I don't think I've ever known him to change his mind about anything. Ever.'

'He's going to change his mind about me, though,' I insisted. 'I'm going to make sure of it. He's the love of my life and I'm not going to let him be the one who got away.'

Things got a bit blurry after that: Jools Holland's face on the telly, Charlotte's friends' goodbyes and good wishes as they all got their Ubers home; even the stupid looping GIF of me and Renzo on that last, horrible night. I must have been sitting on the sofa for quite a while, in a state of suspended animation, because I remember Charlotte coming over, taking my hand, helping me up and asking if I was okay, and me noticing that the house had been restored to some kind of order and realising that she, Xander and Adam must have been clearing up while I'd just sat staring at nothing.

'I'm fine,' I said. 'Got to go to bed.'

Even I could hear my voice slurring into a kind of word porridge.

'Come on, babe,' Charlotte said, and I followed her upstairs, Xander and Adam forming a rearguard in case I toppled over.

I didn't take off my make-up or even clean my teeth. I got into bed, pulled the duvet up to my chin and unlocked my phone – because, obviously, however pissed I was, I couldn't lose the one remaining potential link I had to Renzo – and started swiping through my messages.

There was nothing there to give me hope. Everything from my friends and family was already a couple of hours old. The group selfie I'd posted on Instagram earlier in the evening had a couple of new likes, but there was no like from Renzo. Obviously.

But I sent him a text. Obviously. It took me a few goes, and I know there were still typos and autocorrect errors all through it, because I spotted them when I read it over the next day, sick with hangover and mortification. I told him how much I loved him and was missing him. I promised that if he let us try again I would make everything all right. I begged him to forgive me.

I did every single thing you shouldn't ever do when you've been dumped. The only thing that makes that particular text less toe-curlingly humiliating was that it had company. Twelve almost identical debasing, begging messages in as many days.

Renzo was building up quite the collection.

Chapter Two

It was still dark when my alarm went off. I felt as if I'd only fallen asleep five minutes before, which, while probably not strictly true, was close enough. It was the second Tuesday in January and eighteen days since Renzo dumped me. Which meant we'd been split up for twelve per cent as long as we'd been together. On the plus side, I'd reduced my rate of text messages to him significantly: only five so far this year, if you didn't count the one I sent in the small hours of the first of January, which I didn't, because technically I hadn't been to sleep so it was still the previous year.

On the minus side, he still hadn't replied to any of them. Also, it was raining. And furthermore, it being Tuesday, I needed to be in the office at eight o'clock for the weekly meeting of the buying team at the online fashion boutique where I worked and, having missed three days' work the previous week, I was hopelessly underprepared.

When I say 'missed' three days, I mean I chucked sickies. There, I said it. I'm not proud. But I'd been feeling so wretched, so hollowed-out with misery and hollow-eyed from crying, that when I caught sight of myself in the window of the Daily Grind café on my way to the Tube station and imagined my colleagues asking how my Christmas had been and how Renzo was, and their faces melting into expressions of concern and pity when they actually looked at me, I couldn't face it. So I turned around, went home and got into bed and called my line manager, saying I had flu, and I sounded so grim she totally believed me.

But flu doesn't last forever and broken hearts are not, according to the NHS, a thing. And the small remaining rational part of me knew that however hard it was to get up and face the world, if I focused hard enough, I could lose myself in the challenge of my job and forget about Renzo for a bit. Also, of course, if I didn't turn up to work I'd be sacked and, given that I'd spent three hundred pounds online in the sales, clicking numbly on garment after garment in the hope that one of them would have the magic power to make Renzo love me again, the last thing I needed was to lose my job.

My job. I remembered with a sick thud that work hadn't been going all that brilliantly for me towards the end of last year anyway. Being a fashion buyer sounds like all the fun – 'What, you get paid to shop?' people often ask me in wonder – but actually, while it *is* fun and I do love it, it's not like that at all. It's incredibly target-driven: I spend an awful lot of time looking at spreadsheets and sending strongly worded emails to my suppliers. Months before, I'd had a line of dresses designed in collaboration with an up-and-coming contact of my boss's called Guillermo Hernandez, and commissioned one of my suppliers in China to manufacture them. They were bang on trend, sparkly mini-dresses, perfect for the 'Oh fuck, what am I going to wear to the Christmas party?' market, and the centre of my *You're the Star Tonight* Christmas marketing campaign.

Except the dresses hadn't turned up when they were supposed to, last October, and were still missing in action. Although it was the supplier's fault, not mine, they'd left a hole in my sales figures that I didn't know how to fix. At the time, I'd been too loved-up and happy to do much more than bollock the supplier and cancel the order, but I knew the fallout was going to happen sooner rather than later.

And I knew one thing for sure: when it did happen, I needed to be there in the office to deal with it, not hiding under my duvet at home. That morning, it was the thought of a jumper that got me out of bed. I know exactly how daft and shallow this sounds, believe me I do. But it was one of the more out-there of my recent sale purchases: a super-chunky, outsize knit in an on-trend shade of mauve. If I wore it with black leather trousers and wedge-heeled suede ankle boots, I'd look like a badass but feel like I was wrapped in a duvet – the best of both worlds.

And if I didn't nail the badass thing, at least the jumper would match the dark circles under my eyes.

I pushed my actual duvet aside and got up.

An hour and a half later, I was sitting with my colleagues around the meeting room table. No one had asked about Renzo, although Kris had complimented me on my outfit and Lisa and Sally asked if I was feeling better. Mostly, though, we were all staring apprehensively at the huge platter of pastries in the centre of the table, then at the door, then back at the pastries again.

We all knew what that platter meant: that Barri van der Merwe, founder, owner and Managing Director of luxeforless.com, would be in attendance.

Don't get me wrong, I have the greatest respect for Barri. Especially if by 'respect', you mean 'abject terror'. Barri started his career in fashion on the shop floor of a department store and worked his way up to Head of Marketing before jumping ship, selling everything he possessed, including his beloved loft apartment in Shoreditch and his vintage 1950s convertible Beetle, starting up an online designer fashion outlet store in an already overcrowded market and building it into a success story that allegedly had venture capitalists sniffing around to invest and catapult the business well and truly into the big leagues.

But Barri was also… well, take the thing with the pastries.

'Croissant, anyone?' Kris said, reaching his elegant, lilac-polished fingers across the table, grabbing one from the plate and taking a flaky, buttery bite.

'I'm good, thanks,' I replied. I hadn't had breakfast, but I had found that since Renzo dumped me, the constant replaying of our last night together in my head meant the very thought of food made me want to spew.

'I had an egg-white omelette earlier, I'm stuffed,' Sally said.

'God, I swore I wouldn't touch carbs until February,' Lisa said. But she broke a loose fragment off the end of a pain au chocolat and we all watched as she brought it up to her lips.

'Hungry, Lisa?' We'd all been looking at the food, not the door, and Barri's voice caught us by surprise. 'Why don't we all dig in. Moment on the lips, lifetime on the hips, but life is for living, right?'

Lisa dropped the flake of pastry like it was laced with rat poison, and all the faces in the room turned to look at our boss, and the woman with him.

'Team, I'd like you to meet Felicity,' Barri said. 'She'll be covering Lingerie while Moby Chick is off on maternity leave.'

Lucy, whose baby had been born three weeks early just before Christmas, had done a great job of pretending that Barri's nickname for her while she was pregnant was funny, even though we all knew it wasn't really. Still, we were too scared of Barri turning his acid mockery onto us to say anything.

'Oh my God,' Felicity said. 'This is, like, so amazing. I'm so excited to be working with you all, and with Barri, of course.'

She walked into the room and took a seat between Sally and me, poured herself a coffee and added milk and sugar, then tore an almond croissant in half and put one half of it on a paper napkin in front of her and the other half in her mouth.

'Starving,' she said, through a mouthful of crumbs. 'Excuse me.'

We all watched, agog, waiting for the moment when Barri would make a comment about how many calories our new colleague had just ingested and reduce her to shame, probably tears and possibly, later, vomiting in the toilet.

We'd all been there – I had, anyway. Okay, Kris hadn't, but he was a bit of a special case, being relatively new to the business and still Barri's pet, and blessed with the physique of a racing greyhound and a metabolism that kept him whip-thin even though he devoured a pulled-pork burrito with extra cheese and guacamole for lunch every single day.

I know what you're thinking. But what about the body positive movement? Where's the embracing of diversity? The average woman in the UK is a size sixteen! You can be beautiful and healthy no matter what your size! But you try telling that to Barri. Go on, I dare you. Better still, do it while you're eating something perfectly normal like a tuna mayo baguette, to get the full impact of his corrosive contempt right before he sacks you.

Occasionally I allowed myself to dwell on the impact the culture of my workplace might be having on my self-image, but I never dwelled for long. It was what it was. I loved my job, and whatever hang-ups I had about my body I'd had long before I'd even known Barri existed. This was the fashion industry, and everyone knows it's fucked up. And besides, all those covetable samples we could buy for ten per cent of their retail price were a size eight.

But Felicity didn't seem even slightly bothered about what Barri, or any of us, might think of her. *I don't blame her*, I thought. *If I looked like that, I'd have rock-solid self-esteem, too.* She was a drop-dead stunning size fourteen, with skin like a pearl, curves everywhere and dark hair cascading in natural waves down her back, and the air of unshatterable confidence that you only get if you've never once had to worry about how to pay your gas bill and whenever you go to a nightclub they know your name and let you in straight away.

'Now.' Barri took his place at the head of the table. The smile on his face when he introduced Felicity had melted away entirely. 'You may be wondering why I've joined this meeting today, rather than Lisa managing it as usual. You do all follow the industry's reports on our business, yes?'

I glanced at Lisa and saw her flinch. The moment of confidence that had tempted her to a morsel of pain au chocolat had vanished, and was regretted.

Around the table, everyone's faces were still and scared. Except Felicity's – she was looking calm, interested, even eager.

'This.' Tapping on his iPad, Barri fired up the big screen at the end of the room and brought up an email. 'I received this from a journalist working for *The Draper*, which as you know is the trade publication with which we've always had a close and constructive relationship. They have been contacted by a leading broadsheet investigating allegations of sweatshop labour in our industry. And they want me to comment. Because apparently our supply chain is involved. Would any of you like to suggest what I might say?'

No one said anything.

Barri said, 'Let me read you an extract from the report that's due to be published next week. "Amalia is thirteen. She went to school until last year, but now she works in a garment factory in Dhaka, Bangladesh. She's paid sixty pounds a month to produce dresses that sell for up to twelve hundred pounds in Britain, including on online boutiques such as Luxeforless.

'"No one asked me how old I am," Amalia told our reporter. "They just asked me if I could sew. I can, because my mother taught me. She worked in a factory, too, but she can't any more because the arthritis in her hands got too bad and she coughs all the time from the chemicals they use to dye the clothes. I wish I could go back to school but I have to support my mum and my brothers."'

There was silence around the table. Barri flicked off the screen and said, 'The factory in question supplies several of our brands.' He wasn't shouting, but I could tell how much effort it was costing him not to – his voice was trembling with rage. 'Across denim – Sally, that's your problem – women's formalwear – Tansy, you're in deep shit. I could go on but I won't, although I can mention that this particular manufacturer doesn't work with footwear or lingerie, so Kris and Felicity, you're in the clear, for now. I shall be spending the next few days and weeks on fixing the massive reputational damage this has caused.

'In the meantime, I want you all to prepare an in-depth report into the supply chains of every single one of your brands. I want it detailed, and I want it tomorrow. Got that? And if anything even slightly dodgy is found anywhere, we're delisting that designer.'

He shot one final, poisoned look around the table then stood, drew himself up to his full five foot five, and strutted out.

I could hear my colleagues' long release of breath around the table. I breathed out, too: at least my missing Christmas dresses had gone below the radar. For now.

'I guess we're done here for this morning,' Lisa said. 'Felicity, Tansy will show you where you're sitting and where everything is. If you have any difficulty compiling the reports Barri's asked for, let me know. Because if they're not with him by close of play tomorrow…'

She tipped her head back and drew a finger across her throat. It was a gesture we'd all seen Barri make when he was about to subject someone to a particularly brutal humiliation or, if they were lucky, sack them.

'Shall we?' I said to Felicity, and we gathered up our things and left the meeting room.

As we walked towards our bank of desks, she said quietly, 'He so knew, you know. About the sweatshop labour and the underage thing. He's just furious because it got found out.'

Put that way, it was obviously true.

'I guess he did,' I said.

Felicity wrinkled her perfect little ski-jump nose. 'Way to start my first day in my new job. Jesus.'

I said, 'You'll be fine. He likes you – for now, anyway. We'll go for a drink if you survive the week.'

'Deal,' she replied.

*

Inevitably, it was late when I got home that night, almost nine o'clock, and I was starving. Approaching the house, I could tell by the lights in the upstairs rooms that Charlotte was out, presumably staying over at Xander's, but Adam was in. Not that that was particularly unusual – Adam was generally in, sitting at the computer in his bedroom, tapping mysteriously away on his keyboard.

I went upstairs and knocked on his door.

'Hey, Tans.' He spun round on his wheeled office chair and smiled at me.

'Hey. How was your day?'

Up until last year, Adam had worked from home, coding and mining cryptocurrency – at least, that's what Charlotte had told me. The coding I got, kind of, but cryptocurrency? It seemed dodgy as anything to me, but at least he wasn't baking crack in the cooker. Anyway, he'd recently been offered a job by the firm where Renzo and Charlotte worked, as their head of information security.

'Okay.' Adam, bless him, is a man of few words. 'Yours?'

I rolled my eyes. 'Fucking horrible. Listen, do you fancy popping out to the Daily Grind for a beer? Tuesday's burger night, remember?'

Adam looked alarmed, as he always did at the prospect of having to leave his bedroom and go out where there are actual humans. but he loved a burger, and he was always forgetting to eat.

'Okay,' he said.

Before he could change his mind, I said, 'Great!' and headed back downstairs and out of the front door. Adam followed me a few seconds later, shrugging on a thin denim jacket that wasn't even slightly equal to the freezing, drizzly night.

He didn't seem to notice the cold, though. That was another thing about Adam – he seemed to live in a slightly alternate version of the world from most people. Take his reaction to me. I don't want to sound vain – and believe me, no one is more critical of their appearance than I am – but because I'm tall and I've got long blonde hair, guys tend to react in a certain way when they meet me. Sometimes, like when I met Renzo and he asked for my number after, like, thirty seconds, this worked in my favour. More often, it's just annoying, so much so that I can't even hear the name of the eighties pop band Blondie without wanting to murder the person saying it, immediately and violently. Usually, though, I didn't even notice it any more. But Adam always saw me as just another person, and I liked him for it.

A wave of warmth and noise met us as we pushed open the glass door of the Daily Grind. Without asking, Adam headed to the bar and I wove my way through the crowd until I found a free table. A few minutes later he appeared with a glass of white wine for me and a beer for himself.

'The burger special comes with blue cheese and bone marrow,' he said, wincing. 'So I got a regular cheeseburger for me and the chicken one for you, because that's what you usually have, right?'

'Cool, thanks,' I said, although I would have quite liked to try the blue cheese. Bone marrow, whatever that was, maybe not so much.

We sat in silence for a bit, sipping our drinks, until our food came. My burger looked amazing and smelled even better, but just as I was about to take a massive bite, I remembered what I was going to talk to Adam about, and my throat closed up. I cut the burger in half, picked up a fry and drank some more wine.

'So,' I said. 'How's Renzo?'

Adam said, 'Tanned. He was skiing over New Year's.'

'I know,' I replied. He'd even asked me to go, in what felt like the distant past, but I reluctantly said no, because I've never learned to ski and Renzo's one of those people who go zooming down black runs like it's a badge of honour to break a leg, and I didn't want him to think less of me. Now, the idea that I could have had three nights with him in a chalet in the mountains, kissing and cuddling under a furry blanket as we looked out at the moonlight reflecting off the snow, was almost too painful to bear.

'He's not doing so great at work, though,' Adam said. 'He was down more than two million today.'

My mouth went dry and I took another gulp of wine. I knew from talking to Renzo how brutal the world of high finance could be, and that if he didn't make money for the fund, he'd be out on his ear. Not only would that be horrible for him, but the last connection I had with him, through Adam, would be lost.

'They make losses sometimes though, don't they?' I said. 'All the portfolio managers do.'

'Renzo doesn't. Hardly ever, anyway. He was the top performer last year. His bonus was like…' He mimed a rocket taking off. 'I think he's missing you.'

'Really?'

'Dunno. It's just speculation. But the evidence points that way.'

'Adam,' I said. 'Can I ask you something?'

'Sure. Are you going to eat that? If not, do you mind if I do?'

'Go ahead,' I said, my stomach knotting as my heart ached. 'I'll get us another drink.'

When I got back from the bar, which took longer than it should have because I had to knock back some random bloke who offered to buy me a drink and then hassled me for my number, Adam had finished the first half of my burger and started on the second. He'd picked off the slice of tomato and left it on the side of the plate, so I ate it and took another chip.

I said, 'Listen, you know I want to get Renzo back.'

Adam rolled his eyes. 'Hard not to know. It's not like you don't mention it at least five times a day, every day.'

'I don't!'

Adam looked at me and ate another bite of burger.

'Okay, maybe I do. But if we were back together, I'd stop, and then you'd stop being annoyed by it, right? And Renzo would stop losing money at work, and everyone would be a winner.'

'But he doesn't want to get back with you,' Adam said. 'I mean, I don't even know why he finished with you, but if he didn't mean it he'd have answered those texts you keep sending him.'

Adam and I were mates, but I wasn't about to tell him what had gone wrong between me and Renzo. There was a small crumb of comfort in knowing that at least it hadn't spread around the whole of Colton Capital.

I said, 'I know. Texting him isn't working. It's desperate and stalkerish and I've got to stop doing it. I need to see him, and I want you to help me do it.'

'What, you're going to turn up at the office?'

'No! God, no, not that. I've got a much better idea.'

I picked up one of the remaining chips and took a small bite off the end of it. It tasted great and I managed to swallow it without the familiar sick feeling overwhelming me. Progress. I finished it and took another one.

'So are you going to tell me this brilliant idea of yours or are you just going to sit there stuffing your face?' Adam said.

'I'm not—' I began, and then I saw the expression on his face. Adam rarely makes jokes and he's not very good at them, but when he tries I feel it should be encouraged, so I laughed.

'It's actually very simple,' I said. 'You've got access to each other's diaries, right? Like, for planning meetings and stuff?'

'Yeah, I guess,' Adam replied. 'But I don't really have meetings with Renzo's team. They're investment, I'm IT. Totally different departments.'

'But in theory. Like, if he was taking a client out for drinks or whatever, you'd be able to see from his diary where he was going.'

'Maybe. But he might not put the venue. Or he might just block it out as unavailable. Or he might not put it on his calendar at all if it was out of hours.'

'Come on,' I said. 'There's no such thing as out of hours in that place.'

If there was one thing that had marred the idyllic few months I spent as Renzo's girlfriend, it was how difficult it was to actually get to see the man. He was typically in the office at seven in the morning (after spending an hour in the gym) and rarely left before nine at night, and when he did it was often to attend dinners with clients, which usually went on late into the night. I suspected that sometimes so-called gentlemen's clubs were involved, although Renzo had assured me that entertainment of that nature was frowned upon by HR and couldn't be expensed, and that anyway he'd never look at another woman as long as he had me.

'You're in the same office as him,' I said. 'You get to talk to him every day. If you're, like, getting in the lift together, you could ask him where he's heading and he'd tell you.'

'You make it sound like we're best mates,' Adam objected. 'We're not. I hardly ever speak to him.'

'But you're close enough that you think he's missing me,' I said.

'That's just logic,' Adam said. 'Last year he was a star performer. This year, he's hit the skids. What's changed? You're not together any more.'

Without really noticing, I'd finished almost all the chips. There were only two left, so I took one and pushed the plate over to Adam.

'This is last Rolo territory,' I said. 'Come on. I'm your friend, even if Renzo's not. Don't you want to help me? And help Colton Capital, because if Renzo carries on doing as badly as he is, it would be bad news for the fund, and for you and your bonus at the end of the year.'

'I don't care about money,' Adam said. 'Anyway, they pay me loads.'

I thought, not for the first time, how unfair it was that Adam didn't need or care about money, yet had heaps, whereas I did and was skint. But clearly the prospect of a hefty cheque at the end of the year wasn't going to persuade him. My wine was finished, there was only about an inch of beer left in Adam's glass, and the staff were starting to clear up for the night.

I needed to find a way to get him to agree to my plan, and fast. I thought of Freezer, the neighbours' white cat, who Adam adores. I could threaten to kidnap him and send Adam one of his whiskers every day in the post until he capitulated, but Adam would know I'd never do that. I could offer to do his laundry for him for a whole year, but he knew me well enough to know I'd give up after a couple of weeks. You would too, trust me, if you'd seen the state of Adam's floordrobe.

He finished his beer. 'Right,' he said, sliding down off the stool and putting his jacket on. 'Time to go. Thanks, Tans, that was fun.'

'Adam,' I said. 'Please? Please will you at least try?'

He looked surprised. 'Sure, I'll see what I can do. You only had to ask.'

Chapter Three

Adam was as good as his word. The next evening at half past nine, I got a text telling me that Renzo was still at his desk and that the whole team was putting in a late night, and that Adam himself was heading home. Which was okay by me, because I was still at my own desk in the Luxeforless office, finishing off the report for Barri.

A week later, my spy informed me that Renzo was taking a client for dinner at the Arts Club, which was useful intel but of no practical help, because I wouldn't be able to get in, not being a member. I was desperate, but not so desperate that I couldn't see being turned away by an inscrutable door bitch was not the look I was after.

The following Tuesday, Adam's text revealed that 'the target' (clearly my housemate was getting well into this whole James Bond vibe) was attending an all-day conference, which would finish with 'networking over canapés' in the evening. Again, there was no way I'd be able to crash that one.

And on Friday, my hopes were dashed when Adam texted me shortly after lunch to inform me that Renzo had left the office early to spend the weekend with friends in the south of France.

All in all, it was not a great start – but it was something. Sooner or later, I told myself, the stars would align and I'd be able to turn up at the same place he was, looking my best, as if entirely by coincidence. Our eyes would meet across the room and he'd realise he couldn't live without me.

Or something. In the meantime, though, I had promises of my own to keep.

I shut down my computer, pushed back my chair and stretched my aching shoulders. Some people think a job in fashion is all about glamour, and while I do get to go to events sometimes, and there's the occasional overseas trip, most of the time I'm in the office in front of my computer, just like anyone else.

'Fancy a drink?' I asked Felicity. 'If you don't have plans?'

'Actually, I'm meeting friends later at Annabel's,' she said. 'Why don't we head over there now?'

'You're a member?' Renzo was, too.

'Sure,' she said, picking up her handbag and swishing her hair. 'Come on.'

I followed her across the office and we went into the ladies' together and spent a few minutes topping up our make-up.

'Oh my God, is that a Milk eye crayon?' I asked. 'I didn't even know you could get that stuff here.'

'I bought it in New York,' Felicity said casually.

Humbly, I brushed some of my Primark shadow onto my own eyelids while taking a sideways look in the mirror at my new colleague.

Her handbag was Chanel. Her coat was cashmere. Her jeans fit her so perfectly, making her waist look tiny and her bottom pert and curvy, that they could only have been purchased after several hours of painstaking trying on and must have cost hundreds of pounds.

Samples were a massive perk of working at Luxeforless, and the staff sale was a treasure trove of bargains, but somehow I didn't think Felicity's clothes were knock-downs or freebies.

I could see her conducting a similar sideways assessment of me, taking in my jumpsuit, which I'd bought at New Look but could – if you didn't look very hard – pass for one from the iconic Theory collection, and my battered Stan Smith trainers.

'You're so lucky, Tansy,' she said kindly. 'With your figure, you can wear anything.'

But I knew she was thinking, *That's one hundred per cent polyester.*

She spritzed on some perfume and slid her beautiful coat over her shoulders.

'Ready?' I said.

'Come on then.' She smiled, and we headed for the lift together.

Even though it was me who'd asked Felicity out for a drink and I was technically the senior colleague, having been at Luxeforless for almost two years as opposed to her few weeks, I had no doubt at all who was in charge. Felicity made her way confidently along Piccadilly, dodging the tourists like a pro.

As she went, she threw the odd remark at me: what Kris thought about Lucy's strategy in the lingerie department and how Felicity was going to develop it; what Lisa had said to her about Sally; and, most significantly of all, the lovely chat she'd had with Barri over blueberry and buttermilk cake ('To die for!') when he'd taken her to the patisserie down the road.

If I needed any confirmation that Felicity's tenure with our employer was somehow different from mine and that of the rest of my colleagues', there it was. At the end of my first week at the company, Barri had invited me out for lunch, too. When I asked for extra feta cheese on my superfood salad, he'd raised an eyebrow and said, 'Image matters in this business, you know, Tansy. You've got the look right now. Make sure it stays that way.'

And that freaked me out so much I'd hardly been able to eat anything at all.

'Here we are. Hello, hello, how was your trip home to Barcelona?' Felicity cooed, kissing the intimidatingly beautiful girl at the door of Annabel's on both cheeks. 'This is my friend Tansy. Pru's got a table booked for later but you'll be able to squeeze us in now, won't you, my lovely?'

'Of course, Felicity,' the girl said. 'Follow me.'

So we did, and a few minutes later we were sitting opposite each other in a booth as voluptuously cushioned as Felicity herself, with a bottle of pink champagne reclining in an ice bucket in front of us.

I didn't want to think about how much it would have cost. I did know that when the bill eventually came, though, I'd have to pay my share, and I hoped my credit card had its big girl pants handy, because it was going to need them.

'So, Tansy,' Felicity said, tipping about fifty quid's worth of fizzy wine into our glasses, 'tell me all about you.'

I laughed. 'This is like writing a Tinder profile! All the pressure.'

'Are you on Tinder, then?'

'Not as such,' I replied. 'I mean, I've got the app on my phone. Doesn't everyone? But I was seeing someone until really recently, so I've been kind of inactive. How about you?'

'Well, so,' Felicity said, leaning back in her chair and doing an almost invisible gesture with her head that somehow brought our waiter scurrying over to top up our glasses (*there goes another twenty quid*, I thought, feeling slightly sick), 'I'm single. Although I grew up in the UK, I went to uni in America, because my dad's from there. I studied history of art at Vassar, and I kind of stayed in New York for a bit. But my little sister Pru is here, and my mum, and I wanted to experience the whole London thing as an adult, you know.'

'Does your sister work in fashion too?' I asked.

'Pru? God, no.' Felicity laughed. 'She's not really working at the mo. She's done some reality TV and a bit of modelling and brand ambassador stuff. So she keeps pretty busy. But she doesn't *work* work. I guess I got the ambition and she got the looks.'

I'd already got the sense, obviously, that Felicity's background was a privileged one, but now I realised just how privileged. If her sister didn't need to '*work* work' and moved in the circles that got her on to *Made in Chelsea* or *Britain's Next Top Model*, presumably Felicity could also be a lady of leisure if she wanted to.

I also thought, looking at her perfect, pearly skin, enormous green eyes and full, pouting lips, that either her sister must be off-the-scale stunning, or Felicity had insecurities far deeper than I'd imagined.

'But you're gorgeous,' I protested. She waved a hand dismissively, and the waiter must have thought he was being summoned, because he apparated by our side and filled our glasses up yet again. As the fizz went to my head, I found myself worrying a bit less about the bill.

'So you were seeing someone, but now you're not,' Felicity said. 'Who was he? What happened?'

I said, 'His name's Renzo. He works for a hedge fund – their office is just around the corner, actually. We dated for a few months but we split up just before Christmas.'

'Hookers and blow?' Felicity asked sympathetically.

'What?' I laughed. 'No, nothing like that. Fortunately.'

Taking another sip of my wine and looking around the glittering, opulent room, I realised that, in Felicity, I'd found not only a potential new friend, but also an opportunity. The doors that were open to Renzo but closed to me were, without question, open to Felicity. It sounds shallow, I know, but it was true. In her company, I'd never need to worry about being turned away at the door of a place where I might see Renzo. With her and her model sister, I could present him with a picture of glamour and desirability he would surely find hard to resist.

It felt like I was already being disloyal to my new friend, and somehow even compromising myself, but it was clear: Felicity was the missing piece in my plan to get him back.

The only question was how much I revealed about my idea. I was pretty sure that if I told her, she'd hoot with laughter, order another bottle of fizz and start making a list of all the places where we could hang out in the coming weeks.

But then, I genuinely liked Felicity. I'd have wanted to spend time with her even if winning Renzo back hadn't been part of my game plan – although, admittedly, it would have been at the local pub rather than in swanky private members' clubs. I didn't want her to feel I was using or manipulating her. I genuinely wanted to be friends with her. Since I'd lived in London, I'd had a succession of housemates – most recently Charlotte and Adam, who'd become real friends – but my social circle was way narrower than I wanted it to be. When I'd been dating Renzo, that hadn't seemed to matter. But now, especially with Charlotte leaving, loneliness threatened me like a dark cloud.

Also, if I told her that I was determined to persuade Renzo to change his mind, I'd have to tell her why he'd dumped me in the first place, and I wasn't even close to ready to do that.

So I said, 'We just kind of drifted apart. The hours those guys work – we struggled to find time to see each other, and it seemed like the relationship wasn't going to move on to the next level, you know?'

'I totally get that,' Felicity said. 'When I was in New York, I was dating a guy who worked in the fine art department at Sotheby's. He travelled loads for work – LA one week, Tokyo the next, Switzerland the week after – you get the picture. Getting to see him got to be this massive effort. So I called it a day.'

She looked down at her hands and sighed, and I wondered how much her 'calling it a day' had had to do with her decision to uproot and move back to London.

'I'm sorry,' I said. 'It's tough breaking up, even when things aren't working.'

'Yeah, well. We should hang out together more often. You can show me where to find hot guys in London.'

I rolled my eyes. 'If I knew the answer to that I wouldn't be single, would I? But we can try. And even if we don't find anyone, we can have fun looking.'

'I'll drink to that,' Felicity said, but it turned out we couldn't, because we'd finished the bottle. As casually as you'd get another

round in at your local, she waved the waiter over and ordered
another.

'Pru and her friends will be here soon,' she said. 'You should
stay. Join us for the night. We're going to have some food and then
go down to the basement later and dance.'

I didn't need a spreadsheet to work out what all that would cost.
More champagne, two or three courses and probably wine with
dinner, cocktails to finish the evening off – it was unthinkable. It
would come close to the cost of my monthly rent.

So I said, 'I'd love to, but I really can't. I promised my housemate
I'd have dinner with her tonight.'

I felt terrible lying to Felicity again, but admitting that I wasn't
in the same league as her and her friends felt somehow too shameful
to admit – almost as shameful as admitting the true cause of my
break-up with Renzo.

So I stayed and chatted to her until her sister (who was so
ridiculously hot you'd literally stop and Instagram her in the street)
arrived, and then, after insisting on paying my share of the bill, I
went home to spend the rest of the evening on my own.

Chapter Four

I'd intended to spend the morning making a start on planning my spring/summer collection for the following year. It was my favourite part of my job: putting together a range that would excite the Luxeforless customer, and my head was already full of ideas.

I drained the last of my coffee and turned to my computer screen. No doubt I had an inbox full of emails, but they could wait: the creative force was strong in me for the first time that year, and I was going to make the most of it.

Then Priti from reception came hurrying over, looking even more harassed than usual.

'There's a delivery for you, Tansy.'

'Cool,' I said. 'Is it the fit samples for my workwear dresses from Turkey? I wasn't expecting them until next week.'

'No,' she said. 'It's from China, and it's a fuckload of stuff. Something's gone wrong somewhere.'

Shit. My inspiration forgotten, I jumped up and hurried behind Priti to the reception area, the rubber floor dulling the clacking of our heels.

A fuckload of stuff. She hadn't been kidding. There were six huge cardboard crates crowding the space between the lift and her desk.

Wordlessly, she handed me the delivery note. Some of it was in Mandarin, and made no sense to me, but the translation did.

Luxeforless X Guillermo Hernandez. Five hundred items.

'But these are… These were meant to arrive last year. I cancelled the order when the supplier said they couldn't fulfil it in time.'

And never mind that: the order should have gone, bar a handful of samples for me to check, to our warehouse and fulfilment centre in Dartford, not come to Luxeforless's Soho HQ, which according to Barri embodied the 'edgy yet effortless mood of the brand'.

There was nothing edgy about these enormous boxes, and nothing effortless about sorting out the headache they presented me with. The order had been cancelled. The limited-edition run of Christmas party frocks, which had cost only a few pounds each to manufacture but would have sold on our website for two hundred and fifty pounds, had so little intrinsic value that it was barely worth the cost of returning them to China – and I was under no obligation to do so, anyway, given that the order had been cancelled months before.

'What do you want me to do?' Priti asked, giving one of the cartons a poke with the pointy toe of her camel suede mule, then wincing as her own toes protested at the pressure.

Fuck only knows, I thought.

But I said, 'Let's find space for them in the sample room for now. We can decide what to do once I've spoken to Lisa.'

We looked at each other, and then, by unspoken mutual agreement, we kicked off our shoes before heaving and dragging the boxes into the already crowded space where all the prototype garments lived. The room was already packed with samples in various stages of production, alongside racks and racks of finished garments, all with their labels and tags in place, destined for the staff sale at the end of the season.

So Priti and I had to undertake something like a game of fashion Jenga, as rails threatened to collapse on top of us and piled-up crates of bags and shoes teetered as we heaved them around, before at last we'd slotted my stupid, sequinned, unwanted frocks into a corner.

'That's going to have to do for now,' I said at last.

'I guess,' Priti said doubtfully, shaking her head as she stepped gingerly out of the room, slid into her shoes and made her way back to her desk, smoothing her violet wings of hair back from her face.

I hurried back to my own desk, but the morning had gone, and my inspiration with it. I was just about to leave for my lunch break, which I planned to spend walking through Mayfair on the off-chance of bumping into Renzo, when Barri's voice rang out across the office.

'Could you all gather round, please.' Felicity and I looked at each other, eyebrows raised.

'What's this about?' she asked.

'No idea.'

Meetings involving all the company's one hundred and twenty staff weren't unusual, but they were held on a quarterly basis and scheduled in everyone's diary at the beginning of the year. Whatever this was, it was clearly some kind of emergency.

'I hope he isn't going to take too long,' Felicity whispered. 'I've got an express manicure booked at half one.'

We all shuffled down to the far end of the office, some of us scooting along on our wheeled chairs, others perching on the corners of desks. Felicity and I chose to stand at the back, as far away from Barri as we could get.

'Greetings, gang,' my boss said, hooking his thumbs through the belt loops of his jeans, which were, as always, cut just slightly too snug.

Still, he seemed in a good mood, bouncing up and down slightly on his Cuban-heeled cowboy boots and smiling warmly.

'I've called you all here at short notice because I have a very exciting announcement to make,' he said, and I watched all my colleagues arrange their faces into expressions of eager anticipation.

'As you are aware, here at Luxeforless we take corporate responsibility very seriously. We aim to be an exemplary corporate citizen on a global and local level.'

Felicity's eyebrows had practically disappeared under her fringe. I kept my face still and didn't meet her eyes.

'Our corporate responsibility statement frames our ethos in a manifesto built on three pillars,' Barri said. It was the first I'd heard of any such manifesto; the marketing team must have been working overtime to draft it. 'First, our people. Within Luxeforless, we work tirelessly to promote diversity and equality. We provide a working environment that is supportive and nurturing, giving everyone in the Luxeforless family the opportunity to grow and become their best selves, while promoting a healthy work–life balance.'

Sally, who'd had her annual leave cancelled the week before because she was ten per cent below her sales target, made a sound that turned into a cough but had definitely started off as a laugh.

'Second, our planet. We work to ensure that the workers all around the world who bring our designers' visions to life are treated fairly. Within our own office, we operate as far as possible in a paperless environment.'

This at least was true, thanks to a recent bollocking email from the office manager about reducing stationery costs.

'And third, our community. Luxeforless team members are always an active presence at Pride marches. And some of you regularly volunteer at soup kitchens in the local area.'

True again, but Barri neglected to mention that all these worthy initiatives happened in his employees' own time.

'This is just damage limitation,' Felicity whispered. 'He's trying to whitewash over that scandal about the Bangladesh factory.'

I nodded silently.

'However,' Barri went on, 'I feel that it's time to take this spirit of community involvement up to the next level. I know how deeply you all care about providing opportunities in this industry for those less fortunate than yourselves. I myself started my career folding T-shirts on the shop floor, but I know only too well that talent alone is not enough to ensure success.'

I looked down at my shoes. Every time Barri reminded us of his humble beginnings, I felt a fresh, if grudging, respect for how hard he had worked and how far he had come. If I had anything like his determination and ambition, my life goals would extend beyond getting Renzo back.

But I didn't want to allow my thoughts to go down that path, so I looked up again and carried on listening to Barri.

'Skills-based volunteering is a highly effective way for people to pass their knowledge and experience on to the wider community,' he said. 'Through mentoring, we can enrich our own working lives, too.'

Oh, do stop, I thought. But Barri didn't. He went on for another ten minutes about how Luxeforless was deeply proud – humbled, even – to be launching its most innovative corporate responsibility programme to date. Which wasn't that hard, given that the words 'corporate' and 'responsibility' had, as far as I was aware, been used together for the first time in our office that afternoon.

At last, he cut to the chase. Each and every one of us, he said, would be given the opportunity to take an afternoon every fortnight to spend engaging in a mentorship with an ambitious young person or group of people from a disadvantaged background. If we were interested in taking part, we should set up a meeting with Daria in HR by close of business, ten working days from now.

'That's all, team,' Barri said. 'Thank you for your attention and, once again, for being part of the Luxeforless journey.'

Kris went, 'Woohoo!' and clapped his hands a few times. Some of the admin team joined in and then, reluctantly, so did the rest of us.

Then everyone hurried back to their desks, collected their coats and bags and raced to the lift to make the most of what was left of their lunch break.

'If I dash, I'll still make that mani,' Felicity said. 'My cuticles are fucked.'

I followed the crowd more slowly outside and walked down the stairs to the ground floor rather than waiting for the lift. Wrapping my scarf high around my neck, I threaded my way through the crowds of tourists on Piccadilly Circus and towards Dover Street, where Renzo worked. I knew that my mission was futile – the hedge fund splurged huge amounts on stocks of sashimi, protein bars and salad so that no one needed to take their eyes off what the markets were doing in order to actually leave the office to eat.

I was damned, I said to myself, if I was going to put myself out to help Barri make good the damage his own relentless focus on the bottom line had done to the company's reputation.

He can do one, I thought. I even considered taking an extra-long lunch and having my nails done, like Felicity. She, weirdly for a new starter, seemed to have acquired the cynicism the rest of us felt after a few months working for Barri on her very first day; for me, it had taken several months for the gloss of working for such a prestigious brand to wear off and the reality of Barri's bullying and mismanagement to sink in.

Well, good luck finding people willing to go along with your mentoring idea, I thought. *I'm out.*

And then I remembered Debbie.

It's funny – it had been months since I'd really thought about her, even though we were friends on Facebook and followed each other on Instagram. She occasionally posted pictures of her outfits and spectacular views of Sydney, where she'd moved a decade before. But now, walking down the freezing London pavement, I found myself thinking about a very different street in a very different season.

It had been high summer and peak tourist season when Debbie opened her shop in Truro, the town in Cornwall where I grew up. I was fourteen and absolutely miserable. Until a couple of months before, we'd been living in a pretty little chocolate-box cottage with a view of fields from the window, and I'd been happily settled in at school, getting decent marks and playing on the netball team. But then Mum and Dad dropped a bombshell: owing to unforeseen expenses and Dad's cabinetmaking business not doing as well as they'd hoped, the cottage was going to have to be sold. We were moving closer to town, into a rented house, and Perdita and I would be starting at a new school in September.

It wasn't until I was older that I found out the truth behind this upheaval and the full extent of the financial mess into which Dad had plunged our family. Back then, my parents were still presenting a united front, and the decision was one that I, with typical teenage angst, railed against in every way I could think of. I cried. I sulked. I ranted about how unfair it was.

I may even have uttered the immortal words: 'I never asked to be born!'

But nothing I said made any difference. The move was going ahead, an offer had been accepted on the house, Mum had taken a job in the local supermarket. There was nothing whatsoever I could do to change things.

So, on that sunny Saturday morning, I was sunk in deepest gloom as I meandered down the high street. Some of my friends were going to the beach, but I'd said I had other stuff to do. What was the point, when I wouldn't be seeing them every day once the new school year started? They'd all move on, and forget about me.

My life was over, I thought. There was no point in anything – no point in me.

And then I noticed Debbie's shop, and it made me stop and look up, instead of down at my chipped blue toenails. Even in the bright sunlight, the boutique looked lighter than outside. Everything was white and clean. The simply cut shift dress in the centre of the window made me think of France – or at least how I imagined

France to be. The woman who wore it would be effortlessly elegant. She'd stroll along a boulevard or lounge against the railings on the deck of a yacht, and she'd turn heads without even trying.

I was having my first fashion moment. It was as if an invisible thread pulled me in through the door, and I stood inside and gazed, breathing in the serene atmosphere and the scent of the air, which was a mixture of new paint and some sort of room fragrance, fresh and clean.

I was so transfixed by the displays that I hardly noticed the woman standing behind the counter, carefully draping silk scarves so they spilled out over the rim of a driftwood bowl. But I couldn't help noticing the boy next to her, idly snapping the cash register open and closed to make it ping. I noticed him, and then I tried to look at him some more without him noticing me. He was wearing board shorts and a white T-shirt that was stretched tight over his broad shoulders, but was baggy around his waist. His hair was the colour of wet sand and flopped over his face in a long, shaggy fringe. His hands were long and bony, and looked too big for the rest of him.

Then he said, 'Hello, can we help you?' and I shook my head dumbly and legged it outside again.

After that day, I took to stopping outside the shop whenever I saw something new in the window, just to look. After a couple of weeks, I was brave enough to go in again, just to look. Okay, and sometimes to touch things, marvelling at the way the natural fibres – linen, cotton and silk – felt under my fingers, so different from the scratchy cheap polyester clothes that were all my mum could afford to buy me.

The woman – the owner, I guessed – was always there, rearranging the displays or chatting to customers. She was effortlessly elegant, too, with cropped dark hair and long, smoothly tanned limbs: the perfect ambassador for her brand, although I didn't know back then that that was even a thing. She never asked if she could help me – she must have been able to tell at a glance that there was no way I could afford to buy anything, and guessed that if she spoke to me I'd leave, spooked and shy, and never come back.

The boy – whose name I learned was Joshua – went to the same school as me. But that didn't mean our paths crossed – well, only about as much as your path would cross with Robert Pattinson's when you downloaded the *Twilight* box set.

It took me almost a year to pluck up the courage to speak to Debbie. For the first time, I actually picked something up, rather than just tentatively brushing my fingertips over things.

It was a pendant on a leather band, a chunky, smooth piece of silver that seemed to have been made by splashing the molten metal randomly from a height and leaving it to cool and set, so its shape was organic and asymmetrical.

'That's so beautiful,' I heard myself say, although I hadn't meant to speak.

'Do you like it?' Debbie asked. 'They're made in Malawi, in Africa, by a company that teaches local women craft skills to help lift them out of poverty, so the story behind it is beautiful too.'

I just nodded and smiled, and put the necklace back in the pottery dish where I'd found it.

'You live locally, don't you?' Debbie asked.

I nodded again, and managed to say, 'My name's Tansy.'

'Debbie Valentine,' she said, giving me her cool, slim hand to shake. I'd never shaken an adult's hand before. 'I don't suppose you're looking for a Saturday job, are you? I could really use some help this summer, if it's as busy as last year.'

And that, I suppose, was the beginning of my career in fashion. All through high school, I worked in the shop, at first just folding and tidying, later working on the till and advising customers on their choices, and later still browsing the internet for pieces that I thought would work as part of the Valentine collection.

It sounds cheesy, I know, but Debbie came to have a special place in my life. She wasn't a substitute for my own mother and she wasn't quite a friend, either. But she talked to me like I was an adult, asking me about my life and making me laugh with anecdotes about her own. I sometimes thought, through a fog of teenage angst, that those Saturdays in the shop were the only times I was truly happy.

After Debbie moved to Sydney with her son Josh, we kept in touch. She encouraged me to go to university and study fashion buying management. She arranged for me to do work experience at Vivienne Westwood through a friend of hers who worked there, and the friend knew someone else who worked at Harvey Nichols, which led to another internship and, after I graduated, a job as an assistant in the buying department.

Even though I hadn't seen her for years, I sometimes caught myself wondering, when I was grappling with a problem at work, what Debbie would do. And whenever I thought of her, it was always with fondness and gratitude that she'd given me my first chance to enter such a highly competitive profession.

Now, though, I didn't exactly ask myself what Debbie would have done in my position, partly because she would probably have told Barri exactly what she thought of him long ago and moved on. But I had to acknowledge that the Luxeforless mentoring scheme was an opportunity to help someone in the same way she'd helped me.

I'd passed Renzo's office a long time before, and there had been no sign of him, so I turned and retraced my steps, stopping on the way to buy a tub of carrot and coriander soup. When I got back to my desk, I sent an email to Daria asking her to sign me up.

Year Ten

You know how it is at school: kind of like a pyramid. Or maybe more like a solar system. At the top – or at the centre – there's a little clique of the cool kids. They're generally the ones who are good at sport and do okay academically, even though they take pains not to be seen to be working too hard, because achievement isn't what they're about. They're all about being popular.

They're the ones who hang out in the park in the evenings with their mates, listening to music and – if it's the weekend – drinking bottles of WKD and smoking fags that one of them gets their older brother to buy for them. Often, just having a big brother is a sufficient qualification for entry to the cool kids' clique. They're all good-looking (except maybe the one with the big brother), but in a kind of no-care way. They talk to each other in a type of secret language that sounds just like normal English, except words have slightly different meanings, and if you use a word wrong they look at you in silence for just a second, and then they all laugh.

Surrounding them – like an asteroid belt, maybe – is a satellite collection of boys and girls who want to be part of their group but have never quite made it. They're included in the alpha group sometimes – just close enough to feel the warmth of the sun – but they know, and everyone else knows, too, that they're tolerated for their usefulness and that one false step could mean they get cast out.

Then there are the ones who make no effort at all to fit in – the emos, or the really bright ones who go to code club in the afternoons, or the ones who have an all-consuming interest that raises them above the petty concerns about who's popular and who isn't. And, of course, the ones like Josh Valentine, who don't seem to try and fit in anywhere at all, but do anyway.

Then, making up the base of the pyramid – I know I'm mixing metaphors here but what can I say? English was never my best subject – are the rest. The ordinary ones, who have their own little friendship groups, and muddle along quietly with their lives, hoping that if the inner circle ever recognises them, it'll be for the right reasons, not the wrong ones. Sometimes, randomly, one of them will get incorporated into the popular group, but it rarely lasts – just as quickly as they were sucked in, they're spat out again.

And then there are the outcasts. The fat boy with thick glasses who once wet himself in Year Three and has never lived it down. The girl whose mother has mental health issues and can't get it together to buy her school uniforms or even wash them, so her clothes are always ill-fitting and dirty and everyone whispers that she smells of BO. The twins whose parents are refugees and who barely speak English, and just sit at the back of the class and watch the other kids with wide, wary eyes.

I was in the base of the pyramid – just. I knew that one false step would get me chucked into the outcasts. At only fourteen, I was already five foot nine. I towered over all the girls and most of the boys no matter how much I slouched to hide my height and my breasts, which seemed enormous compared to the other girls'. And I'd arrived at the school suddenly, when my parents had to sell their cottage and move to a rented house in a grotty part of town. Even though I never told anyone what had happened, they all seemed to know anyway and assumed I looked down on them, even though I didn't (no more than someone as tall as me had to, at any rate).

I was terrified of them, and painfully shy, and my fear and awkwardness were interpreted – I suspect deliberately – as stand-offishness. I had no friends. I sat at the back, next to the twins from Somalia, and made myself as small and inconspicuous as I could. I ate the sandwiches Mum made me, because she was too proud to have me on free school dinners, alone at break time, pretending to listen to music or read a book.

But really, I was watching the cool kids – Anoushka, Ben, Kylie and all the rest of them – trying to figure out what they were doing right and I was doing wrong. I knew perfectly well that I was as likely to fly to the moon as join their group, but I tried to understand their language, the subtle cues that set them apart, so I could behave a little more like them and be a little more accepted, a little less different.

Most of all, I watched Josh. He seemed to drift in and out of the cool kids' group, not because they chose to cast him out, but because he didn't particularly care about the secret language or the contraband fags, or about fitting in. But, even though I was a constant presence in Debbie's shop at weekends, whenever he saw me there or at school, it was like he didn't notice me at all.

And that was fine by me. I didn't want to be noticed – I wanted to be invisible.

But then suddenly, when I'd been at Trelander Academy for almost three terms and had just turned fifteen, I did get noticed. I got noticed not just by one of the 'in group' but by Connor, Kylie's big brother, the one who bought the illicit booze and fags from Mr Nabi's corner shop.

Connor, the absolute apex of cool. He was way, way cooler even than Josh: the sun in the solar system, or a star floating high above the pyramid.

He was coming out of the shop, carrying two blue plastic bags rattling with bottles, and I was going in to buy a pint of milk for Mum. Because I'd got into the habit of slouching, I was staring down at my shoes and didn't see him until we almost bumped into each other.

'Sorry.' I sprang away from him like he was carrying a horrible, infectious disease.

'Sorry?' he echoed. 'Is that all you've got to say for yourself?'

I looked up at him. He was taller than me – not by much, admittedly, but it was something. He was wearing grey tracksuit bottoms, a faded green T-shirt and a baseball cap backwards over his buzz-cut hair. His eyes were crinkled up against the sun and I could see a gap between his front teeth when he smiled.

The smile took my breath away and I found that 'sorry' literally was all I had to say for myself.

He stared at me for what felt like hours, and I felt my face growing scarlet and my palms getting damp and clammy. I should have said, 'Excuse me,' and brushed past him into the shop, bought the milk and gone home. But I couldn't. I couldn't even move – it was like my shabby silver ballet pumps had been replaced with concrete boots.

At last, he said, 'So. Coming?'

I nodded mutely and followed him up the road, relieved to be able to move, even though my legs still felt strange. I followed him all the way to the park, where Kylie, Anoushka and all the rest of them were slumped against the railings. Josh was there, too, and I felt a small thrill of gladness that he'd seen me singled out by Connor.

'Here.' Connor handed over one of the blue carrier bags. 'You lot can have this. This one's for me and her. We're going for a walk.'

I couldn't look at them – I could only stare down at my feet again. Then Connor took my hand in a grip so firm it was almost rough, and led me away.

Behind me, I heard Anoushka say, 'Well!' and the rest of them burst into amazed laughter.

We didn't walk far – just to the other side of the park, where it dipped down to a stream with fields on the other side. Connor leaned against a stone wall, half-sitting, half-standing, and I hesitated a moment before joining him. Only then did he let go of my hand, which was hot now from his grip.

He took a bottle out of the carrier bag, opened it with his teeth, took a deep swig and then passed it to me. I didn't know what I was expected to do – should I wipe the neck of the bottle or not? Did he mean me to drink, or was I just holding it for him while he rolled and lit a fag? I took a tentative sip of the sugary, fizzy blue liquid, trying not to grimace at the taste, and then handed it back to him.

I suppose we must have talked while we worked our way through that bottle and three more, but I can't remember anything he said. I don't think I said much at all – I was too bewildered by what was happening, and, later, by the way the drink made the edges of everything go soft and unfocused.

And then, when he kissed me, talking didn't matter any more.

We kissed for a long time, until my bum cheeks went numb from leaning against the cool stone and my face was stinging from his stubble. But I didn't care about that – I was oblivious to any physical sensation except the sweet stickiness of his lips on mine, the insistent questing of his tongue, the feel of his hand snaking under my school shirt and the panic as I wondered how far to let it go, and how to tell him to stop.

I didn't have to, in the end. He let me go, glanced at his watch and lit another cigarette. Then he said, 'I gotta go. Meet me here tomorrow?'

I nodded mutely and he turned and walked away, leaving me there.

I'd kissed boys before – of course I had, I wasn't that tragic – but Connor wasn't a *boy*. He was a man. He was eighteen. He had a driving licence and a job. I wasn't sure I even liked him, but I was so in awe of him I'd have done anything he wanted – anything at all.

So there was no question of my not going back to meet him the next day, and the day after that, and most days for the next three weeks. The WKD alcopop wasn't a regular thing, fortunately – I wasn't the greatest student ever but even I wasn't about to acquire an afternoon alcohol habit before I'd even sat my GCSEs. Sometimes he brought packets of crisps, or Mars bars, and once a bag of chips, hot and greasy and saturated with vinegar.

We never went out anywhere. Our relationship, such as it was, involved meeting by that stone wall, talking for a bit and then kissing each other. And of course, as time went on, the kissing led to other things.

Chapter Five

Finally, January had come to an end. It didn't mean that the long, depressing winter was anywhere close to over, but it did at least mean payday – and not a moment too soon. My rent was due, my credit card was hovering dangerously close to its maximum and I'd been living on beans on toast.

Daria's assistant came round the office as she always did, depositing the precious little sealed blue and white payslips on our desks and, as I always did, I opened mine straight away. Felicity, I noticed, chucked hers in her drawer without even looking at it.

'Hey,' she said. 'Fancy coming out tonight? Pru's mates are all in Gloucestershire for the weekend but she's had to stay in town because she's meeting some boy off Toffee she likes for brunch tomorrow. And it's Friday, so…'

'Go hard or go home?' I suggested. 'What's Toffee, anyway?'

'It's a dating app,' Felicity said. 'You know, like Tinder, only it's…'

Then she stopped, and looked uncomfortable for a second.

'It's what? Never mind,' I said hastily, when she continued to look awkward. 'I was just being nosy.'

'No, it's fine.' Felicity squeezed hand cream into her palm and massaged her cuticles, and the smell of freesias filled the air as if spring had made an early appearance, but she still didn't quite meet my eyes. 'Toffee is for... well, people who are privately educated, that's all.'

'A dating app for posh people?' I hooted. 'That's hilarious. So much for social mobility. I can't believe that's a thing.'

Then I cringed even more, realising how rude and insulting I was being not only to Pru and her potential date, but also to Felicity herself. And also, a small, shameful part of me was wondering whether Renzo, who'd been to boarding school in Milan, might make the cut and whether, by lying about my own education, I could, too.

'Yes, well,' Felicity said. 'It is. And Pru's on it.'

There was an awkward silence while I wondered whether I needed to apologise, or say I was busy that evening. Rationally, I knew that going home would be the wiser choice for me, by far.

But then my phone buzzed. Adam. *Target has confirmed reservation at the Cuckoo Club, 10pm. This is not a drill. Repeat: this is not a drill.* For good measure, he'd added a hashtag: #notadrill.

I couldn't help laughing at how seriously he was taking Operation Get Renzo Back.

'Have you been to the Cuckoo Club?' I asked, faux casually.

'The what now?' Felicity said, tapping it into her phone. 'God, I am so out of touch. No, but it looks cool. Let me check with my sis.'

Evidently Renzo's choice of venue cracked the nod from Pru, because it was all arranged within minutes. Effortlessly, Pru secured us a place on the guest list and a table booking, without us having to guarantee the thousand-pound minimum spend. Which was obviously a massive relief to me, although I'd have sold my own hair if it guaranteed I'd see Renzo again.

And tonight I was going to.

The afternoon crawled on. I checked my phone compulsively for updates from Adam, but he sent nothing more. I inventoried my wardrobe in my head, running through outfit after outfit and failing to decide what I was going to wear. I wished I hadn't been too skint to have my eyebrows threaded during the week, and now there would be no time.

At last, five thirty came and Felicity headed off to the flat in Chelsea she shared with her sister to get ready, and I got on the Tube to go home to Hackney and do the same.

I had three hours, I told myself. Heaps and heaps of time. I'd shower first and wash my hair, then let it air-dry while I did my nails. Then I'd decide what to wear, do my make-up, get dressed and head off. I'd treat myself to an Uber, I decided, so I wouldn't need to take a bag big enough for emergency Tube shoes.

It was all going to be fine. I was going to see Renzo. Somehow, I'd make it okay. He'd look at me the way he used to, and kiss me, and everything would be back to how it was, except without any secrets. I needed to believe it, to keep the faith.

Standing in the damp fug of the Tube carriage on my way home, I allowed my mind to wander back to the first time I'd been out with Renzo. I remembered walking into the restaurant where I was meeting him, my knees literally trembling with nerves so I felt like I could hardly balance in my four-inch stiletto heels. I remembered saying, 'You have a reservation for Renzo Volta?' amazed that I was able to get the words out, my mouth was so dry. I remembered goosebumps springing up all down my spine when I took my coat off, because I was wearing a backless jumpsuit. When I followed the maître d' to our table – the maître d'! I'd never been anywhere that had one of those before – I felt heads turn to look at me, and felt horribly self-conscious, wishing I'd worn something less out there.

It felt like the longest walk ever to the back corner of the restaurant, where he was waiting at a table for two. He was wearing an open-necked purple shirt that made his eyes gleam like topaz. He was too gorgeous to be real. But when he saw me his whole face lit up in a delighted grin that made him seem suddenly much less intimidating.

And then he stood up to greet me, but his hip bumped the table, and the cocktail glass he'd been drinking from tottered and fell, spilling clear liquid everywhere. A green olive rolled along the polished wood and bounced to the floor.

He looked at me and I looked at him, and we both burst out laughing.

'*Che cavolo!*' he said. 'What is wrong with me? I'm never nervous like this on dates. You look so gorgeous, and here I am making a fool of myself.'

And, as waitresses descended with napkins to clean up the mess he'd made and he ordered fresh drinks for us both, I felt my own nerves evaporating. He'd been scared, too! He was sweet, and self-effacing, and he could even be awkward. It was right at that moment, not even five minutes into our first date, that I realised I might fall in love with him.

And now I was going to see him again.

Charlotte wasn't in when I got home, which was gutting because I'd come to rely on her advice when it came to Renzo, before it had all gone wrong.

But Adam was. He wasn't in his bedroom as usual; he was downstairs in the kitchen – with the doors to the garden wide open, making the whole house Baltic cold – staring out into the darkness.

'Adam!' I said. 'What the hell are you doing? It's bloody freezing in here.'

He turned round. Instead of his usual, 'Hi, Tans,' he said, 'You're home. Good. I need your help.'

'Adam, what the… I need to get ready. You know, I'm going to see Renzo.'

'Yes,' Adam replied. 'But first you need to rescue Freezer.'

'What? Where is he? What do you expect me to do?'

Adam didn't say anything. He just pointed out of the door and upwards, and I could see a furry white body in the ash tree that was half in the neighbours' garden and half in ours, clinging to a branch about ten feet up.

'So a cat's climbed a tree,' I said. 'What's the drama?'

'He went up after a squirrel, and now he can't get down. He's been there two hours. He's stuck.'

I said, 'He's not stuck! He got up, he can get down again. Logic, right?'

'Cats climb up trees using their claws. They hook into the bark to get them up. But they won't climb down backwards because they can't see where they're going, and their claws don't give them purchase facing down. I googled it.'

'Okay, but can't Luke sort it? Or Hannah? I mean, he's their cat.'

'They're away for the weekend,' Adam replied. 'I said I'd look after him. And now look what's happened.'

'So go and get him.' I could quite clearly see the route Adam could take: hand on the top of the fence, climb up, grab the branch below where Freezer was, scoop the cat, repeat the process in reverse order. Job done.

Adam said, 'I can't. I'm afraid of heights.'

I looked at my normally inscrutable housemate, clutching his arms around himself as if he was cold, although I knew it couldn't be that, because this was the man who didn't even own a proper coat. I thought about the manicure I'd planned, and the face mask that would take fifteen minutes to give me a luminous glow, and the multiple outfits I needed to try on before making a decision.

'Oh, for God's sake,' I said. 'Okay. I've got this.'

'Shall I hold your bag?' Adam offered.

'Thanks. And my coat.' I handed them both to him and stood, shivering, while I tried to work out whether I'd be better off with my boots on or off. At least I was wearing jeans. But the route from ground to fence to branch to cat suddenly looked a bit less easy than it had when I was imagining Adam doing it.

'Right, Freezer,' I said. 'I'm coming to get you.'

I put both hands on top of the fence and Adam gave me a leg-up, and seconds later I was crouching precariously on its narrow top, clutching a branch of the tree for balance. Reaching up to a higher branch, I carefully stood up and assessed my options.

I could lean across the gap and try and grab Freezer with one hand, but that would mean risking falling, dropping him, or both. Or I could climb into the tree myself, but then I'd have to find a way to get down one-handed, while carrying a squirming, frightened bundle of fur. And claws. Let's not forget the claws.

I chose the first option and reached over as far as I could. I could just about touch the cat's front paws, but not quite.

'Come on, Freezer,' I pleaded. 'Come just a bit closer and we'll get you down.'

Freezer ignored me. Instead, he stood up from his crouched position and backed away slightly.

'No, Freezer, be sensible,' I heard Adam say, far below me.

I edged carefully along the fence, closer to the cat. He edged carefully away.

Then we both watched in horror as he somehow turned himself around and took off at speed along a branch in the opposite direction.

'For fuck's sake, Freezer, come back!' I said.

But he didn't. Instead, he took a flying leap off the branch, landing safely on the roof of Luke and Hannah's shed, and immediately sat down and started to wash himself.

'You little bastard!' I said.

'He's okay, Tansy, you did it!' Adam said.

I can't remember how I got down from there, but a minute later I was back on solid ground, my legs trembling with delayed fright. Adam and I went back inside, and a few seconds later Freezer followed and started to twine himself around Adam's legs, mewing hungrily.

'I think I can give him some tuna, just this once, don't you?' Adam said.

'I think you probably can,' I replied, and took myself off upstairs to get ready.

I definitely didn't have time to paint my nails, I decided – I'd just take off the chipped polish that had been on all week. My face pack could work its magic while I did that. But first I needed a shower.

An hour before I was due to meet Felicity, I was standing in my bedroom in my pants, hair and make-up done, surrounded by half my wardrobe. I'd rejected the silver-grey jumpsuit I'd worn on my first date with Renzo, for obvious reasons. The red dress I'd worn on our last night together was out, too – I didn't even bother taking it off its hanger. But nothing else I owned seemed right.

The weight I'd lost meant that my hipbones jutted unattractively, spoiling the line of my favourite black mini-dress. I was too pale, even with all the bronzer I'd slapped on, for my backless white shift. More than anything, I realised, I wanted to put on my pyjamas, make a cup of tea and spend the evening on the sofa. More than anything, that is, except seeing Renzo.

In the end, I settled for a tuxedo dress I'd bought in my sales haul thinking it would be suitable for work, but which had turned out to be ridiculously short and cut almost down to my waist in the front. Then I spent a few minutes dithering over black bra, leopard-print bra or no bra before throwing caution to the wind and going without. I added pointy, high-heeled ankle boots and dangly earrings, and I was ready to go, although I didn't feel it.

In the taxi on the way, I stalked Renzo online more avidly than I had for days. His Twitter feed was boringly impersonal, taken up with musings about the state of the markets. ('Critical blow to Goldilocks thesis in Q2 as sequential average unit value growth stalls'. No, me neither.)

He hadn't posted on Facebook since a generic Happy New Year message on the first of January – or possibly he had, but had put me on a limited profile. There was no way to tell, but at least I hadn't been blocked or defriended, which was some comfort.

His Instagram was more fruitful, in a masochistic way at least. I scrolled through views of snowy mountains from his skiing holiday, the wine list at a restaurant he'd been to, a car a friend of his had bought. There were no pictures of women, apart from a family group of him with his sisters from Christmas Day, which I supposed was something.

I scrolled back up to his most recent posts, and as I did so, a new one appeared: a cocktail glass full of clear liquid which I guessed must be dry martini, because there was an olive in it, too. But I wasn't looking at the drink – I was looking at the background, which I instantly recognised from the Cuckoo Club website. He'd turned up. He hadn't changed his mind.

In just a few minutes – if the bloody cab driver would hurry up – I'd be in the same room as him. I'd have my chance to talk to him and make everything all right.

*

Felicity and Pru were already at our table when I arrived. Felicity was wearing a skin-tight zebra-print dress with sheer mesh insets, her amazing boobs spilling out over the top. Her hair was straightened into a perfect sheet of shiny black. Her face was impeccably highlighted and contoured; her lipstick was an on-trend matte coral and her eyelash extensions were so long they cast actual shadows over her cheekbones.

Pru was wearing a tiny gold suede mini-skirt with a backless black top held in place with criss-crossing gold chains, and thigh-high platform boots, and if anything she looked even more amazing than her sister.

My long-sleeved black dress, which had felt fashion-forward when I put it on in my bedroom, now made me feel underdressed and drab.

Still, the two of them welcomed me like a long-lost third sister, kissed me on both cheeks, told me I looked stunning and filled a glass for me from the inevitable bottle of pink champagne.

'So, tell me about this date you've got tomorrow,' I said.

'Oh my God,' Pru gushed. 'He's really, really hot. He went to Eton. Divides his time between London and Dubai. He owns six polo ponies and he collects vintage Aston Martins. He's called Phillip, but I can get past that.'

'Nice work, little sis,' Felicity said. 'And speaking of hot, look over there.'

Carefully, so as not to seem to be looking, we did.

And of course, it was Renzo. Tall, tanned from skiing, still wearing his work suit but with no tie and his shirt undone. Sipping a cocktail and laughing the way he did that made you want to laugh too, even if you didn't understand the joke.

My Renzo. Seeing him literally took my breath away. I felt sick, my heart pounded in my chest and I could feel sweat snaking down my back under my too-warm dress. I couldn't look at him and, also, I couldn't not.

But I forced myself to turn away and I manufactured a casual laugh. 'That's my ex, the one I told you about.'

'Oooh, really?' Felicity said. 'Well! I can't believe you let that one get away, Tansy! Are you going to go over and say hello? Invite him over for a drink, maybe?'

'Go on, babe, take one for the team,' Pru urged.

'I don't think I can,' I replied. Literally, I didn't think I could. If I stood up, I thought my knees would give way and I'd collapse on the floor in an embarrassing heap. It was all I could do to keep the air going in and out of my lungs on a semi-regular basis. 'You know, it's awkward sometimes, with exes.'

'Looks like you might not have to,' Felicity said. 'Don't look, but he's coming over here.'

I didn't look. I picked up my glass and drained the lot in four big gulps, then instantly worried I'd get hiccups.

Pru filled it up straight away like the good woman she was.

'Hello,' I heard Renzo's voice, right above my head.

I swivelled round on the faux-crocodile skin seat, ever so slowly, looked up at him and smiled, my heart hammering so hard I was certain he could hear it. I didn't stand up, or try to kiss him hello.

I just said, 'Renzo! Hi! It's so great to see you. These are my friends, Felicity and Pru.'

Amazingly, my voice sounded quite normal. Renzo aimed the floodlight beam of his smile at Pru, then at Felicity, and I saw them both bask briefly in its heat.

Then he said, 'Tansy, could we talk for a second?'

Shit. I was going to have to stand up.

'Of course.' But I didn't move, because I couldn't.

'Come on, babe,' Felicity said to Pru. 'I'm dying for a wee. And maybe a sneaky fag. Shall we?'

As far as I knew, neither of the sisters smoked. I sent desperately grateful vibes in their direction as they slithered out of the booth and vanished into the crowd.

Renzo took Pru's place next to me.

'How are you?' I asked. 'I mean, how have you been? Since…'

'I'm okay. I'm fine. Work, travel, same old. I'm good. But I saw you, and I thought we should talk.'

Once again, my heart went from zero to a hundred in seconds, like Renzo's Lamborghini.

'Go on,' I tried to say, but no words came out.

'Last year, last time we saw each other,' he went on, 'I said some things I shouldn't have. I'm not proud of it. I don't believe in treating people like that, especially people I care about. So I wanted to apologise.'

In my heart, a whole squad of cheerleaders were doing somersaults and waving pompoms. But my head wasn't quite there yet.

I said, 'Okay. It wasn't the best. But it wasn't your fault, not at all. It was my fault. I should have been honest from the beginning. I should be the one apologising. That's what I've been trying to do. I'm sorry about all the texts and everything. I hope you don't think I'm a nutter. I—'

Renzo reached over and touched my hand. I could feel that it was icy and damp and I hoped that was why he didn't take it and wrap it in his warm, dry one. I was gazing up at him, transfixed by his hazel eyes and wondering how they managed to be clear and opaque at the same time.

'That's what I wanted to say,' he said. 'Just that I behaved badly, and I'm sorry.'

I said, 'Does that mean we… That we can try again?'

He paused a beat. *If I drop dead right now, I won't care*, I thought. *I'll die happy and full of hope.*

'I'm not sure, Tansy. I don't know how to feel about you now. What to think. Not after... You know.'

I don't know how I did it, but I managed not to break down. I didn't cry. I didn't beg him to change his mind and give me another chance. I didn't even apologise again. I just sat there and looked at him for a long moment, and he looked back at me. And then he smiled – a sad, intimate smile that was like an invitation to fall in love with him all over again – before standing up.

I gathered my dignity close like a warm coat on a cold night, and I said, 'Okay. I'll wait for you to decide. I won't contact you again.'

Renzo paused, and I wondered whether he was going to say something more, something that would offer me a crumb of comfort. But he just said, 'Thank you.'

Then he turned and went away, back to his friends. Without his warm body next to me, I felt suddenly cold.

Seconds later, Felicity and Pru returned. They must have been hovering close by, wanting to know what happened but also not wanting to leave me sitting alone like a loser. They slid into the booth, one on either side of me.

'What gives?' Felicity asked.

'Are you okay?' Pru said. 'You look like you've seen a ghost.'

'Are you getting back together?' Felicity demanded.

I said, 'No, we're not. We were just chatting, clearing the air a bit. You know how it is.'

Again, I was relieved how normal I managed to sound.

'Well. Time for another bottle, I feel,' Felicity said.

For a moment, I considered making my excuses and leaving. But then I thought of Renzo watching me go, knowing that it was our conversation that had made me run off. Knowing that he still had that power over me. Maybe even suspecting that I'd only been there in the first place in the hope of seeing him and having the conversation with him that hadn't turned out quite the way I wanted it to.

So I didn't. I stayed, I drank, I danced. Occasionally, in my peripheral vision, I saw Renzo looking at me, but I didn't look back. I talked to a man called Charlie and a man called Ed and a man called Simon, and danced with them all and even tried to flirt a bit, although my heart wasn't in it. I drank some more. A lot more.

I watched Felicity dancing with a tall blond man in a red shirt, and laughed when she came back to our table and said, 'Married. He didn't even bother to take his wedding ring off. What a doughnut.'

After that, we drank and danced some more, and then it was three in the morning and chucking-out time, and Renzo had left without me noticing, and I realised with a hollow, sick sense of loss that I might never see him again. We paid our bill and because it was payday I put it on my normal bank card, not my credit card, and only winced a bit at the total. We got our coats and said goodbye in the freezing drizzle, and Felicity and Pru got a black cab to take them home to west London while I waited for an Uber to take me back east. But it was surge pricing and the wait was almost ten minutes and I was cold, so I started walking, thinking I'd get the night Tube, but then I went the wrong way because I was pissed, and I found myself walking and walking, aimless and numb.

Some kind of internal GPS must have kicked in, because after a while I realised I was almost halfway home and might as well keep going.

And so I walked, my feet automatically moving and my mind far away. The image of Renzo was so clear it was almost as if he was there next to me, although of course he wasn't. I couldn't allow myself to imagine that he ever would be again – that I'd ever feel his warm arm around my shoulders or hear his laugh, or lose myself in his greeny-gold eyes.

It was half past five when I eventually unlocked the front door. I didn't feel drunk any more and I was very conscious of how cold I was and that my feet hurt almost as much as my heart.

I went straight upstairs, took my clothes off and slipped under the duvet, shivering and veering between hope and despair until finally I fell asleep.

Chapter Six

The next day I slept until almost midday, occasionally drifting awake and then forcing my eyes closed again so I could carry on with the muddled dream I was having in which Renzo had told me he still loved me, but he told me over the phone and he was somewhere in a Tube station and I kept going from one of the six exits to the next, unable to find him, and when I ran I almost tripped over in my high heels and my feet hurt more and more.

It was that that finally woke me up. My feet were throbbing, and the duvet cover had actually stuck to my right heel where a blister had burst. Also, my head was pounding, I was hungry and I had a WhatsApp from Mum.

One thing at a time, Tansy, I told myself. So first, I got up, had a shower and got rid of last night's make-up. I put plasters on my feet and swallowed two paracetamol with water.

I put on jeans, trainers and a grey Gucci sweatshirt of Renzo's that had ended up in my suitcase when we were packing after our last, idyllic holiday in Switzerland. I'd like to say it still smelled of him but it didn't, although it had until I put it through the wash a week before because it was getting downright rank.

Then I went downstairs and scrounged in the kitchen for food. Since he'd been gainfully employed with unlimited access to smoked salmon, rare roast beef and sushi in the work fridge, Adam had been buying even less food than he used to. Apart from one tin of tuna, a box of teabags and some porridge oats, the cupboard was basically bare.

But it was okay – I'd just been paid. So I could treat myself to a proper coffee and brunch at the Daily Grind. I put my phone in my bag, reminding myself to read and reply to Mum as soon as I'd eaten. Then I shrugged on the lovely warm shearling coat that had been one of last winter's samples from my favourite supplier, and strolled up the road.

Last night's clouds had cleared, and it was one of those radiant, crisp winter mornings that make you think spring isn't far away, even though you know there's another two months of lip-chapping wind and horizontal rain to get through first. Parents were out with their children, all wrapped up in bright fleece jackets as they scooted along the pavement. Joggers had their sunglasses on for their lunchtime runs, even though they still wore gloves and beanie hats. Dogs in their cute little dog coats were dragging their owners in the direction of interesting smells.

The Daily Grind, predictably, was rammed. It was owned by Luke, our next-door neighbour, who also owned Adam's cat friend Freezer, and I instinctively glanced behind the bar to see if he was there, knowing he'd find a table or at least a stool for me, before I remembered that he and his partner Hannah, a teacher at the primary school up the road, were away.

But Yelena, the waitress, clocked me as soon as I walked in. She smiled, waved and gestured, and soon I was sitting on a stool at the end of one of the long tables in the centre of the room with a double espresso she'd brought without me having to ask. I used to drink cappuccino all the time before I met Renzo, but he told me off very sternly and said that no proper Italian would drink anything other than espresso after eleven o'clock, and now Yelena knew it, too.

'Avo smash on wholemeal, Tansy?' she asked.

'Yes, please,' I said automatically, then realised that wasn't going to cut it. 'Actually, no, I'd like a sausage sandwich with a fried egg.'

Yelena smiled. 'Heavy night?'

'You could say so.' We laughed, and I drank some coffee and flicked through a magazine that someone had left on the table. Normally I'd have been checking my phone, but right now, in this warm, safe space, I didn't want to.

I was frightened of what I'd see, and what I wouldn't.

There would be no message from Renzo, that was for sure. The idea made me feel sick and hollow with sadness. There wouldn't ever be again. There was no point in hoping. And the WhatsApp notification from Mum made my phone feel like an unexploded bomb in my handbag.

Don't get me wrong, she's my mother and I love her. And I love my younger sister Perdita and her husband and their two kids, and when the baby Perdita was due to have in a few weeks was born I knew I'd love him or her too.

It's my dad I can't stand.

Every bit of happiness and stability I remember from my childhood was created by Mum, or later by Debbie. Everything else was down to him. The rows, the fear. The bailiffs turning up at our door and taking away the iPod Nano Perdita had saved up her babysitting money for months to buy.

Dad was what I guess you'd call a problem gambler, although I just called him a selfish bastard. Mum called him her husband, and so she stayed with him, even though it broke her a tiny bit more every year that she did.

'Sausage sandwich and eggs. Enjoy, my darling.' Yelena placed the plate in front of me, aligning a napkin and cutlery alongside it. 'Anything else?'

'This is wonderful, thank you.' I knew that I needed to eat quickly, before I thought more about what Mum might be asking me for and my throat closed up and my stomach started to churn. So I pushed her from my mind and focused on my breakfast.

'Anything else? Another coffee?' Yelena asked when she came to clear my plate.

'Nothing thanks, just the bill. That was amazing.'

Yelena came over with the machine and I passed her my Visa card and waited while she tapped it on the screen. There was a pause, and then she said, 'Sorry Tansy, there seems to be a problem here. Let me try again. Sometimes our system goes down and…' She shrugged. 'No, it's not going through.'

But I've just been paid! My mouth was suddenly as dry as paper, and tasted sour from the coffee.

'Shall we try another one?' I took my credit card from my purse and handed it to her. I could see my hand shaking, and I felt an awful, familiar sense of fear and shame.

'There we go,' Yelena said. 'All done. Thank you darling, come again soon.'

'Have a good rest of the weekend,' I said.

I walked back out through the glass doors into the sunshine and breathed in great lungfuls of cold air. It didn't help. I felt as if my head was floating above my body, and my legs didn't seem to be working properly. I looked down at my trainers and forced them to move, one in front of the other, again and again until I was home.

I made it up the stairs and into the bathroom before I was sick.

When I'd cleaned my teeth and drunk some water, I felt a bit better. I went into my bedroom and closed the door, sat hunched on the bed and took out my phone.

What to do first: check my online banking, or read Mum's message? Each would hold equally bad news.

The banking app won. It was as bad as I feared. My salary had gone into my account yesterday as it should have done. But, as they should also have done, a bunch of direct debits had gone out. My rent, council tax, the gas and electricity, my phone subscription and gym membership. And, of course, my share of the bill from the previous night.

'Two hundred and twenty-nine pounds,' I whispered in horror. It was fun money to Pru and Felicity, and I had no doubt Renzo had spent even more. But to me, it was a big deal – a seriously big deal.

What were you thinking, Tansy? Were *you even thinking?*

I hadn't been, of course. At first I hadn't been thinking about anything except Renzo, and then I'd been too pissed to think about anything much at all.

And my credit card payment from the previous month. Another six hundred and ten pounds. How had I even done that? How had I spent that much?

But I knew how. The night out at Annabel's. The clothes I'd bought. The pizza with Adam. The times I'd been to the supermarket and casually bought extra stuff to donate to the food bank, because it was the right thing to do and there were so many people worse off than me. Even the carrot soup I'd had for lunch yesterday, which I'd stuck on my credit card because I wasn't sure my salary would have reached my current account yet.

Desperate to escape from the horror of the numbers in front of me, I swiped to Mum's message.

Hello love, hope all is well with you. We've had a lot of rain here but at least it's got rid of the ice on the pavements. Gwenda next door had a nasty fall and we thought she might have broken a hip, but it was just badly bruised. I've been walking Pebble for her while she rests up. Perdy's not got long to go now – will you be able to come down for a few days when the baby comes?

No, not a chance, I thought glumly. A train ticket to Cornwall at short notice would be a hundred pounds at least, and it was a hundred pounds I didn't have. Last week, yesterday even, I'd have stuck it on a credit card, along with presents for my sister and the new baby. Now, that seemed reckless to the point of craziness.

I scrolled further down Mum's message. I could tell from her stilted, formal tone what was coming, and sure enough, there it was.

Your father's been bad again.

'Bad' – I knew she meant it not in the sense of wicked or misbehaving, but in the sense of poorly, like an illness.

He's been so much better since Christmas, really trying hard. He promised things would change this year, so I haven't been as careful as I should have been.

I knew what that meant, too – not careful with money, not watching every penny, which Mum did automatically anyway, because she had to. 'Careful' meant hiding her purse in a different place every week, logging out of her online banking every time she used it and changing the password so frequently she often forgot it herself, because she couldn't leave it written down anywhere.

You know I hate to ask, but would it be possible to let us have a couple of hundred pounds, just to tide us over? I've asked work for extra hours but there's nothing right now, with it being winter, and of course Perdy isn't able to help. Don't worry if it's difficult, we'll manage! Do tell me all your news soon. Dad sends his love.

'Like I need his fucking love,' I muttered. 'I need money.'

I needed money, and not for the first time. A year ago, I'd been in this exact same situation. It had been Christmas that brought on that crisis. A trip home and wanting to spoil my family with the nice things they could never afford themselves: toys from Hamleys for Rosie and Arthur, perfume for my sister, a cashmere cardigan for Mum, a supermarket order with an organic free-range turkey and a case of prosecco, even a *Peaky Blinders* box set for Dad.

And then, like now, when the humble, apologetic request came from Mum in January (*I know how much you've already done for us, love…*), my bank account had been empty.

Perdita couldn't help, because she had two kids and no job and only just managed to get by herself. Perdita's husband Ryan could probably have spared a hundred quid, but I remembered my sister telling me tearfully that they'd had a blazing row about it just recently, during which Ryan had said his own wife and kids were his fucking priority, and did she want to save for Rosie and Arthur's university education, or did she want to keep pissing money away on a deadbeat?

Which I'd thought at the time – and still thought, to be honest – was harsh but fair.

When I'd hit on the solution, it seemed like a genius one. I could make extra cash, working from my bedroom in the evenings. Quite a lot of extra cash. It was easy.

Of course, it didn't turn out to be anything like as good an idea as I first thought.

For a horrible few months, I was Tansy, junior buyer for formal-wear at Luxeforless, during the day, and someone else entirely by night: Saskia, a girl men could talk to and watch online.

Webcam work was easy at first – easy and lucrative. It made me feel powerful and in control. So what if, when I thought about it properly in the cold light of day, I felt dirty and ashamed? So what if I was afraid to meet strangers' eyes in the street in case they recognised me? So what if one of the punters started bombarding me with gifts and requests to meet in a way that went from being a bit creepy to full-on stalking, even turning up outside our house? I was able to help Mum, and I was even able to buy nice things for myself.

And then I met Renzo. After the first time he kissed me, I knew I couldn't do it any more. My body was no longer an object I could detach from, a resource I could exploit – even if it was for the good of my family. I was alive with desire for Renzo; physically and emotionally connected to a man for the first time in ages, and the idea of sharing that part of myself with anyone else but him was impossible – it was horrifying.

Besides, I knew deep down how he would react if he found out. And I was right. When I told him, at his work Christmas party, right after he told me he loved me for the first time and I couldn't bear there to be secrets between us any more, after months of feeling guilty for hiding it, he flew into a white-hot rage. Right there, in front of his colleagues and my friends, he said terrible things to me. He called me a slag and a whore. He pushed me away from him with his eyes shut like he couldn't stand to look at me.

My whole body burned with shame remembering it – because he was right. I'd sold myself for money. Even if no physical contact had taken place, that was what I'd done.

And I could never, ever go back to doing it again. No matter how desperate things got.

*

My eyes stinging with unshed tears, I put my phone down, got up off my bed and went back out onto the landing. *If only Charlotte was here*, I thought, *she'd know what to do*. But Charlotte had been spending more and more nights at Xander's flat, as the date of their departure for Thailand grew closer. Adam's door was closed, but I knew he wasn't asleep – even on weekends, he was generally up at eight o'clock, tapping away on his computer with the blinds closed, the room in darkness apart from the glow of the screens.

I knocked on his door.

'Come in.'

As I'd known he would be, Adam was there, on his wheeled chair, Freezer curled up on his lap. The cat opened one eye – the green one – and peered at me, then curled up again and put his paw over his face.

'So that's the gratitude I get for rescuing you,' I said.

'He's very grateful,' Adam protested. 'He's just expressing it through the medium of sleep.'

'One of his core skills,' I said. 'Along with eating tuna and getting stuck up trees.'

'And purring.' Adam scratched Freezer behind the ear and I heard a low rumbling sound, like a Harley-Davidson revving in the distance. 'He's an ace purrer.'

'Fancy a cup of tea?' I asked.

Adam turned away from the screen to look at me, rolled his shoulders and yawned. 'Go on then.'

Relieved, I hurried downstairs. I waited impatiently while the kettle boiled and the tea brewed to a deep tan colour, the way Adam liked it, then added milk and three sugars and poured a glass of water for myself.

As I put the mug carefully down on his desk, Adam asked, 'Are you feeling okay, Tans?'

Shit. He must have heard me throwing up.

'I'm all right. Hung-over.'

'Good night?'

'It was all right. I ended up walking home all the way from Mayfair, which was maybe not the brightest idea.'

Adam raised his eyebrows. 'Maybe not.'

'Listen, Adam, how do you make money trading bitcoin?'

'You want the long answer or the short answer?'

'Short, I guess.'

He smiled. 'Buy low, sell high.'

'No, but seriously. How do you?'

'Tansy, *seriously*,' Adam said. 'Why are you asking me this?'

I sat down on his bed and put my water glass down on the floor. Then, without any warning at all, I started to cry.

'Shit.' Adam wheeled his chair over to me, sending Freezer leaping to the floor in a huff, and patted my shoulder awkwardly. Bless him, he'd seen me crying enough times over the past few weeks, but his shoulder pats weren't getting any less awkward.

'Shit,' he said again. Then he got up and went to the bathroom and came back with a roll of loo paper. 'Don't cry.'

'Sorry.' I blew my nose and wiped my eyes, but I wasn't done. Another sob built in my throat and I put my face in my hands and cried some more, while Adam patted and shushed like an out-of-practice nana trying to comfort a new baby. Freezer jumped up onto the bed and butted his head against my hand as if he was also trying to console me, which made me cry harder.

Eventually I stopped, blew my nose again and said, 'I'm really sorry, Adam.'

'It's okay. All part of the service. Do you want to tell me what's the matter? It's not just Renzo, is it?'

'No. It's… I've got myself into a bit of a mess.'

Adam looked appalled. 'You're not…?'

For a second I couldn't think what he meant. Then I laughed. 'I'm not pregnant. Jesus, that would be a proper fucking mess.'

Weirdly, the realisation that I could be having Renzo's baby – or making the decision not to have it – but I wasn't, cheered me up considerably.

I took a deep breath. 'I've got myself into a hole with money. I'm skint, and Mum's asked for some cash, and I can't help her. And I feel terrible about it. I don't know what to do.'

Adam said, 'Is that all? God, you had me worried there for a second. Just tell me how much you need.'

'I can't take your money, Adam.'

'Why not? I've got lots.'

'I just can't. I'd never be able to pay it back, for one thing.'

'That doesn't matter.'

'Yes, it does. It matters to me. I can't do it, Adam. But I'm so grateful to you for offering.'

He shrugged. 'I want to help. If you change your mind, please let me.'

'I will.' I stood up, giving Freezer a final stroke. 'Thanks. You're a good mate.'

We looked at each other for a second, then I turned and left the room. I could hear the rumble of Adam's chair wheeling across the floorboards as he moved back to his computer.

Whether it was his kindness or having had a good old weep, or realising that, however awful things were, at least I wasn't up the duff, I was feeling almost positive as I crossed the landing to my room.

I opened my wardrobe and took a deep breath. If I hesitated, I'd be lost. I pulled out the red dress I'd worn to Renzo's Christmas party, the night we split up, and threw it onto my bed. That, at least, I'd never want to wear again. The grey silk jumpsuit I'd worn on our first date was next, then the designer scarf he'd bought me in Paris and the white wool coat I'd splashed out on when we were in Zürich together. Several more dresses followed, and – after I'd given it one final, loving stroke – my shearling coat. From the bottom of my wardrobe I pulled pairs of shoes, some unworn and some almost new. There was the Prada handbag I'd bought with my webcamming money but never used, because I didn't feel as proud of it as I'd expected to – it felt tainted, somehow.

Hands on hips, I surveyed the pile. There were about twenty items there. Some I'd put straight on eBay with a Buy it Now price, so I could send Mum some money right away and tide myself over for a couple of weeks. Some would go to specialist retailers of 'pre-loved' designer fashion, which would take longer but give me a better price. The next morning, I took a load of the garments to the dry cleaner – another hit for my long-suffering credit card – and spent most of the day photographing the rest of the items and listing them online. It was something – a start, and not a bad one – but it wasn't enough.

That evening, I put on my coat, telling myself that wearing it just one last time would make no difference to its value, picked up my handbag and an empty Selfridges carrier bag and headed for the Tube station.

I'd been to the Luxeforless office on weekends before, once when I'd planned to work from home over the weekend and discovered I'd left a vital file on my desk, once when I'd needed to prepare for a Monday-morning photoshoot, and once when I'd lost my mobile and had become convinced I must have left it by the coffee machine. (I hadn't. It had been in my coat pocket all along.)

But this felt different. I felt furtive and guilty as I tapped in the passcode to let myself into the downstairs reception area, which was dark and silent. My footsteps sounded extra-loud on the marble floor as I approached the lift, then changed my mind and headed for the stairwell instead.

The office was dark, too, empty and still. But the alarm wasn't armed: instead of a flashing red LED on its panel, there was a steady green one. My breath caught in my throat and my heart hammered. I stood there in the gloom, listening intently, but I couldn't hear a thing.

What if there were burglars in the building? There was computer equipment worth tens of thousands of pounds filling the banks of desks, not to mention the merchandise in the sample room. For a second I imagined myself being ambushed by men in leather jackets, overpowered and left there, tied up and helpless, until the cleaners arrived in the small hours of Monday morning.

Don't be ridiculous, Tansy, I scolded myself. I didn't know much about the MO of your average burglar, but I was pretty sure that if they were planning a heist on the Luxeforless office, they'd need a van or something to transport their swag in, and the street outside had been empty.

One of my colleagues must be here, catching up with work or picking something up, just as I had. But then why were all the lights on their dim, energy-saving, out-of-hours setting? When I'd come in alone over the weekend, the first thing I'd done was switch them to their daytime brightness setting to banish the creepy shadows that filled every corner.

I didn't switch them on now, though. I walked silently through the deserted space, past the meeting rooms and the banks of desks, almost all the way to the closed door of Barri's office at the back of the room, and I saw no one.

Reassured, I turned and retraced my steps. Whoever had left last on Friday must have forgotten to set the alarm, that was all. It happened sometimes – there'd been an angry email about that very thing from Priti just a few months ago.

Still, I tried not to make a sound as I let myself into the sample room, pulled the door to and turned the light on low. The rails were groaning with garments on hangers, the floor stacked with boxes of shoes and bags. There was almost no room to move; the next staff sample sale was only a month away, and then the room would be half-empty again, waiting for more merchandise to come flooding in.

To make more space, someone had opened the crates sent by my Chinese supplier and crammed the unwanted dresses onto a rail, still in their plastic sleeves. I checked the swing tag on one, a rectangle of matte-black card embossed with the silver Luxeforless X Guillermo Hernandez label, bearing a price sticker.

Two hundred and fifty pounds. At our sample sale, the dresses would be priced at twenty-five pounds. Online, they'd fetch at least a hundred and fifty. We weren't supposed to sell on samples we'd purchased in the staff sale, but everyone knew it happened. I'd assuaged my guilt about it by sending a few garments every season to Mum and Perdita, pretending to myself that they might want to keep them for themselves, even though I knew that the chances of my mum or my sister ever wearing a floor-length cerise velvet evening gown or a feather-trimmed lace cocktail dress were somewhere between slim and none.

Well, pretence or no pretence, I couldn't keep Mum waiting a month. Her situation was desperate. When the sale happened, I'd just have to slip extra cash for the dresses in with my payment for whatever else I purchased. Which would mean I'd have to *have* cash – but that was a problem for another day. I'd find a way somehow.

I slipped five dresses off the rack and stuffed them into my waiting yellow carrier bag, wishing I could squash down my guilt as easily. It wasn't stealing, I told myself. I'd repay the money and no one would be out of pocket. And, most importantly, Mum would be able to pay the rent and not get a Section 21 notice from her landlord through the letter box along with all the other bills and final demands I'd seen her crying over, month after month.

It was done now; there was no other way.

I turned to leave the room, suddenly desperate to get home, back to Adam, a cup of tea and normality. Then I heard the alarm beep six times in rapid succession – the familiar tune I'd played so often when I left the office late.

Seventeen-five-thirteen, star – the date when luxeforless.com had gone live for the first time.

I froze again, rigid with fear. Then I heard the double chime the lift made when it arrived on our floor and – almost against my will – I pushed the door open a crack and peered out.

A figure in a cashmere coat and boots, a bright wool scarf wound high above the collar, was hurrying into the lift. I couldn't see their face, but I'd recognise that glossy fall of dark hair and croc-embossed leather tote bag anywhere.

It was Felicity.

Chapter Seven

Don't you hate it when it's Saturday, you were looking forward to a long, lazy lie-in and you find yourself pinging awake at seven in the morning? I mean, how is seven o'clock on a Saturday even legal? It was still dark outside, for God's sake. And it was raining. And the weekend, which should have felt packed with fun and possibility, just felt grey, dull and depressing.

I almost wished it was Monday, so I'd at least have something useful to do.

The past few weeks had dragged by. A few times, Adam had texted me to let me know Renzo's plans for the evening, but there was nothing I could do about them. Apart from one raucous but bittersweet night out at the Prince George to wish Charlotte and Xander bon voyage, I'd been too skint to go out. If it hadn't been for Adam's Netflix subscription I'd literally have spent every night at home staring at the walls; as it was I spent every night at home staring at the telly.

I rolled over in bed, pulled the duvet up over my head to shut out the sound of rain pattering against my window and cars swishing along the street outside, and closed my eyes.

It's only sleep, Tansy. You've got this. Anyone can sleep.

But I couldn't.

Reluctantly, I stood up, pushed the duvet aside and slid my feet into my slippers. Adam's room and the room that used to be Charlotte's were both closed and silent.

Downstairs, I switched on the lights, the telly and the radio for a bit of company, and dropped two pieces of bread into the toaster.

I looked at my phone, but I had no new messages. I'd been expecting to hear from Mum or Perdita that the new baby was coming, but there was nothing yet. I opened Facebook and saw an event reminder for Sally's birthday drinks at a pub in south London that evening, from seven thirty. She'd invited everyone in the team, and all of us were going apart from Felicity, because it was Pru's birthday too and she was off to a far more glamorous location to celebrate that. It was seven thirty in the morning now, and my God, those twelve hours might as well have been a lifetime.

Is there anything more depressing than a rainy Saturday when you've got no one to snuggle up and watch Netflix with, no one to go for brunch with, no one to have lazy afternoon sex with?

If there was, I couldn't think of it.

I spread a thick layer of peanut butter onto a piece of toast, sprinkled it with salt and Tabasco sauce (don't knock it till you've tried it), and carried the plate, a mug of coffee and my phone over to the sofa.

If I planned carefully, I could fill those twelve long hours, and then the day would be over.

I could watch a box set or read a book. I could bake something, but there was no one who'd eat it except Adam. I could make soup. A huge pot of nourishing soup that I could take to work with me for lunch to save me spending a fortune in Pret every month. I could go to the gym, even though it would be full of preening Instagrammers drinking protein shakes. But then I remembered I'd cancelled my membership as part of my new austerity regime.

If Charlotte had been here, we could have gone out for a coffee together, or to the cinema, or even just hung out drinking tea and chatting. But she wasn't here: she was basking on a beach somewhere exotic with a man who adored her.

I could start getting ready for Sally's party at five thirty – five, even, if I painted my nails as part of my preparations. And then I'd be with other people, at least. I'd have fun.

And then, I thought grimly, it would be Sunday and I'd have the same problem all over again – a long, lonely day stretching out before me.

Through the French doors, I could see the grey morning brightening slightly. I looked out and saw that the rain had stopped and the clouds were breaking apart, revealing a pale, cold sky.

I could go outside, then, at least.

I put my breakfast things in the dishwasher, showered and dressed in jeans, my purple jumper and boots. I looked at myself in the mirror and grimaced. I was hollow-eyed and pale. My eyebrows needed tinting and my hair needed a trim, but both those things would have to wait until next payday at least.

I put on tinted moisturiser, swept on some bronzer, added mascara and a slick of matte-pink lipstick, so at least I looked a bit less like a ghost, even though I still felt like one. I put on a woolly hat and my old, shabby grey coat. (God, I missed my beautiful shearling, but the proceeds from its sale were paying Mum's rent, so I couldn't complain.)

Putting my phone and my keys in my bag, I left the house and walked to the bus stop with no real idea where I was going.

I'd get on the first bus that arrived, I decided, and stay on it until I got somewhere interesting.

Just my luck; I'd misjudged which bus stop to wait at, and instead of a route heading into town, the bus route fairies gifted me the 276, which was headed out into deepest suburban east London. But I'd made my decision and there was no going back, so I got on and went up to the top deck.

Instead of getting my phone out and flicking idly through my social media, I looked out at the streets of Hackney creeping past the windows. I breathed and I watched. I was in no hurry; I had nothing special to do and nowhere important to be. I could just be here, on my own in the warm. I studied the signs above the shops the bus passed: fried chicken shops, betting shops and charity shops, mostly, with the occasional ethnic food store, on-trend coffee shop or vegan restaurant.

I listened as stop after stop was announced, enjoying the sound of the names: Marsh Hill, Crowfoot Close, Wick Lane. I let myself wonder where the marsh had been, what crow had been important enough to have a street named after it, and whether there had once been a candle factory somewhere nearby.

Then the electronic announcement said, 'Roman Road Market.'

Almost before I registered that I'd made a decision, I was down the stairs and waiting for the doors to open. But my mind wasn't on whether centurions wearing cloaks and helmets had driven chariots down a track here two thousand years ago. I was thinking about clothes.

When I was first in London, working as an unpaid intern and staying with Debbie's friend Sasha, she'd brought me to Roman Road Market. It was high summer then, and we bought fresh cherries from a stall and ate them out of brown paper bags as we strolled along. I had forgotten all about that day, but now it came back to me in a rush, so clearly I could almost taste the ripe sourness of the fruit, smell the incense drifting out of shop doors, hear the stallholders shouting, 'Three for a pound! Only one pound for three. Four for you, beautiful!'

It had been packed, I remembered. It had taken Sasha and me the best part of an hour to make our way from one end of the market to the other.

'If you want to learn about fashion, Tansy,' she'd said, 'places like this will teach you far more than college or work experience. Look at that young woman there – her entire outfit probably cost her under a tenner. But she's nailed it.'

The girl in question had been wearing what looked like an old nylon nightie, with battered Doc Martens, a feather boa and a trilby hat almost covering her hair, which was bleached and dyed into a rainbow of pink, lilac and silver. She looked fabulous. And this was long before unicorn hair was even a thing.

There had also been second-hand clothes stalls, I remembered. Sasha had bought a pair of tailored wool trousers with a Chanel label in them for fifteen quid, and I'd found a fringed, beaded shawl that might or might not have been a 1920s original but looked the part. I loved it so much I still hadn't been able to part with it, even though I hardly ever went anywhere I could wear it.

I might find a new coat, I thought, jumping off the bus and hurrying down the road, following the signs directing me to the market. Or a handbag to take the place of the one I'd sold, one I could take genuine pleasure in this time. Or, at the very least, find inspiration for my new collection.

The only problem was, I was too early. It was still not yet ten, and the market hadn't opened properly for business. Stallholders were heaving armfuls of clothes onto garment rails, arranging jewellery on tables, draping scarves over mannequins and plonking hats on their wooden heads. But no one was selling anything. The man at the discount French Connection stall I'd had my eye on sent me away with a curt, 'Ten thirty we open, love. Not a minute before. Have a cuppa and come back.'

So I followed his advice and headed across the road towards a coffee shop, but before I got there, I stopped. I may have gasped. There was a girl, a few years younger than me, setting out her stall. She herself was stunning, about nineteen or twenty as far as I could tell, with a bright red, side-swept, angular pixie cut (the sort you can only get away with if your bone structure is literally perfect), multiple piercings in her ears and sparkly false eyelashes. She was wearing a denim playsuit over ribbed scarlet tights, a vintage faux-fur coat over that, and stripy wristwarmers to protect her hands as she arranged her garments in the biting wind.

She was striking, for sure, but the things she was lifting out of a blue Ikea bag and onto a rickety frame lined with hessian were something else again. I stopped to look, and then I found myself staying and gazing.

There were jeans, most distressed or destroyed, and heavily embellished with beading, criss-cross lacing and embroidery. There were skirts made from alternating panels of denim and bright silk.

There was a black lace evening dress with a deep swish of fringing around the bottom of the skirt, and another, a white dress that was…

I came closer and looked. Yes, it was made from old wedding dresses: panels of silk, lace and tulle in shades of white, cream and ivory, the whole thing a spectacular, unique creation that would make you feel like a princess in a fairy tale the moment you put it on.

Everything was custom-made, I realised, and upcycled from other garments. As different as they could possibly be from the mass-produced sequinned frocks I'd taken from the office sample room. (*What the hell was Felicity doing there that night, anyway?* I wondered for the thousandth time.)

'I'm not open,' the girl snapped. 'And no photography.'

She turned back to her bag and lifted out a tailored, emerald-green silk shift and arranged it on a hanger.

'Are these your designs?' I asked.

'Look, I'm busy, innit. Come back in half an hour.'

I suppressed a smile. I'd worked with enough designers in my time to know that some of them – actually, a lot of them – could be total divas, but I didn't think I'd ever met one as downright rude as this.

I stepped back a little and watched as she took out a portable garment steamer and ran it over the dresses so the creases dropped away. Then she adjusted the fall of each garment on its hanger, turned one dress around so the embellishment on the back was visible, and carefully arranged a necklace over another. Her attention to detail impressed me.

At last, she stepped back, surveyed her work and nodded. Then she picked up a coffee cup from the table, took a sip and grimaced.

'Cold?' I said. 'Can I buy you a fresh one?'

'Look, I thought I told you to… Oh, all right then. Macchiato, two sugars. And a custard Danish.'

She stared defiantly at me, daring me to point out that she was taking the piss. But I didn't. I smiled and said, 'Sure thing.'

The queue in the coffee shop was long and, ridiculously, I worried that I wouldn't be able to find her stall again, or that she would have packed up and spirited everything away. But she hadn't, of course. When I got back with her drink and pastry, and a coffee for myself, she was with a customer.

'Could I try that on, please?' the woman asked, pointing up at the green dress.

'No.'

'Er… Is it not for sale?'

'It's for sale,' the girl said. 'Just not to you. Not your colour, and a size too small.'

'Oh.' The woman actually blushed. 'I'm sorry.'

'Here,' the girl said, as if making a huge concession. 'You can try this one.'

From the rail behind her, she produced an ice-blue dress in a similar style, handed it over and gestured to a curtained-off corner of the stall.

The woman looked doubtful for a second, and I didn't blame her – the idea of getting my kit off and getting into a cocktail dress with only a flimsy curtain to protect me from the cold wind and the eyes of the passing crowd made me shiver, too. Then she looked longingly back at the dress.

'No refunds, no exchanges,' the girl said. 'Cash only.'

Reluctantly, the customer disappeared behind the curtain. I handed over the cardboard cup and the paper bag and the girl nodded, but didn't thank me.

'My name's Tansy,' I said.

She narrowed her eyes and sipped her coffee, and for a second I thought she wasn't going to respond. Then she replied, 'Chelsea.'

But that was all she had to say. We waited in silence for a couple of minutes, until the customer emerged from behind the curtain, looking chilly but with an expression on her face that told me she'd seen a version of herself in the mirror that she hadn't thought was possible. Her face said, 'I can look beautiful!'

'I'll take it,' she said aloud. 'It's incredible. I've never… How much is it, by the way?'

'One seventy-five,' Chelsea replied, folding her arms as if challenging the woman to argue.

But she didn't. She counted the cash out from her purse – looking briefly panicked that she wouldn't have enough, and scrabbling around for change – and handed it over without hesitation. She would have paid twice as much, I knew. She'd probably have parted with a kidney in exchange for that frock.

Chelsea folded the dress and placed it carefully in an unbranded brown paper bag and passed it to her.

'Thank you,' the woman gushed. 'Thank you so much. I'll be back.'

Chelsea did the hard stare thing again, unsmiling, eyes narrowed. 'You're welcome,' she said reluctantly.

The woman practically skipped away, clutching her purchase to her chest.

Chelsea turned back to me. 'Now, what do you want? You're not shopping.'

'No, I'm not,' I said. 'I just wanted to ask you a couple of things about your work. You make all these yourself?'

'Yeah.'

'Have you been doing it for long?'

'Three years, since I left school.'

'You're not at college?' I asked, amazed that someone with no training could be this good.

'Nah. Look, why are you—'

Then another customer interrupted us, and a few minutes later she left, two hundred quid lighter, clutching the fringed black dress in a brown bag and smiling like it was Christmas.

I said, 'I work in fashion, too. I'm a buyer at Luxeforless, you know, the online boutique?'

Chelsea nodded, her mouth full of custard Danish. She didn't say anything, but I could see a spark of animation in her face for the first time. I knew what she was thinking: this could be her big break. Her clothes could be stocked in a high-end online store.

I said, 'Would you be able to meet up, during the week maybe, when you're not so busy? I'd love to find out more about you.'

'Okay.'

I reached into my bag and rummaged around, hoping there was a business card in there somewhere. And then I thought, *she won't contact me. However eager she is, she'll be too frightened of being knocked back. She'll keep my card and stare at it every day, and maybe she'll dial the number and hang up when it rings, or compose an email and never press send, and eventually, one day, she'll look for my card and not be able to find it. But I won't hear from her. She'll carry on doing what she's doing and either she'll survive or she won't.*

So instead, I took out my phone. 'What's your number?'

She recited it and I saved it, and again, I saw that flash of longing and fear in her eyes and, again, I was pretty sure I knew what she was thinking. *She's not who she says she is. And even if she is, she'll never call.*

The Ninth Date

Two weeks after Renzo and I got back from Paris, I had an idea. We'd been out together four times since then, twice for cocktails and dinner at swanky restaurants in Mayfair, once to see *La Bohème* at the Royal Opera House (I'd never been to the opera before, and to be perfectly honest I didn't have a clue what was going on, but I loved sitting there next to Renzo, admiring the costumes and the set and soaking up the atmosphere), and once to the cinema and then for dinner at Pizza Express.

Each time (except the pizza and movie night, which was my treat), Renzo had made the restaurant reservation or bought the tickets, and each time we'd spent the night together afterwards at his flat.

So for our ninth date I decided to plan something different. After spending hours trawling the internet and studying reviews on TripAdvisor, I booked two nights at a hotel in the Cotswolds. I told him to take the afternoon off work and meet me at Paddington station at midday on Friday, but refused to give him any more details, saying only that he should pack for two nights away and that the rest would be my surprise.

I was practically hyperventilating with nervous excitement as I waited for him on the concourse, my little wheelie suitcase at my feet and a carrier bag with snacks and two small bottles of cava in my hand. It wasn't the vintage champagne Renzo bought for us when we were out, but it was fizzy and reasonably cold, and I hoped it would make the train journey feel like a romantic celebration.

You know how it is when a relationship is still quite new: it seems like everything is possible, everything is thrilling, yet at the same time everything is still so uncertain. What if some crisis erupted at Renzo's work and he wasn't able to make it? What if I'd messed up the train tickets somehow and we were supposed to leave from Marylebone or somewhere? What if I couldn't find him in the crowds of people? What if he told me he'd changed his mind, not just about the weekend but about me?

I checked my phone again and again, making sure I knew the numbers of our reserved seats and the address of the hotel where we were going off by heart. I was just tapping through to WhatsApp to see if there was a message from him, and the platform for our train was just being called, making fresh panic surge inside me in case we missed it, when Renzo appeared in front of me.

'There you are,' he said, wrapping me in a hug that made all my worries melt away.

As always, I felt a thrill of happiness when I saw him. He was wearing his work suit, although he'd taken off his tie. His hair was swept back from his face in a glossy black wing. His perfect teeth flashed in a grin of pleasure as he looked at me. He seemed to have arrived from a different world to the crowds of sweating tourists and harassed families – almost too perfect and glossy to be real.

'All set?' he said. 'Come on then, you'd better tell me where we're going.'

And I realised I'd been standing there like a lemon, staring at him without saying a word.

'Platform ten,' I said, and he took my hand and we hurried along together and found our seats.

'So when are you going to reveal the mystery destination?' he asked, as I twisted the cap off a bottle of cava and passed it to him. 'I even brought my passport, in case we were getting a flight somewhere.'

I laughed. 'Nothing as ambitious as that. We're going to Chippenham.'

I watched his face carefully for a flicker of disappointment, but there wasn't one, so I went on, 'The place where we're staying is in a little village near there. It's really picturesque, apparently. There's lovely countryside around, so we can go for walks and stuff. Maybe even hire bicycles, if we want. But mostly just chill.'

Our eyes met and he smiled, reaching for my hand again and caressing my palm with his thumb. We both knew what 'just chill' meant. Walks and cycling were all very well – on our second date, we'd been for lunch at a country pub, and he'd surprised me by being able to name all the birds we'd seen and lots of the plants, too – but what I really wanted was to spend long, languid hours in bed with him.

'Here we are,' I said a couple of hours later, paying the cab driver who'd brought us from the station. 'The Cow and Bell.'

The pub, with its golden stone front half-concealed by ivy, was just as pretty as it had looked on TripAdvisor. A fat ginger cat was perched on the front step, and the door stood open to a hallway that looked gloomy in contrast to the brilliant sunshine outside.

We picked up our bags and walked in, Renzo ducking his head as he passed under the low beams. To one side of us was a bar, the sounds of clinking glasses and muted conversation drifting out; to the other was a door to a lounge where I could see chintz-covered sofas and little spindly-legged tables. In front of us was a desk holding a computer, a visitors' book and a brass bell.

I hesitated, but Renzo walked confidently forward and pressed the bell, and a few seconds later a woman with dyed red hair scraped back in a ponytail emerged from the bar.

'How can I help?'

'I've booked a room. Tansy Barlow.'

'Let me see.' The woman squeezed behind the desk and sat down, tapping the keyboard. 'Barlow, for two nights, here you are. I'll just take a credit card for any extras, if I may. You're in room four, just up the stairs and to your right. Breakfast is served between seven and nine in the bar area. Enjoy your stay with us.'

'Thank you,' I said, accepting a key with a large wooden fob with a number 4 on it.

Renzo didn't say anything, but he picked up our bags and I followed him up a narrow, squeaking staircase that smelled a bit of that morning's breakfast and a bit of cat, and slotted the key into the door of room four.

Already, my heart was beginning to sink, and it sank still further when I opened the door. The room, which had looked small but comfortable in the pictures online, was tiny. There was just enough space to edge between the double bed and the wardrobe. A framed print of a cow hung above the bed, and thick net curtains covered the window. A small table held a television and a tray with a little kettle, sachets of teabags and instant coffee, and tubs of long-life milk. I glanced into the bathroom and saw a cramped shower, washbasin and loo. It was oppressively hot.

Neither of us said anything. I couldn't bear to look at Renzo. Part of me wanted to pretend everything was okay; another part didn't want him to think I didn't know it wasn't. Objectively, of course, it was fine: it was a perfectly comfortable room in a modest country hotel. When I went abroad for fashion weeks, I stayed in far, far worse places than this. If I'd come here with Dale, my boyfriend at university, we'd have thought this was quite the lap of luxury.

But I'd known as soon as I walked in that Renzo wouldn't see it that way. The contrast between this and the enormous suite where we'd stayed in Paris couldn't have been greater.

I didn't just feel disappointed; I felt ashamed. This was my surprise, the romantic weekend I'd planned for us. And this was the best I could do.

Renzo went over to the window and tried to open it, but it was locked. I sat down on the bed, and a second later he joined me and put his arm around me.

'I'm sorry,' I said, feeling myself choking up like I was about to cry.

But he laughed, gave my shoulder a little squeeze and turned my face gently towards his. 'Why would you be sorry? You don't have to apologise for anything. Do you want to stay? Or would you rather find somewhere else?'

'We can't leave. I've paid for the room in advance.'

'Sunk cost fallacy,' he said.

'What?'

'It's a thing in behavioural economics. The money's gone and we're not going to recover it by staying here if we don't want to.'

He took out his phone, tapped the screen a few times and I saw the number for Colton Capital appear on the screen.

'Yeah, it's me,' he said. 'Get one of the EAs to book me a suite at Babington House, would you? If they haven't got one, a superior double will do. And a table for two in the restaurant tonight, please. And they can throw in a few spa treatments, too, since it's a late booking. Okay? Thank you. *Ciao.*'

'What if they're full?'

'They won't be full. Come on then, if we're doing a runner, let's do it fast. Shame you didn't ask me to drive us up, but we'll get the woman downstairs to ring for a cab.'

'But what will we say to her?'

'Whatever we want. It's no skin off her back, she's got the room paid for.'

We picked up our cases and went downstairs again. Renzo pinged the bell and the woman hurried through from the bar as she had before.

I handed back the key.

'I'm awfully sorry, but there's been a change of plan. We don't need the room after all. Could you order a taxi for us, please?'

'Back to the station? I hope everything's all right.'

'No, to Babington House,' Renzo said, and I felt my face flame with embarrassment.

She looked hard at us. 'I see.'

We spent that night in an enormous, air-conditioned room in a stunning converted barn, with a free-standing bath in the middle of the floor and a crystal chandelier hanging over the bed. We ate a delicious dinner in the restaurant, and Renzo ordered a two-hundred-pound bottle of claret to go with it. The next day I had a facial, a massage and a pedicure while he worked out in the gym, and then in the afternoon we explored the grounds together before going back to our suite and having exactly the sort of long, lazy shag I'd imagined, before showering, dressing and getting a taxi to a nearby restaurant that Renzo said was owned by a celebrity chef and had a Michelin star.

Our dinner there was even better – seven courses of small dishes that quite honestly looked like they'd been arranged on the plates by an artist. I had quail for the first time in my life, and ravioli that the waiter grated fresh truffle over at the table while I watched in awe. Renzo made me try one of his sweetbreads, which I thought was the most heavenly thing I'd ever tasted until he told me it was some unmentionable bit of a sheep. There was a bread waiter who kept coming round and pressing different kinds on us: bread with caraway seeds, bread with sundried tomatoes, bread with caramelised onion, and three different kinds of butter to have with them. There was even a pre-pudding that they brought before your actual pudding, so I was too full to have more than a tiny spoonful of my rich chocolate soufflé. And, best of all, I was having too much fun to worry about all the calories I was hoovering up.

In bed that night, after we'd had slightly wild, slightly drunken sex, Renzo held me in his arms and said, 'You must let me pay for stuff, *fragolina mia*. I don't mind. It's cents on the dollar, it really is. I like doing cool things, and I love having you to share them with.

Whatever you want us to do together, you must just tell me and I'll sort it, or one of the girls in the office will. Okay?'

'Okay,' I replied, resting my head drowsily on his shoulder. 'Thank you so much for this. It's been amazing.'

'It's my absolute pleasure. This was your idea, anyway. I should be thanking you.'

And as I drifted into sleep, I couldn't help feeling sad that I hadn't had the pleasure of treating him.

I knew he meant what he'd said: whatever I wanted to do, we could do. Whatever I wanted to have, I could have. He would casually take out his black American Express card and that would be that. He never needed to worry about it being declined, or feel guilty because he couldn't afford extra groceries for the food bank that week, or go without stuff he wanted because his family needed his help.

As long as I was his girlfriend, I could live a life I'd only ever been able to dream of. But was I – could I ever be – good enough for him?

Chapter Eight

As it turned out, I didn't contact Chelsea the following week because three things happened. Only one of them was good.

First of all, on Sunday, while I was lying in bed recovering from my hangover after Sally's party, Mum called to tell me my sister had gone into labour. I spent the day glued to their WhatsApp updates, and by the evening I had a new nephew.

Meet Calum, Perdita texted under a picture of her beaming, tired face and the tiny bundle clutched to her chest, starfish hands poking into the yellow blanket Mum had crocheted for her newest grandchild. *He weighs seven pounds four ounces and he can't wait to meet his auntie Tansy. My foof is in tatters and I'm in love.*

So I went to work on Monday with an overnight bag packed and asked Lisa if I could take a couple of days' holiday, which she could hardly refuse as I had loads owed to me. I got the evening train down to Cornwall, trying to read the new *Vogue* on the way but unable to concentrate, distracted by the excitement of seeing my sister, the new baby and my older niece and nephew, while fighting with resentment at knowing I'd have to see Dad, too, and hide my feelings about him so as not to upset Mum.

'You'll have to wait until the morning to meet Calum, love,' Mum said firmly when she picked me up at the station. 'A new baby's disruptive enough for Arthur and Rosie without you turning up at nearly midnight and waking the whole house.'

I noticed how tired she looked after her double shift at work, and that her ancient hatchback had developed an ominous-sounding new rattle when she changed gear. But I didn't say anything – I just let her chatter on about how adorable her new grandson was, how the neighbour whose dog she'd been walking was up and about again, and how I'd got much too thin and she hoped I wasn't going to be getting that eating disorder thing again.

'I'm fine, Mum,' I said. 'Don't worry about me. I've just been busy at work. You know I lose weight when I'm stressed.'

'And what about that boy you were seeing? The one with the Italian name.'

'Renzo. We broke up before Christmas. It was, like, a mutual thing. I'm okay.' I felt the familiar ache of loss, and wondered whether to tell her that it was only temporary, a lovers' tiff, and we'd be back on track in no time. But I knew I didn't believe that enough myself to convince her that it was true.

'If you say so.' She glanced at me, then swung the car into its parking space, expertly squeezing in between number eight's Skoda and number twelve's Peugeot.

Sometimes, when I was feeling particularly stressed about needing to help Mum out with money, I caught myself thinking, *Why don't you sell the bloody car?* before remembering that not only was it the only way she could manage to work her irregular shifts, but it was the one thing in her life that made her feel independent and in control. And then I felt absolutely wretched with guilt for having had the idea in the first place.

I said, 'Is Dad...?'

'Asleep, I expect. He was up late last night.'

If I hadn't already known what that meant, the grim set of her lips would have told me. But the house was silent and unlit, and we both went straight to bed. Mum asked me if I needed anything to eat but I lied and said I'd had a sandwich on the train, and took a glass of water upstairs.

As I lay in the darkness on the lumpy single mattress, I began to hear a faint, arrhythmic sound above the rush of the wind. It was so quiet I had to strain my ears to realise it was there at all, and then it became clearer and clearer. *Click.* Pause. *Click, click.* Pause. *Click.* Then a longer gap. Then, *Click click click click click.*

Dad. Jesus. The betting shops being closed didn't stop him, Mum's rage and despair hadn't stopped him, the birth of his new grandson hadn't stopped him. He was downstairs gambling on the computer while Mum slept. Gambling away the money I'd sent Mum just days before from the clothes I'd sold on eBay, sinking all of our lives deeper into peril. And I knew that nothing I could say or do would stop him, either.

Mum had done her best to shield me from the truth for as long as she could. But it was impossible not to realise that something serious was going on.

It wasn't just the whispered (and sometimes shouted) rows, the expression on Mum's face when bills came through the letterbox, the need to sell our cottage and move to the rented house. There were other things, too. The appointments Mum arranged with the GP, even though Dad assured us he wasn't ill. The time Mum frogmarched him out of the door one evening, her expression as grim as his was sheepish, announcing that they were going to a meeting. Mum constantly having to hunt for things – her purse or the card reader for the online banking or the little slips of paper she wrote the password for the computer on every time she changed it – because either she'd forgotten where she'd hidden them or Dad had found them and hidden them somewhere else.

She'd tried, she really had. She'd tried everything, and nothing had made a difference. And there was no point me going and confronting Dad now, in the middle of the night. He might stop for half an hour, or until tomorrow morning, but he wouldn't stop for good. I knew that for certain and I was sure Mum did, too.

So I lay there in the dark, my jaw clenching tighter and tighter and my eyes burning, until eventually I fell asleep.

Mum and I left early the next morning, before Dad was up, and she drove me to Perdita and Ryan's, where I spent the next two days cuddling my adorable, squidgy new nephew, making cups of tea for Perdita and binge-watching *Fireman Sam* with Rosie and Arthur.

Oh, and changing nappies and cleaning up sick and wanting to stuff cotton wool in my ears as Rosie, who was understandably unsettled by her little brother's arrival, acted out with yet another tantrum.

Sometimes, when I was jammed like a sweaty sardine on a Central Line Tube on a summer afternoon, or when Barri was in one of his moods, or when it was Saturday night and I had no money to go out and no one to go out with, I looked at my sister's life with envy. She'd never been to university; she'd married her high school sweetheart, settled down in a little three-bedroom house with a garden and as soon as Arthur arrived, she'd given up her job in a call centre with evident relief and settled down to be a stay-at-home mum.

But, as I watched those two days go by in their unchanging rhythm: the morning feed, the older kids' breakfast, the battle to get everyone wrapped up warm for a trip to the park, the nutritious lunch of cheese and tomato sandwiches rejected and thrown onto the floor, another battle over nap time and another over bath time and a truly epic one over bedtime, I thought that if I never met anyone I wanted to have kids with it wouldn't actually be so bad.

And then I remembered Renzo and thought what an amazing dad he'd be, and found myself feeling broody all over again. I remembered the soppy expression he got on his face when he talked about his sisters' kids, and the photos he'd shown me of him cuddling one of his nephews, who had ice cream smeared all over his face. I imagined him cuddling our baby and blowing raspberries on her tummy like Ryan did. I imagined him looking at me the way Ryan looked at Perdita when she was feeding Calum, like, *My God, look at this amazing thing we've done together.*

And then I remembered that my chances of ever having sex with Renzo again, never mind procreating with him, were non-existent, and I came back to earth with a bump – and not the baby kind.

So, to be honest, it was a relief when I got back to the office just before lunch on Thursday. The team had all signed a 'Congratulations, Auntie!' card for me, and tied three blue balloons to the back of my chair, which made me laugh and then almost cry. I'd pulled my chair towards my desk and was starting to work through my mountain of unread emails, when I heard Felicity's voice behind me.

'Hello!' she cooed. 'Lovely to have you back. We missed you. How was the baba?'

'Adorable. But he thinks sleep is for the weak. I'm shattered.'

She laughed. 'Fancy a bite to eat before you get stuck in here? We could try that new vegan place that's opened round the corner.'

I thought about my carefully planned lunch budget, and then realised I'd forgotten to pick up a sandwich on my way in, and I was hungry.

'Go on then.'

'My treat,' Felicity said.

'But—' I started to protest, and then I remembered the cost of my return train ticket, the gifts I'd taken for my sister and the baby (and the older children, so they wouldn't feel left out). And anyway, Felicity had already got her coat on and was waiting impatiently for me, so I followed her to the lift and out into the street.

The café was just around the corner, as she'd promised – an ultra-feminine place with little curly-legged tables and chairs, the floor tiled in delicate grey and white that must have been a nightmare to keep clean, and a counter painted in rainbow pastel stripes and piled with cupcakes on tall stands. It was crowded with women – I counted just two men, one bearded guy who looked like a true believer, and a bloke in a suit who looked like he'd been dragged there on sufferance by his female boss – but with her usual skill, Felicity spotted the only free table and nabbed it.

'I have to say, vegan food isn't normally my cup of tea,' she remarked, studying the menu. 'But it's so on-trend right now, and you have to admit this place is fabulously Instagrammable.'

'It's lovely,' I said. 'Thanks for suggesting it. I feel a bit bad, given I've been out of the office for most of the week, but you've got to eat, right?'

Eat. Looking at the menu, I felt an old, familiar anxiety that I thought I'd put to bed years ago. With men, strangely, I was fine, but eating with women always freaked me out, like whatever I chose would mean a judgement: either, 'No wonder she's getting a bit podgy,' or, 'She was anorexic, you know, she's obviously not over it,' or anything at all in between.

A waitress came over with a carafe of water with cucumber slices floating in it, and an iPad. 'What can I get for you ladies?'

I looked back down at the menu, panicking slightly.

'I'd like a kale salad,' I said. Kale, my old buddy. I knew where I was with kale. Not fighting the urge to ram my fingers down my throat as soon as I'd finished my lunch, is where.

'The black bean and walnut burger, please,' Felicity said. 'With sweet potato fries – actually, no, make that regular fries. And extra chipotle mayo.'

How, I agonised. How the hell did she manage to give no fucks at all about what people thought of her, wear her self-assurance as easily as a leather biker jacket that went with everything and eat stuff because it was what she wanted, not what she thought other people would think it was okay for her to eat?

I sipped my water. 'So what's been going on in the office while I was away?'

Maybe if I initiated a chat about work, I'd find a way to ask her what she'd been doing in the office that Sunday night, sneaking around as furtively as I'd been.

'Same old, same old,' Felicity said. 'His highness threw a strop at Sally because her mood boards were too vanilla. We've got to quit using so many coffee capsules or we'll be going back to instant. And Daria sent out a stroppy email because only, like, three people have signed up for that mentoring thing.'

So it was going to happen, after all. Daria's email would be sitting in my own inbox, still unread.

I opened my mouth to say, 'Hey, listen, I came into work a few Sundays ago to pick up some stuff, and you were there. What's going on?' But I bottled it. I couldn't ask her without telling her why I'd been there myself, and that would open a can of worms that was definitely best left firmly closed.

Our food arrived and I forked up some seed-strewn green leaves, while Felicity picked up her burger with both hands and took a massive, squelchy bite. Incredibly, she managed to look both elegant and sexy while she chewed, wiping a smear of guacamole from her chin with her napkin.

'May I have some salt for my fries, please?' She seemed to have summoned the waitress with the tiniest glance.

'How was Pru's birthday?' I asked, folding a kale leaf carefully with my knife and fork before eating it.

'Aww, so fab! Bless her, it was a total surprise. We drank eight bottles of fizz between six of us and then we went on to Loulou's and someone sent over a bottle of Beluga voddie, so of course we had to have that too. I was hanging so badly next day, I chucked a sickie and didn't get out of bed for thirty-six hours except to spew some more.'

I laughed. 'Sounds like it was fun.'

'It was epic,' Felicity sprinkled salt liberally over her fries, then picked up five of them in a bunch and put them in her mouth. 'Anyway, so, I was reeeally pissed. Did I mention I was pissed?'

'You did.' I wondered where this was going.

'So I don't remember too much about the actual night. Not after about eleven, anyway. But yesterday, the weirdest thing happened. My phone rang, and it was a new contact that I'd saved without remembering.'

'That must have freaked you out.' I looked down at my salad and poked it a bit with my fork, spearing a cherry tomato and a cube of tofu.

'It so did! It was, like, surreal. Incoming call from Renzo, and I was, like, I don't know anyone called Renzo, and then I realised I did.'

'You met him when we were out a couple of weeks ago,' I said. I tried to smile, but the shape my mouth was making felt more like a snarl.

'Exactly!' Felicity ate some more of her burger as if nothing untoward was happening at all. 'So I realised he must have been at Loulou's that night too, and asked for my number. And I must have given it to him while I was shitfaced, because obviously normally he'd be off limits, Tans, of course he would.'

When Adam called me Tans, I didn't mind – I even quite liked it. But Felicity doing it now – while she was telling me this – was so not okay that it made me think about how it would feel to tip the carafe of cucumber-infused water over her carefully un-done up-do.

'Right,' I said. 'But you did. Give him your number, I mean. And he called you.'

Sophie Ranald

'He did. That voice! I can so totally see why you… But anyway. I let it go to voicemail, and I haven't rung him back, because of course I would never do that without checking if you were okay with it.'

I put my knife and fork together on my plate at five o'clock, the way Debbie had told me was the right way, with the prongs of the fork facing upwards.

'Obviously it's fine! Renzo and I are so over, we're ancient history. I just want him to be happy. And you too, of course.'

My voice sounded normal, even though inside I was screaming, *No! Forget your stupid pride! Tell her you're still in love with him and you want him back! Tell her why he dumped you! She'll understand – she's your friend!*

'Oh, Tans.' Felicity swooshed the last of her fries through the last of her spicy mayo. 'I'm so glad I told you this. I've been stressing about it so much, but I should have known you'd be cool with it.'

'Of course I am!' I took a big, determined gulp of cucumber water. 'On you go! Call him back!'

'Maybe you could be bridesmaid at our wedding!' Felicity trilled, gesturing for the bill.

'I'd be honoured,' I said through gritted teeth. 'Godmother to your first child as well, maybe?'

She raked a perfectly manicured hand through her fringe and laughed again, like I'd just said the wittiest thing ever.

'Tans, you're the best. Thanks for being you.'

'Thank you so much for lunch,' I said, and we walked back to the office with our arms linked, even though it felt like going for an afternoon stroll with a Dementor.

Chapter Nine

All that afternoon, I tried to focus on work. But I couldn't: I kept imagining Renzo and Felicity together, his lips brushing her lush, creamy shoulders, his hands around her waist, her dark hair tumbling over his pillow. I hit 'reply to all' on an email that should have gone to just the sender, and sent forty people outside Luxeforless a confidential spreadsheet. I spilled water all over the meeting room table, soaking my poor supplier's grey wool trousers. I kept having to go to the loo and cry.

Although I had loads to do and had been planning on staying late to catch up, when five thirty came I shut down my computer, picked up my bag and left as fast as my legs would carry me. There was no point in staying – no point in anything, really. I just wanted to go home, get into bed and hide there until I had to get up and face the world again.

Tempting as it was, I didn't call in sick the next day. I had too much to do, and too much to lose. But I did find myself running horribly late, because not only did I oversleep and take twice as long as normal to hide the dark rings under my eyes, but the Tube stitched me up by being out of order, so I had to get a bus to Bethnal Green and then a different line from there.

The bus took me past Roman Road, and I remembered that I needed to get in touch with Chelsea soon. *I'll take a look at some numbers over the weekend*, I promised myself, *so I can have an idea in my head about the prospects for her business before speaking to her.* Then I had a better idea – a much better idea.

I bought a coffee on my way into the office, mindful of Barri's orders to cut down on Nespresso consumption, and it was almost ten before I got to my desk. Felicity hadn't arrived yet, but Kris and Sally were there already, looking intently at their screens and tapping on their keyboards.

I opened my emails, resolving to spend an hour working through the messages I hadn't had time to read and respond to the previous day. Quickly, before my courage could desert me, I sent a message to Lisa saying that I'd discovered a really exciting young designer, and I'd love to have a chat about potentially listing her collection on Luxeforless.

And then I opened the Gmail account that I used for my personal stuff, just, you know, in case.

I had twenty new messages in my promotions folder, all of which I deleted unread, tempting as it was to check out the new offers from Boohoo, Missguided, The Outnet and all the rest of them.

There was only one new message in my main inbox, from debbievalentine73@hotmail.com. Just seeing her name made me smile – it felt like a hug from the other side of the world, right when I most needed one. Debbie rarely emailed, but when she did her messages were long and chatty, full of gossip about people I'd never meet. I always tried to reply in a similar vein, which meant I wouldn't have time to write back until I was at home that evening.

Still, I'd allow myself to read her email at least, and then I'd settle down to some proper work.

My dear Tansy

I'm writing this sitting on my balcony, drinking a glass of chardonnay and watching the sun set. There are two crested pigeons on the balustrade, having a good old flirt. The male keeps puffing up his chest and cooing longingly at the female, and she coos back, then flutters a little way away so he has to flutter after her and carry on the seduction process.

But enough of the pigeon erotica!

It's been such a glorious summer here. I've been going to outdoor yoga classes in the park, and in spite of wearing factor 50 sunblock every day I've got really brown. Josh has been surfing every day, when he's not practising or playing gigs, and his hair is almost white-blond from the sun. Do you remember that Sun-in stuff, or are you too young? When I was a teenager we all used to spray it on our hair and then sit outside, and after a week or so your hair might have lightened a few shades, but it would be like straw and full of split ends. Happy days!

I've been on a few dates with Ben, a bloke from my wine-tasting group. He's good-looking and funny, and I do like him a lot, but I'm not sure whether I'm ready to ramp things up in terms of seriousness. I've been single for so long, you know, I'm quite used to not having a man in my life, and the idea of having to cook and clean for anyone other than Josh seems like a bit too much of a commitment!

Which brings me to the reason for this email. You know how when I moved out here, I always said I knew Josh might decide Australia wasn't for him, or just feel the need to spread his wings a bit? Secretly, of course, I hoped he'd stay forever, but I suspected wanderlust would get the better of him sooner or later. He's been travelling quite a bit over the past few years, seeing lots of New Zealand and South East Asia, and even spent a couple of months in South America with friends, but he always came home to me.

Now, though, he says he's ready for a bit of a longer-term adventure. It's partly because the band is splitting up. Nicola wants to pursue a solo career, apparently. Will's decided he needs to grow up and put that law degree of his to some use, and Amber's been offered a job in Singapore. It feels like the end of an era! Almost seven years, they've all been together, since they started The Pollinators while they were at uni, and I guess they've all realised that if they were going to get a big break it would have happened by now, and of course in the meantime Josh has managed to make a living producing other bands, and he sees that as his real career now.

Anyway, to cut a long story short, Josh has decided the time has come for him to return to the UK and spend some time working in London. He's hoping he'll be able to find freelance production work, or get some gigs as a session musician, but of course he won't have an actual job lined up when he arrives, which will make finding a place to stay a bit tricky, especially judging by what you've told me about the property rental market there!

So I wanted to ask you, as a huge favour to an old friend, if it would be possible for him to stay with you for a bit, just until he finds his feet? He has money saved up, so he'll be able to pay his way, I promise!

Do let me know what you think.

Debbie had been so kind to me, and so much of the modest success I'd achieved in my career was thanks to her, that saying no to her request was out of the question. But oh my God. I couldn't have Josh Valentine as a housemate. Not after everything. I couldn't. The idea made me go cold with horror.

Almost as cold as Barri's voice, right behind my left shoulder, saying, 'Got a minute, Tansy?' Lisa was hovering expectantly next to him. Shit. Already I was regretting the email I'd sent with such enthusiasm half an hour before. Already I wished I'd been less effusive, less keen to big myself up as the person who'd discovered the new genius young designer who would be the talk of London Fashion Week in a couple of seasons and maybe even grace the cover of *Vogue*.

But I believed in Chelsea, and I was desperate for Barri and Lisa to see what I saw in her designs: not just her talent, but her grit and determination, too. I wanted them to meet the girl I'd seen on Roman Road, truculent to the point of rudeness, but so passionate about her work she wouldn't even let a customer try on a dress she wasn't certain would suit her.

So I snatched my phone up off my desk and, following Lisa and Barri to the meeting room, I quickly scrolled through my Instagram to Chelsea's feed. It wasn't much – the quality of the photos wasn't professional or anything – but I hoped it would be enough to persuade them that she was at least worth a second look.

Barri sat down at the head of the table. Lisa perched in the seat to his right and opened her laptop. I sat on his other side, fighting back a sneeze as his cologne invaded my sinuses. It was something weirdly sweet and feminine – fruity, almost – and I felt a brief pang of longing for the mossy, musky aftershave Renzo wore.

'So,' Barri said, raising a perfectly threaded eyebrow in a manner that clearly indicated that this had better be good. 'You've discovered the next Sarah Burton, have you?'

I gave what I hoped was a composed, professional smile, remembering the advice Debbie had given me all those years ago about dealing with difficult customers: *Aim to please, but always manage expectations.* Barri wasn't a customer, but God only knew he was difficult.

'I might not put it quite that strongly,' I said. 'But I think she has talent, yes. I think there's something here we could work with.'

I explained how Chelsea repurposed reclaimed garments into creations of her own, and how she seemed to have a real gift for making women feel and look amazing. I waffled on a bit about how I knew Luxeforless saw itself as an incubator for talent, and mentioned Guillermo Hernandez and the big break we'd given him, even though privately I thought he was about as talented as my left sock, which had a hole in it that had been annoying me all day as my toe poked through it into the coldness of my boot. I talked about how sustainability was increasingly an issue in fashion, and how a high percentage of plastic waste in our marine ecology was the result of disposable, polyester-based clothing. I cited some research I'd found that said twenty-five per cent of women believed turning up at an event and seeing someone else wearing the same dress was the most socially awkward thing that had ever happened to them, and that Chelsea's unique creations would address that sector of the market.

If I say so myself, I really gave it some.

So much so that Barri's first, snide comment was, 'Are you telling me how to do my job?'

Inwardly, I flinched. Outwardly, I hoped my positive-but-not-hyper face didn't waver.

'Of course not,' I said. 'I'm the ladies' formalwear buyer. This is *my* job.'

It was quite a zinger, and it hit home – but not in the way I'd intended.

Barri raised both eyebrows this time. 'Oooh,' he said. 'Isn't that me told?'

Fuck. I'd antagonised him. Instead of being assertive, I'd been confrontational. I could feel my chances of selling the concept to him sliding out of my grasp as swiftly and surely as spaghetti slipping off a fork when there's loads of olive oil on it and you don't know how to do that windey thing with a spoon – and I knew exactly how that felt, because it had happened to me once, mortifyingly, over dinner with Renzo.

'Let's take a look at her work, anyway.' Lisa tried to defuse the situation.

With a grateful smile at her, I tapped my phone to life and put it on the table between them.

'I saw this dress being sold,' I said. 'The customer was in love with it. She'd have paid fifty per cent more for it, no problem. And look at this – customised denim. It's retro, kind of nineties but also so now. Every piece she makes is unique, a one-off in terms of design and fabrication. Take this bridal gown, made of vintage wedding dresses. When you think of the environmental impact of yards and yards of silk only being worn once—'

'Tat,' Barri said. 'Tchotchkes. Are we running a high-end online boutique here, Tansy, or an Oxfam shop? You tell me, since you know the business so well.'

I opened my mouth to protest, but Lisa intervened.

'Do you feel this chimes with any of the current trends we've identified?'

It didn't. Not really. It wasn't boho, or eighties structured tailoring, or athleisure or utility. It was something different – something I really believed was special.

'Not exactly,' I said. 'But must we always be trend-led? Isn't there a case for making trends, rather than following them?'

But I already knew I'd lost them. I'd pissed Barri off, and Lisa – no matter how much she talked the talk about supporting her team – knew it and wasn't going to put her arse on the line alongside mine.

'And what about the supply chain?' she went on. 'Where does the fabric come from to produce a proper range? And the manufacture? She makes all these garments herself, right? And the embellishment? Or does she have a lock-up somewhere with people working for her?'

'I don't think so,' I admitted. 'But the fabric's reclaimed. The cost of sourcing it would be close to zero.'

'But you'd have to source it in the first place,' Lisa said. 'And the cost of that, and the challenges of scaling the range…'

She shrugged, and Barri pushed my phone away from him as dismissively as if I'd interrupted our meeting to show him a picture of Freezer the cat.

I knew it was game over, but I gave it one last shot.

'There are challenges, of course. But surely the benefit of being the first to list an exciting new line would outweigh the drawbacks of having to start from scratch with her supply chain? I mean, we could…'

I'd run out of steam.

But it was okay. Barri was on hand to pick up where I'd left off.

'We could tell our majority shareholder we're donating the entire profit from this financial year to the Cats' Protection League,' he said. 'Or spunking it all on the staff party. Or taking it out of the bank in used fivers and using it for compost. How d'you reckon that would go down, Tansy?'

I shook my head mutely.

'Like a bucket of cold sick, that's how,' Barri said. 'I'm done here. This girl's business is entirely unsustainable. The sooner she gets herself a job flipping burgers at McDonald's, the better.'

He stood up, tucking his tablet under his arm, and headed for the door.

Then he turned and delivered one parting shot: 'You might want to spend more time focusing on your sales figures. They've been disappointing, to say the least.'

I stood too, fighting back tears of anger and disappointment. But Lisa touched my arm.

'I'm sorry,' she said.

'Don't be.' Her kindness brought my tears closer to the surface. 'You're right. And Barri's right. Chelsea's stuff isn't right for us.'

'If she's as talented as you think,' Lisa went on, 'she'll find a way to succeed in the industry. Well, if she's talented *and* determined *and* lucky. And there's another thing you could do for her, you know.'

'What's that?'

'Tell her about the mentoring scheme. You've volunteered, right? Daria's interviewing candidates over the next couple of weeks. There's still time for her to take part.'

'But won't Barri—'

'Barri won't know,' Lisa said. 'He's not going to be involved in it, day-to-day. He hasn't got time and anyway, to be perfectly honest…'

'He's not that interested?'

'Well, I wouldn't put it quite like that. But…'

'Okay,' I said. 'I'll talk to her. Thanks.'

I walked slowly back to my desk, feeling utterly deflated and somehow ashamed, as if I'd made a fool of myself. So far, I'd managed to stay pretty much beneath Barri's radar: I'd done my job as well as I could, even if I hadn't been an outstanding performer. My sales figures weren't what they should be – but nor were anyone else's. All my colleagues were discounting lines, scrabbling to make their targets, blaming Brexit and weak consumer confidence for the slow-down in sales.

But now I felt as if I had a different target to worry about: one painted right on my head. If Barri had taken against me, my days at Luxeforless would be numbered.

If my financial situation that morning had felt critical but stable, now it was in need of intensive care.

I read Debbie's email again, skimming past the chatty parts this time and focusing on the bit that made me feel all cold and knotted up inside: the bit about Josh.

He has money saved up, so he'll be able to pay his way.

The extra rent Josh would pay, once Charlotte stopped paying for the room to be kept empty for her in case her travel plans went wrong, would ensure I didn't get deeper into a financial hole.

Presumably musicians – or even music producers, although I wasn't entirely sure what one of those actually did – worked antisocial hours, which at least meant that if Josh moved into Charlotte's room for a few weeks, I wouldn't have to see too much of him.

Even if I didn't want to help Josh, I did owe a huge debt of gratitude to his mother, and – unlike my other debts – this was one I could quite easily pay. And besides, Josh, like Chelsea, was only trying to make his way in a competitive, uncertain world. And tempting as it was to make it even harder for him, I didn't want to upset Debbie or bring bad karma on myself.

My work emails still unread, I opened the WhatsApp group that had just me, Charlotte and Adam as members, and sent a quick message telling them what Debbie had asked. If either of them said no, it would be game over and out of my hands.

Can we sublet Charlotte's room to the son of my old boss, who's coming out from Australia? He's annoying, but not actually a drug dealer or anything. He'll pay his share of rent and bills and move out ASAP. He's arriving in a couple of weeks and might stay a month or two max. If you guys say it's a problem, I'll tell Debbie no. WDYT?

Then I determinedly put my phone aside and cracked on with work. I didn't check WhatsApp again until lunchtime, and there was a response from Charlotte.

*Of course, babe, whatever you want. So long as I can tell him to
sling his hook if I dump Xander and come home – or move into his
room and revenge-shag him, haha! Thailand is incredible, sunshine
24/7. Well not at night obvs. X incredible too. Love you, C x*

Adam didn't respond on WhatsApp, but he'd sent me a text.

*Fine about the room, so long as he likes cats. Reservation made
by the target for two tonight at Nobu, 8.30pm. Didn't want
to say but I promised full disclosure. Sorry to be bearer of bad
news – or is it for you??*

It wasn't, of course. But I noticed Felicity return from her lunch
break with a bulging Selfridges bag, and when I went for a final wee
before I left the office well after seven that evening, she was doing
her face in front of the mirror, wearing a black Roland Mouret
dress that she certainly hadn't had on when she'd drifted into the
office that morning.

The colour on her face when she saw me wasn't just down to
her Nars blusher, but she styled it out.

'Short-notice date!' she said. 'You know how it is! If only I'd
worn my lucky pants, ha ha!'

'Ha ha,' I echoed hollowly, and headed for home.

Year Ten

One day at school, I overheard Kylie and Anoushka talking in the toilets.

'So is she actually your brother's girlfriend?' Anoushka asked, and I froze, silent behind the cubicle door, wondering whether they were talking about me or someone else. I didn't know which would be worse.

'Girlfriend?' Kylie sneered. 'Of course not. Connor wouldn't go out with *that*.'

'But they go off together practically every afternoon,' Anoushka said. 'Here, give me some of that lip gloss.'

'Lend me your eyelash curlers, then. She's dead easy, he says. Went to second base the first time he met her. She's a slapper.'

'So are they… you know?'

'You won't believe what he told me.' Kylie's voice dropped to a whisper. 'He says she…'

Someone flushed the toilet in the next-door cubicle, so I couldn't hear what she said next. But I'd heard enough. My whole body felt flooded with shame. If they were talking about me, it meant everyone was. The whole school would know stuff about me – probably stuff that wasn't even true.

All that day, I was sure eyes were watching me everywhere I went, whispers beginning as soon as I was out of earshot, waves of giggles suddenly stopping when I walked into the classroom.

I didn't go to meet Connor that afternoon. I went straight home and closed my bedroom door and did my homework, and when Mum called me for tea I said I wasn't hungry.

Connor didn't have my mobile number – he hadn't needed it, he'd just had to say, 'See you Thursday,' and know I'd be there. So, after a couple of days, he came to find me as I was leaving school.

'Where've you been?' he asked. 'Been ill?'

'Just busy.' I ducked my head.

'Busy. Right. Come on.' He roughly took my hand and I let myself be led away. I don't know why. Maybe I felt I owed him an explanation. Maybe I was flattered that he'd gone to the trouble of seeking me out, even though he must have known exactly where I'd be. But I went.

Leaning against the wall, he asked again, 'So what's up? I waited for you and you never came.'

I felt a thrill of something that was part guilt for having abandoned him, part happiness that he'd been there, waiting for me.

I replied, 'They were talking about me. About us. Your sister and her mate.'

'So? Why do you care about a couple of girls gossiping? I don't.'

You don't have to, I thought. *You're so far above them, nothing they say can hurt you. But it can hurt me.*

But I just said, 'I don't know.'

'Tansy, look at me.' He put his strong fingers around my jaw and tilted my face upwards. 'They're just kids. Ignore them. You and me, we've got something special. Haven't we?'

'Have we?'

'Course we have.'

Then he kissed me. His mouth didn't taste of chocolate that time, or vinegar or blue WKD, just of cigarettes. I wasn't enjoying his kiss, and I felt myself wondering if I'd ever enjoyed it. But I let him carry on. I let him do more than he'd ever done before, until my knickers were round my ankles and my school skirt up around my waist and his jeans were unzipped, and he moved my hand down underneath his boxer shorts.

'Feel that. That's how much I love you.'

I was only a kid, but I wasn't stupid. I knew perfectly well this wasn't about love. But, at the same time, I lacked the willpower to say anything to make him stop. Maybe I knew he wouldn't; maybe I thought that since the other girls believed I was having sex with Connor, I had nothing to lose by letting it happen. Maybe I thought that if I let him do it, he really would love me.

I don't know. I can't remember what I was thinking; only the hard stone of the wall pressing into my back, the aniseedy smell of the cow parsley around our feet, the sudden stab of pain when he pushed himself inside me.

It didn't last long. I leaned my head back and closed my eyes against the sun, and heard his breath coming faster and faster until he made a sound that was more than a groan – almost a shout – and stopped.

He moved away from me and I felt a hot gush from inside my body. I didn't say anything – it hurt so much I knew that if I opened my mouth I'd cry. But I opened my eyes.

Connor was doing up his belt; the clink of the buckle sounded very loud in the still afternoon. He lit a cigarette and the smoke blotted out the smell of the cow parsley, but not the smell he'd left on me, damp and somehow clammy, like the way the changing rooms smelled at school when we got ready for swimming.

'See you around,' he said. 'I guess.'

I didn't reply. I closed my eyes again and waited, watching the red spots the sun made dance across my eyelids, and waited, listening carefully until I was sure he'd gone. He hadn't said anything about meeting me there again, not that I expected him to. He didn't say anything more to me at all, and nor did I.

When I opened my eyes at last, I could just see his red T-shirt disappearing over the hill, and that was the last time I ever saw Connor there.

Chapter Ten

The following week, I finally made good my promise and called Chelsea. She didn't answer, so I left a voicemail: 'Hi, this is Tansy calling. We met at your stall on Roman Road a couple of weeks ago. I'm sorry it's taken me so long to get in touch, I've been kind of busy. My sister had a baby, and work, and… yeah, anyway. I'd love to meet up with you and chat about what you do, and see if there's an opportunity to work together. Give me a call back when you can.' And I recited the eleven digits of my mobile number.

If she didn't ring back, I decided, I'd try one more time and then leave it. Maybe she didn't need my mentorship. Maybe she was happy making and selling a handful of amazing, unique garments a week to women who felt like princesses in them, like some kind of street-market fairy godmother. And even if she did, I wasn't sure what I could actually do to help her.

But thoughts of helping Chelsea – whether it was welcome or not – were at least a distraction from my endless, futile preoccupation with Renzo. Renzo and Felicity. The two of them at Nobu, where he'd taken me for our first date. Remembering every detail of that night – and imagining Felicity there, maybe even in the same chair where I'd sat, eating the same food, seeing the same wicked half-smile on Renzo's face when she made a joke – was agony. I spent most of the weekend trying to blot the picture from my mind, and failing.

So at last, that Sunday, I filled in the empty hours of the afternoon sitting at the kitchen table with my laptop, drinking coffee and tinkering with a business plan for Chelsea. Reluctantly, I had to conclude that Barri and Lisa had been right. However many times I tweaked the numbers on my spreadsheet, it was impossible to see how her business could be made into something viable.

I worked until evening, then got up, stretched, poured a glass of water and looked unenthusiastically at the contents of the fridge before fishing out a tub of hummus, cutting up some cucumber and pepper and shoving a frozen pitta bread in the toaster. It was almost six – soon I'd be able to have a bath and go to bed without feeling totally tragic.

Just a lot tragic.

Returning to my laptop, I scrolled through my social media. Charlotte and Xander had posted loads of pictures from Thailand, where they were spending a week at a fabulous-looking lodge right on the beach before heading to Bangkok and then on to Cambodia. I scrolled through pictures of plates piled with juicy pink prawns, Charlotte's feet half-buried in sand, their bed swathed in mosquito netting like a bridal veil, and imagined being there with Renzo.

Everything, I thought gloomily, ripping off a strip of bread and raking it through my hummus, came back to Renzo. I'd resolved to get him back, but now Felicity had got him, and my chances seemed to have gone from remote to zero. It had been more than three months since he dumped me; soon it would be four. Soon, if I wanted to carry on counting the hours and days, I'd need to set up another of my stupid spreadsheets.

I clicked on Felicity's Instagram feed. There she was, making a silly face in a fitting-room mirror. And there, sweating in a Nagnata sports bra after a hot yoga session and tucking into a massive bowl of out-of-season fresh berries and double cream to refuel (#virtuous, she'd posted, presumably ironically, #mybodyisatemple). And there again, her dark hair tangled up with Pru's as they made their best duck faces for the camera, clinking glasses of pink Pol Roger fizz together (#sistersofinsta #pamperday #restylane). Knowing what I'd suspected for a while – that the sisters' plump, dewy complexions weren't just down to good genes and sunblock – was no comfort to me. I couldn't afford work like that myself, so I'd just have to carry on looking more and more haggard with every passing day.

And there was a photo without Felicity in it, of grey sky looming above bare branches, a flash of green grass in the distance and a wrought-iron railing in the foreground. She'd written just one word alongside the image: #view.

Except it was a #view I recognised, because I'd looked out over it so often myself, in various states of quiet happiness, giddy laughter and nervous excitement. I'd even seen it while bending over, the cold steel of the window frame digging into my hips, glimpsing Renzo's reflection in the window as he kissed his way tenderly down the length of my spine.

It was the #view from the balcony outside Renzo's bedroom.

Felicity wasn't just dating Renzo. They were sleeping together. It was serious. I squeezed my eyes shut to try and block out the image of them in bed, their dark hair tangled together on Renzo's pillow, their secret smiles – but I couldn't. I slammed my laptop closed and stood up again, stretching the tension from my neck and shoulders. I'd started the year resolving to get him back, and now it was almost a quarter over and I'd achieved nothing. Less than nothing, because now he was with someone else – someone I'd inadvertently introduced him to. Someone who I'd practically given my blessing to to go after him. Someone who was *meant* to be my friend, who I'd have to see every day at work for the foreseeable future and pretend to be happy for.

I picked up my phone and an empty pint glass from the cupboard and was wearily climbing the stairs when my phone buzzed in my hand with an incoming text.

Hi, got your message. Wanna meet up?

Chelsea didn't waste any more words in texts than she did in person, I thought, with the beginnings of a smile. I replied in the same vein.

Sure, love to! Where and when?

Maybe, after I'd been to Daria's meeting, I could suggest she come into the office and show her around.

I'm free now. Now? Really? The front of the girl was quite something. It was Sunday evening, for God's sake. I could be putting my baby to bed. I could be lingering over a final glass of wine at the tail-end of a sumptuous lunch with twelve of my closest friends. I could be in a cab on my way back from the airport, having spent the weekend shopping in Milan.

Except, of course, I wasn't.

Right, okay. Let me know where and I'll tell you if I can make it.

Her reply flashed up straight away: an address that sounded like a flat in a council estate. (Wadsworth Heights. I mean, you just know, don't you? I did, anyway, given I'd spent my teenage years on Mitchell Crescent.) And then a postcode, which I had to read a second time because at first I thought she'd somehow guessed my own address and was trolling the fuck out of me.

But no – the last two letters were different. It must be pretty close by, though. And it was; when I clicked through to Google Maps, I saw that the place she wanted me to go to was on the Garforth Estate, and literally five minutes' walk from our house.

Wow, right, looks like we're almost neighbours! I can be there by 7.

To that, the only reply I got was an 'okay' emoji.

I took off my dressing gown for the first time that day, brushed my hair and teeth and thought about an outfit that would project the right message: professional, creative, accessible. A leather skirt, thick woolly tights and a jumper, maybe, with a cross-body satchel. Or wide-legged trousers and some sort of floaty, layery thing going on, with a crochet coatigan and a faux-fur bolero.

Then I said, 'Fuck it,' and pulled on yoga pants, a sweatshirt and trainers, and an ancient parka I hadn't worn in ages.

It was freezing, I was in a hurry, and Chelsea would just have to take me as she found me.

Every day for the past nine months, I'd walked past the Garforth Estate on my way to the station. Its three grey towers and four low-rise blocks were so familiar I could almost have drawn them from memory, but I'd never actually walked through the estate before. This dark, drizzly night wasn't exactly the ideal introduction. Without sunshine to show the cheerful window boxes planted on balconies and the clean washing flapping in the cold breeze, without children kicking a football underneath the NO BALL GAMES sign, without neighbours pausing to chat on the concrete walkways, it felt desolate and almost sinister.

Unnerved, I hurried to what Google Maps told me was the centre of the three tall blocks of flats, found the lift and pressed the button for the sixth floor. I turned the wrong way at first, hearing a barking dog through the door of number 609 and *Antiques Roadshow* blaring out from number 610, and inhaling the mouthwatering waft of roast chicken from 611 before retracing my steps and knocking on the door of 606.

The woman who opened it was unmistakably Chelsea's mum, but also totally not the person I expected to see. She had the same killer bone structure and the same 'don't you mess with me' stare. Only she was a good five stone heavier than her daughter, with the kind of ageless skin that could have made her anything from thirty to sixty. She was wearing a sea-green satin dress, fitted perfectly to her ample figure, with a pleated frill snaking from her right shoulder around her waist to finish in a kind of bustle at the back. On her head was a matching hat – a stunning design that Meghan Markle would have been proud to wear.

I held out my hand and said, 'My name's Tansy Barlow. I'm here to see Chelsea.'

'Mariella Johnston.' The woman gave me her hand to shake, and it was cool and soft.

I could see Chelsea hovering impatiently in the background behind her, but clearly Mrs Johnston believed in standing on ceremony.

'Won't you come in,' she said, 'and have a cup of tea?'

'Thank you. That would be lovely.'

'And maybe a slice of my cherry cake. I baked it yesterday.'

I saw Chelsea roll her eyes and shake her head.

'That's so kind. I'd love to.'

A few minutes later, the three of us were sitting around a small table in the world's cleanest kitchen, drinking strong, milky tea and eating proper old-school cake studded with glacé cherries so red they were practically luminous.

'This is delicious,' I said. 'So do you sew as well as bake?'

'Do I sew!' Mrs Johnston laughed. 'I taught this girl of mine to sew. When she was just a little thing of ten she was making her own dresses to wear to church on Sundays. Not that you'd get her to go near a church any more. Godless child.'

Chelsea rolled her eyes again and said, 'Mum!' But the look that passed between the two of them was loving.

'I taught her to sew, my mammy taught me and her mammy taught her. I wouldn't be surprised if it went back even further than that. We love clothes in this family. Maybe because we're all such good-looking women.' She shouted with laughter again.

I was beginning to wonder whether Chelsea's taciturn silence wasn't so much unfriendliness as the result of having grown up being unable to get a word in edgeways.

'Is Chelsea your only child?' I asked.

'I've got a bro—' Chelsea began, but it was hopeless.

'My Nathan's seventeen,' Mrs Johnston said. 'Three years younger than her. He's the clever one, so bright, ever since he could walk he's been into everything. Always top of the class in primary school. He was going to be the first one in the family to go to university. The teachers all said he'd be a lawyer one day, or a judge, or one of them bankers. He's a good boy, really.'

Which, I thought, was a mother's hopeful way of making excuses for a son who'd gone off the rails a bit.

But it was none of my business, so I just asked, 'What do you do for work, Mrs Johnston?'

'Most important work there is! Bringing new life into the world! I'm a midwife. For twenty years I've worked right up the road at Homerton Hospital. And…' She looked at her watch and put her teacup firmly down in its saucer, 'I'm on shift in twenty-five minutes. So I shouldn't be sitting around here in my Sunday best, chatting away!'

She stood up and bustled out of the room, and Chelsea cleared away the tea things. A few minutes later her mother returned, dressed in a dark blue shirt and trousers with a lanyard around her neck.

'I'll love and leave you girls,' she said, kissing her daughter's cheek and shaking my hand again. 'Don't you stay up too late, missy, you've work in the morning.'

'Work?' I asked, once the front door had closed. 'But I thought…'

'Thought I spent all my time designing dresses? As if. I work on the till in Superdrug on one of them zero-hours contracts. The Jobcentre made me take it.'

'So how do you find time for your other work then? The dresses?'

She grimaced. 'In between. Sometimes zero-hours does literally mean zero hours, you know.'

I imagined her getting up in the morning for her shift, coming home afterwards, sewing, drawing or cutting out patterns late into the night, going to work again the next day and repeating the process until it was the weekend, when she had to be manning her stall in the market. And if she wasn't wanted for shifts, sewing and sewing all day. I felt exhausted just thinking about it. Exhausted, and also overwhelmed, because the challenges she faced were even greater than I'd thought.

'May I see where you work?'

Chelsea shrugged and stood up. The way she ducked her head, instead of boldly meeting my eyes as she usually did, made me wonder if she was embarrassed, and if so, why. I followed her down a short corridor into what I supposed had once been a bedroom. It wasn't now, though: it was set up entirely for dressmaking. One wall was lined from floor to ceiling with shelves, on which fabric and second-hand garments were arranged neatly by colour. On the opposite wall was a garment rail holding about twenty finished dresses. A sewing machine stood on a trestle table in the centre; there was just about enough room to move around it.

'I sleep in the front room now,' Chelsea said. 'Nathan has his own room cos he's a boy, even though he ain't hardly here.'

I edged carefully around the table to the rail of dresses and looked at them, more closely this time. The work was even better than I remembered, the garments beautifully cut and finished. The labour that had gone into each one was astonishing.

'Wow,' I breathed. 'You've got serious talent. But you know that, don't you?'

Chelsea ducked her head again. Then she raised her eyes and looked directly at me. 'So, you gonna sell my stuff then? On your website? Along with Balenciaga and Alexis Mabille and all them?'

Damn. I knew that was what she wanted more than anything, and I knew that it wasn't going to happen.

I said, 'See, the thing is, Luxeforless is fundamentally a volume business. I mean, it's not like Primark where you're talking thousands or tens of thousands of one item, but it's still volume. We sell designer stuff, sure, and some of it's high-end, but when we list a line, we need to know that it's going to sell at least ten or twenty identical pieces, maybe more in the popular sizes. I don't think that's where you want your business to be, really, is it?'

'I could,' she insisted. 'I could make more things. I could work harder. Mum could help me.'

I knew this was impossible, and she must have known it too.

'What I really wanted to talk to you about, though, is this new initiative my boss has come up with. It's all about helping young people who are just starting out in the business. The idea is, you'd work with a mentor – that would be me, I guess – and learn a bit more about how a fashion company works – all the boring stuff like budgets and forecasts and merchandising and things. And do some work experience at Luxeforless, and maybe at some of our suppliers. It's, like, a way of supporting people to gain a foothold in the industry who wouldn't have had the opportunity otherwise.'

I'd hoped I sounded encouraging, but I could hear my voice tail off as I saw the expression on Chelsea's face. *Shit, she's going to cry*, I thought.

'Fuck off,' she said. 'And stop wasting my time.'

Chapter Eleven

Three weeks passed, and I didn't hear from Chelsea again. To be honest, I hadn't expected to. Felicity's Instagram feed continued to be populated with images of her in fabulous clubs and restaurants, wearing fabulous clothes, only now she was accompanied less often by Pru – whose own feed informed me that things with Phillip from Toffee were hotting up – and more often by Renzo. Although she hardly ever showed his face in her pictures, there were glimpses of his flat, his car, the back of his head. Each image was like a punch in the stomach, but I couldn't help looking at them, torturing myself with the knowledge that, if only I'd done things differently, it could have been me with him still. If I hadn't resorted to webcam work. If I hadn't told him about it. If I'd been a better girlfriend to him, so that when I told him, he didn't mind. If I'd had a chance to see him just one more time, and maybe… Round and round the thoughts went in my head, all those pointless, painful *if*s.

Felicity herself was perfectly friendly at work, but she'd stopped offering me sweets when she bought them to snack on at her desk, and she didn't stop by my workstation to chat any more, or invite me to come out with her and Pru and their friends. And because our friendship seemed to have cooled so much, I realised I'd never have an opportunity to ask her what she'd been doing in the office on that Sunday night in February, when I'd spotted her going into the lift.

I'd replied, a bit reluctantly, to Debbie letting her know that of course it was absolutely fine for Josh to come and stay for a while – as long as he wanted, I'd written through gritted teeth – in fact, I was really excited to see him again after all these years, and please pass on my email and WhatsApp details. She'd thanked me profusely, but I had heard nothing from him.

Maybe, I thought, he'd changed his mind. Or maybe, like any normal, functioning flipping adult, he'd found a place to stay with friends of his own, not some random his mother had known years ago.

But then, when I was eating my lunch in Soho Square on a blissfully, unseasonably warm March day, I received a text message from him.

Hey, Tansy! Josh Valentine here. Thanks for the invite to crash at your place, really appreciate it. My flight lands tomorrow just before 6am. Guess by the time I make my way from Heathrow to Hackney you'll have left already for work! Any way I can pick up the key somewhere? No worries if not, I can just hang out and explore London for the day, and catch up in the evening. I don't want to put you to any trouble!

Fucksake, I thought. *How arrogant – how typical! Just like he used to be, expecting everything to happen the way he wants it to, without any effort on his part. Doesn't bother making contact until he's practically in the air and expects to swan in and be welcomed like a long-lost friend.* And there was no way I could let Debbie's precious only son hang around London all day on his own, no doubt jet-lagged and with a massive suitcase to lug around. He'd be mugged or get lost, for sure. I'd have to wait in until he arrived, or ask Adam if he could work from home for the morning.

Then I remembered that the next day was Friday.

No problem. Odeta, our cleaning lady, will be at the house from nine until twelve, so she'll let you in. Have a safe flight, looking forward to seeing you.

I wasn't, not even slightly, and I also thought yet again how Adam and I could save more than a hundred quid a month if we dispensed with Odeta's services and did the cleaning ourselves, like most other people.

But when I'd mentioned it to Adam, he'd looked horrified and said, 'But Tans, I don't know how to clean. And anyway, think how precarious Odeta's situation must be feeling right now, with Brexit and everything. She told me the other day some people graffitied "Fuck off home to Romania" on the front door of her house. Well, the house she and her boyfriend share with about eight other couples. If you can't afford her I totally understand; I'll keep paying her wages until you can.'

And so that was that – Odeta had stayed and I'd carried on paying my share.

I felt oddly nervous on my way home from work the next evening. Not just about seeing Josh, but about the disruption to what had become normality. We'd never been much of a party house. Adam, Charlotte and I all worked hard, and put in long hours, and the most we'd ever really been up for together was a quiet drink down the Prince George, pizza night at the Daily Grind or an Indian takeaway in front of the telly.

Now, our sedate routine was going to be disrupted. If grown-up Josh was anything like teenage Josh had been, he'd have loads of mates who he'd want to bring round – and maybe even acquire a girlfriend in short order, too. It would mean change. He might want to use the bathroom at times that clashed with mine. He might come home late after gigs and start drunkenly making toast and set off the smoke alarm. He might snore.

Pull yourself together, Tansy, I told myself firmly. *He's Debbie's son, you owe it to her to be nice to the bloke. Take him out for a pint, get to know him a bit. He might not be so bad. You've grown up in the past eleven years, you've changed. He probably has, too. Stop being a wuss.*

Still, walking back from the bus stop, I felt exactly like my fifteen-year-old self had felt walking to school in the morning: all hollow and sick with apprehension, half-expecting the crowd of teenagers hanging around outside McDonald's to start laughing and taunting as I passed. They were surrounded by a cloud of smoke from the joint they were passing around, and I wondered if one of them could be Chelsea's brother Nathan.

They didn't laugh or taunt, although one of them said, 'Some legs you got there, girl,' and in spite of myself, I laughed.

So it was with a sense of determination and a sunny smile plastered onto my face that I unlocked the front door and went upstairs. But the smile was wiped off immediately when I stepped onto the landing and immediately tripped over a discarded bright yellow trainer.

'Oh, for fuck's…' I picked it up. It was by Allbirds – a brand I knew because it was developing quite the cult following and Kris was in talks with the manufacturers in New Zealand about us stocking it – and it was absolutely fricking *huge*. Either Debbie's son favoured flapping about in footwear like a clown, or he'd put on a serious growth spurt over the past decade.

I put the shoe down and looked around. Also on the landing were, in no particular order, an open guitar case, five T-shirts in assorted colours, an aluminium water bottle, three jars of Vegemite, a bottle of Bombay Sapphire gin half falling out of a duty-free carrier bag, a tub of hair pomade and a tube of Berocca.

And, coming through the door of Charlotte's old room, music was playing – the kind of music that sounds loud even when it isn't. It might have been Dire Straits, or Led Zeppelin, or one of those bands your dad used to listen to that are suddenly cool again, if you're the kind of person who wanks endlessly on about the superior sound quality you get from vinyl.

I walked determinedly towards Charlotte's door – well, Joshua's bloody door, I supposed – ready to tell my new housemate kindly but firmly to please get his shit together.

Then, in the doorway, I stopped. The bedroom looked as bad as the landing – worse, even. A backpack had spewed its contents out over the floor: jeans, more T-shirts, a down gilet, a sleeping bag, two pairs of sunglasses, a trilby hat, the guitar that presumably belonged in the empty case and various bits of tech: a laptop, a tablet, headphones and a tangle of chargers.

Poking out from one end of Charlotte's duvet was a pair of enormous feet, and from the other, almost covered, a shock of dark blond hair.

Josh was fast asleep.

Call me a sucker, but I couldn't bring myself to wake him up and give him the bollocking he deserved. He'd had an awfully long flight, after all. He'd be jet-lagged and probably homesick. We were going to have to live together, for a few weeks at least, and there was no point starting things off on an unpleasant footing. Tomorrow was Saturday, and I'd sit him down over a cup of tea and read him the riot act. In a friendly, hospitable way, obviously.

I carefully picked up the stuff on the landing and ferried it into the bedroom, one item at a time, treading softly so as not to wake its owner. I found the portable speaker the music was coming from and turned it off, then froze, wondering if the lack of sound would wake him when the sound itself hadn't, but he didn't move.

I retreated back onto the landing and paused. It was hard to know what to do next. Normally, I'd have had a shower, changed into slobbing-around clothes and gone downstairs to watch telly. But in my ideal, old-normal life, I wouldn't even be there on a Friday night. I'd be having a cocktail with Renzo before going on to dinner somewhere amazing and then back to his to spend all night in his arms in bed.

Or, more recently, I'd have been getting glammed up for a night out with Felicity and Pru. But both those ships had sailed.

Now I was home, on my own, but with a stranger in the house whose presence made me feel uncomfortable about taking my work clothes off and going to the bathroom wrapped in a towel.

Or was I alone?

Adam's door was closed, but I gave it a gentle tap and, seconds later, he opened it and stepped out to join me on the landing, looking narky as anything.

'Tans,' he said. 'Listen, this just isn't on.'

'I know,' I soothed. 'Look, I've cleared some of the stuff up. I'm sure he'll sort it out in the morning. Why don't we go downstairs and put the kettle on, or head out for a drink?'

Privately, I thought Adam was being a bit melodramatic. I mean, it's not like he was Mrs Perfect Housewife, either. I'd seen the face on Odeta sometimes when she went into his room to clean.

'Not the mess, Tans. Who cares about that?'

'So, what…?'

Adam didn't say anything. He just pointed, and I noticed his hand was actually trembling, as if he was in the grip of an emotion so strong it couldn't possibly be provoked by something as trivial as an untidy house.

I looked where he was telling me to look, and saw what I'd missed when I first tiptoed into Charlotte's old room.

There, on the pillow next to Josh's sandy head, was Freezer's white one. He was fast asleep, too.

*

It was almost ten when I woke up the next morning and, in spite of a mild hangover, I felt fantastic. The night before, to help calm Adam down, I'd insisted we go out for some food and a few drinks, and we'd found a street food market a couple of roads away in a cavernous space that used to be a deeply dodgy nightclub before the council shut it down.

Once Adam had finished chuntering about people who stole other people's cats – which was entirely unreasonable, given that Freezer wasn't, and never had been, his – and got over his anxiety about food hygiene after I'd pointed out the Scores on the Doors five-star rating, we'd had a great time. When we got home, Josh's bedroom door was closed, although the shower tray was damp so at least he wasn't dead. I hadn't been so bothered any more about taking my make-up off and walking back to my room in my pants, and I'd fallen into bed and slept for ten solid hours.

Now, though, I'd have to get up and deal with the reality of my new housemate. Also, I needed a glass of water and a wee. So I put on a dressing gown and went to the bathroom, hovering outside for a bit to see if I could identify who was home and where they were. But the house was entirely silent – Adam and Josh were either still asleep or out. Or, in Adam's case, immersed in the world that existed behind his bedroom door and, beyond that, behind his computer screens, which I sometimes thought was his real home.

I showered and dressed, not bothering to dry my hair, and went downstairs, through the still-silent house. The early spring warmth hadn't broken, and the sky outside was a clear, radiant blue. I even opened the back door to let in the air, which in my head smelled of flowers even though I knew it smelled of London and traffic and a bit of the foxes Hannah had said had made a den down the end of their garden.

I made a cup of coffee and drank it sitting at the table in the kitchen, warm in my leggings and jumper even though the morning was still cool. Suddenly hungry, in spite of all the smoky aubergine dip and grilled lamb I'd eaten last night, I opened the fridge. It was depressingly empty, apart from the bottle of gin I'd seen amid Josh's stuff, some bags of wilting salad leaves and a carton of fat-free cottage cheese I'd bought. I know this makes me sound like a freak, but I genuinely do like the stuff. I didn't fancy it, though – I felt like a proper breakfast.

Not avocado on toast and poached eggs. A Proper Fucking Breakfast.

I was hovering by the fridge, considering what exactly I felt like eating and where I might go to get it, when the front door crashed open and Josh blew in like a tsunami. The size of his sneakers had given me a clue to how tall he was, but it hadn't prepared me for the reality. He was about six foot four, all loose, gangly limbs, floppy hair and perfect teeth. His shoulders filled the doorway and his voice filled the entire house, so it felt like there wasn't room in the place for the two of us, never mind Adam and a part-time cat as well.

'Hey, Tansy!' He gambolled over and enveloped me in a hug, even though, judging from his long-sleeved Lycra top, shorts and trainers, he'd just been out for a run. *Yep, definitely a run*, I thought, feeling the damp fabric against my cheek. 'I'm so sorry about the state I left the place in yesterday! I'm mortified. I got in and I'd just started to unpack when in strolls this adorable white cat, and I sat on the bed to give him some fuss and the next thing I knew it was five in the morning and I'd been crashed out for, like, ever.'

Disarmed, I said, 'That's okay. Been out for a run?'

'You bet! It's glorious out there. I was expecting it to be freezing and drizzling, but it's not. And your local park is dead cool, there are swans and everything.'

'Coffee?' I gestured towards the machine.

'Not right now, thanks – I made myself one earlier. I'm going to grab a shower, and then head out and explore London. But first I'll need some breakfast – I'm starving. Where's good around here? And will you join me? My shout.'

I hesitated.

'Come on,' he urged. 'A proper English fry-up.'

It was like he'd read my mind. My mouth watered at the prospect, despite my reluctance to spend any more time in his company than I absolutely had to. But he was my new housemate – it was the least I could do to be polite. And besides, at the back of my mind, the glimmering of an idea had appeared. 'Go on, then.'

I didn't bother putting on any make-up – not for Josh Valentine, of all people – but while he was in the shower I quickly dried my hair. By the time he came downstairs, dressed in faded jeans, a dark blue jumper and those giant trainers, I was as ready as I needed to be.

'So, where's your go-to for breakfast?' he asked as we stepped out into the street.

It was colder than it looked – although the sun was shining, there was a brisk breeze that ruffled my hair, and I saw Josh shiver.

'I guess it's still really hot in Sydney,' I said.

'Sure is. Hard to believe I was surfing last weekend. Still, I expect I'll toughen up.'

'We'll go to the Daily Grind. It's just up the road, and they do killer breakfasts there. If there's space for us, that is.'

But it was almost eleven o'clock; the breakfast rush was over and the bottomless brunch crowd hadn't yet arrived, so we were able to get a table right by the window, with sunlight spilling onto its burnished copper top.

'Morning, Tansy,' Yelena said, putting menus and a carafe of water in front of us. I noticed her looking intently at Josh, and I knew exactly what she must be thinking. *Someone got lucky last night.* Of course, with Josh sitting right there, I couldn't explain that I wouldn't sleep with Josh if we were the last two people left on the planet and humanity's only hope of saving itself from extinction.

'This is Josh,' I said. 'He's staying with us for a few months, while Charlotte's travelling. So I guess you'll be seeing quite a bit of him.'

'You certainly will,' Josh added, 'if the food here is as good as it smells. I'd like a flat white, please.'

'A double espresso for me, please,' I requested automatically.

'And are you ready to order food?' Yelena asked. 'Or shall I give you five minutes?'

'I'm ready,' Josh said. 'I'd like the full English, with scrambled eggs and extra hash browns and wholemeal sourdough toast.'

I looked down at the menu. Suddenly, the type went all strange in front of my eyes, blurring and jumping, and I wasn't in the Daily Grind any more but in the canteen at school, sitting all alone, opening my lunchbox as quietly as I could, but knowing that there was no way I wouldn't be noticed; no way I'd be ignored. Then, I'd tried my hardest not to look at Josh. Now he was sitting right there opposite me and I had no choice.

How can you look so bloody relaxed? I wondered. *How can you smile, like this is totally normal?*

Yelena was still standing there, I realised, patiently holding her pencil at the ready over her order pad.

'Uh… I'll have the same as him, please.' At least it meant I didn't have to gather my thoughts enough to make an actual decision.

'So,' Josh said when she'd gone, 'looks like you come here often.'

The cheesy line made me blush, and at the same time feel absolutely furious. How could he – how dare he – provoke that reaction in me? He wasn't Renzo, and it was Renzo I wanted. The two of them couldn't have been more different: even though Josh was fit, in a kind of loose-limbed, lanky, surfer sort of way, he had none of the magnetic power that Renzo had. If Renzo was a black panther, sleek and self-possessed, Josh was a grinning, playful golden retriever.

'Oftenish,' I replied, hoping that he hadn't noticed the blush. 'It's just up the road, after all, and our neighbour, Luke, whose cat you met, owns the place.'

So after that, our conversation moved along neutral lines. Josh asked about the area, and about my work, and I asked how Debbie was doing, and about his plans for exploring London. As we ate our breakfast, I found myself relaxing a bit. Maybe I could put the past behind me – be a grown-up, be friendly and polite and do the right thing for Debbie until it was time for him to move out, for Charlotte to return and for everything to go back to normal.

Then, out of nowhere, Josh asked, 'So, are you seeing anyone right now? I mean, sorry if it's a personal question.'

'Not at all,' I said stiffly. 'I was, but we broke up just before Christmas.'

'Rubbish timing,' he sympathised. 'Me too, as it happens. Paige and I were together for three years, but I guess it just got to the point where we wanted different things. She was keen to settle down and stuff, and I just wasn't ready. I wanted to see some more of the world first. So here I am.'

'Here you are,' I echoed. And, looking at his white, even teeth and his smiling eyes, the deep greeny-blue of seawater, the ghost of an idea I'd had earlier resurfaced. *He could be useful.* It wasn't kind; it wasn't particularly fair, but I didn't have to care about that. It wasn't like he'd treated me fairly. I had a goal: I was going to get Renzo back. And if Josh could unwittingly help me with that, and there was some collateral damage, so be it. He deserved it.

Year Ten

I'd thought things at school were bad before, but I'd had no idea
– no idea at all.

It started the very next day, when I walked into the classroom
and saw Kylie, Anoushka and their friends all whispering together
by their desks. When they saw me, the room immediately went
quiet, and they stared at me. Then Anoushka whispered something
to Danielle, one of the girls on the periphery of the group, and
they all giggled.

'Slag,' I heard Kylie not-quite-whisper.

'Slapper,' Anoushka hissed. She wasn't even bothering to pretend
she didn't want me to hear. 'Bag of chips and a Mars bar and she's
anyone's. Or so they say.'

'She goes like a train, I'm told,' Kylie said, turning to the group
of boys behind her – Ben, Josh, Luke and a few others. 'You should
all have a go. So long as you don't mind Connor's sloppy seconds.'

There was more laughter. One of the boys said, 'Gross.' Another
said, 'Yeah, but I still would.' 'Any hole's a goal,' laughed another.

Then, just as I was wondering whether it was physically possible
to simply drop dead, or whether I could run away and hide under
my duvet and never come out again, Mr Brodrick showed up and

told us all to get into our seats and quieten down before he started doling out detentions.

After that, everyone started calling me Bike Barlow, even in front of the teachers. I wasn't part of the invisible majority any more; I was firmly in with the untouchables. However hard I tried to keep my head down and go back to being invisible, they sought me out. At lunchtime later that week, when I brought tuna sandwiches in for lunch, Anoushka said, 'Something stinks in here. Must be Bike Barlow's fanny,' and immediately I stopped feeling hungry.

At home that night, I told Mum I didn't want any dinner, and went to the room Perdita and I shared. I couldn't tell my little sister what was happening; she was still in junior school, safely untainted by my reputation, and I didn't want to worry her. Besides, I felt too ashamed to admit what had happened to anyone who loved me.

I took off my clothes and forced myself to look in the mirror. My face was a blank, white moon broken only by my wide, frightened eyes and the tight line of my mouth. My hair was still scraped back in a ponytail. My breasts looked huge, obscene and incongruous like lumps of uncooked dough on my chest.

I remembered a thing I'd read somewhere – in a magazine, or maybe in one of the books about 'grooming' and 'deportment' that seemed to have been gathering dust on the shelves of our school library since the 1980s.

Stand tall. Glance down. If you can see your belly button, you need tummy-toning.

I could see my belly button all right. I gripped the flesh of my abdomen and squeezed hard. *On a toned body, you can never pinch more than an inch.* Another fail.

I pulled on a T-shirt that used to be baggy on me, but was tight now and barely covered my bottom, and padded through to the bathroom.

I stepped gingerly on the scales and watched the black digital numbers flicker and settle. Ten stone eight pounds. Well, there might not be much else I could change, but I could change that.

The next day, I told Mum I'd make my own lunch from now on. I peeled a carrot, cut it up into sticks and shoved it into one of the bags Mum used for our sandwiches, together with an apple. And at school, I locked myself into a toilet cubicle and ate there, surrounded by the smells of industrial bleach and Impulse body spray.

It was surprisingly easy to hide what I was doing from Mum. It helped that her radar was so finely tuned to Dad: where he was going while she was at work, where the money was draining away to, how to keep changing the password on the computer and hiding her chequebook. She was constantly stressed, distracted and exhausted, and when she asked me how things were at school, it was easy to just say, 'Fine,' and watch the concern on her face turn to relief and then concern again as the next worry jumped into her mind. When she said, 'You'll turn into a horse, love, eating like that,' I hissed that raw fruit and vegetables were good for you, everyone knew that, and if she carried on nagging me about what I ate I'd get a complex and it would be all her fault.

I was not the nicest teenager there's ever been, it has to be said. After the long, lonely summer holidays had dragged past, I walked into the classroom, filled with dread about what the new term had in store for me. But things felt different.

Kylie said, 'Hi, Tansy,' as casually as if she said it every day.

Anoushka said, 'I like your hair like that. Cool.'

Astonished, I muttered a thank you and sat down, confused but also secretly delighted. Maybe it was okay. Maybe they'd forgiven me – as I'd longed for them to, even though, if I allowed myself to think hard enough about it, I knew I'd done nothing wrong.

Then, at break time, Danielle approached me.

'Tansy?' Her tone was shy, almost wheedling.

I looked up from the copy of *Glamour* magazine someone had left in the canteen. I'd have told her to get lost, if I'd been one of the cool kids. But I wasn't, so I couldn't.

'Hi, Danielle.'

'Listen, Kylie and Anoushka asked me to come and talk to you. They reckon they couldn't, cos you'd tell them to eff off. But they're sorry they've been bitchy to you. Anoushka was, like, literally crying earlier, she feels so bad.'

She wasn't the only one who'd felt so bad she'd literally cried recently, I thought. But I said, 'Oh, really?'

'Tansy, look, I know they've been cows to you. Me too, if I'm honest. And I'm sorry as well. We all really want to make it up to you.'

Every bit of me was on high alert. I knew deep down – I was quite certain – that I shouldn't, mustn't trust her. Danielle, of all people, who the inner circle used to do their dirty work. But at the same time, she looked genuinely remorseful. I knew her parents were getting divorced and she was going through a tough time. She was right – if it had been one of the ringleaders, I might well have told them where to go. But for Danielle, with her acne and her bitten nails, and her way of pressing her elbows into her sides all the time so no one could see the damp patches her nervous sweat left on her school shirt, I felt genuine pity.

'That's nice,' I said cautiously.

'Look, they've asked you – we've asked you – if you want to come to the cinema with us on Saturday. We're going to see *The Dark Knight*, you know, the new Batman movie? And afterwards we're going to McDonald's, and we might try and get into the Moon and Cow. I know, like, fat chance, but Luke's sister's a barmaid there and he reckons we might. What d'you think?'

I'd passed Kylie and Anoushka in the street on Saturday evenings before, and even to me they looked eighteen if they looked a day. Danielle? Not so much. But I didn't say that. My defences were down, but I was still on a hair-trigger of awareness that I was being played.

'Depends whether the manager also turns a blind eye, I guess. But it sounds like a fun night. I hope you guys enjoy.'

'No, but, Tansy,' Danielle persisted, 'we really want you to come. Kylie said she wants to make things right between us all.'

'I want to make things right, too,' I admitted.

'So you'll come then?'

'I don't think so. I'm kind of busy.' Yeah, I was. Staring at the four walls of my room and doing ab crunches.

Danielle looked crestfallen, almost panicky. 'Please, Tansy? Please will you come?' She leaned in close to me, so close I could smell the fruity mousse she'd used on her hair. 'You see, it's not just them. I promised I wouldn't tell you, but it's Josh. He says he'll only come if you do. Look.'

She fished her phone out of her blazer pocket, pressed a few buttons and showed me the screen. On it was a text.

Can't be arsed with Batman *if I'm honest. But if you ask Tansy Barlow I might change my mind. She's well fit.*

I gazed at the screen for a second, overwhelmed by what I read – but not so overwhelmed that I didn't commit the number instantly to memory, to store away like a precious gift.

In spite of the rush of elation and amazement I felt, I could see what was going on. Kind of. If Josh liked me – my God, Josh Valentine, liking *me* – and had imposed my presence as a condition of turning up to see a movie and eat burgers with Kylie and her crowd, they'd have invited their mums along if that was what it took to get him. Josh – too cool even for the cool crowd – was a serious prize. Except he didn't like me. There was no way he did. Was there?

'If Josh wants to hang out with me, why doesn't he ask me himself?'

Danielle visibly relaxed. 'Search me. I guess he's shy. And he said you're, like, a total ice maiden when he sees you when you work at the shop on Saturdays. Maybe he thinks that in, like, a group, it would be different.'

Maybe in a group, it would. Maybe if Josh and Luke and the other boys were there, I wouldn't feel like such an outcast. And I could meet Josh's eyes, talk to him, smile at him. Not feel ashamed to be in the same room as him.

'Okay,' I said. 'I'll come.'

Chapter Twelve

'Good morning, everyone,' Daria addressed the group filling the Luxeforless boardroom. 'I'm so excited to welcome you all here today for the official launch of our mentorship scheme.'

The mentors, sitting on the right-hand side of the room, looked at the group on the left with encouraging smiles, and the mentees looked anxiously back.

'Over the coming months, you'll be working together to exchange knowledge and experiences in a way that I know will be equally rewarding and challenging for all of you. I can't emphasise enough that this is a two-way process, and that mutual trust and openness are essential to the success of the programme.'

I glanced sideways again, wondering which of the assembled girls and boys would be allocated to me. A couple of them had come in suits, which I thought was sweet and showed seriousness. Most were in jeans and jumpers, and a handful were in clothes I thought they must have designed themselves, none of which were as striking as Chelsea's designs.

'Most importantly, I want you all to know that I and Jules and the whole team at HandsUp Mentorship are here to guide and support you. And, of course, in six months' time this first phase of the programme will come to an end and we'll have a partaaay!'

Everyone went, 'Wooohooo!' a bit tentatively.

'And now,' Daria went on, 'it's the moment you've all been waiting for. We've assessed our mentees' goals and talents – which, let me tell you, are highly impressive – and matched them up with mentors whose skill sets best complement them. It's been a bit like coupling up on *Love Island*, let me tell you.'

There was a ripple of laughter at this, although of course it was nothing like *Love Island* at all.

'So, without further ado, let me introduce the first of our mentors. Kris Cross…' Kris's name always made me giggle. Seriously, what were his parents thinking? '… is the footwear buyer at Luxeforless. Kris graduated from Central Saint Martins here in London, but he's worked in Tokyo and Paris as well. Highlights of his CV include a stint in the merchandising department at Manolo Blahnik.'

Kris stood up. He was wearing, presumably in honour of the occasion, red patent thigh-high boots over his skinny jeans, and a flowing cream silk shirt. His head was shaved and his beard neatly trimmed. I'd got so used to his appearance over the years it barely registered with me, but now, seeing him through the mentees' eyes, I realised how intimidatingly out-there he might seem.

'Kris has been paired with Alfie Blake, whose family have been cobblers for almost two hundred years. Alfie's goal is to take the family business to the next level and future-proof it for the next generation.'

One of the boys in suits, the one with ginger hair who'd been alternately blowing his nose and sniffing throughout Daria's presentation, stood up, looking terrified.

'Gents, please go through to the next-door meeting room, where you can help yourself to coffee and pastries and get to know each other. Next up we have the brilliant Savita Patel, one of the newest arrivals in our Digital Design team. Savita is…'

Daria carried on, and I watched as pair after pair was formed, until there were only five of us left: a slim blonde girl wearing fishnet tights under her ripped jeans, another boy in a suit, Devon from Marketing, Mischa from the Content team, and me.

Something was wrong. There weren't enough mentees to go round. I wondered if Daria had noticed. She must have – even the two remaining mentees had, I'd seen their heads duck together as they briefly whispered to each other – but she was calmly carrying on as if everything was going exactly according to plan.

Devon got the girl with the ripped jeans, smiling warmly and giving her a quick hug as they went off together.

'Mischa started her career interning at *Vogue* when she was just seventeen.' Daria glanced down at her notes. 'She's since worked at *Elle* and *Harper's* and been published at The Pool, all while working on a novel. We've paired her with…'

Not much of a surprise there, I thought. It looked like I hadn't been considered good enough to be trusted with any of these bright young minds. So why had I even been allowed to come to the meeting? I felt an angry flush creep up my neck and sting my cheeks. Was it some ruse of Barri's to humiliate me as punishment for standing up to him?

'Tansy, I'm sorry,' Daria said. 'It looks as if…'

Then we both turned, hearing the clatter of heels on the floor outside. The glass door burst open and a voice I recognised said, 'I got delayed. I'm not too late, right?'

*

It was mid-afternoon by the time I got back to my desk. Felicity looked up from her computer screen and asked, 'So how did the do-gooding go?'

'The do-gooding was good,' I said. 'I got paired with a super-talented girl called Chelsea, who actually lives just round the corner from me, so I'll even get to sneak off home early some afternoons after I've met with her. Look, I'll show you some of her work on her Insta feed.'

I didn't tell Felicity how late Chelsea had been, and how awkward I'd felt, left alone in the room on my own. I didn't relate what Chelsea had said when we were alone, sitting across from each other with cups of tea.

She'd looked down at her mug and muttered, 'I'm sorry.'

'Don't apologise,' I replied. 'You're here now, that's the main thing.'

'Mum said I had to come,' Chelsea said. 'I told her what happened when you came round to the flat, and she gave me the biggest telling-off ever. Like, ever. She properly bit my head off, and told me if I carried on throwing away opportunities like that I'd never get anywhere in life.'

'Harsh.' I sent up a silent prayer of thanks to Mrs Johnston.

Chelsea met my eyes. 'But true. You wanted to help me and I told you to...'

She looked down again.

'Look,' I said, 'accepting help is tough, especially when it's not the kind of help you think you need. And it might not be – this whole thing might turn out to be a total waste of both our time. But it might not. And you did change your mind – you applied for the scheme and they chose you. You should be bloody proud of yourself. Now let's put that behind us and decide how we're going to work together. Right?'

'Right.' Chelsea had flashed her rare smile.

'Nice stuff.' Felicity said now, handing me back my phone. 'Bit niche.'

She was trying to sound indifferent, but I wondered whether she was a bit jealous, deep down, regretting not volunteering. That could account for how subdued she seemed. Or, of course, it might be something else. Something to do with what she'd been doing in the office that Sunday night. Maybe, if I had some time alone with her, I'd get the chance to ask her about it.

'Fancy a drink after work?' I asked. 'We could go to that new place in Soho. They do cocktails and crazy golf.'

'Crazy golf?' Felicity laughed like I'd suggested she join me for a happy meal at McDonald's. 'Not really my kind of thing, to be honest. And anyway, I'm busy tonight. I'm going out for dinner with… But thanks for asking.'

'You're going out with Renzo? Cool.' I forced a smile. 'How's that going?'

Renzo, I thought with a pang, would absolutely love cocktails and crazy golf, being insanely competitive and naturally good at anything remotely sporty. *I took him bowling,* I remembered, *and he didn't even mind that I won.* That was the first night we kissed. The first time he called me *fragolina* – little strawberry – which became his pet name for me. I wondered if he had a pet name for Felicity, and what it was. The idea was almost too painful to bear.

'Good. We're having fun together. You know, taking things slow. It's early days. And he's off to New York for a week tomorrow with work.' She rolled her eyes and then said, 'Thanks for asking.'

I wasn't going to get anything more out of her, even if I genuinely wanted to know the details of her and Renzo's fledgling relationship. Which I kind of did, in a masochistic way, and kind of didn't. Like when you've got a ragged cuticle and no nail clippers to hand, and you know that if you grip it with your teeth and pull it will be gone and stop annoying you, but it'll also hurt like hell and probably bleed all over your clothes.

Except a torn cuticle would heal, and my heart was showing no signs of doing that. I wondered whether, if I'd originally told Felicity my true feelings for Renzo, she'd have told him to sling his hook.

I wasn't sure. After all, it wasn't like we were close friends, or had even known each other that long. We were colleagues who'd been out a couple of times, that was all. She didn't owe me any loyalty. And, given the choice between going out with Renzo and pissing off a woman she barely knew, and turning down the chance of dating a man who was by anyone's standards a hell of a catch – well, what would you do?

What would I do? Because, I realised, I was now in exactly the same position Felicity had been in. In getting back the man I thought of as mine, I'd be stealing her boyfriend from her. Or at least, I would be if he was a possession, like a car, rather than a human being capable of making his own choices.

Wearily, I forced my attention away from this dilemma, and returned to my emails. It was all far too flipping complicated. At least with an order for fifty dresses that had turned up in navy blue instead of black, I knew where I was.

Chapter Thirteen

As the days passed, I began to get used to Josh being there. But it still felt strange to see him emerging from the room I continued to think of as Charlotte's each morning, dressed in his running gear. The smell of his shower gel and deodorant in the bathroom still sometimes brought me up short, surprised. And the fact that someone, for the first time since I'd moved in, was actually using the kitchen, was downright bizarre. There was actual food around: blocks of cheddar and feta cheese; vegetables that needed to be peeled, chopped and cooked before you ate them; jars of curry paste and miso and anchovies, which weren't there to be spread on toast or eaten with a spoon while standing by the open fridge door.

And he seemed to take up so much space. It wasn't just his height, and it wasn't that he was untidy – he wasn't. It was more that when he was home, I was constantly conscious of his presence. He played the guitar sometimes, and even though he used headphones and an amp, the sound of the strings was audible from my bedroom. He talked to people on the phone, not loudly or late at night or in any way antisocially, but it made me aware that there was another presence in the house. The house felt alive, I realised, for the first time in ages. It felt like a home where people did more than just shower, sleep and drink coffee. It felt comforting – and that, together with Josh's always-on smile and casual good humour, made me sometimes almost forget that I hated him, and why.

The next Friday, the first batch of samples arrived for my new collection. Even though this was my fourth season at Luxeforless (if you don't count the weird in-between bit we call 'cruise' in the industry, when a load of linen trousers and straw trilbies go up on sale in the middle of winter and hardly any of our customers buy them, but we have to list them anyway because everyone else does), it still gave me a huge thrill to see the garments I'd worked on in the flesh for the first time. Well, in the fabric, I suppose, if you wanted to be literal about it.

I'd asked Chelsea to come along and see the unveiling. She was on her best behaviour, standing back as we arranged the samples on a rail and checked the quality of the workmanship, the cut and whether the colours were true to the swatches we'd sent the supplier. She listened intently as we discussed launch dates and pricing models, and asked Abi, the lead designer, some intelligent questions about why a particular fabrication, length or detail had been chosen. Then she thanked us all politely (for her, anyway; the word 'Thanks' was definitely used, and that was good enough for me) and said she'd better be off because her shift at Superdrug was starting in an hour.

By five thirty, I was done. It had been a good day – a good week, really. One of those that made me remember why I loved my job, in spite of all the whingeing I did to my colleagues and, far more often, in my own head, about management, which we all knew meant Barri.

'Hey, Tans,' Felicity said when she saw me putting on my coat. 'Fancy Annabel's tonight? Pru's chap's with his olds in Gloucestershire this weekend, and so she's gone off to a spa for a freebie they've been offering her for ages.'

And Renzo's in New York with work, and that means you're at a loose end, I thought. With him away, my original motivation for hanging out with Felicity and her sister was null and void, so to speak. I liked Felicity, I enjoyed her company, but part of me suspected that her reason for asking me to come out with her that night was no purer than my own had originally been: she had nothing else to do. But my finances wouldn't stretch to another massive night in Mayfair, even if I'd wanted to go more than anything. And, thinking about it, I found that I didn't want to, funnily enough.

I was tired, the nice kind of tired you feel at the end of the week when you've worked hard and done well. I was wearing flat shoes and battered leather trousers that definitely weren't Annabel's-ready, my hair was scraped up into a knot because it needed a wash, and the idea of going home and spending the best part of two hours trying and failing to make myself look my best had absolutely zero appeal.

'Let me just check…' I glanced at my phone and there, like a message from the gods of Friday night dullards, was a message from Josh.

Hey Tansy, you in tonight? Adam and I are, and I'm cooking.

I said, 'Ah, I'm so sorry but I can't. Bonding sesh with my new housemate. I've hardly seen the poor bloke since he arrived and I feel a bit bad. Maybe another time?'

'New housemate?' Felicity asked. 'You never mentioned him before.'

'No, well…' I remembered the flash of inspiration I'd had, which I'd yet to act on, and hesitated for a moment. I could sow a seed in Felicity's mind, without actually committing myself to anything, or even bending the truth.

'Well what? Is he hot?'

'Yeah, I guess so. Yes, he is. But the weird thing is, I knew him when I was at school. Had a massive crush on him, in fact.'

'Oooh!' Felicity said. 'Awks, much? Or does he feel the same way? Might love blossom over the tumble dryer?' Felicity had shown no sign of feeling any guilt about dating Renzo, or any concern that I might want to get back together with him. But I could see that, from her point of view, a hot former crush turning up in my life would solve a lot of problems.

I smiled in a way that I hoped was enigmatic, and pulled a loose strand of hair out of my up-do. 'We'll have to see. Have fun tonight, anyway. Tell Pru I said hi.'

Then I texted Josh, thanking him, saying I'd be home before seven and asking if he needed me to pick anything up from the shops.

I made my way home through the Friday evening crowds, stopping at the off-licence near home for a couple of bottles of Australian shiraz, because even though it was clearly shittier shiraz than Josh would be used to, it seemed like the polite thing to do. And the tactical one, too.

When I opened our front door, the first thing I saw was Adam. He was hovering on the stairs, a look of outrage on his face. I began to say hello, but he waved a hand dismissively and pointed frantically towards the kitchen.

Oh God, I thought. The last thing I needed was for Josh to do something that would piss Adam off enough to make him move out. Finding another new person to make up the rent, which even after just a couple of weeks I'd come to count on, was far more than I was able to deal with right now. Whatever Adam was freaking out about, I'd have to deal with it and try to defuse the situation.

I walked quietly into the kitchen, then stopped.

Josh was standing by the kitchen counter, where a huge, gleaming chef's knife lay on the chopping board. And he was holding Freezer upside down in his arms.

My brain, already on high alert thanks to Adam, segued directly into panic mode as my eyes interpreted the situation.

He's going to murder the cat!

I froze, my heart pounding and my thoughts whirling. What was going on? Had Josh and Adam had some kind of row, and Josh was holding Freezer hostage? Was he engaged in some kind of satanic ritual? And exactly what the hell was I going to say to Luke and Hannah if so much as one of Freezer's whiskers was harmed in our house?

Then my rational side kicked in as I took in the details of the scene. The pile of vegetables on the counter. The faint, fishy smell in the air. And most of all, Josh and Freezer's demeanour. From the doorway, I could hear thunderous purring. The cat's white paws were floppy, his eyes blissfully blinking. And Josh was singing to him. Well, not singing exactly. Rapping.

'Hey, yo, Freezer, you da geezer

You da pussy, you da dude
But I ain't allowed to give you food
You're one eye's blue and one is green
Yo, Freezer, you done owned the scene
I ain't been in Hackney long
Man, I know I get shit wrong
But the one thing I know is that
Freezer be the pengest cat.

'But no prawns for you, right, mate? They're human food.'

And he turned Freezer the right way up again, put him on one of the kitchen chairs and scratched him behind the ear.

'Hello,' I said, limp with relief. 'I brought some wine.'

'Cool! I just opened a beer, and I was starting dinner when this dude turned up and started demanding seafood.'

'We're not supposed to feed him,' Adam said, stepping past me and sitting down. Freezer immediately made himself comfortable on his lap, and Adam's face brightened. 'He belongs to the neighbours, and they don't like it.'

'Shame,' Josh said. 'And he was being so persuasive, too.'

He picked up a paper package and carefully unwrapped it, tipping a load of raw prawns out into a bowl. Freezer mewed, jumped down off Adam's lap and put his paws up against the cabinet door, stretching up as tall as he could get. Adam looked furious.

'What are you making?' I asked, partly curious and partly desperate to end what looked like turning into an epic cat popularity contest.

'It's called camarofongo,' Josh said. 'Well, kind of. It's similar to a thing I ate when I was travelling in the Dominican Republic.

It's prawns, plantain, tomatoes and shedloads of garlic and butter. Hope you haven't got a big date tomorrow.'

'Not much chance of that. Need a hand with anything?'

'Grab yourself a drink – there's a cold bottle of white in the fridge – and then we can peel these beauties,' Josh said. 'I got them at the market down the road. It's awesome there.'

'What, you mean the wholefoods place? You must have paid about two quid a prawn.'

'Not there, the proper market off the high street. Seems like that's where the locals shop.'

Not this local, I thought, impressed. Whenever I'd been through the street market, I'd been too intimidated by the array of exotic vegetables I'd never seen before and had no idea what do with, and too daunted by the eagle-eyed women scrutinising the fresh fish and haggling over the price with the stallholders, to ever buy anything. Clearly Josh was made of sterner stuff.

I sloshed some chardonnay into a glass – it smelled rich and oaky, far superior to the dodgy red I'd bought – and joined him at the counter, watching as he expertly peeled and beheaded a prawn, sliced it down the back and pulled out a slimy black thread.

'Kind of gross,' he said, 'but satisfying too. If you don't fancy doing this, you could chop some garlic.'

'I'll help you with those.' I picked up a prawn and copied him, only considerably less expertly. He was right – it was both gross and satisfying.

When they were all done, we washed our hands and Josh took another beer from the fridge, passing one to Adam, who was reading something on his phone. Freezer had given up on the idea of persuading us that he was definitely, totally allowed prawns, and had gone to sleep on Adam's lap.

'I'd offer to help too,' Adam said. 'But...'

'Never disturb a sleeping cat,' Josh finished good-naturedly. 'A good rule to live by.'

Adam didn't say very much after that. He kind of retreated into himself, as he often did, and sat in silence while Josh whirled around the kitchen like something off *MasterChef*, chopping garlic, sautéing onions, soaking rice and making a salad. *Typical Adam,* I thought – he wasn't being deliberately rude, it was just that if he didn't have anything to say, he said nothing.

I set the table and drank more wine while we chatted. Well, Josh chatted, mostly. I heard about how he'd been to the Tower of London and St Paul's and a bunch of museums, had been running every day and gone as far as Little Venice, and how cool it all was.

His enthusiasm made me remember how I'd felt when I'd first arrived in London: all fired up with excitement, convinced that my life here was going to be brilliant in every way. My career would go from strength to strength. I'd date loads of hot, eligible blokes before meeting the hottest and most eligible of them all. I'd live in a stylish apartment and later in a spacious house with a garden where my children could play and a spare room where Mum could stay when she came to visit.

Musing on all this, I fell a bit silent, and while we ate our meal, which was lush – spicy, but not too spicy, the prawns sweet and juicy – Josh tried to bring Adam out of his shell by asking him about work, but got mostly one-word answers. I felt bad for him

– he'd gone to all this trouble and one of his new housemates was cripplingly shy and the other sunk in gloom.

So I made myself say, 'That was amazing, Josh. Aren't we the lucky ones, getting a housemate who's an ace cook?'

Adam smiled reluctantly. 'Well, I'm certainly not complaining.'

It wasn't long before every last prawn, cucumber slice and grain of rice was gone. I cleared the table and stacked the dishwasher, and thought about putting the kettle on, but opened another bottle of wine instead.

Then we heard the familiar sound of Hannah and Luke's back door opening, the rattle of cat biscuits in a bowl and Hannah calling Freezer's name. Like lightning, the cat sprang off Adam's lap and shot out through the window that we always left open just wide enough for him to get through, no matter how cold it was. We heard the scrabble of his claws on the fence, and Hannah saying, 'Come on, little one. Dinner time.'

'Quite the routine you've got going there,' Josh said. Then he yawned hugely and said he was going to go up to his room, and wished us good night. Adam stood up too.

'I've just opened this.' I waved the wine bottle. 'Stay and chat for a bit.'

'Okay.' Adam sat down again, leaning back on his chair and putting his feet up on the one Josh had vacated, visibly relaxing now that it was just the two of us.

I filled up our glasses, sipped, waited until I heard the bathroom tap stop running upstairs and Josh's bedroom door close. Then I found a Spotify playlist of noughties rock, which I knew was Adam's favourite, and turned the volume up, not so loud it would disturb Josh but loud enough to drown out our conversation.

'Look,' I said in a rush. 'I know this is going to sound crazy, but hear me out. You know how you promised to tell me where Renzo was going so that I could show up in the same places as him and see him there?'

'I didn't just promise,' Adam objected. 'I delivered. Seriously good intel, almost every day since January.'

'I know, you've been brilliant. I'm really grateful. Only thing is, it hasn't worked out like I hoped it would.'

'How do you mean?'

'Well,' I said. 'It's like this.'

And I explained how the wheels had come off in a major way when Renzo had asked Felicity out.

Adam looked at his hands, then took a gulp of wine. I could see he was concerned, but also on the verge of laughter.

'It's not funny,' I said. 'Come on. I've got a broken heart and you're giggling away like you're watching *Sausage Party*.'

'Sorry, Tans,' he said. 'I'm not laughing at your broken heart, I promise. It's just… you know.'

'Okay,' I said. 'So my genius plan to get him back went tits up. But that means I need a better one, and I think I've got one.'

'You're going to jump into the fountain by Piccadilly Circus and pretend you're drowning, and he'll come past on his way to work and rescue you?'

'Nope.'

'You're going to break into his apartment and take all your clothes off and wait in his bed?'

'Fuck, no!' My face burned with embarrassment at the thought.

'You're going to chuck acid in this Felicity woman's face like that girl who went to prison last summer?'

'No! God, of course not! I'd never do anything like that. I don't want to hurt Felicity. She's my mate. Kind of.'

'But you've got no problem with trying to take her bloke off her.'

Adam's logical mind was back to full function, I noted. I'd preferred it when two and two were making five.

'I don't want to take her bloke off her, Adam.'

'Then what do you want?'

'I just want… I guess I just want him to realise he made a mistake, and he still loves me.'

'And what happens then? He dumps Felicity and breaks her heart. And then maybe she decides to pull a stunt to get him back herself. It could carry on forever, like a game of ping pong.'

'Adam! Hear me out, okay? I've got a plan. It's not a great one, but it's all I've got. It might just work, and if it does, Felicity will find someone else. She's only been dating Renzo for, like, five minutes.'

'Whereas you were dating him for, like…'

'Six months! That's half a year. It's almost one-fiftieth of my whole life. He and I were serious. What we had was really good.'

'Okay, fine,' Adam said. 'Tell me this genius plan of yours.'

'It's pretty simple. If Renzo finds out I'm seeing someone else, he might get jealous and realise he still likes me.' Now that I'd said the words, I could hear just how stupid the scheme sounded, and I could tell from the look on Adam's face that he thought so, too.

'It's not great,' I admitted. 'But, like I said, it's all I've got. It's worth a shot, surely?'

'But you're not seeing someone else.'

'Well, no. But I kind of told Felicity I was. And if you were to tell Renzo, and if he was to see me and Josh together, he might…'

'Hold on,' Adam said. 'You and Josh aren't a thing, but you want me to tell Renzo you are, and then you're going to parade Josh around under Renzo's nose and hope he changes his mind?'

'Kind of. I mean, yes. That. You know how competitive he is. If he thinks another bloke's got me, he might think, game on, and try to win me back.'

And then Adam asked the question I'd been dreading. 'What went wrong with the two of you, anyway? If things were so wonderful, why did he suddenly dump you?'

I felt the familiar hot rush of shame cover my entire body. Part of me was relieved that at least Renzo hadn't told Adam himself – but now it meant that I would have to. There was no way I could lie to him, no way of sugar-coating it to make what I'd done seem less tawdry and humiliating.

So I told him the truth.

'I totally understand if you don't want to be my friend any more,' I finished, once I'd blurted out the whole sorry story of Mum's debt, my financial crisis, turning to webcam work to make ends meet, giving it all up for Renzo and, finally, confessing to him about it.

Adam listened silently, occasionally taking a sip of wine while I talked.

At last he said, 'But Tans, that's awful.'

'I know. I feel absolutely sick remembering it. What was I even thinking?'

'Not that! Don't be ridiculous. I mean, it's horrible that such an industry even exists, that there are men out there who think they've got a relationship with some random woman on the internet who's desperate for cash. It's fucking grim. But Renzo, reacting that way – ugh.'

He literally shuddered.

'But he – it was a shock,' I protested. 'He'd just told me he loved me. And then he found out I wasn't the person he thought I was.'

'Bullshit,' Adam said. 'I'm sorry, but that's just stupid. So you have a past. Doesn't everyone? It's not like he's some kind of Trappist monk, is he, swanning off to strip bars all the time to perv over pole dancers?'

'That's different. I was his girlfriend.'

'Yeah, so the guy's got some ridiculous Madonna or whore dichotomy going on in his head. I mean, seriously. That's the most unreconstructed, offensive thing I've ever heard, and I've heard a few since I started working in that place.'

It had never occurred to me before that Adam disliked Renzo, or felt uncomfortable with the brash, macho culture I knew was the norm in his workplace. Now I realised how difficult it must be for him to keep his head down and ignore some of his colleagues' attitudes. He wasn't keeping quiet now, though.

'If I were you, Tansy, I wouldn't touch that man with someone else's ten-foot bargepole,' he ranted on. 'God. What are you think-ing? Where's your self-respect? He's shown you who he is – believe him. How can you even entertain the idea of going out with him again? You've had a lucky escape! And now you're going to go chasing after him and try to get him back? Are you completely nuts?'

I'd never heard Adam talk so passionately before. It was bizarre – as if Freezer had sat up and started lecturing me about my love life.

How dare he, I thought. Who did he think he was, telling me that the man I was in love with was a horrible person and I was stupid to want a relationship with him? He was bang out of order, and I was going to tell him so just as soon as I could find the words. And figure out what on earth 'unreconstructed' meant.

Then I paused. I didn't want to fall out with Adam – and not just because the loss of our friendship would leave a massive hole in both our lives. As I'd said earlier, this plan was the only one I had. It might be shit, but I had to try it. And to do that, I had to persuade Adam to help me. I only had one weapon and, damn it, I was going to use it.

I poured the last of the wine into our glasses.

'Adam, you know when I walked in the front door earlier. You looked like something terrible was happening. Like you'd seen a ghost, or the kitchen was on fire, or something.'

Adam said, 'But he…'

'Josh was cuddling Freezer. And singing to him. Freezer's a cat, Adam, come on. You might not be Renzo's number one fan, but at least he doesn't murder small furry animals for shits and giggles and sleep with anyone who scratches him behind the ears. Freezer does, but you still love him, right? You'd love him whatever he did. Maybe even if he suddenly decided he liked Josh more than he likes you.'

Adam winced.

'I know. That's how I feel. I understand you think you've got my best interests at heart and I can't tell you how grateful I am that

you're my friend. But I'm a big girl, and I can make my own decisions about what's right for me. And what's right for me is Renzo.'

Adam shook his head and scowled, so I changed tack.

'Just think about it for a second. If Josh is out with me, then
he's not going to be here, sneaking prawns to Freezer and letting
him sleep in his bed and maybe even throwing bits of scrunched-up
tinfoil for him to chase. Is he?'

Adam shook his head again, but he wasn't scowling any more.
It was time to play my final card – the one I didn't feel bad about
playing, because I meant it absolutely sincerely.

'If you don't want to say anything to Renzo, that's fine,' I said.
'Honestly, it is. I respect your decision. You don't have to look at
his diary any more, or tell him anything about me. It won't change
anything between us, it really won't. I care about you too much for
that. We'll still be mates, whatever happens.'

Adam was still shaking his head. *If he doesn't stop doing that
soon it's going to work loose off his neck and go flying across the room
and one of computing's finest minds will be lost forever*, I thought.
But fortunately, he paused, then rolled his eyes again and nodded.

'Sheesh, Tans. Okay, I'll do it.'

Chapter Fourteen

I woke up the next day with a thumping headache and a foul taste in my mouth that was partly down to the huge amount of garlic Josh had used in our food, but mostly down to the copious amount of wine me and Adam – to be fair, it had mostly been me – had drunk. Fortunately, because it wasn't like me to think so far ahead, I'd remembered to put a pint glass of water by my bed before I fell asleep. Congratulating myself on my boy-scout-worthy levels of preparation, I reached across for it. In my hung-over, half-asleep state, I thought it would be possible to drink some without actually sitting up. It wasn't, of course.

I tipped the whole lot over my pillow, my duvet and, mostly, my head.

'Shit! Fucksake!' I sat up, wide awake, dripping like I'd been for a swim. The bed was soaked. There was no question of necking a couple of paracetamol and going back to sleep now – not until I'd changed the sheets and rotated the mattress so I had a dry bit to lie on, anyway. And if basically waterboarding myself hadn't finished me off completely, moving a mattress would, the way I was feeling.

Reluctantly, I got up and walked, dripping, through to the bathroom with my empty glass. While I brushed my teeth, I remembered the details of my conversation with Adam the previous night. Could I pretend to Renzo that Josh was my boyfriend? What had seemed like a stroke of genius after a bottle of wine appeared completely ridiculous in the cold light of day.

Or did it? I turned the idea over in my mind. But the more I thought about it, the more problems I could see with it. If Renzo were to be made jealous of my new relationship, and his macho pride sparked into action, he'd have to see me and Josh together. And that would mean more trips to Annabel's and Nobu and God knew where else, which I couldn't afford and, as far as I could tell, nor could Josh. Not that I'd let him pay, of course, even if he could.

Where else can I see Renzo? I wondered. *Where does he go that doesn't involve spaffing hundred of pounds away on cocktails and food?* He went to work, obviously, but I couldn't think of anyone less qualified than me to seek employment at a Mayfair hedge fund. He went to the gym, but that was at work and for staff use only. He sometimes took clients to Gaslight, the so-called gentlemen's club where the evening's entertainment consisted of knocking back bottles of overpriced vodka while watching beautiful Eastern European pole dancers get their kit off.

I could try and get a job there, I thought, and for a split second it seemed like a brilliant solution. I couldn't dance, but even though I'd never been to a strip club, I suspected that you didn't exactly have to be the next Darcey Bussell to qualify. But then I remembered how Renzo had reacted when I told him about my webcam work. If that was a dumping offence, then gyrating in my smalls without even a broadband connection between me and the watching eyes would be a total deal-breaker.

For a second, I allowed myself to think about the inherent hypocrisy of Renzo's position on this, but I brushed the thought aside. Gaslight was work; his girlfriend was his personal life. He had different standards about the two things, and that was just how it was. But becoming an exotic dancer in my spare time was a non-starter.

And then, of course, there was the problem of Felicity. In order for me to get him back, she'd have to lose him, and making that happen went against all the rules of friendship. Unless, of course, I changed my tactics entirely and tried to persuade Josh to make a massive play for her and steal her away from Renzo, leaving the field wide open for me. But I knew Felicity well enough to know that she would never entertain the idea of dating a penniless (at least compared to Renzo) musician, however blond and fit he was. And I suspected, too, that that would be a game Josh wouldn't be willing to play.

I trudged gloomily downstairs. The whole thing was hopeless. My relationship with Renzo was over, and I was just going to have to suck it up and tell Adam I'd changed my mind and the whole thing was a terrible idea. That would make him happy, at least.

I flicked the kettle on and investigated the bread bin. There was a new kind of bread in there, I noticed, not the ordinary stuff I usually picked up from the supermarket but something with seeds in it and a dark, chewy-looking crust that looked like it would require some serious muscle to get through, instead of pre-cut slices falling limply from plastic wrap. Josh, I concluded, had found a local artisan bakery as well as the food market.

I poked around in the cupboards some more and found palm-oil-free peanut butter, Vegemite, a box of organic free-range eggs and a vacuum pack of coffee with a label on it that said 'Daily Grind House Blend'. In the fridge was a brown paper parcel that smelled enticingly of bacon. Adam's instant noodles and my wilting packet of kale looked distinctly unappetising by comparison.

But helping myself to Josh's bread was one thing; his bacon and special coffee were off limits, I decided. My own crumb-filled tub of low-fat spread and the scrapings from my Marmite jar were going to have to do.

Then I heard feet on the stairs and Josh himself appeared, wearing his running gear.

'Morning!' he said brightly. 'You okay?'

'I've felt better,' I admitted. 'Opening that second bottle, and then polishing it off with Adam, was probably not the smartest thing I've ever done.'

He laughed. 'Sympathy. Why don't you join me for a run? It's guaranteed to cure even a force-ten hangover. Trust me, I've tested the theory extensively.'

I opened my mouth to tell him that that was the daftest idea I'd ever heard in my life, then closed it again. Was it actually so daft? Since jacking in my gym membership, I'd barely done any exercise, and I missed the healthy, virtuous glow it gave me. And it had worked, not just at getting me a bit more toned and muscular, but at making me feel better about my body.

And besides, hadn't Josh mentioned running all the way along the canal, as far as Regent's Park? That was right near where Renzo lived. I imagined loping athletically along, my hair in a ponytail, possibly wearing a crop top that showed off the six-pack I'd magically developed, my skin glowing with fresh air and well-being and –

crucially – Josh by my side. I imagined us passing Renzo, and me giving him a casual wave, then turning to laugh with Josh while Renzo wistfully watched the two of us disappear into the distance.

Okay, that would mean being able to run about five miles, and I supposed the same distance back again, but you had to start somewhere, didn't you?

'Why not?' I said. 'Just let me get myself sorted. But you have to promise to go really, really slowly, because I am seriously unfit.'

'You don't look it. But of course, slow as you like.'

Ten minutes later, I met Josh by the front door, having resisted the temptation to have a shower because really, what kind of idiot showers *before* exercise?

'Ready?' he asked, tucking his keys into the pocket of his Lycra shorts. They were pretty tight, I noticed – obviously, being Lycra – and showed off his muscular thighs and also his… *Stop staring, Tansy!*

'I guess,' I said.

He opened the door and we stepped out into the cool, bright morning. I wasn't sure what I'd expected – that he'd walk as far as the park and then maybe do some stretches or something – but he took off straight down the road at what was clearly an easy jog for him, but felt alarmingly fast to me. I trotted after him, my legs feeling wooden and clumsy.

'First couple of hundred metres are the hardest,' he said, sounding not even slightly out of breath, 'so we may as well get them over with.'

'That makes sense,' I panted. *I'm not going to ask him to slow down*, I vowed to myself. *I'm going to keep up if it kills me. Which it probably will.*

But, to my surprise, by the time we swung through the wrought-iron gates into the park, it had started to feel a bit easier. I was still breathing hard, but it seemed normal now. My legs were getting used to the rhythm, my trainers thudding evenly on the path as I kept step with Josh, although I could see that it was costing him almost as much effort to keep at my speed as it was costing me to keep up with him. The beauty of the morning helped: the mist still hanging over the pond, but clearing everywhere else, revealing a radiant blue sky. The clouds of bright pink blossom on the cherry trees. The flock of green parakeets that whirled, screeching, over our heads.

Josh pointed all these things out to me, unnecessarily, because I could see them for myself and was too out of breath to respond. But his constant stream of chatter distracted me from the pain, and soon we'd completed a circuit of the park.

'That's about three kilometres,' Josh said. 'Enough for your first time, I reckon, unless you'd like to go round again?'

My pride said yes, but my legs definitely said no. 'Let's head home.'

'Sure,' he said, and turned back out through the gate. I managed to stay alongside him all the way to the end of the road, when he said, 'Sprint finish? Come on, I'll race you to the door.'

And he took off, his long legs scissoring effortlessly and his arms swinging, his hair flying out behind him.

'Bastard!' I gasped. 'That's not fair!'

I forced my tired legs into the most activity they'd done for months, chasing after him as fast as I could go. Which was surprisingly fast. For a few seconds, I felt like I had when I was a kid on sports day, racing because I wanted to, because it was fun and I was determined to win.

And Josh let me – I'm sure of it, because there was no way that I, unpractised and unfit as I was, could outrun him. Just before we reached our house, I drove my legs into a final burst of speed and edged past him – and then it all went pear-shaped. My rhythm broke, I tripped over my own trainers and face-planted on the pavement at Josh's feet.

'Oh my God,' he said. 'Are you okay? I'm so sorry, that was totally my fault. You poor thing. Here.'

He held out his hand and I took it, letting him help me up on my trembling legs.

'Ouch,' he said. 'That's got to hurt.'

I looked down and saw blood trickling down my calves from where I'd taken the skin off both knees. He was right – it hurt like a bitch. It was all I could do not to cry. I was torn between embarrassment, pain and fury that Josh had persuaded me to do this stupid thing against my better judgement. Which, of course, I ought to have known was absolutely typical of him.

But Josh didn't seem to notice my inner turmoil. He guided me inside and sat me down at the kitchen table, then tore two squares of paper towel off the roll and soaked them under the tap.

'Here, this should do for now,' he said. 'I've got plasters and antiseptic and stuff upstairs. I'll just—'

'Honestly, don't worry.' I didn't feel like I was going to cry any more, thank God – his concern was so over the top it was almost funny, and I started to giggle. 'It's just a scrape. I promise I'll live.'

'A mere flesh wound,' he said, kneeling down in front of me and smiling up at me. 'Let's try and clean it up, though.'

The wet paper towels stung when he touched the raw places on my knees, but his warm hand on my calf distracted me from that. I stared at the top of his head as he carefully dabbed away at the blood. I don't know why – whether it was his gentle touch or the sudden presence of his body so close to me, all big and male and slightly sweaty and just *there* – but I felt warmth flood my face.

'Thanks, Florence Nightingale,' I said, when at last he'd finished. Then I looked up, and saw Adam. He was standing halfway down the stairs, watching us. There was no way of telling how long he'd been there.

*

I barely saw Josh all the next week. On the house WhatsApp group, where we'd occasionally post if we were in the mood to cook and wanted to know who'd be home, or if Odeta had pointed out that we were out of Fairy Liquid and someone needed to replace it, or if we fancied popping out for a beer, Josh's responses were generally, 'Sorry, I'm going out with some mates tonight.'

For someone who'd just arrived in London, whose mum worried that he'd be lonely and not know anyone, he seemed to have a bottomless store of these 'mates', I thought, rather sourly. I wondered who they were: fellow Aussie travellers, I supposed, unless he'd got himself set up on Tinder in record time and was managing to actually meet girls, rather than just exchange messages with people who turned out to be in relationships already, or who ghosted you the moment you began to feel any connection with them, which had been my experience when I'd briefly attempted to date a couple of years before.

Anyway, his arrival in the house didn't exactly make things any livelier, and Adam and I carried on pretty much as we had before he moved in. Adam worked late most days, and then sat in his room tapping away on his computer, sometimes with Freezer curled up on his lap, emerging only to make himself a bowl of instant noodles.

I spent the evenings alone downstairs, flicking idly through the channels on the telly and trying – usually unsuccessfully – to resist the urge to stalk Renzo and Felicity on social media until it was time to FaceTime Mum and Perdita in Cornwall and go to bed.

Then, on Friday, a message from Josh popped up on my phone.

A mate of mine (another bloody mate!) *has invited me to a gig tonight. Fancy coming along? He works for a bank in the City and it's in aid of a charity called Street Cred – something to do with helping young men from underprivileged backgrounds get into work and training, so a good cause! Should be fun too – Cross Wires are playing.*

I'd never heard of Cross Wires, but I was pretty sure I'd heard of Street Cred somewhere before. I typed it into Google and found a website with lots of feel-good stuff about outreach and opportunities for disadvantaged – and, I got the sense although it wasn't spelled out, disaffected – youths.

So far, so worthy. But right where the site mentioned sponsors, there was a clickable link. I clicked it and, sure enough, there was the Colton Capital logo right at the top. I could remember quite clearly now how Renzo had spoken about the firm's work with the charity.

While I'd been searching, Adam had replied to Josh. *Sorry, gigs aren't really my thing, so I'll pass. Thanks anyway! Some of the people from work are going though. Some of the people from work?* I tapped quickly through to my private text conversation with Adam and sent a row of question marks, and he replied seconds later: *Yeah, R will be there. And yeah, I mentioned you had a new bloke. He didn't look too happy about it.*

An opportunity to see Renzo without Felicity – who'd already told me she'd managed to get an evening hair appointment to have her lowlights done – was far too good to pass up, even if it would mean an evening trying to be nice to Josh.

Sure, I typed, *I'd love to join you. Let me know the details.*

Josh replied with the time and venue, which was a pub in Shoreditch I'd never been to – not that that was any surprise at all, given that I barely went out anywhere any more. I figured out that if I left work on time, I'd be able to go home and get ready before meeting him there.

What the hell do you wear to charity gigs? I wondered. Jeans and boots would be the order of the day for a normal gig, but was this different? Was it more like a charity ball? I had no idea, and there was no one I could ask, so I spent the rest of the afternoon frantically googling images of previous events, growing more and more nervous at the prospect of seeing Renzo and getting the sum total of fuck all work done.

At home in the shower, as I slapped a deep-conditioning treatment on my hair that was supposed to work miracles in under three minutes and frantically shaved my legs, I still hadn't made up my mind what to wear. I imagined Renzo noticing me across the crowded room, his eyes widening in surprise and pleasure – because although I knew that he was going to be there, he had no way of suspecting that I was. I pictured him walking towards me, and me smiling back, making my way through the crowd, wearing… what?

What? The question repeated itself over and over in my head as I stood in front of my wardrobe ten minutes later, still no nearer making a decision. A leather mini-skirt seemed like a good option, but my legs were too milk-bottle white to carry it off without tights, and tights were… Well, they were a question that was currently vexing the entire fashion world, and I wasn't clear where I stood on the matter. Sheers were back, everyone knew that, but somehow I just couldn't imagine myself rocking Kate Middleton-style hosiery at a gig, charity or not.

If I opted for a longer length, I could leave off the tights, but a midi-skirt, however on-trend, didn't seem right. Fashionistas might nod approvingly, but Renzo? 'God, I love how hot she looks in that mid-calf pleated plaid skirt of hers,' said no man ever. And tonight, definitively and unapologetically, I was dressing for Renzo.

Or was I? Wasn't there an element of reverse fashion psychology to consider? What if, in the scenario in my head, I looked so effortlessly put-together, so comfortable in my own skin, that he would never guess the torment of indecision I'd gone through while making up my mind?

'Jeans and boots it is,' I said aloud.

I still had my beloved high-rise, slim-fitting cropped jeans. When Sally passed the sample on to me, she said that even after spending half an hour in front of the mirror trying to convince herself that they suited her, she'd had to admit defeat. But when I tried them on, I knew straight away that these were the holy grail for me. They made my bum, which in reality is washboard-flat however many squats I do, look pert and peachy. Even though cropped jeans normally look stupid on me, because with my height they look like I hadn't got the memo that everywhere stocks tall ranges now, these skimmed my ankles at just the right level. I'd had a massive tussle with my conscience about keeping them, rather than including them in my latest fundraising eBay upload, but in the end the jeans had won.

I put them on, added a crocheted crop top I'd found in a charity shop, which I'm pretty sure dated back to the last time bare midriffs were a thing in the nineties, and slipped my feet into faux-snakeskin kitten-heel mules.

And then, glancing at my watch and realising that if I spent any more time finessing my outfit I would be seriously late, not just a bit late, I legged it down the stairs and out to the bus stop.

I couldn't see Renzo when I arrived, and I didn't spot Josh immediately, either. Then I realised that that was because I'd been scanning the room for his tousled dark blond head in a corner somewhere, standing alone waiting for me. But he wasn't alone, or with the only person in the crowded bar he knew. He was right in the middle of the room, surrounded by a huge group of laughing, chatting people.

Seeing him there, I suddenly felt as small and lost as I had at school, when he was at the centre of the group that included Kylie, Anoushka and all the rest of them, and I was invisible out there on the sidelines – if I was lucky. All my excitement at the prospect of seeing Renzo melted away, and I wanted nothing more than to turn around and get back on the safe, warm bus and go home. But it was too late. He'd seen me.

His hand raised high above the crowd in a wave, he made his way towards me, effortlessly breaking a path through the packed room without pushing or shoving or treading on toes, as I would have done.

'Tans! So great you could make it!' he hugged me like seeing me was the best thing that had happened to him all day. 'This is just the warm-up act, but how awesome are they? They're four of the guys who Street Cred have helped over the past few years. They're working on an album, Matt says. I asked if they needed a producer, but I reckon they're out of my league.'

I'd felt so out of my league myself that I'd barely noticed the music. But now I saw the group on stage: a guy with dreadlocks, an Asian boy with glasses and two others in the background, one playing drums and the other on a brass horn of some kind. The sound was mournful, almost melancholy, a haunting tune without any words.

'What do you reckon?' Josh asked. 'Talented, or what?'

I had no idea how to gauge musical skill, but I said, 'They sound amazing. What is it, some kind of post-punk, new-wave indie sound?'

I had no clue what the words actually meant, but they sounded okay, so I went with them. It was too late to say anything else, anyway.

'Nailed it!' Josh said approvingly. 'Now, let me buy you a drink and introduce you to Matt and the rest of the gang.'

A few minutes later, I too was included in the big group at the centre of the room, a cold bottle of lager in my hand, listening to one of the women talk about a sewing cooperative she'd set up for asylum seekers, paying the living wage to make a line of ethically produced underwear. It was hard to hear her over the music, but I leaned in and listened, fascinated.

Then, with a final, haunting chord from the lead guitar, the set came to an end. Applause erupted around me, and someone handed me a fresh drink. I glanced around the room, remembering why I'd come.

And then I saw Renzo.

He was standing alone in a corner by the bar, like I'd expected Josh to be. In his work clothes, he looked as uncomfortable and out of place as I'd expected to feel, before I'd been so warmly welcomed and included. There was a glass of red wine in his hand, and I saw him wince as he sipped it.

Then he looked over and clocked me, and his face changed, lighting up as I'd imagined it doing. For a second, I thought about excusing myself and hurrying over to him. But Harriet was telling me how hard it was for the women, many of whom had been brutalised and lost their whole families, to integrate into a new community, and how she had volunteer teachers coming in to do English conversation classes, and I was too interested to interrupt her.

And when her story finished, the main act started setting up on stage and I looked around again for Renzo. But he wasn't there. He'd left, and I didn't even know whether he'd noticed that I'd been there with Josh.

The Thirteenth Date

I woke up in Renzo's flat one Saturday in August. We'd been out the night before with some of his mates from his previous job and what he'd promised would just be a quiet drink, a catch-up and a chance for me to meet some of them had turned into multiple rounds of cocktails, a lavish dinner at Sketch (which I'd seen mentioned on Instagram by some of the celebrities I followed and never, ever dreamed I'd go to myself) and then on to a club for dancing. Some of Renzo's friends had announced that they were going on to Stringfellows, and for a second I'd wondered with the beginnings of panic whether he was going to want to go too or, worse still, expect me to accompany him.

But he'd just said, 'I don't need to pay good money to look at beautiful naked women. I've got the real thing, right here, for free.'

And we went back to his flat and had the sort of slightly wild, slightly drunken sex I was beginning to expect after nights out with him. I'd wondered with a shadow of concern whether his frenetic energy (and the fact that it took him way longer than normal to orgasm) was due to anything stronger than the many cocktails we'd drunk together, but I told myself that even if it was, it was none of my business. He was a grown-up, and able to make his own decisions about his own body. And anyway, it wasn't like taking cocaine was a regular thing for him. I'd have known if it was, I reassured myself; and if occasionally he used it to let his hair down after a stressful week, who was I to judge?

Even though I definitely hadn't indulged in any illegal substances myself, I woke up feeling absolutely foul on that glorious, sunny summer's day. My head was throbbing like my brain wanted to burst out of my skull. My thighs ached like I'd done a hundred lunges, which I certainly hadn't, and I was baffled as to why until I remembered how he'd bent my legs high over my head and held my ankles while we had sex. It must have felt like a hardcore yoga workout at the time, but I'd been too pissed and turned on to notice.

And speaking of which… As I mentally assessed the state of my body, a new kind of pain made its presence felt, and with it vanished any hope of going back to sleep until my hangover was better. I got out of bed and tiptoed towards the bathroom, but then the tiptoeing turned into a sprint.

'Fuck,' I muttered. 'Fucking fuck you, cystitis, you utter fucker.'

There went the prospect of leisurely morning sex, lazy afternoon sex after we'd had something to eat, and possibly even sex again before we went to sleep. We'd only been going out for two months, after all, and we didn't see each other every night, so when we did it still felt as if we were making up for lost time.

But the thought of anything other than a cold flannel going anywhere near my poor sore bits made me want to howl with misery. I turned on the tap to run a cool bath, wondering briefly whether there was any chance of Renzo's flat containing anything that even vaguely resembled bicarbonate of soda, tea tree oil or cranberry juice, then immediately dismissing the idea. Renzo was about as likely to buy tea tree oil as he was to get the night bus home. If he'd ever bought a carton of cranberry juice it would have been to make Cosmopolitans, and they hadn't been fashionable since the dark ages of about 2006, long before I was even legally allowed to drink. I necked a couple of paracetamol with water from the tap and lowered myself tenderly into the bath. The cool water and the painkillers helped a bit, and by the time I heard Renzo's feet on the floor outside, I was feeling a bit better.

'Christ,' he said, pushing open the door. 'I feel like all kinds of shit.'

Even with charcoal shadows under his eyes and his hair sticking up all over the place, he was still the most beautiful man in existence.

'Me too,' I said. 'When I've had my bath I might go back to bed. I think I've… Do you think you could maybe…'

I know, totally pathetic, but I couldn't bring myself to come out and tell him what the matter was. It felt too intimate, not in the way sex was intimate, but in another way that was deeply personal, almost shameful. I wondered if we'd ever reach a point where I could casually ask him to add a pack of tampons to the weekly shop, saying carelessly, 'Not the applicator ones, they ming.' I couldn't imagine it at all, but I supposed we'd get there eventually. Maybe.

But he wasn't listening to my fumbling attempt to explain why I was lying in the bath at eleven in the morning, wan and sorry for myself like a hung-over Lady of Shallot. He switched the shower on to boiling and stepped in. Seconds later, the rich, fruity smell of the Creed shower gel he used billowed out into the bathroom. On his skin, I loved it, but now it seemed unpleasantly cloying.

I levered myself out of the bath, wrapped a huge velvety dove-grey towel round my shoulders and went to sit on the bed, and I was still there, not properly dry and certainly not dressed but feeling slightly less like I was about to die, when Renzo reappeared. He'd shaved and fixed his hair so it fell in the familiar glossy sweep across his brow. He dropped his towel onto the floor and opened the wardrobe, stepping quickly into boxer shorts and jeans, then pulling on a pale blue and white sports shirt.

'Should I get dressed too? Where are we going?'

'I'm going to the pub.'

'What? Surely you don't feel up to drinking now?'

He laughed. 'Man's gotta do what a man's gotta do. It's the opening day of the Serie A season and Lazio are playing SPAL. I'm meeting some mates at one, and it's half twelve now. I'll just have a few beers.'

'Do you want me to come?'

'You?' He looked at me in surprise. 'God, no. You'd hate it, *fragolina mia*. Bunch of men swearing at a TV.'

'Okay. I'll get dressed then, and go home.'

He sat next to me on the bed and put his arm around me. 'Hey, you don't have to go anywhere. If you're feeling like crap, stay here, relax, have a nap. I'll be home by six. We could just have a chilled night in.'

I looked at the bed. The sheets were rumpled after last night and no longer clean, but still they looked like the most inviting thing ever. I could sleep for a couple of hours and then stagger to a pharmacy and get some good strong drugs, and by the time Renzo came home I'd definitely be feeling better. We could order a takeaway and watch a movie and chill, like he said.

'Great idea,' I said.

'Here's a key. Maybe if you're feeling better you could make us some dinner? I'll be starving when I get back. *Molta fame*. There are loads of shops just down the road. Or just stay in bed, if you want.'

He kissed me and strode out.

I collapsed onto the bed like I was made of melting jelly. I felt hot and cold, knackered and wide awake. I needed to eat, but I wasn't sure what – if any – food there was in Renzo's kitchen. I'd never been in the flat alone before, I realised.

With that thought, any chance I'd had of sleep was gone. It's not like I wanted to snoop; I didn't, at all. But knowing that I was there by myself made me want to get up and explore, and imagine what it would be like to feel I belonged there.

Ten minutes later, I was dressed in the denim skirt and vest top I'd stuffed into my bag the previous day so I wouldn't have to do the walk of shame in the low-cut red chiffon shirt and thigh-length skirt I'd gone out in. I wished I had more stuff at Renzo's flat – the contents of my make-up bag were nowhere near up to the task of making me look like I hadn't been dead for several days, and the can of deodorant in my handbag was empty so I had to nick some of his, which made me smell like a very fragrant bloke.

I made the bed, went through to the kitchen and poured a glass of water from the dispenser on the front of the fridge. Everything in the flat was super-high tech: there were USB sockets everywhere, a wine chiller under the copper-topped counter and a whole cupboard full of space-age appliances including a food processor, an ice-cream maker and a bread maker, all still in their boxes, unused.

On a shelf was a row of cookbooks: *Gastronomy of Italy, Essentials of Classic Italian Cooking, The Food of Italy, La Cucina: The Regional Cooking of Italy* and a few more. I opened one at random and saw, in swirly writing on the first page: *Buon appetito, Polpetto! Looking forward to many feasts together. Love Minty.*

'Well, stuff you, Minty,' I muttered. 'You're not around now, and I am.'

The books all looked unused, too, their spines stiff and their glossy pages unmarked by splashes of grease or tomato stains. In the fridge were a few bottles of beer, a pint of milk, a pack of coffee beans, a tub of olives and two lemons. The freezer was empty apart from ice and bottles of gin and vodka. The cavernous larder unit held only a pack of amaretti biscuits, a couple of jars of chickpeas, a bottle of olive oil and a box of muesli. When I opened the box, wondering if I could face eating some for breakfast, a moth fluttered out.

Well, if I was going to cook for Renzo, I'd have to lay in some serious provisions. Feeling suddenly faint and queasy again, I sat on one of the tall stools by the counter and sipped my water. I needed to go out anyway, I reasoned, to get to a pharmacy and see if they could give me anything stronger than paracetamol, and to the supermarket to invest in a stash of cranberry juice.

I flicked through one of the cookbooks. Most of the recipes seemed to assume that I had the entire contents of a farmers' market at my disposal and several hours to spend reducing stock and rendering fat, not to mention the ability to use the pasta maker I'd spotted in the gadget cupboard.

I had none of those things, but there was a Waitrose nearby, so I'd have to manage as best I could. I took photos on my phone of a couple of the simpler-looking recipes and, after another agonising trip to the loo, ventured out.

It was half past two when I staggered back to the flat, buckling under the weight of carrier bags from the supermarket, the pharmacy, the butcher, the deli and the wine merchant (and reeling with horror at how much money I'd spent). Although Renzo's own wine fridge was nothing if not well stocked, I didn't want to fuck up and open something that was a precious gift from a client or had cost Renzo two hundred pounds, so I'd bought a bottle each of red and white.

I unpacked everything onto the kitchen island and opened the photos of the recipes on my phone rather than risking spilling something on the virgin pages of the books, and got to work.

I made a tiramisu, beating the mascarpone cheese and eggs together by hand with a fork because I didn't want to be the first person to use Renzo's snazzy electric mixer. That was simple enough, and the espresso maker – which at least I knew how to use – was well up to the job of making the 'good, strong coffee' the book stipulated the sponge biscuits ('savoiardi are far superior', the recipe said sternly, hence my trip to the deli) should be soaked in.

Once that was in the fridge, awaiting only a grating of 'best dark chocolate' over the top, and after I'd taken more painkillers washed down with a pint of cranberry juice, I turned to the next recipe.

'A classic, authentic ragù alla bolognese is quite different from the tomatoey imitation you might be used to eating in Britain,' lectured the writer, who I was beginning to hate quite a lot. So I chopped onion, carrot, celery and pancetta into tiny cubes, crushed garlic, browned ordinary minced beef and veal mince (which I'd had to go to the butcher to get), mixed everything together in a huge pan and, after figuring out how to make Renzo's state-of-the-art induction hob turn down to 'an almost imperceptible, trembling simmer' without it beeping furiously at me, went to wee for what felt like the billionth time that day.

I remembered Mum telling Perdita and me, when we were teenagers and she was going through a phase of making everything from scratch, which I'd thought at the time was just one of her hippy things but now realised was a very necessary money-saving strategy, that if you can read, you can cook. Maybe that's true, but no one tells you that if you can't cook, having to read how to do everything makes it take five times as long.

It was half past four already. If Renzo got back when he'd said – or if he was early – and was starving, the food wouldn't be nearly ready: the recipe stipulated three to four hours of imperceptible simmering. So I dashed out again and spent a small fortune on marinated artichoke hearts, prosciutto, fennel salami and a cured meat thing called bresaola – which the nice woman in the deli assured me was as authentic as it got – and arranged it all on a platter.

I sliced more garlic and put it in a little dish ready to be rubbed with olive oil and salt over slices of freshly toasted sourdough bread. ('The silver foil-wrapped slugs of garlic bread beloved of 1980s dinner parties would be an insult to any true Italian,' dissed the recipe.) Yet more garlic went into a dressing to go on the salad I made with no fewer than five different kinds of lettuce, paper-thin slices of red onion and ripped-up basil leaves. I grated most of a wedge of what I thought was parmesan cheese but turned out to be called Parmigiano Reggiano into a bowl.

I drank another pint of water and more cranberry juice and took more of the good strong drugs from the chemist. I had a shower and shaved my legs with Renzo's razor and dressed in my denim skirt and the top and knickers I'd bought on Marylebone High Street earlier because I could see no sign of a washing machine anywhere in the flat. I put on more make-up. I set the table – a huge, asymmetrical slab of glass surrounded by eight white leather chairs.

I lit candles, even though it was only six and still light outside. I stacked the dishwasher, hoping that I was doing it right. I checked my phone again and again, but there was no message from Renzo. Six thirty came and went. I stirred the sauce for the pasta and put salt ('a good handful – Italians use water as salty as the Mediterranean sea') into a pan ready to cook the fresh spaghetti I'd bought. I wiped the counter tops and drank more water. I looked at the half-full bottle of white wine I'd opened to put in the pasta sauce and felt a fresh stab of hot pain, and hurried to the bathroom again.

Then there was really nothing more for me to do. The tide of motivation – the urge to prove myself to be the perfect girlfriend – that had carried me through the day was ebbing. I tried calling Renzo, just the once, but his phone went straight to voicemail. I was determined not to ring or message him again after that; he was with friends, he'd said he would be home early, I didn't want to look needy.

In a cupboard in the spare bedroom, I found a silky silver throw, the designer tags still attached. I carried it through to the living room and curled up on the sofa to wait, needing the comfort of its warmth even though the night wasn't cold. I found an old episode of *RuPaul's Drag Race* on my phone – Renzo's home entertainment system being a mystery to me – and plugged in my earbuds.

The bang of the front door woke me, hours later, even though I hadn't been aware I'd fallen asleep. I heard footsteps on the wooden floor, heavy and uneven, then a crash as something heavy – a phone or a set of keys – fell to the floor.

'Renzo?'

'Nil–nil. What a fucking shit show. What a waste of fucking time. *Che cazzo de casino!* Viviane was shit and Mora was worse, and Simone – Christ, what a waste of fucking money.'

He stormed in from the hallway. His shirt was stained and I could smell sourness – beer, sweat or a mixture – coming off him.

'I cooked dinner,' I said humbly, struggling up off the sofa. 'There's pasta and ragù and salad and pudding. And if you're hungry now, there's some salami and stuff.'

I looked doubtfully at the platter I'd arranged, on which some of the cold meats were curling dry and others sweating grease.

'I'm not hungry, babe,' he said. 'I ate earlier. What I need now is a shag and a sleep. Come on, come to bed.'

Chapter Fifteen

When I got to work on Monday morning, a week later, Felicity was already at her desk, her computer powered up and a glass of what looked like pond slime next to her. I said a bright and breezy good morning, and asked how her weekend had been.

'Okay,' she said. 'Quiet. I spent a lot of time in the gym.'

'In the gym? Really?' As far as I knew, my colleague's idea of healthy living didn't extend very far beyond the occasional hot yoga class and kicking off brunch with a virgin mary before hitting the fizz.

'Yup.' She took a sip of the slime and grimaced.

'What the hell is that stuff?'

'It's the High Fidelity Power Protein shake. Tastes fucking rank, but I expect I'll get used to it by about week three of the programme.'

'What programme?' I sipped my cappuccino and switched on my own computer.

'You haven't heard of Fidel Blake? I'm amazed – he's got, like, two million followers on Insta. Although of course he only takes on a select number of new clients. A few of Pru's friends use him. Bettina lost a stone and a half and two dress sizes in the first three weeks.'

A stone and a half in three weeks. The numbers on my app had stayed the same for a while now; I'd been a bit lax about entering all my daily calories and I remembered I hadn't even stepped on the scale that morning. I'd been feeling okay about it – good, even, like the monster in my head had retreated for the moment to leave me in peace. But hearing Felicity's words made it prick up its ears and stir, knotting my stomach with guilt and anxiety and spoiling the taste of my milky coffee.

'What does he do?'

'Works miracles, obviously.' Felicity laughed and sipped some more slime. 'I've gone for the Elite Ripped package. Three personal training sessions a week with Fidel, all my meals and shakes delivered and motivational calls to keep me going whenever I need them. But there are lower-tier deals, too. Like, you can download a personalised training schedule and upload pics of your food before you eat it and he tells you if it's okay.'

'It sounds hardcore,' I said.

'Well, it gets results. Especially the programme I'm doing. It's called the Ten-Week Accelerator. If my body fat isn't down below twenty per cent by the end, I get my money back.'

Intrigued in spite of myself, I asked, 'How much does it cost? And what do you get to eat?'

'Fidel doesn't come cheap,' Felicity admitted. 'But obviously everything's included in the seven hundred pounds a week.'

'Seven hundred…?' Well. Even if I hadn't known what a terrible idea it would be for me, I knew now that Felicity's regime was as far beyond my reach as bench-pressing my own body weight. Even what my body weight would be after completing Fidel Blake's Elite Ripped Ten-Week Accelerator programme.

'So for the first four days I don't eat anything,' Felicity carried on, glancing at her phone even though I suspected she'd committed the entire ordeal that lay ahead of her to memory already. 'Just the shakes. But they're totally nutritionally balanced, with optimal amounts of protein, fat and micronutrients, tailored to my unique body composition. I'm on day three now. So on Wednesday I get some eggs, a superfood salad and another shake. Thursday's a high-carb day. Breakfast is chia seed and carob power porridge, and apparently it's orgasmic. Friday's a high-fat day, with salmon for lunch, and then on Saturday I'm allowed booze again – any white spirit, with a zero-calorie mixer. Reckon I'll need it. And Renzo's back from Singapore this weekend, so we can celebrate.'

A vodka and soda didn't sound like much of a celebration to me, even if it was with Renzo. Although, if it were possible to swap places with Felicity, I'd happily have taken the agonising workouts and green slime if he came as part of the deal. For the millionth time, I had to subdue my resentment of her – after all, I'd basically given their relationship my blessing.

But that wasn't the only thing troubling me. Felicity's lush curves, the way she ate without self-consciousness or fear of being judged, her effortless sensuousness, all seemed such a fundamental part of her. If I was like that, there's no way I'd want to change it by embarking on a ten-week marathon of slime and squats. It was like Nigella Lawson saying she'd gone vegan.

But I knew all too well how I would leap to my own defence if someone asked – as they had done so often when I was enduring one of my own 'I like the gym, and anyway, steamed butternut squash is a carb, don't you know anything?' phases – if I was okay.

So I asked gently, 'Is there something in particular that's made you decide this is right for you?'

Felicity shrugged and smiled. There was a bit of green stuff caught between her perfectly straight, pearl-white teeth. 'Summer's just around the corner. Pru's friend Jonty was talking about a week on his yacht in Cannes in May and he asked if I'd like to come. I thought I might invite Renzo. So, you know, I want to look my best.'

I imagined Felicity wafting round the deck of a yacht in a bikini, with a sarong draped around her hips, sipping a glass of whatever people sipped on yachts. In my head, Renzo appeared behind her, wrapped his arms around her waist and swept her off to their stateroom, or whatever the hell the places where beds are on yachts are called. In my head, she looked amazing. And she was – there was no way a skinny, ripped version of her would have looked better.

But I just said, 'Blimey. Well, good luck with it.'

'I'll need it,' she replied grimly. 'How was your weekend, anyway? How's your new housemate?'

I took a deep breath. Now was the moment I'd rehearsed over and over, unable to decide what, if anything, I was going to say. My choices were clear: I could tell the truth about Josh – that he was just a housemate – or I could elaborate on the fiction I'd talked to Adam about, in the hope that what I told Felicity would get back to Renzo and prompt him to do… something.

'He's nice,' I said. 'A musician. He's looking for freelance session work, playing guitar with bands, and he's talking about finding a studio to do some production work.'

Felicity raised a perfectly microbladed eyebrow. 'When you say nice…?'

'That kind of nice,' I said. It was perfectly true – by any reasonable person's standards, Josh was attractive. 'He's hot. Tall, blond, amazing green eyes. Like I said, I knew him when I was a teenager in Cornwall, before he moved to Australia with his mum. It's kind of weird seeing him all grown up.'

'A surfer dude. Nice indeed. I can just imagine it – a thwarted teenage crush, years pass, you think of each other occasionally, wondering what if…? Then suddenly, you come back into each other's lives and – bam. It's like he never left. All the old passion is reignited, only now the sweet boy has grown into a man.'

I laughed. 'You should be writing for *Take a Break*.'

'No, no. If it was *Take a Break* he'd have run off with your sister, leaving you broken-hearted. Desperate for a baby, you'd have turned to a sperm bank and then, when he returned from his long, lonely years in Australia, regretting the terrible mistake he'd made, and met your son for the first time, you noticed their identical green eyes and you realised… God, I love that magazine. It's my guilty pleasure. I always buy a copy to take with me to the hairdresser because they only have bloody *Vogue* and *Harper's*. Anyway, so you and this – what's his name?'

'Josh. Josh Valentine.'

'Valentine! That's just perfect, you couldn't make it up. "Me and My Valentine", the story would be called. So you're taking things up where you left off?'

Of course, that's when I should have told her. I should have laughed off her funny little made-up romance and fessed up that there had never been anything between me and Josh – outside of my own wistful teenage imagination – and there wasn't going to be now. In the interests of absolutely full disclosure, I could even have told her that I wasn't in the market for a new boyfriend because I still wasn't over the old one.

But I didn't. I said, 'We'll have to wait and see. I'm not rushing into anything.'

'Well then, I'll hold off buying a new hat for your wedding until you tell me different. That's so exciting, though! When do I get to meet him? We must make a plan to go out next week when I'm back on the booze. I can't wait to tell Renzo.'

Job done, I thought. There didn't need to be anything between me and Josh – Felicity's enthusiastic embellishment of the story she'd made up with almost no prompting from me would be all I'd wanted. By tonight – or whenever Felicity next WhatsApped him – Renzo would believe that I was newly and blissfully loved- up with an old flame from my past. And I hadn't even had to fib. I felt bad about misleading Felicity – or rather allowing her to mislead herself – but I pushed my guilt aside. And as for Josh – well, if he ended up being a pawn in my game, that was too bad. It wasn't like he'd never played by those rules himself.

It was almost nine thirty; I had a call with a supplier in Shaoxing at ten and our departmental meeting was about to start. Hopefully, Barri wouldn't decide to gatecrash this time. I turned to my email and, as if summoned like Lord Voldemort, there was his name right at the top of my inbox with a red 'urgent' flag alongside it. My heart sank as I clicked on it, wondering what I'd done wrong this time, but to my relief the message was to the whole of the buying team, not just me.

Guys, I need your sales figures for year to date updated and your budget forecasts completed with detailed cost and scenario analyses by close of play today. No excuses.

It was typical of my boss's communication style that there was no salutation on the email and no sign-off. Barri liked to appear far too busy for such fripperies and, to be fair, he probably was. But then how long did it actually take to type 'Hi' and 'Thanks'?

'Shit,' I muttered to Kris as we all gathered our things and headed for the meeting room. 'I'm supposed to be meeting my mentee this afternoon. Guess I'll have to blow her out and do that stupid forecast instead. It was only meant to be due on Friday.'

'Good morning, everyone,' Lisa said as we all took our places around the meeting room table. 'Just a quick one today, as I'm sure you'll all have seen Barri's email and know we've got a busy day ahead of us. There are no announcements from the management team meeting, so I just wanted to make sure you were all okay to deliver the work he's asked for.'

No one said anything. There was no point asking if someone else could meet Chelsea that afternoon – she was my responsibility. If I didn't get my forecast done I'd have to cancel – that was all there was to it.

Then Sally said, 'Do you know why he's asked us to do this? I mean, it's a normal part of our jobs, but why's it so flipping urgent all of a sudden?'

Sally had happened to mention to me that, thanks to a cancellation, she'd managed to get an appointment to have platinum highlights at a nearby salon with a stylist who'd done Emilia Clarke's hair and normally had a three-month waiting list. So I could understand her frustration at having to sack off having her hair transformed in favour of tearing it out over a spreadsheet all afternoon.

'I…' Lisa paused. 'Well, it's not official but it's not confidential either, so I suppose you may as well know. Barri's been approached by a venture capitalist who's interested in buying into the business. As you know, he received a round of funding four years ago, which allowed us to move into this office and expand into menswear, footwear and lingerie. This latest injection of cash would take the business up to a level where we'd really be able to start to compete with the major players in the market. The investor is doing his due diligence before making a decision, and so has requested all this information.'

'Does that mean Barri's selling Luxeforless?' Kris asked.

'Certainly not,' Lisa said. 'I know he'd want me to reassure you all – and I'm sure he will do so himself once things are a bit more certain – that this should be seen as an opportunity, not a threat. Investment at this kind of level brings the potential for real growth, not just for the business, but for all of us. The VC investor in question – I definitely can't name any names at this stage – has worked with some major players in the industry and transformed them from promising mid-level businesses to household names.'

Which she couldn't name either, I thought, because otherwise we'd all have been on Google the second we left the meeting, figuring out who Luxeforless's new shareholder was going to be.

'What about Barri?' I asked. 'Will he still… I mean, will he be as hands-on as he's always been?'

Will he still bully us all mercilessly and taunt us with his platters of pastries in meetings, was what I meant.

'Barri is widely respected as the founder of Luxeforless and the vision behind the business,' Lisa said, as if she was reciting from a PowerPoint presentation, which, for all I knew, she might have been. 'In every meaningful sense, he *is* Luxeforless. The vision behind the company is his, it remains driven by his boldness, creativity and integrity. I'm sure that any cash injection the enterprise received would be conditional upon his remaining at the helm of the management team.'

Definitely a PowerPoint presentation, I thought. *Probably one written by Barri himself.*

'Any more questions?' Lisa asked, looking relieved that she'd got that spiel off her chest, word-perfect. She glanced around the table and we all shook our heads. 'Good. Then shall we all crack on? If we end up needing to pull a late one, Daria's promised to order in some sushi.'

We all filed out and headed back to our desks. It was only when I was sitting down, checking my phone, that I noticed a text from Chelsea saying that she wouldn't be able to meet me that afternoon because something urgent had come up (actually, her message said, *Can't make today, soz, problems.*). It was then that I realised something strange. Felicity hadn't said a word the whole time we were in there. Not a question, not a smile, not a widening of her eyes. She'd sat there silently through it all, staring down at her hands like she'd never seen a manicure before – except when she'd been tapping, almost stealthily, at her phone under the table. No one else had seen, but because I'd been sitting right next to her, I had.

Chapter Sixteen

The next day, Josh got an easyJet flight to Belfast, where he'd landed a short-notice gig working on an album for a singer called Ruby Wells, whose regular producer had pulled out at the last minute. Actually, Josh told me, her regular producer, who was also Ruby's boyfriend, hadn't pulled out at all when he was shagging the bass player, who was now pregnant. So the whole thing had blown up into an almighty mess a week before Ruby's contract stipulated that she was due to deliver her album to her record label, and reinforcements were being called in from all over to replace the musicians who'd been sacked and the people who'd taken sides that weren't Ruby's.

And, at the same time, Adam was packed off to a cybersecurity conference in Berlin for three days by Colton Capital.

The house, which I'd worried would feel crowded with the two of them there, felt empty and almost unnaturally quiet without them. Each evening when I got home from work, Freezer's little white face appeared at the window looking for his friends, but when he saw that it was only me there, he turned around and flounced off back home in a way that was quite frankly insulting.

I guess I should have enjoyed having the place to myself – being able to wander around in my pants and hog the bathroom for hours and watch *Say Yes to the Dress* on the sofa downstairs without someone asking what the fuck this shit was and being able to eat kale salads without Adam saying he was going to order a curry and did I want some.

But I found I missed them.

I missed the glimmer of light through Adam's open bedroom door and the sound of his chair wheeling around on the wooden floor. I missed seeing him in the kitchen in the mornings, eating toast over the sink so he didn't have to put a plate in the dishwasher and asking, 'Coffee, Tans?'

And, although Josh had only been living there for a few weeks, I'd got used to the smell of his shampoo in the shower, the twang of the strings as he tuned his guitar and even his muddy trainers on the shoe rack in the hallway. I could have gone out, since my Prada bag had sold at last and I was relatively flush, but I wasn't feeling the vibe. I tried going out for a run in the park, but it wasn't so much fun without Josh, and I gave up and headed home after ten minutes.

I even missed the regular, tense stand-offs I'd witnessed the boys having in the kitchen in the mornings when Freezer dropped in for a fuss and wound himself around four legs instead of just Adam's two, purring and miaowing. The two of them practically had a tug-of-war over who'd get to give him the three cat treats that were all Hannah had said he was allowed, because the vet had noticed him getting a bit podgy.

I found myself turning off all the downstairs lights and going up to bed early, so that the house would be in darkness. But then, with only the faint glow of my bedside lamp lighting the top floor, strange shadows seemed to crowd in on me. The normal noises of the house – the creak of a floor joist as the evening cooled, the tick of a radiator pipe, the swish of car tyres on the road outside – all jerked me from sleep even though they were the same sounds I heard every night. And when at last the house was silent, I could hear the *click, click, click* of Dad's computer mouse in my head, even though he was hundreds of miles away.

I pressed my eyes shut and began counting slowly backwards from one hundred, trying to focus on the 'now' like a mindfulness app I once downloaded said to do. I forced my awareness back to my breathing, to the familiar sounds of the house.

Then my phone buzzed, jerking me into alertness again. I hoped it would be Chelsea – my last three texts to her had gone unanswered, and I was getting concerned. But it was a WhatsApp from Felicity: *Meeting Pru and Phil at Home House tomorrow at 10. R might join us. Fancy coming? Bring your new chap?*

I tapped out a quick reply saying I'd love to, but I didn't know whether Josh was free – which was true, I wasn't even sure whether he'd be back from Northern Ireland – and then I watched random YouTube make-up tutorials until eventually, long after midnight, I fell asleep and had horrible, disconcerting dreams all night. Most of them I don't remember, but in the one I do, Adam and Josh were at Chelsea's market stall having a proper bitch fight over a beaded red dress. What that meant about what was going on in my subconscious mind I don't even want to know.

The crash of the front door woke me just after nine o'clock, and I heard the familiar tread of Josh's feet on the stairs. Honestly, what was it about the man that he couldn't move around the house without sounding like a herd of stampeding elephants? I huddled down under the duvet and tried to go back to sleep, but it was no good; I could hear him doing what was presumably his version of tiptoeing as he went to the bathroom, then to his bedroom and started unpacking his stuff.

I got up and went to the bathroom myself, showered, dressed and followed the smell of toast and coffee downstairs.

'Morning,' I said. 'How did the job go?'

'It was good,' Josh said, pouring coffee and yawning hugely. 'I'm knackered, though. We had to pull an all-nighter last night to get the last track recorded. I came straight from the studio to the airport. Talk about full-on. But Ruby's a pro. You'd never know from her vocals that she was going through a messy break-up, except on the song she wrote at the last minute.'

'What, she wrote a song about her boyfriend cheating on her?'

'She did. It's called "Love Rat". I guess if that gets to number one there'll be no chance of them getting back together.'

I laughed. 'No, I guess slagging someone off in song lyrics is a pretty definitive way of telling them to fuck off to the far side of fuck.'

'And when they get there, fuck off some more. It's a great track though, really raw. How have things been here?' he asked, spreading peanut butter on a piece of toast.

'You should try Tabasco sauce and salt on that,' I said. 'Trust me. It's the future.'

'Salt and what now?' Josh sounded incredulous, but he obediently reached for the salt cellar and the sauce bottle, sprinkled cautiously and took a bite. I watched his face go from doubtful to ecstatic.

'My God. What else haven't you told me?'

Loads and loads of things, I reflected, feeling suddenly guilty. But I just gave a modest shrug and asked him more about how his week had gone, and he asked me the same.

'Not too bad,' I said. 'Work's been kind of intense. I've been home in bed by ten every night, I've been so knackered.'

There was a sudden scrabble at the window that made me jump, but it was only Freezer. He hopped down and scampered over to Josh, every furry white bit of him seeming to say, 'Thank God! You're back! You won't believe what I've had to put up with while she's been in charge!'

'Hey, little dude! I missed you.' Josh picked him up and scratched his ears, and the cat writhed blissfully in his arms, purring like a power tool.

'For fuck's sake,' I grumbled, 'he's been throwing shade at me the whole time you were away, and now look at him.'

'Aww, Freezer, have you?' Josh cooed. 'Come on! We love Tansy. Tansy's our mate. Isn't she?'

Speak for yourself, I thought, annoyed at his presumption. *I wasn't your mate back at school, and I'm not now.* Freezer didn't seem too convinced, either, peering sideways at me out of his green eye, like he didn't believe a word. But, slighted as I felt at being dissed by a cat, I had another handsome male I needed to focus on winning round – and he was neither Josh nor Freezer.

'Fancy coming out with me tonight?' I asked. 'My colleague Felicity and her sister and some of their mates are going to Home House. It's swanky as, you'll like it.'

'Will I?'

'You might,' I conceded. 'And even if you don't, apparently the cocktails are off the scale. I got paid yesterday, so it's my treat.'

'Go on then,' Josh said. 'But if we're going to have a massive night, I'd better catch up on some sleep today.'

'Cool, you have a good rest.' *And don't even think about spoiling my plan by being too knackered to come out tonight,* I added silently. An hour later, I was on a bus heading towards Bethnal Green. I'd find Chelsea at her stall in the market, I hoped, and I'd try to talk to her there and check that she was okay. If something had gone wrong in her life, maybe I'd be able to help. And if she'd just decided she'd had enough of being mentored by me, I'd at least know, and I'd have to tell Daria that I'd failed in my attempt to nurture and support a promising young designer.

I stopped on the way and bought two macchiatos, a custard Danish for Chelsea and something that was advertised as a high-protein oat and chia seed muffin (but looked like it had come out of the wrong end of a cow) for myself.

My mentee was at her stall as I'd hoped, arranging garments on a rail. She must have been working harder than ever, I thought; there were at least ten completed dresses that I hadn't seen before, many of them made from sari silk in dazzling colours.

'Spring/summer collection's looking good,' I said.

Chelsea spun round and glared at me. 'What are you doing here?'

I held out the coffee and pastry, and she hesitated for a second, then took them. 'I was worried about you when you didn't return my calls.'

'Been busy, innit.'

'I can see that. These are stunning.' I picked up one of the dresses and admired the cut.

Chelsea smiled, even though it looked like it took some effort. 'Thanks.'

'How are things going at work? And how's your mum?' I asked, casting around the little I knew about her life to try and tease out what the problem – if there was one – could be.

'Work's shit. Mum's shittier.' She took the dress from me and put it back on the rail, then started to fiddle around, smoothing non-existent creases from things.

'Chelsea? Is your mum okay? She's not ill, is she?' If that was the problem, it was way beyond my powers to do anything about it.

'Nah. She's fine. Just knackered, like me.'

Cautiously, I put a hand on her shoulder. 'You can talk to me, you know, if something's bothering you.'

She flinched like I'd burned her. 'Look, will you just…'

Then she stopped. I could see tears welling in her eyes, and as I watched they spilled down her cheeks, carrying rivers of mascara with them.

'Hey,' I said. 'It's okay. Here, take this.'

I shoved the paper bag with her Danish pastry in it at her.

'You're giving me cake? What are you, Marie fucking Antoinette?'

'There's a napkin in there,' I said gently. 'You look like you might need it.'

'Oh. Right.' She looked at me, then at the bag, then started to laugh, but within seconds her laughter turned to sobs.

I knew that a full-on hug would be even less welcome to her than it was to Adam, so I just stood next to her and patted her shoulder a bit while she wept into the paper napkin. After a while I passed her the one from my muffin, too.

'The fuck is this?' she said, sniffing. 'It smells like that compost they use on the allotments.'

'I know,' I said. 'I was going to eat it, but I think I've changed my mind.'

Chelsea blew her nose and wiped her eyes. 'Don't do it. Get some proper food down you.'

She tore her Danish in two and handed half to me. I took a bite. I don't know if she meant to, but she'd given me the bit with most of the custard in it.

'God, that's good.'

'See?' she said.

'Okay, fine. I'm eating. Now you can tell me what's wrong.'

Chelsea looked stricken again, and for a second I thought she might be about to start crying again. Then she squared her shoulders and set her jaw.

'It's just… This. I'm working my arse off, with my day job and sewing every spare bleeding second, and sometimes, like today, I look at it and I think, what the fuck is this all for?'

'What do you mean? Your work is amazing. Look how happy your customers are. You should be really proud.'

'Yeah, but being proud isn't good enough, is it? Do you even know how long it takes me to make a dress? Like, two or three days. Even a week, for the ones with beading and shit. And I sell it for a couple of hundred quid – maybe two fifty, and sure, the customer's happy and I'm happy, but then I sit down and do the maths and I'm like, I make more money per hour in my day job. And that's minimum wage.'

She didn't need to tell me all this, of course – I'd worked it out for myself. So I just nodded sympathetically and kept listening.

'And I'm like, am I going to be stuck doing this forever? I've got no qualifications. All I can do is work a shitty zero-hours contract in retail, and this. And if this doesn't work, I've got nothing.'

I opened my mouth to come up with some kind of reassuring platitude, but I couldn't think of anything that didn't sound hollow. And anyway, Chelsea was in full flood.

'And then there's Nathan.'

Nathan? I scratched around desperately in my mind until I remembered. The beloved son who Mrs Johnston had said was 'a good boy, really', with all that implied.

'Your brother? What's happened to him?'

'Nothing,' she spat. 'That's the whole problem. Nothing happens. He smokes weed and he hangs out with his mates, and some of them are dealing, and he hasn't been to school in ages, and it just feels like he's got no future, either.'

'It's difficult, I know,' I said, trying to sound sympathetic but wishing I had more of a clue what I was on about. 'I mean, I know young men like him are disproportionately likely to leave school without—'

'Young black men,' Chelsea spat at me. 'Say it like it is.'

'Okay, young black men. I'm sorry if I offended you.'

She laughed again, but it wasn't a happy laugh. 'It's more that you tried not to.'

I did a rueful gesture that was part shrug, part smile and part nod, and waited for her to carry on.

'I just want to make Mum proud,' she said. 'Of me and him, both. But she says she can't show her face in church any more because everyone thinks her boy is a gangster. And I'm a failure.'

'You are no such thing! You mustn't even think that way, Chelsea. I mean, Luxeforless wouldn't have chosen you for the mentoring programme if they – if we – didn't think you had incredible potential. You weren't thinking of dropping out, were you? Because of the way you're feeling? Because I for one would be absolutely gutted if you did.'

Chelsea's face brightened like the sun coming out. 'Really?'

'Of course.' I could have kicked myself for not realising straight away that that was one of the things worrying her. 'I've got a meeting with the marketing team on Wednesday, so why don't you join me for that?'

'Okay,' she said. 'Yes, I will.'

'And,' I went on, encouraged by her smile, 'tell your mum to go to church tomorrow with her head held high. It's not like she's done anything wrong, and even if she had, they're meant to be all about forgiveness, aren't they?'

'I guess,' Chelsea said. 'I'll talk to Mum tonight. And I'll see you next week. Thanks for the coffee and… everything.'

I waved her thanks away and reminded her that she could call me any time she needed to talk. Just as I was leaving, Chelsea pressed one of her plain brown bags into my hand.

'Take this. It's a present. It's your size.'

I opened my mouth to protest and offer payment, then thought better of it.

'Thanks,' I said. 'You're amazing, you know that, right?'

And this time, she did let me give her the very briefest of hugs.

Chapter Seventeen

I was tempted to open the bag Chelsea had given me on the bus home, but I resisted and made myself wait until I was in my room. Then I lifted the tissue-paper parcel out and carefully unwrapped it. She'd given me a dress made out of silk scarves, pieced together so that their floral, paisley and geometric prints complemented one another perfectly. It had a draped cowl neckline, spaghetti straps that turned into criss-cross lacing down the open back, and an asymmetrical hanky hemline that came down to mid-calf at its longest and was just above my knees at the shortest bit. The colours were coral and jade and silver, with accents of vivid saffron yellow, and even though none of them was from the same palette, they still worked together like they'd dreamed of meeting in their previous lives.

I put it on straight away, and watched my face in the mirror break into the delighted smile I'd seen on Chelsea's other customers. I looked like me, only better. Me, without boobs that were either too big or not big enough. Me, without collarbones that made me look like a wire coathanger. Me, without my skin all sallow and tired.

I took a selfie in the mirror and sent it to Chelsea with a whole load of emojis. I didn't need to add a message – I was pretty sure she'd understand what I meant. She'd intended the gift to be a thank-you, but I felt as if I hadn't done nearly enough to warrant such a gorgeous present, with all the hours that had gone into making it, and – more importantly – that I still had to earn the trust Chelsea had placed in me.

I'll find a way, I promised her in my head. *Somehow, I'll make you the famous designer you deserve to be. And if I learn that one person at church has been mean to your mum, I'll personally hunt them down and twat scones at them until they apologise.*

I spent almost three hours getting ready to go out that evening. I showered and shaved and exfoliated every inch of myself, and slathered on fake tan. I put a protein treatment on my hair, wrapped it in cling film, covered it with a towel and left it while I soaked my hands in hot water, oiled and trimmed my cuticles and painted my nails (fingers silver, toes electric blue). I put a radiance-boosting mask on my face and peeled it off (although whoever makes these things and tells you they peel off in one piece is the biggest liar ever – it wasn't so much peeling as picking the thing away, one tiny piece at a time, until I lost patience and washed the whole lot off with a flannel).

When my nail varnish had dried, I rinsed my hair, dried it, sprayed sea salt spray on it and tonged it. I put one kind of primer on my face and another kind on my eyes and brushed on foundation and concealer until a blank mask looked back at me from the mirror, and then I used contouring powder, highlighter and blusher to sculpt my features back on the way I wanted them to look.

I tightlined my eyes, wincing and trying not to blink as I ran the eyeliner over the inside of my top lids. I put on four different coloured eyeshadows: smoky grey, peacock blue, dark green and sparkly silver. I swished on wings of black liquid eyeliner and held my breath as I stuck on false eyelashes over my mascaraed real ones. I powdered and pencilled my eyebrows, lined my lips in rose pink then filled them in with a matte liquid lipstick.

I inspected my face from all angles and wished I felt beautiful, but I didn't. I felt like a girl who'd overdone the slap because she was desperate to look prettier than she was.

But it was too late to change anything, and at least I had a killer dress to wear. I spritzed on some of the Miu Miu scent I'd bought at the duty-free shop in the airport on my way home from that last, wonderful holiday with Renzo before stepping into the dress, tying the laces at the back and zipping on my favourite silver shoe boots. I slipped a few silver rings onto my fingers and tucked my keys, phone, credit card and lipstick into the little silver clutch Mum had given me for my eighteenth birthday, remembering with a pang how she'd said, 'Every woman needs a good bag for best,' and I'd imagined the hours of overtime she must have worked to pay for it, even though it was only from Next.

And then I went downstairs.

Josh was eating spaghetti at the kitchen table, wearing jeans and a black shirt. When he saw me, he put his fork down and stared.

'Blimey. You look… different.' Then he hastily added, 'You look great, I mean. That's a nice dress.'

I thanked him, told him how it had been given to me, and explained how the different panels of silk had been cut on the bias and sewn together with the seams in exactly the right places so it would hang properly.

'You sound like Mum,' he said. 'A frock's never just a frock with her, it's a piece of art she has to analyse.'

'Well, she got me started in fashion, remember? So I guess I do sound like her when I wank on about it.'

'You're not wanking on, you're being passionate. Now, you should eat something before we go. There's loads more of this on the hob.'

I realised I hadn't eaten since sharing Chelsea's pastry that morning, and I was starving. Then I looked at the oily red sauce coating the pasta, and imagined it splatting over my cheeks and down my dress.

'You know what they say,' I objected. 'Eating's cheating.'

'Don't be daft,' Josh said. 'You don't want to be totally shitfaced after two cocktails. Put a tea towel round your neck and have some food.'

So, feeling like a messy child wearing a bib, I did. It was delicious – I ate a huge bowlful and was about to have a second helping when I remembered that I might be going to see Renzo, and suddenly felt queasy with excitement and apprehension. It was half past nine. In an hour, I might be talking to him.

Before that, he'd see me with Josh, and I knew what I wanted him to think.

'So do we get the Tube?' Josh asked. 'Where is this place we're going, anyway?'

'Mayfair,' I said. 'But I'm in taxi shoes, so we'll get an Uber.'

'Right, then.' Josh tapped his phone. 'Give me the address and I'll order one while you get your coat.'

*

Felicity, Pru and Phillip were already there when we arrived, seated at a table in a room so designer-fabulous that Josh muttered, 'Oh my God, it's like the Battlestar Galactica in here!' clutching my arm in a way that made me wonder if he was almost as nervous about the evening as me. I spotted Felicity across the room and said, 'This is it, we're going in,' and dragged him over.

I'd never met Pru's newish boyfriend before and I wasn't sure what I had been expecting, but it was definitely not the slightly chubby, balding bloke sitting next to her. But when he stood up, flashed an impressive set of veneers in a massive grin like meeting me was the best thing that had ever happened to him, and greeted Josh the same way, adding in a voice so posh it was almost comical how delighted he was to meet us both, and how he couldn't wait for all of Pru's friends to be his friends too, I totally got what she saw in him.

Within a few seconds, he and Josh were having a good old natter about golf, which I never even knew Josh could play, and music, which Phil seemed to be both knowledgeable about and mad keen on. Felicity ordered a bottle of Bollinger and one of vodka to celebrate the end of her alcohol-free week, and I seriously hoped she wasn't planning to sink the lot herself or things would get far messier than I'd bargained for, Renzo or no Renzo.

'But I need to know,' Pru gushed, caressing my dress with a fingertip, 'who this is by? I have to have one. Everyone has to have one. Actually, they don't. Let's keep it our little secret.'

'A young up-and-coming designer called Chelsea Johnston,' I said.

'Chelsea… Wait, is that the kid you're mentoring at work?' Felicity said. 'You never told me she was that talented.'

You never asked, I thought. But I said, 'Yes, she shows a lot of promise.'

Pru said, 'Promise? If you told me that was by Salvatore Ferragamo I'd have believed you. Stand up, Tansy. I'm Instagramming the fuck out of that.'

I stood and did a bit of a twirl while they both admired the dress, then sat back down again, this time on the end next to Josh, while Phillip ordered a round of cocktails and some edamame beans for Felicity, who'd announced that she was about to faint from hunger.

'I texted Fidel,' she said, 'and I'm allowed edamame, as long as they're not salted.'

Which pretty much defeated the whole point of them, I thought, trying not to make comparisons with the huge bowl of pasta I'd eaten before we left.

But before Felicity had the chance to eat her snack, she was interrupted by the buzzing of her phone.

'Renzo's on his way,' she said eagerly. 'He's in a cab now. He came straight from the airport.'

'Aw, that's so sweet,' Pru said. 'He must have really missed you.'

'And I've missed him.' Felicity smiled a secret little smile. 'I can't wait to get reacquainted. I ordered a load of lingerie and other stuff online, which should be waiting at his apartment. It's full of surprises for him, I can tell you.'

I tried to smile, but felt hollow and sick inside. The sex Renzo and I had had together had been amazing, but it had been pretty vanilla, too. Apart from wearing nice underwear and having a Hollywood wax (and oh my God, it was nothing like the regular minge maintenance I'd done before), I hadn't done anything exotic for him at all. The attraction I'd felt for him – and I believed he had for me – had been so raw and powerful that introducing handcuffs or sex toys into the mix just never seemed necessary.

I remembered the first time we'd slept together, on the weekend away in Paris that had effectively been our fourth date. We'd both just stepped out of the shower (because, obviously, Renzo hadn't just booked any old hotel room but a luxury suite with two bathrooms).

I was wrapped in a fluffy white bathrobe; he only had a towel round his waist. I felt a flutter of excitement and desire looking at his bare chest, ridged with muscle and dusted with dark hair. His naturally olive skin was deeply tanned and I could see a line of paler skin just above where the white towel began.

It was as if an invisible thread – or maybe a magnet too powerful to resist – pulled me towards him. I crossed the room and touched him with a fingertip, tentatively, as if his skin might burn me, tracing a line down from his collarbone over his chest and the smooth muscles of his abdomen, down to where his tan ended, looking at him all the time and smiling.

Then he kissed me, his mouth hot and hungry on mine. He pulled the robe off my shoulders and his hands found my breasts, his palms brushing over my nipples, which were already hard in anticipation of his touch. Seconds later, he'd pushed me back onto the bed and was kissing me all over, exploring my body with his mouth and his hands, his desire raw and consuming, overwhelming my own.

'*Amore a prima vista*,' he'd murmured, looking down at me. 'That's what it was, when I met you, love at first sight.'

I remembered his first, hard thrusts inside me – a brief stab of discomfort, then pleasure beginning to build and build. I remembered how fragile he'd made me feel, as if I might split in two with the force of his fucking. He'd finished before me, but I was too happy to care.

Maybe that was the problem, I thought morosely. Maybe if I'd been more adventurous, more exciting, spiced things up a bit more, he and I would still be together. But then I remembered Adam's words: *some ridiculous Madonna or whore dichotomy going on inside his head.* And I wondered whether Renzo might not react as well to Felicity's saucy purchases as she hoped.

'Earth to Tansy.' Josh topped up my glass of champagne, and I realised I'd been sitting in silence, lost in the memory.

'Oh God, I'm so sorry. I was miles away.'

Literally. Miles away in a hotel in Paris, nine months in the past.

'Come on, let's go and dance.'

He took my hand and led me onto the dance floor, where couples and groups of women were swaying uncertainly to the music. It was too early in the evening for full-on partying – the DJ was getting things warmed up with 'Girls' by Rita Ora, and pink lights were washing over everything.

Josh didn't sway uncertainly. He let his body move with the music, utterly uninhibited, grinning with pleasure like he didn't care if people thought he looked stupid. Except he didn't – he looked rhythmic, graceful, powerful. I tried to move my body in time with his, but I've always been a crap dancer and I wasn't drunk enough to forget it.

The more I thought about leading with my hips and keeping my upper body still and moving my feet slightly but not too much, and letting my head follow my hips and my hands move the opposite way, which is what the 'dancing for complete and utter numpties' videos I watched on YouTube a few years back said one should do, the more confused and self-conscious I got.

'Sorry,' I said to Josh over the music. 'I've got two left feet, no sense of rhythm and I'm tone deaf.'

He grinned and did a little sort of shimmy thing that should have looked ridiculous but didn't. He seemed to have no problem at all moving his hips, I noticed. Then he put his hands on my waist and pulled me a bit closer to him. Not so close we were touching, and he didn't do any of that fancy shite you see on *Strictly Come Dancing*, like trying to spin me around or lifting me over his head or anything (thank God, because I would have totally, literally died right there). He just kind of moved me nearer to him, so that I could feel what his body was doing and follow it.

I didn't get it at first. Our knees bumped together. I stood on his toe. I wasn't sure what to do with my own hands, so I kept them dangling foolishly by my side. But then I relaxed, let myself touch his back or his arm and connect with his movements, and suddenly something clicked. I won't say I looked good – I'm pretty sure I didn't – but I felt better, and I was concentrating too hard on what the music was telling me to do to feel awkward.

And then I saw Renzo.

He'd just walked in, and was glancing around. He was wearing black jeans, a silvery-grey shirt and trainers. He hadn't shaved, and even across the room I could recognise the familiar signs of tiredness in his face – the slightly tight, drawn lines around his mouth, the way he was squinting a bit as he scanned the room. I had no problem at all believing that he'd come straight from a long-haul flight and a week-long business trip that had involved a hell of a lot of entertaining and not much sleep.

I wished I could smooth the tiredness from his face with my fingers, massage his tight shoulders the way he liked, run him a hot bath and maybe join him in it and, much later, lie next to him and gaze and gaze at him while he slept. Although I wouldn't murder him, obviously, not like one of those psycho stalkers you read about who watch people sleep. I wouldn't even murder Felicity, if she was sleeping there next to him, tempting as it would be.

'Ouch,' Josh said, and I realised I'd trodden on his toe again.

'Sorry. I got distracted.'

Whatever power the music had had over me had melted away. My body felt stiff and awkward again and I wished, pointlessly, that I'd had time to dash to the loo and refresh my lipstick.

I saw Josh's eyes flick over my shoulder and realised Renzo must have spotted the others and be making his way towards the table.

'Hey, Tansy,' Josh said, and my eyes snapped back to him.

And then he kissed me.

It came completely out of the blue. I literally couldn't have been more surprised if he'd slapped me in the face. But he didn't do that, of course. His hands still on my waist, he gently pulled our bodies together. Then his hand slipped up my back – I could feel its warmth through the gaps between the lacing on my dress – to cradle the back of my head. Instinctively, I looked up at him, and he smiled. His hand moved around to caress my cheek and then – bam – he was snogging the hell out of me.

I mean, I don't want to make it sound as if it was one of those awful, awkward kisses you had as a teenager, like wrestling with an octopus holding a Hoover filled with spit, because it wasn't. It was a perfectly good kiss – even a great one. Josh's lips were not too dry and not too wet. His jaw against my cheek felt hard, but smooth. There was tongue – mine as well as his, if I'm being entirely honest – but not too much. It was the Goldilocks of kisses.

But the intensity of it, as well as the unexpectedness, took my breath away.

When I was able to summon back the power of rational thought, I pulled my head away, and Josh made no attempt to keep it there. He just smiled down at me again, and there was something like triumph in his face.

I was raging. At him, for taking for granted that he could kiss me and that I'd enjoy it – and for being right about that. At myself, for letting him – and for getting so lost in the moment. But, I realised, he'd only done what I wanted him to do. Not just the kiss, but it being so public, with Felicity, Pru and most of all Renzo right there to see physical proof of the relationship I wanted them to believe there was between Josh and me.

'There,' he said. 'Shall we go back to our table?'

I nodded in agreement, relieved not just because my legs suddenly felt all wobbly and my ankles were turning over in my high heels. I let him lead me back across the room, his hand now burning hot against my back.

'Quite the shapes you two were throwing there,' Pru laughed. 'Renz, you know Tansy, of course, and this is Josh.'

'Good to meet you, mate.' Josh extended his hand and Renzo shook it, but the expression on his face was like he'd just grasped a bag of ice.

I forced a radiant smile onto my face and said how nice it was to see him again, and Renzo said, 'Likewise,' only without any smile at all, radiant or otherwise. Felicity took the vodka bottle from the ice bucket and splashed some into her glass and Renzo's, missing slightly and slopping the icy liquid over the table. The bottle was more than a third gone, I noticed – she must have been giving it some while we were dancing. Her lippy had rubbed off, so I realised she hadn't been able to resist the just-permitted snacks. There was a shiny patch on the side of her nose and smudged mascara under her eyes.

'I'm desperate for a wee,' I said to her. 'Coming, babe?'

'Sure,' she said, the word sounding mushy and slurred.

I grabbed my bag in one hand and her arm in the other, and we made our way around the bar and down a flight of stairs to a ladies' room so sumptuous I would have spent ages going, 'Oooh!' and Instagramming everything from the toiletries to the taps, if I hadn't been so worried. Because now, her poise all stripped away, it felt like Felicity was my friend again, and she needed me.

'Shit.' Felicity stood in front of the mirror like she was looking at a ghost. 'What a fucking mess.'

She swayed, and her reflection did, too.

Then she gripped the edges of the basin and vomited lumpy green vodka into it, retching and heaving like she was never going to stop.

Year Ten

I spent the next three days veering between excitement, doubt and panic. I put the number I'd memorised into my phone as soon as I could, and I kept looking at it, like it was a treasure I'd found and picked up, unsure whether it was okay for me to keep it. I thought about sending a text, just a casual one, telling Josh I was looking forward to seeing him, but I resisted. I was going to play it cool – well, as cool as I possibly could.

Inside, though, I was light years away from cool. I asked Debbie if I could leave work early that Saturday afternoon, and spent hours getting ready. I painted my toenails yellow. I put on the white broderie anglaise puffball skirt I'd found on a sale rail, and a pink T-shirt. I borrowed Perdita's denim jacket, which was too small for me but suited the shrunken jacket trend. I wished I had a pair of wedge heels to wear, but then remembered that if I did, they'd make me taller than Josh, so I settled for flip-flops instead. I put on masses of pink lip gloss, which my hair kept sticking to. And at last I was ready.

I told Mum to expect me back by ten – if we did end up managing to get into the pub, I'd be home way later than that, but I'd cross that bridge if I came to it.

'Have a good time, love,' Mum said. 'It's lovely to—'

And then she stopped. I knew what she was going to say – it was lovely to see me going out with mates, like a normal teenager, not the friendless pariah I'd become. But she was too tactful to call attention to that.

'It's lovely to see you looking so pretty,' she said instead.

I got the bus into town, opening my bag over and over again to check my face in my hand mirror and also to check the money in my purse, even though I knew exactly how much was there. I had enough for a cinema ticket and a small popcorn, and just two pounds spare after that. If we went for burgers afterwards, I'd have to say I wasn't hungry and just have a Coke. And if we went to the pub after that – well, again, I'd have to cross that bridge if I came to it.

But in the event, I didn't even have to buy the movie ticket.

I got to the cinema ten minutes early and there was no one I knew waiting there. I checked my phone, but there were no new text messages. I didn't know Kylie, Anoushka or Danielle's numbers – the only one I had was Josh's. And I wasn't going to text him – not yet, anyway. That would just be too tragic.

I walked round the block, but when I got back there was still no sign of anyone, so I walked round again. It was five past five now. I wished I smoked, so I could join the nonchalant-looking older teenagers who were leaning against the wall, puffing away. Five more minutes passed – the film had already started. Maybe they were late on purpose: too rebellious to sit through the ads and trailers. For me, going to see a movie was such a rare treat that I'd happily have done so, but maybe they were different.

At almost half past five, my resolve snapped and I texted Josh.

Hey, it's Tansy. Not sure where you guys are? I'm waiting outside the Plaza.

Ten more minutes passed. No one came, and there was no reply. I tried to convince myself that there'd been some kind of mix-up: that I'd got the date wrong, or the plans had changed and no one had been able to contact me to tell me, and at school on Monday they'd be full of laughing apologies.

But in my gut I knew that wasn't true.

So, when my phone eventually beeped with an incoming text, I was horrified but not exactly surprised.

You really think I'd go out with the town bike? Haha — you're not just a slag, you're stupid, too.

Chapter Eighteen

It was Tuesday, that horrible, slow hour between our morning meeting and the time when everyone could start thinking optimistically about lunch. Sally was in the kitchen making a round of coffees. Kris was filing his nails. Lisa was off site and incognito, checking out a hot new designer's work in Brighton. I was staring mindlessly at the sales forecast document on my computer, willing my mind to focus on whether the additional cost of having pockets added to a line of work dresses would earn itself back in sales.

But my mind wasn't on pockets, in spite of the conversation I'd had earlier with Customer Care, who'd reported a whole spate of emails from women saying that if we cared one jot for feminism, all our garments would have pockets, and when were we going to do something about it.

My mind was on other things: so many that I couldn't narrow it down to one, resolve it and move on to the next.

After our team meeting earlier, Lisa had lightly touched my arm and said, 'Barri's asked you to drop into his office later for a chat. I thought you'd want to hear it from me first.'

Normally, the prospect of a one-on-one 'chat' with Barri, which invariably meant a telling-off of major proportions, would have made me feel like vomiting with fear. Actually, it did now, too, but there were so many other things worrying me that even Barri's wrath seemed relatively insignificant.

More even than Barri, or pockets, or Chelsea and the doubts she'd expressed about her future and her brother's present, what had happened on Saturday night was weighing on my mind.

A series of images, short bursts of them like an Instagram Story, kept playing over and over in my head. Except, unlike on Insta, they hadn't conveniently deleted themselves after twenty-four hours: the memories were as fresh as they'd been when they happened.

I remembered Renzo's face when Josh and I came back to our table, cold and immobile. I remembered Felicity crying after she'd been sick, saying over and over again, 'What am I doing, Tansy?' I'd helped her repair her face and guided her back to our seats, but by then Renzo had left, and Pru had taken her sister home in a taxi. Felicity wasn't in the office that day, and she hadn't been on Monday either. She'd called in sick, and she hadn't responded to any of my texts.

And I remembered Josh. Josh had kissed me. I'd let him, and I'd liked it. I'd liked it a *lot*. In those few moments, while I was in his arms, it was like the past had never happened: like no one existed but me and him. Not even Renzo.

It had felt familiar, somehow, as if I'd always wanted to be kissed in that particular way and now it was happening. But it had been new and thrilling, too. I could still remember my heart hammering so hard it was as if it might burst right out through the silk of my dress. There on the dance floor, we'd held each other close and kissed and kissed, and part of me had been like, *What the fuck do you think you're doing?* Whether that was meant as a question for myself, taking the crazy idea of pretending he was my boyfriend further than I'd ever intended, or for him, taking liberties that I hadn't expected him to take and doing nothing to stop him, I couldn't say for sure.

But a far bigger part had been like, *Don't stop. Don't ever stop.*

Josh and I had got a taxi home, too, but there had been no more snogging. He'd opened the car door for me, and when I thanked him he'd given me a little secret smile and brushed my hair back from my face, his touch like an electric shock. After that, I'd kept my eyes fixed on my phone, checking for updates from Pru, and Josh had chatted idly about the night and the sights that flashed past the cab's windows, apparently entirely unconcerned about what we'd done. When we got home he offered me tea, but I said no, thanked him for a lovely evening and went up to bed, my head spinning from more than just the Veuve Clicquot we'd drunk, which I had no idea how I was going to reimburse Josh for.

The next morning, I'd waited until I heard him leave for his morning run before getting out of bed myself, showering and dressing at warp speed and getting the Tube into town, where I spent the day wandering aimlessly around the shops, not buying anything and not even taking photos on my phone to remind myself of trends that had sold poorly and been discounted early.

I treated myself to a salt beef sandwich at the counter in Selfridges, checking my phone anxiously for a reply from Felicity, or a message from Pru, or a sign from Renzo of what was going on in his mind, but there was nothing. There was a message from Josh, saying that he was heading into Camden for a gig that evening, and did I fancy coming along. I thought about saying yes, but there was no point in going somewhere with him where there was no chance of Renzo seeing us. If he tried to kiss me again, I had no idea what I would do. Let him? Lead him on? Kiss him back? Enjoy it? I didn't know the answer to that – I didn't even know what I wanted the answer to be. So I declined, saying I was too knackered to go out two nights in a row, with work the next day.

Eventually, when the shops were shutting and I reckoned the coast would be clear, I headed home and went straight to bed.

But Josh was my housemate; I couldn't avoid him forever. At some point, the opportunity for another kiss would present itself, and I'd have to decide what to do about it. I could either carry on the pretence, whether at home so that Adam would see and hopefully report to Renzo, or when I was out with Felicity, or, ideally, in front of Renzo himself. But I couldn't work out how I could make that happen, and anyway, a tiny voice in my head was scolding me. *You're using him. You snogged him just so Renzo could see, no matter how much you liked it. You're letting him think you're into him when you're not. You're no better he was, back at school…*

And even when I reminded myself that he had done exactly the same thing to me, eleven years before, the voice wasn't letting me off the hook.

You were kids, it insisted. *It's ancient history. Let it go. Tell him Saturday night was a mistake, and move on.*

But then I remembered the cold immobility on Renzo's face, and how I'd thought, *It's working. He's jealous.*

Maybe if he saw us together just one more time, that would be enough. He'd left early, while Felicity was in the bathroom with me. Maybe that disloyalty would be enough to make her dump him? Or maybe they'd already had some kind of falling-out, and that was why she'd got so drunk. She hadn't been coherent enough to tell me. Why the hell wasn't she answering my messages?

And so my mind spun uselessly on and on, like wheels on an icy road, gaining no traction at all.

I forced my attention back to my screen and saw the meeting invitation. *Fuck*. Barri wanted to see me in ten minutes. All at once, the queasy fear my other concerns had kept at bay came rushing back. I dashed to the loo, brushed my hair and put on some lipstick, although I didn't bother topping up my eye make-up, because the victims of one-to-one 'chats' with Barri ended up in tears more often than not.

I will not cry, I told my reflection firmly. Whatever he's going to have a go at me for – poor sales figures, sloppy reporting, the potential last-minute addition of pockets screwing up my budget – I'd respond calmly, stating my case as well as I could. I'd put a brave face on it. At least I could take comfort from one thing: he wasn't going to humiliate me about having put on weight, the way he had Lucy, forcing her to reveal that she was pregnant before she'd even told her mum.

But my face, white and wide-eyed, didn't look even a tiny bit brave.

I returned to my desk, gathered up a notepad and pen and my phone, and made my way to the back of the office where Barri had his lair. Juanita, his PA, gave me a smile that was carefully, blandly sympathetic, and waved me in.

I'd never actually been into Barri's private office before, only glimpsed it from outside. As was fitting for the founder and CEO of a major (well, not major yet, but Barri was all about the image) online fashion retailer, it exuded high-camp fabulousness. The floor was dark, polished parquet, partly covered by an enormous shaggy white rug. A full-length cheval mirror stood in one corner. In another was a gilt chaise longue upholstered in shocking pink velvet; in another, a retro drinks trolley was laden with bottles that I noticed could do with dusting. Enlarged, framed prints of vintage fashion drawings crowded the walls, which were painted lime green. A black glass chandelier illuminated it all.

Barri's desk, a simple three-sided slab of glass holding nothing but his iMac, stood at the far end, and behind it was Barri himself. He was wearing pale pink jeans so skinny I feared for his manhood, a faded Led Zeppelin T-shirt, a cream dinner jacket and tan brogues with Cuban heels that did little to help his lack of height. His hair, which I'd noticed before was thinning on top, was carefully coiffed and gelled so it almost, but not quite, covered his scalp.

I don't want to give the impression that I was perusing all this at my leisure. Far from it. I paused in the doorway for only a second or two, my knees literally trembling, before he said, 'Close the door behind you.'

I did.

He strolled out from behind his desk and sat on the pink sofa, stretching one arm along its elaborately curved, gilded back, before giving the seat next to him a little pat to invite me to sit there.

If I hadn't known beyond any reasonable doubt that Barri was as gay as a rainbow, I'd have had a #MeToo moment, right there. But I did, so I didn't. It was a different kind of fear that threatened to overwhelm me as I walked the few steps it took to take a seat next to him.

'Thank you for taking time out of your busy day to meet with me, Tansy,' he said.

'That's okay.' I just managed to get the words out, my mouth so dry my tongue felt like an enormous lump of cotton wool.

'I had a call from Guillermo Hernandez last week,' Barri began conversationally.

I nodded, but didn't say anything. Now I knew what I was here for. *Say anything*, I urged myself desperately. *Say whatever you think he wants to hear. Just keep your job, otherwise you're screwed.*

'Guillermo is a very dear friend of mine, as well as a supplier,' Barri went on, looking admiringly at the polished toe of his shoe as he rotated his ankle in leisurely circles. He wasn't wearing any socks, I noticed. 'As you know, trust is central to the relationships we build in this business. So when he told me he felt that trust had been betrayed, and wept – literally wept down the line to me, Tansy – I was devastated.'

'Why does he feel that way?' I asked, although, with an icy certainty that was spreading outwards from my stomach and making me start to shiver all over, I was pretty sure I knew the answer.

'One of Guillermo's assistants here in London happened to notice, through a Google alert that she has, naturally, set up to monitor brand perception, a listing on eBay.'

Shit. Shit just got real.

'Yes?' I just managed to say.

'It was a garment from last year's limited edition party collection, which we – which *you* – failed to deliver in time to list. A piece that would have retailed at two hundred and fifty pounds, advertised for sale to the best offer, or buy it now for one fifty. And specifying that it came brand new with tags. Not just Guillermo's tags. Luxeforless tags, too.'

I tried to take a deep, steadying breath and failed. Instead, I stammered out, 'But Barri, you know this is a thing. Lots of our samples get sold online, and the remaindered stock, too. People think it's, like, a perk of the job.'

'They *did*,' Barri said.

He leaned back further against the padded velvet, having a little wiggle to make himself more comfortable, and then he went on, almost placidly, still not raising his voice.

'I know how competitive this industry is, Tansy. I know how hard you girls and boys – and non-binary individuals, of course – work to secure a foothold in it. I know that sometimes we all have to make sacrifices – a shoe you adore, for instance, sold on after a couple of wears. The dress of your dreams, but you gift the sample to a friend. I know this happens. It's fine. You're all brand ambassadors. You love and wear our pieces, and then sometimes you pass them on for others to enjoy.'

I knew where this was going, but still I tried to put my case to him. I did. I tried my best.

'But there's so much,' I stammered. 'The samples we get from outside the EU, which are cut or marked so they can't be sold on as new. The remaindered stock – there's always some, however hard we try to plan for minimal waste. It happens. People do sell things they don't want.'

'Not. Any. More,' Barri spat. He no longer sounded serene; he sounded irate. 'As of today, I'll be introducing a new policy. All samples, and all unsold merchandise, will be destroyed. I can't have our brand and our suppliers' labels devalued in this fashion. There's perks of the job and then there's *taking the piss*.'

'I see,' I said, hoping this would be the end of it, but knowing that it wasn't.

'Oh, you do see? Then perhaps you can explain to me how Guillermo's assistant managed to purchase a BNWT item on eBay for twenty-five pounds, which, if I'm not mistaken, equates to some ten per cent of its list price? Brand new, with tags?'

'I have no idea,' I whispered.

Fuck. Mum must have been desperate.

'But I know. It was quite easy, with a bit of homework, to trace an eBay seller moving what I might call industrial quantities of Luxeforless merchandise from an address in Truro, Cornwall. A Mrs Belinda Barlow. She has a five-star seller rating, I'm told. Imagine how Guillermo feels about some call-centre worker from Essex turning up at the local karaoke night down the Slug and Slapper in a piece that's meant to be high-fucking-end?'

I felt like a badger whose number has come up in the badger cull, and now the sniper's searchlight was blinding me, the bullet about to be fired. But instead of freezing and crouching, I broke cover.

'Barri,' I said. 'I know a lot of the people who work here come from privileged backgrounds. I don't. I know you don't either. That's why it's so amazing that you've built this business up from nothing. It's one of the main reasons why I wanted to work for you. It's why I volunteered for the mentorship scheme. My mum struggles like mad, at home in Truro. The money she makes selling those clothes is often the difference between paying the rent and not being able to. I appreciate that you feel boundaries were crossed, and I'm sorry for that. But I don't want to be the reason my colleagues can't benefit from wearing and enjoying – and yes, making a bit of profit from – their own samples and returns any more. If there are guidelines you feel should be put in place, please tell me what they are and I'll be the first to comply.'

It was quite the speech, and I was all out of breath when I finished. I looked hopefully at Barri, and in return I received a sneer so despising I might as well have been shit on his croc-embossed shoe.

'Do I look like I'm running a fucking Oxfam shop?' he said. 'Get out. Tell your chavvy family that if they ever sell a single item with my label on it again, I'll have my lawyers on to them and you'll be out of work. You're on a final warning right now. Goodbye.'

And he waved his buffed-nailed hand at me as I stumbled out in floods of tears.

Chapter Nineteen

I spent the rest of that day ricocheting like a ping-pong ball between my desk, where I attempted to work, and the loo, where I kept having to sneak off to cry in peace. Except there wasn't much peace, even there – there was always someone doing her face at the mirror, or a couple of people who'd slipped in for a quiet chat, or Halle from Marketing being sick after eating her lunch. She thought she was being discreet, too, but everyone knew she had a problem, same as I'm sure they knew I'd been given a roasting by Barri, and kept weeping at my desk, but wasn't telling anyone what it was about.

I could have, obviously – Sally or Lisa would have been sympathetic. But being able to buy designer clothes cheaply when otherwise, on our salaries, they'd have been as far out of reach as the moon – and get samples for free – and either wear or sell them was a massive perk of the job. Now, thanks to me, everyone would be losing that privilege. I felt almost as bad about that as I did about the prospect of telling Mum that a significant source of her income was about to dwindle to nothing.

I'd sent her a parcel just the previous week, I remembered. An adorable purple knitted rabbit for her to pass on to Perdita for the baby, and some clothes for her to sell. I wasn't sure if she'd got around to photographing and listing them yet, but I was going to have to ring her and tell her not to, or to take them down if they were already on eBay. I wouldn't – couldn't – tell her the full magnitude of what had happened. I'd have to make something up, let her think that it was just a temporary blip until things got back to normal. But I knew that, for now at least, Barri would be keeping a watching brief on the site, and anything at all she offered for sale would get spotted and I'd lose my job. And if that happened, even the fifty quid or so a month I was able to scrape together once my normal living expenses were accounted for would be lost to Mum, too.

Back at my desk, I automatically checked my phone. Nothing from Felicity. A quick note from Josh: *You ok? Seems like that was some epic hangover – when I got in on Sunday you were already (still??) sparko.*

Sunday – and the night before – seemed like a lifetime ago now.

I couldn't think what I wanted to say to him, so I ignored the message for now, even though his concern made fresh tears well up in my eyes.

My phone vibrated with another incoming message, this one from Adam. *You free tonight? Beer at DG at 7?*

His words made me realise two things: first, that whatever awkwardness I'd worried about there being between us had passed. This was typical of Adam – he said what he thought with no filter whatsoever, but he'd never bear a grudge. He'd told me what he thought about Renzo; now, it was over to me to go ahead and do what I was going to do. He wouldn't mind either way – and he'd promised to help me if he could, and if he could, he would. And that led me to realise the second thing – that Adam's steady friendship was just what I needed right now. If I needed to confide in him, I could, and he'd listen without judgement. And if I decided to keep this current crisis to myself, he wouldn't ask me over and over what was wrong.

See you there, I replied.

Another thing about Adam is that he's fanatically punctual. Although it was only just after ten past seven when I arrived at the Daily Grind, he was already almost halfway down his beer, and there was a cold glass of chardonnay and a small tube of Pringles there on the table waiting for me.

I could have kissed him, but I contented myself with giving his shoulder a squeeze and saying, 'Thanks, you're a hero,' as I plonked myself down, took a big gulp of wine and ripped the foil off the crisps, shoving four of them in my mouth at once before offering them to him.

'Carb crisis?' Adam said, taking a Pringle and biting it carefully in half.

'Word.' I took four more and stuffed them in my mouth.

'Want me to get more?'

I looked regretfully at the tube. 'Nah, I'm good with these.'

Adam drank some beer and ate the other half of his crisp.

'So, your man was asking about you today,' he said casually.

'My – you mean Renzo?'

'No, I mean Elon Musk,' Adam teased. 'Although it's getting a bit hard to keep track, to be fair. I might need to write an app.'

'Adam! Stop taking the piss or I won't buy you another beer.'

Adam made a contrite face at his empty glass, and I hurried over to the bar and got us another round.

I considered feigning indifference when I returned to our table, where Adam was engrossed in his phone, a shard of sour-cream-and-onion-flavoured extruded potato forgotten in his fingers. But there really wasn't any point. He'd see straight through me.

'Right,' I said, wiggling onto my bar stool. 'Hit me with it.'

'Okay, so you know how Colton Capital works,' Adam began. 'Everyone's portfolio's monitored, minute by minute, so the boss can track performance in real time. But it's more about monitoring trends longer-term, on a day-to-day and week-by-week basis, and obviously monthly and quarterly too.'

'Got you,' I said, although I wasn't sure what relevance Colton Capital's performance management strategies had to me.

'So at the beginning of the year, Renzo's numbers dropped off a cliff, as I mentioned to you,' Adam went on. 'But in the interim, his record has stabilised. It's not back to where it was in quarter four of last year, but it's not been miles off.'

Ridiculously, I felt both a glow of pleasure that it had been when Renzo was going out with me that he'd done best and after we broke up that he'd done worst, alongside a prickle of resentment that his relationship with Felicity had upped his game.

'Go on,' I said.

'So,' Adam continued obediently, 'I started to track trends. Because that's what market analysis is all about, at its heart. Seeing how things adjust, and noticing patterns, and then working out what's going on to make them move the way they do. I did a spreadsheet. Would you like to see it?'

Grateful as I was for his efforts, I felt that if I never saw another spreadsheet in my life, it would be too soon.

'Just tell me,' I suggested.

'Okay, so.' Adam tapped his phone's screen and I saw a series of graphs flicker to life. I knew that all the numbers were right there in his head, but he wanted the chance to admire his own handiwork. 'We see a series of significant peaks and troughs. I've controlled here for the normal movement of the markets; all other things being equal, what this represents is Lorenzo Volta's emotional state – or at any rate, the way his emotional state impacts on his decision-making – over the period from last summer through to today.'

I couldn't resist. 'Oh, go on then, show me what you've got.'

Adam slid his phone across the table, and I leaned in and had a good look.

It was weird as fuck. All the dates that were important to me were so imprinted in my memory that I didn't even have to check them on my own phone, and I knew that they were accurately reflected in Adam's figures. There, following a steady upward trajectory last summer, was an even higher peak correlating with the time when Renzo had first asked me out. The line stayed highish for a couple of weeks, wavering a bit before veering upwards right around when we'd had that first amazing weekend together in Paris. It stayed high after that – sky-high – right until just before Christmas, when it dropped way down and stayed there for a week.

'Whatever position he held the day before the Christmas break was a disaster for him,' Adam said. 'And then he went away for a week, so he wasn't trading and it remained static. But take a look at the figures for January.'

I did. I saw the graph veering up and down – never achieving the heights it had before, but not plumbing the depths either. I couldn't be sure, because I'd erased all those desperate, mortifying messages from my phone, but I suspected there was a pattern revealing itself.

'And here,' Adam said. 'Sudden peak.'

I nodded. That was the Monday after I'd seen Renzo at Annabel's. The night he'd met Felicity. It could mean something or nothing.

'Now we see a slight upward trend,' Adam went on, far too engrossed in the figures he'd plotted to notice how I was feeling about them. 'Fairly steady, from January through the first quarter. Not as high as we were looking at last autumn, but a reasonable performance, although there was a noticeable dip a couple of weeks back. But look at today.'

I didn't need to say anything; the red line said it all. That very morning, Renzo's position in the markets had dived big time.

'Are you sure?' I asked. 'I mean, couldn't it just be, like, random volatility, or something?'

'Potentially.' Adam took his glasses off and polished them on a paper napkin. 'Only it's not. Because he spoke to me.'

'He did?' My heart was hammering eagerly in my chest. 'What did he say?'

'He said, "So you guys have a new housemate?" Adam recounted. 'And I said, "Sure we do, how did you know? He's Tansy's ex from way back."'

'You never did?' I gasped.

'Yeah, well, I thought it might help you. A bit of creative exaggeration, you know. I told him his name's Josh, and he's been living in Australia, and he was in a band that had a number one single.'

I yelped with laughter. I knew that Josh's band had never even come close to emerging from obscurity, never mind making the charts. Who knew Adam had such a talent for invention?

'And what did he say?'

'He said, "Not so much ex, by the looks of things." And then I got called into a meeting, so he didn't say anything else, and he was narky as hell all day. And look at those numbers, going down and down.'

I felt a flash of pity for Renzo. I knew how passionate he was about his job, how proud he was of being Colton Capital's top performer, how much the admiration of his colleagues and the validation of a massive annual bonus meant to him. It must be torture for him to find himself at the mercy of his emotions like this, his judgement clouded, his natural impulsiveness turning into reckless risk-taking. *He must be really miserable*, I thought, and his terrible results would only be making it worse.

'He won't get sacked, will he?'

'Not if he gets his shit back together,' Adam said. 'He's had a few strong weeks this year, after all.'

'So you'll carry on talking to him about what's going on between me and Josh?'

'Maybe. What is going on, anyway? What did the two of you get up to over the weekend that got Renzo so worked up?'

I pressed my hand against my face. I didn't want to tell Adam that Josh and I had snogged – that the physical evidence of another man in my life had triggered the cataclysmic fall in Renzo's performance at work – even though it was pretty much the reaction I'd hoped for. I knew that Adam – no matter that he wasn't exactly Josh's number one fan – would take a seriously dim view of me actually getting physical with him in order to make a point. And if I said that it had all been Josh's idea – nothing to do with me at all, honest, guv – Adam would feel the same about him, and his attitude towards Josh would segue from mild resentment to outright dislike, making the atmosphere in the house seriously toxic.

I was saved from having to say anything by the urgent trill of my phone in my handbag. My heart leaped with hope – Renzo? But it was Josh's name that flashed up on the screen. I turned it so Adam could see who was calling, then answered.

'Hey, Josh.'

'Tans. Are you still at work?' He sounded out of breath, like he'd just got in from one of his runs.

'No, I'm just up the road, in the Daily Grind. Adam and I popped in for a quick one.'

I felt a twinge of guilt, because we should have asked Josh to join us, but we hadn't.

'Thank God,' Josh said. 'How soon can you get home? It's Freezer.'

'Freezer? What, has he gone AWOL again?'

'No. He's here. But he's sick, and the neighbours aren't home.'

'Fuck. Sick how? Never mind, we'll be right there.' I didn't ask for more details – there was no point. It would take as long for him to explain as it would for us to leg it out and get back to the house. I cast a panicky glance towards the bar, but Luke wasn't there.

'We're on our way right now,' I said.

I didn't need to hurry Adam along – he was already on his feet, his phone stowed away, rushing towards the door.

Together, we walked round the corner and into our road, faster and faster until our walk had practically become a sprint.

'Fuck,' Adam gasped as I panted along in his wake, feeling sweat beginning to snake down my spine from anxiety and the early summer heat. 'If something happens to him…'

'I know. What would we tell Luke and Hannah?'

'Never mind about them. It's Freezer I'm worried about. What if he's in pain? What if he…'

He couldn't voice the rest of that thought. He kept powering along, but I noticed him brush his cheek with the back of his hand and heard him sniff. Adam crying was almost as worrying as whatever was happening to Freezer.

Still, in spite of his distress, Adam hadn't lost the ability to use his phone. The device looked like an extension of his arm as he tapped the screen, simultaneously striding along like an Olympic power-walker and fishing in his pocket for his keys.

'Hannah gave me the number for the vet last time they were away,' he said. 'But they're closed already. There's an emergency number to call.'

I knew he would have memorised it effortlessly, and he was dialling as we reached the house.

But Josh was already outside, holding a cardboard box carefully in his arms, tapping away at his own phone.

Seeing the box gave me a jolt of horror. What if we were too late?

But Josh said, 'They're expecting us at the emergency vet. There's only one nearby that's open twenty-four hours. I've ordered an Uber.'

The car arrived seconds later and we all piled in. Josh handed the box containing Freezer to Adam, who cradled it on his lap. From inside came a plaintive yowl.

'I guess we don't have a cat carrier,' Josh said. 'I didn't have time to look for one, anyway, so I just grabbed the nearest thing – this box was in your room and I put one of your T-shirts in, too, so it smells familiar for him. I hope you don't mind, mate.'

Adam shook his head. Josh could have ransacked his bedroom and made off with his new iPad Pro and he wouldn't have cared at that moment. 'What's wrong with him?'

'He hasn't been hit by a car, has he?' I asked.

'I don't think so,' Josh said. 'I'm pretty sure it's not that. I came out of the shower and he was in your room – the door was open and he was lying there on the floor, twitching and howling. He was kind of drooling, too. I think it might be some kind of seizure. But I don't know. I just thought I needed to get him to a vet straight away.'

The cardboard flaps of the box looked like they'd been torn open, their jagged edges leaving enough of a gap to give Freezer air. Adam peered down, lifted a corner and said, 'He's conscious, anyway. But he's still twitching. And he's clawing and biting at my shirt. He's not right.'

Then he lowered the flap carefully back, as if he couldn't bear to look any more.

'Do cats get heatstroke?' I suggested tentatively. 'It's been so warm, maybe if he wasn't drinking enough water…'

Josh and Adam both shook their heads. They didn't know, and neither did I.

The rest of the journey took less than fifteen minutes, but it felt like an eternity. The cab crawled through unfamiliar streets, choked with traffic, before eventually turning into a side road and stopping.

'Animal hospital,' the driver said. 'I hope your cat will be all right.'

Thanking him, we trooped into the vet's waiting room. I hung back and Josh and Adam walked to the reception desk together and gave their names and Freezer's. Josh filled in a form, while Adam held the cardboard box. I could see his shoulders trembling, either with suppressed sobs or with tension.

'The vet will see you now,' the receptionist said.

I watched as the two boys pushed open the door to the consulting room and carried Freezer in, hesitating.

'Coming, Tans?' Adam said.

Suddenly, I felt not just superfluous, but almost like an intruder. It wasn't that Freezer wasn't my cat – he wasn't Adam's either. It was partly the knowledge that, for whatever reason he had formulated in his feline brain, Freezer didn't like me and, given the choice, probably wouldn't have wanted me there. And partly, it was knowing that if something was terribly wrong and an awful decision needed to be made, it should be made by Adam and Josh, who loved him.

'I'll wait here.' I perched on a plastic chair and watched as the door closed, straining to hear the murmurs of conversation from inside. But I couldn't make out a word. For ten minutes, I just sat there, not even looking at my phone, just watching the featureless expanse of pale yellow-painted wood, wondering what was going on behind it and fearing the worst.

Then I heard a shout of laughter.

The door burst open and Adam and Josh came out, both grinning and shaking their heads. Josh was carrying the box now.

'He's fine,' they both said together.

'But what...?' They were too busy paying the bill and thanking the receptionist to explain, so I had to wait until we were all in another taxi, heading home.

'What happened?' I demanded.

'The vet tipped him out of the box, really carefully, in case he was injured,' Josh said.

'And he sat right down on the examination table and started licking himself,' Adam went on.

'She asked about his symptoms, and whether he had any history of feline epilepsy, and she listened to his heart and looked in his mouth.'

'And palpated his stomach, in case he'd eaten something toxic.'

'But she couldn't find anything wrong. And Freezer was just sat there, having a good old wash.'

'And then,' Adam said, and even in the dark car I could see a blush creeping up his neck, 'she looked at the label on the box.'

'And she said, "He's off his face on catnip."'

'Mortifying, or what?' Adam said. 'I'd actually forgotten I'd even ordered the stuff for him. Extra-strength Canadian catnip buds. The parcel must have got held up in customs, in case it was weed or something.'

'And Odeta must've left it in your room.'

'And Freezer found it, and broke into the box.'

'And was like, "This is the good shit, right here."'

'Oh my God.' The release of tension, as well as the absurdity of the picture their words painted, made me start to giggle, and that set the two boys off too. By the time we got home we were all weak with laughter and I felt positively exhausted from all the drama.

The lights were on in Luke and Hannah's house so, as soon as he was released from the box, Freezer hopped out through the window and scaled the fence, already shouting for his supper.

'I guess I'd better pop round and tell Hannah what happened,' Adam said, ducking his head and blushing again at the prospect. 'Their lights are still on, and I heard her talking to Freezer.'

'Shall I put the kettle on?' I asked.

'I don't know about you two,' Josh said, 'but I could do with a drink. I bought a bottle of seriously good whiskey when I was in Ireland. Fancy a drop?'

'Oh, go on then,' Adam said. 'I'll go next door first, though, and confess to Hannah that I gave her cat an overdose.'

'I'm sure she'll be fine with it,' I said. I was sure, but at the same time I was glad explaining to Hannah was Adam's job, not mine.

'It's not your fault, mate,' Josh said. 'He was basically high on his own supply.'

Adam headed out into the night, and I heard his polite tap on next door's knocker.

'He'll be ages,' I said. 'Hannah never lets anyone leave until they've had a drink and something to eat. And the two of them can chatter on about Freezer for hours.'

'In that case…' Josh carefully unpeeled the seal and eased the cork out of a squat, dark green bottle and sloshed some golden liquid into two wine glasses. 'We really ought to be drinking this stuff out of cut crystal tumblers, but we'll work with what we've got. Ice?'

'I don't know. Are you meant to have ice with it?'

'Purists say not, just a bit of water. Ideally filtered. But I like ice in mine, and I won't tell anyone if you do, too. Hell, have ginger ale in it if you want.'

I laughed. 'We haven't got any.'

'True. On the rocks it is, then.'

I sipped my drink and almost choked. 'Bloody hell. What is this stuff? It tastes kind of burnt.'

'That's the smokiness from the peat. It's meant to taste like that. Would you rather have a glass of wine?'

'No.' I sipped again, and this time I could begin to see the point of the drink. It was heady and warming and tasted somehow incredibly grown-up. 'I think I could get to like this.'

'It's good to try new things,' Josh said easily. 'You never know what you'll discover you like.'

He looked at me, smiling slightly, and I knew he wasn't talking about the whiskey. He was talking about our kiss – as strange and unexpected as the taste of this drink, and as surprisingly moreish.

'That's a very profound observation,' I said carefully, taking another, larger gulp of whiskey and trying not to choke as it seemed to set fire to my throat.

'Is it? I was just talking about single malt.'

'Of course you were.'

We looked at each other. He was still smiling, and I felt myself smile, too. Our eyes met, and held together for what felt like the longest time, until I broke away from his gaze and looked back at my glass. *Why the hell am I feeling like this? I hate him. He humiliated me*, one part of me protested vehemently. *Hate away*, the other part argued back. *But he's the key to getting Renzo back. Do you want that, or don't you? And besides*, added the inner voice – which by now I was thinking really needed to STFU – *you liked kissing him. A lot. Didn't you?*

'But we could talk about something else, if you like,' Josh said. 'We could talk about what happened in the club the other night.'

Or what happened at the Plaza cinema eleven years ago.

'We could.'

'Tansy, I know you only recently split up with your bloke. I don't know if you're ready to start something new. I don't know if I am, either. But what happened that night – it felt great, to me.'

The smile that had felt so natural just a minute before felt kind of forced now. If I was going to do this – use my feminine wiles to play him – I had to do it now. And I found I didn't have a clue how.

I wasn't sure I even had any feminine wiles. Whatever they were.

'It felt great to me, too.' I tried to do a sort of fluttery thing with my eyelashes, which I kind of needed to do anyway, since my eyes were watering a bit from the whiskey. I was sure my mascara must be smudging down my cheeks. 'But Renzo – it's all really recent, like you said.'

'He certainly didn't look best pleased when he saw you with me,' Josh said, and my heart jumped with renewed hope, just like it had when Adam had shown me his graph in the Daily Grind earlier.

'It's over between us,' I said. 'There's no going back, even if I wanted to. He's dating Felicity now.'

'But do you want to?' Josh pressed.

I couldn't lie to him, I realised. However much I wanted him to play along with my plan, that would be going too far. I couldn't lie, but I could let him draw his own conclusions.

I reached my hand across the table to him and said, 'I don't know. It's really hard. I just don't know.'

'Well then.' Josh covered my hand with his, then turned it over and caressed my palm with one finger, running it up the sensitive skin to my elbow, then back down again. All over my body, my skin prickled at his touch. 'Maybe you should think about it a bit.'

'I don't want to rush into anything,' I blurted out.

'Who said anything about rushing? I'm in no hurry.'

Shit. Why did everything he said make me think he meant something else? The idea of him not being in a hurry made me think irresistibly of other things he might do, slowly and languorously, taking his time. *Like he took his time over that prank at school.*

'I think…' I began, and then we heard Adam's keys in the door.

'Oh good, you guys are still up. I'd love to try some of that Connemara malt if it's still going. Freezer's fine, and Hannah's cool with what happened. She thought it was hilarious, actually, and she said she'll reimburse us for the vet's bill.'

'I think I'll head up to bed,' I finished.

I said good night and went to my room, but I couldn't fall asleep for the longest time, because I could hear their voices downstairs, not being loud or lairy or anything, but chatting and laughing and clearly having a good old male bonding session.

It made me feel somehow unsettled, although I couldn't identify exactly why.

Year Eleven

Over the next few months, my life developed a new routine that was fulfilling in a grim sort of way. I ate my apple and carrot every lunchtime, until I began to enjoy them so little that I threw quite a lot away, so then I reduced my allowance to half an apple and half a carrot. I bought packs of sugar-free gum from Mr Nabi's shop and chewed it, savouring each little white pellet until all the flavour was long gone. I cooked dinner for Perdita and me when Mum was at work and Dad was out, and then said I wasn't hungry. After my sister had gone to sleep, I lay on our bedroom floor and did sit-ups and leg-raises, first fifty, then a hundred, then more and more.

I worked hard at school and was amazed to find I enjoyed it. When Mr Brodrick praised me, I didn't care so much about being called 'Bike'. I perfected a distant stare when I saw Kylie, Anoushka and their crowd looking my way and sniggering. In bed each night, I made a bridge across my hipbones with my forearm, and loved measuring the increasing empty space beneath it.

One Saturday at work, Debbie closed the shop early and offered me a cup of tea.

'Yes, please,' I said, then added automatically, 'Just black. No sugar.'

She set one of her simple, perfect white china mugs down in front of me and said, 'Tansy, are you okay?'

'Of course I am,' I said. 'Why are you asking?'

'Everything all right at school?'

School. I thought of Josh, hanging out with Kylie and Anoushka and their elite crowd, and I wondered what he'd told her about me. I wondered whether she knew the names they called me, and why. I treasured those weekend days in the shop, surrounded by beautiful things, and I knew that the small amount of money I brought home mattered hugely to Mum. If Debbie knew what I was really like, if Josh told her what everyone said about me, it would all be gone. And if I told her about the trick he'd played on me, my relationship with Debbie would surely be finished.

I wondered whether Josh knew about the thoughts I'd had about him, how I'd imagined him talking to me, taking my side against his friends, maybe – maybe even telling me he liked me. But that was impossible. At school, and on the occasions, rarer now than they used to be, when he came into the shop, I blanked him totally.

'Of course,' I said again.

'Okay,' Debbie replied. 'Only you've lost some weight, and I wondered…?'

'Wondered what? I'm just being healthy. My body is a temple, right?'

Amazingly, Debbie blushed. She'd used the phrase herself, when she'd gone on one of her hardcore juice fasts that involved no solid food, only smoothies made from celery, spirulina, spinach and whey protein, along with five litres of water and two hours of yoga a day. I'd have loved to try it myself, but I had no money for spirulina and wasn't sure what whey protein was, and the yoga book I'd found in the school library said you should stick dental floss up your nose and pull it out again to clear your passages, which grossed me right out.

'Okay,' she said. 'So long as you're sure.'

'I'm sure.'

Then she sighed, took another sip of her tea, and said she had something to tell me. She was selling the shop, and she and Josh were moving to Australia in the summer once he'd finished his GCSEs.

'It's a massive change for us both,' she said. 'But an old friend of mine moved out there a few years ago, to Sydney, and opened a business there. It's thriving, and she's looking for someone to manage a second branch. I've loved living here, but I get itchy feet, and it's time to start a new chapter.'

'Right,' I said, a million questions crowding into my mind. Why Australia? Why now? What did Josh make of leaving his little gaggle of friends behind to start over at a new school where he'd be the new, awkward, frightened one? Not that I could imagine Josh ever being awkward. And most of all, what about me? Why was she leaving me? Had I done something that had made her hate me, along with everyone at school? What would I do without those tranquil weekend mornings spent working and learning, the only time in my life I felt truly happy?

'There's not a lot more I can teach you, you know, Tansy,' Debbie said gently. 'If you really want a career in fashion, you need to broaden your horizons. I've talked to a friend in London who can arrange some work experience for you over the summer, if you want. You could stay with her for a couple of weeks. And if your exam results are good, you could go on to sixth form college and then university. You don't have to stay here if you don't want to.'

I looked up at her, and past her to the shop window. It was February and raining, the wind battering against the glass and driving litter along the high street. *You don't have to stay here.* It was the first time it had occurred to me that I didn't; that there was a future for me away from school, away from Dad, away from the memory of Connor and Josh and the things people said about me.

'When I was your age, I felt like I'd never be grown up,' Debbie said. 'I felt like I'd never be in charge of my own life. But things change. This too shall pass.'

It was a typical Debbie remark – a philosophical platitude that she'd read in a book somewhere and was trotting out to make me feel better. But, even though it was on the tip of my tongue to ask how in control of his life her son was feeling right now, being whisked away to the other side of the world because his mum was experiencing itchy feet, it worked. I thanked her and said good night and went home, and over the next few weeks I worked and studied harder than I'd ever dreamed I could. The vision I had in my mind of London, working a summer internship, escaping from Truro and my classmates' mocking laughter and the stress and misery of life with my father, was a beacon of hope that grew more real each day.

*

At school, I found myself gravitating towards the clever kids, the ones who were being tutored for their exams, did music lessons in the afternoons and spent break times tapping away on laptops. I wasn't clever myself, I knew that – anything I managed to achieve would be through hard work and single-mindedness, not through innate talent. And I was still too much of an outcast to make friends with anyone. But, sitting next to Fawzia and Faaruq, the twins from Somalia, an open book in front of me and my little bag of carrot sticks in my lap, I felt a kind of insulated peace, if not any real sense of belonging.

Kylie, Anoushka and the rest of them weren't focused on exams – not one bit. Anoushka and Luke were an item now, and spent every second when a teacher wasn't watching glued hip to hip, snogging passionately. All the girls were obsessed with the Year Eleven leavers' ball, endlessly practising their make-up and getting the train to Plymouth on weekends to try on dresses in Jane Norman and Miss Selfridge. I sometimes thought wistfully that if things had been different, I might have been going to try on dresses, too, planning what colour I'd paint my nails and speculating about whose invitation I'd accept to the ball.

But my life was what it was, and no one would be asking me to any dance, so I did my homework and chewed my gum, relishing the sound of my rumbling stomach. I signed up for Mr Brodrick's extra maths classes and saved up to buy *Vogue* every month, learning the styles of the big-name designers, and, later on, all the minor ones too, as industriously as I did my school work.

And every morning I felt either savage pleasure or wretched disappointment when I stepped onto the bathroom scale. A low number gave me a sense of achievement as warm and satisfying as a good result in a test; a higher one meant only a quarter of an apple at lunchtime. My belly bore permanent bruises where I pinched the skin over and over, tighter and tighter, because if an inch was good, less than an inch must be even better.

One afternoon in May, after school finished for the day, I hung back as I always did, waiting for Kylie and Anoushka and their crew to leave. I'd learned that if I went ahead of them, they could run and catch me up, and their taunts would follow me all the way home. So I loitered by the gate until I was sure it was safe to go, and then I walked slowly towards home, my bag of books dragging on my right shoulder.

I could see their little group far ahead of me, Luke's arm draped around Anoushka's neck, Kylie and Danielle punching each other's arms and shrieking, Josh and Ben idly kicking a football back and forth, a few others tagging along, hoping to be included. Then Josh broke away from the group, waved and came jogging back towards me.

I froze, looking around for a place to hide. But the wide road was lined with terraced houses on either side; there was nowhere to go. I fixed my gaze straight ahead and kept walking.

When he was a few yards away, he called out my name. My actual name, not the cruel nickname I'd been given. I ignored him.

'Hey, Tansy,' he said again, but I didn't stop.

He fell into step next to me, and I walked on as if he wasn't there. Ahead of me, I saw Anoushka and Luke peel off and go into Luke's house, while the others split up at the crossroads, going right and left. I could hear their laughter drifting back towards me.

'Tansy? Earth to Tansy!' Josh stepped in front of me and turned around to face me, so I had no choice but to stop.

'What do you want?' I demanded.

Josh looked just the same as always, lean and lanky, his dark blond hair dishevelled by the wind and his tie half undone. He'd 'shot up', as Debbie put it, over the past few months and his trouser legs and shirtsleeves were too short. He was smiling like him stopping to talk to me was a totally normal thing to do, even though we both knew it wasn't.

'Do you have a date for the leavers' ball?'

I couldn't have been more surprised if he'd gone down on one knee and proposed marriage, but I fought to keep my face impassive.

'Don't be stupid.'

'Will you come with me?'

For a second, a whole new future opened up in front of me: a future in which I'd be wearing a dress that didn't come from a high-street store but was unique and beautiful, my hair coiled in a perfect up-do, surrounded by laughing friends who liked me, my arm around the waist of a handsome boy.

Then reality closed back down with a snap. I remembered what he'd done before – the cruel trick he'd played on me. I remembered how eagerly I'd gone along with it, how I'd let myself be lured into the trap against my better judgement, because I wanted so badly to believe that he liked me.

I wasn't going to fall for that again.

'Are you fucking kidding me?' I said, made brave by months' worth of pent-up hurt and anger. 'I'm not playing your pathetic little game.'

And I stepped deftly past him and walked on, leaving him standing open-mouthed and alone in the street.

Chapter Twenty

Things changed yet again after that night. Before, I'd had the sense that Josh and Adam were engaged in a kind of love triangle with Freezer at its apex, and even worried that they might challenge each other to a duel over his favours at any moment.

Now I was living in a house with a three-way bromance going down.

Take this typical scene a couple of weeks later. I came downstairs on my way to work and found Adam and Josh in the kitchen. They both had slices of Josh's special organic sourdough wholemeal toast spread with the palm-oil-free peanut butter he'd bought, and cups of espresso from Adam's fancy new coffee machine. But their toast was going soggy on their plates and their coffee cooling in their mugs, because they also had a fishing-rod cat toy with a bunch of feathers on the end, which Freezer was chasing round the kitchen, occasionally doing wild pounces or dramatic skids on the tiled floor.

Both of them were watching him with identical soppy grins on their faces.

'Look at this, Tans,' Josh said. 'It arrived this morning. He thinks it's the best thing ever.'

'Come on, little dude.' Adam made the toy go again and, after a dubious glance in my direction, Freezer pursued it, leaping in the air and coming down with all four paws on the feathers, before turning upside down and savaging it with his hind legs.

'You got the birdie!' Josh cooed. 'You clever cat!'

'Freezer, the mighty hunter,' Adam said, glowing with pride like a father watching his baby take its first steps.

'We should really give him treats when he catches it,' Josh said. 'It reinforces their predatory drive, I read online.'

'We'll have to ask Hannah,' Adam replied.

'He is adorable.' *And so are the two of you, you big dafties,* I thought, forgetting for a second how unadorable Josh had been to me in the past. 'Right, I'm off.'

'Have a good day,' Josh said, but he was watching the bundle of feathers and Freezer, who was crouched low, his bottom wriggling as he prepared to pounce.

'Some mates of Josh's are doing the quiz at the Prince George tonight. Fancy coming along?' Adam asked.

'With Adam on our team, we're sure to win,' Josh said. 'Bloke's basically a walking Wikipedia.'

Adam ducked his head in a modest *aw, shucks* gesture, but I was pretty sure it was true.

'I'll try,' I said. 'Depends how work goes.'

The prospect of being with Josh – who'd no doubt nail all the questions about music and sport – and Adam – who knew everything else – and being left to humbly answer the odd question about *America's Next Top Model* wasn't the most appealing thing ever.

But, on the other hand, I'd noticed the expression on Adam's face the night before, when he'd come home late from work and found Josh and me sitting on the sofa together watching *Queer Eye*. We hadn't been canoodling or anything – we hadn't even been touching each other. But there we were, next to each other, our feet up on the coffee table next to the remains of a chicken salad I'd made, and Adam had looked at us with an expression on his face that was not unlike the way he looked at Freezer when he pounced on his feathery toy.

If I did manage to nail a tricky quiz question, Josh would high-five me, maybe even hug me. And I'd hug him back. And Adam would see, and tell Renzo. A price worth paying, surely.

But, as it turned out, I didn't make it to the pub that night. Just as I was shutting down my computer at half six, my phone buzzed with an incoming text. Chelsea.

You free?
Sure. What's up?
Can you come round the flat?

Bollocks. Typical Chelsea – she wasn't going to communicate anything significant in a text. But it was on my way home, after all.

Give me 45 minutes.

Chelsea's staccato texting style was catching, I'd found.

Soon, I was in the lift on the way up to the sixth floor of Wadsworth Heights. The estate felt different now, in the twilight of a summer evening. It hadn't rained for weeks, and people at work had stopped saying how gorgeous the weather was and started moaning about how they simply couldn't bear the heat any more, it was too much. But here, everything seemed to have been brought to life by the heatwave. I could smell the mouthwatering savouriness of a barbecue. Windows were open to let in the warm air, children's laughter was drifting up from the playground next to the car park and people were sitting on plastic chairs outside their front doors, smoking and chatting.

The door to Chelsea's mum's flat was closed, though, and I knocked tentatively. It was opened by a boy who I guessed must be Nathan – a lanky, handsome lad wearing low-slung jeans and a hoodie pulled up over his baseball cap. *He must be roasting in this weather*, I thought fleetingly.

He stared hard at me, unsmiling. In spite of what I knew about him, he looked like a boy trying to look tougher than he was.

'Hi, I'm Tansy. I work with Chelsea.'

'Nathan.' He held out his hand for me to shake and smiled a sudden, warm smile, his cool street demeanour slipping for a second so I could see the sweet boy Mrs Johnston had described. 'They're through here.'

He showed me to the bedroom that Chelsea had told me used to be hers, where she did her sewing now, but he needn't have – I could have found my own way there just by following the whirr of sewing machines.

Chelsea and her mother were both in there. Mrs Johnston was still in her work uniform, a scarf tied over her hair, bent over a machine as she fed a swathe of mustard-coloured silk under the needle, rapidly and expertly. Chelsea was at the table, fixing a pattern to a piece of midnight-blue velvet, her mouth full of pins. The room wasn't immaculately tidy as it had been before, with everything squared away. It was – well, not chaos, exactly. But there were several empty teacups scattered around, drifts of snipped-off thread littering the floor, garments in various stages of production hanging on rails and lying in roughly folded piles.

'Evening,' I said. 'Wow, looks like you've been busy.'

Neither woman said anything. Chelsea waved a hand at me, then carried on pinning as fast as she could. Her mother snatched a piece of fuchsia lace from the pile next to the machine and reached up to the shelf above her for matching thread.

'Come into the kitchen,' Chelsea said, once the last pin had been removed from her lips and stabbed through the pattern and fabric.

Her magenta hair was frizzing a bit over her sweating forehead and her eyes were red-rimmed. She rolled her shoulders as she left the room, then they dropped back into the hunched position I guessed they'd been in for many hours.

'I'm fucking knackered,' she said, pouring two pint glasses full of water from the tap and handing one to me. 'I can't drink any more coffee, I'm rattling. And it's too hot.'

She pulled her T-shirt away from her body and sniffed it.

'Jesus. I haven't showered since before my shift last night, or slept.'

'Okay,' I said. 'Drink your water, and tell me what's happening.'

She gulped the whole glass down in one go, then refilled it and necked some more.

'So, a couple of weeks ago some posh bird came by my stall and bought, like, four dresses,' Chelsea said. 'She wanted to take more but I said no, cos I was running low on stock and for all I knew she was going to sell them on on eBay or something. I've had that happen before. I sold a jacket for one fifty and, the next week, I saw a woman wearing it. I didn't recognise her – and I know all my customers – so I asked her and she said she got it online for three hundred. Not cool.'

'Not cool at all,' I said with a shiver of guilt.

'Anyway, so this woman,' Chelsea went on. 'Turns out she's one of them influencers on Insta. She didn't sell the dresses. She wore them. She wore them to, like, The Ivy and shit, and she tagged me in her posts when she did. And next thing I know, I've got a queue outside my stall. All these rah girls going, "Babe, this is so, like, authentic," and buying up my whole stock.'

'But that's brilliant! You're hitting the big time!' I didn't want to tell Chelsea that I was about ninety-nine point nine per cent sure that the original posh bird was Pru, and that it was the dress I'd worn out a few weeks ago that had sparked this sudden spike in demand.

'Yeah, it would be fucking brilliant if I could keep up,' Chelsea said. 'But I can't. I've got no stock, so people are putting in orders, and they all want them, like, yesterday, because they're off to Provence or Marrakesh or Indo-fucking-nesia for their holidays, or they've got a wedding in Gloucestershire that they need a "real statement piece" for. And they've paid deposits, and Mum and me have been working our bloody tits off and we're still miles behind, and I'm meant to have forty dresses done by next Saturday and it's more likely that England will win the shagging World Cup.'

She slumped into a chair and put her head in her arms, her shoulders starting to tremble with fatigue, or tears.

'It's okay, Chelsea,' I said. 'We've got this. We'll make a plan.'

'What plan, though?' she demanded. 'Mum and I are working flat out and there's no way we'll get everything finished in time. I've been working for twenty hours solid and Mum for twelve, and we're both due on shift at six tomorrow. And if I don't keep up making my regular stock I won't have anything to sell when people come by the stall and then it'll be game over.'

I saw her point. I was about to tell her to calm down again, but she was in full flood.

'And I know what people are like. I see it all the time at work. Someone comes in wanting to buy Nip and Fab pads and we've sold out, and they throw all their toys out the pram and demand to see the manager and start slagging us off on Twitter. And that's just normal people like us – how badly are these girls going to kick off if they don't get their outfit for their flash wedding on time?'

'They'll go to Harrods and buy something else,' I said. 'But obviously, you don't want to let anyone down. Let's take this one step at a time.'

'I haven't got time!' Chelsea snapped. 'I need to be back in there, working.'

'No, you don't. You're running a business now. You need to think like a manager. Remember that last mentoring session we all had together? Remember the bloke from that incubator fund who said the biggest mistake entrepreneurs make is carrying on like they did when they were one-person bands and not learning to outsource when growth is happening? That's happening to you, right now. Admittedly it's happened sooner than we expected, and we don't have mechanisms in place to facilitate it, but you and I need to be working right now to find them.'

Chelsea looked up at me. She was still super-stressed, but there was a new calm and purpose in her face. I only wished I was feeling calm myself – but I carried on.

'Now. Tell your mum to step away from that machine and get some rest. I don't know about you, but if I was having a baby tomorrow morning, I wouldn't want the midwife to be so knackered she went in there like she was cutting a seam. Would you?'

Chelsea winced and giggled. 'Hell, no.'

'Right. And have a shower yourself, if you want. And let's order in some food. I bet you haven't eaten in ages.'

Chelsea didn't say anything, but her stomach let out a massive rumble that was enough of an answer.

I picked up my phone. 'What do you want? Fried chicken? Burgers? Ramen?'

'Pizza,' she said. 'With salami and red onion and chilli and a stuffed crust. If you don't mind?'

'Works for me.'

She shuffled out, and I started putting in an order for food when I heard an almost inaudible cough.

I looked up and saw Nathan hovering in the doorway, looking hopeful. He reminded me a bit of Freezer when Adam rattled the Dreamies packet.

'Hungry? I'm just ordering in some Domino's. What do you fancy?'

'Mega Meatlovers,' he said shyly. 'If that's okay? That shit is peng.'

'Of course. And for your mum?'

'She likes ham and pineapple,' Nathan said. 'Freak.'

I laughed. 'I'm not keen on pineapple on pizza myself. But hey, each to their own, right?'

I tapped in our order, adding some garlic bread and wedges for good measure, reassured to hear the sound of water pattering in the shower tray. At least Chelsea was getting in some self-care. But she needed more than food and a freshen-up: she needed her entire business rescuing, and I wasn't sure how – or even whether – it could be done.

I took my tablet out of my bag and logged into my email. I thought about my suppliers in East Asia, and the ones in Turkey. Probably, I could call in some favours somewhere, but even if Kuan-Yu in Taipei or Erdal in Istanbul were willing to help, I wasn't sure they'd be able to. Chelsea's order was tiny by their standards, and it wouldn't be financially viable for them to take a handful of machinists off the production line to make up fewer than a hundred garments using what was basically scraps of random fabric, rather than the vast bolts of cloth they usually worked with. The couturiers in Paris used suppliers for fine embroidery who were better able to cope with small-scale orders, but their work came at a crazy price – all the profit Chelsea could hope to make would be wiped out in labour costs.

And then I saw a LinkedIn invitation that had been hanging around in my alerts for ages. I tapped on the red dot while my brain hummed hopelessly in search of a solution.

'Harriet Dawson would like to connect with you…' Harriet who? I was pretty sure I didn't know anyone called Harriet. I clicked and read it, and my brain clicked, too. Harriet. The woman I'd met at the Streets Ahead gig I'd been to with Josh, who'd so fascinated me with her description of the charity she'd started that I'd even forgotten Renzo was there.

'*Stitch Together helps refugees and asylum seekers integrate into their new communities… Many of the women have amazing needlework skills… We work with partners who pay the London living wage…*'

I did a series of rapid calculations, first in my head and then on a spreadsheet. Paying a skilled seamstress to make up her garments, even allowing a generous ten hours for each dress, would make Chelsea a decent profit. And what was more, the project had the potential to scale up. If Pru's friends wore the dresses on their holidays or to their swanky weddings and got noticed, and more orders flooded in, suddenly there could be the beginnings of something viable.

I tapped out a rapid-fire email to Harriet, then tweaked the numbers on my spreadsheet some more. Soon, I was so engrossed that I barely noticed Chelsea emerging from the bathroom, wafting fragrant steam, and Nathan answering the door and returning with boxes of pizza that smelled even better.

'I think we can make this work,' I said triumphantly.

Chapter Twenty-One

To be honest, I've never been much of a birthday person. When I was very little, Mum used to make the usual amount of fuss, baking cakes and arranging parties at which I remember Pass the Parcel and Musical Bumps featuring heavily. After we moved to Cornwall, it all got a bit more complicated. Already, Dad's little problem was becoming a big problem, and money was always tight.

Mum tried her best, but I was getting too old for fancy cakes and party games. Trips to the cinema followed by McDonald's just couldn't happen, and even though Mum did her best with craft-based activities, treasure hunts in the garden, home-made sausage rolls and falafel balls, because she couldn't bring herself to shop at Iceland like other mums on a budget did, I could see my classmates' reactions turning from bewildered to sneering.

And when we moved house and changed schools, I told her, abruptly and probably hurtfully, that she needn't bother any more. It was just as well, because there certainly wasn't a child at Trelander Academy willing to risk social death by turning up at my party, and Mum would have made her courgette cake and veggie burritos for nothing.

At uni, my birthday was always a non-event, falling as it did right in the middle of exams, when everyone was in peak stress mode. Not that I had a huge cohort of friends falling over one another to go out with me and get bladdered on cheap lager before staggering home via the kebab shop.

My last birthday, when I turned twenty-six, had been a bit better. Lucy at work had hers the day after and, because she was pregnant and off the booze, we'd gone out after work with Sally, Kris, Lisa and a few others from the office to a restaurant that specialised in puddings and shared more than twenty between the ten of us, and it had felt deliciously subversive knowing how furious Barri would be if he found out we were indulging so shamelessly.

Actually, with hindsight, it's possible Kris ratted on us, because Barri's comments about Lucy's expanding waistline ramped up from goading to downright vicious after that.

But this year, I wasn't expecting much. *Twenty-seven isn't a landmark birthday anyway*, I told myself, fighting back a twinge of disappointment when Josh told me he was flying to Belfast to record a single with Ruby the night before and didn't know when he would be back. *Even for a fake boyfriend, that's pretty fucking shoddy,* I thought, before remembering that until Facebook reminded him on the day, he probably wouldn't even know it was my birthday.

So I got up in the morning, same as on any other day, went downstairs and made myself a coffee. Adam had left for work already. In the unlikely event that anyone was going to send me a card, it wouldn't arrive until the postman did, hours later, and I'd only see it when I got home. And, same as any other day, I got the Tube to work, fighting the urge to have a good old cry of self-pity.

I was cheered up by a beautiful bunch of flowers on my desk – pink roses and peonies, my favourite – with a note from Debbie wishing me a happy day. I was surprised and touched, and felt a fresh twinge of guilt about Josh. *This can't carry on forever*, I told myself firmly. At some point, the charade was going to have to end. I'd have to give up on Renzo and move on with my life.

Just not yet.

At the desk next to mine, Felicity was eating hard-boiled eggs out of a Tupperware box, looking as morose as I felt.

'God, that stinks,' Kris grumbled.

To my surprise, instead of slapping him down with a sassy comeback, Felicity snapped the box closed, marched off to the kitchen with it and returned empty-handed, looking as if she, too, might be on the verge of tears.

'Happy now?' she said.

Kris flushed. 'I didn't mean you to…'

'Well, I did,' Felicity snapped. Over the hum of our computers, I heard her stomach give a massive rumble.

You ok? I tapped out to her on WhatsApp. *Fancy popping out for lunch? Or for a drink later?*

She glanced down at her phone, then up at me. 'Sorry, I'm busy. Are you doing anything nice for your birthday?'

'Guess not,' I said. 'I might share a bottle of wine and a takeaway with my housemate, or something. Rock and roll.'

'What about your chap? The handsome Australian?' It was an innocent enough question, but there was a bit of an edge to her voice.

'He's out of town with work.' I sighed, picking up my phone again to text Adam. 'I suppose we'll do something to celebrate when he gets back. Whenever that is.'

We both returned to our screens and the day dragged slowly by. A smattering of birthday wishes appeared on my Facebook wall. Adam replied, saying he was working late but suggesting I meet him at the Daily Grind at eight, which meant I'd have to stay late at the office too, because I was pretty sure that if I went home I'd never summon up the energy to leave again.

I had a meeting with the marketing team about the promotional shoot for my new collection, which was normally one of my favourite parts of my job. Today, though, I couldn't manage to get excited about the location, a disused gas works in Nottingham, or the selection of head-shots the modelling agency had sent over, or the stylist's vision of 'an urban dystopia brought to life by glamour'.

I emailed two of my suppliers to chivvy them about late deliveries, and my words were more acid and less diplomatic than they needed to be. I sent Daria the update she'd requested on the progress of my mentoring relationship with Chelsea, but something stopped me from mentioning that, even as I wrote, there were eight women, hailing from Syria, South Sudan, Eritrea, Albania and Zimbabwe, all working busily to fulfil the orders that had flooded in from Pru's friends and Instagram followers.

I'm not sure what prevented me from sharing what was, after all, a bit of a coup for my mentee. Maybe it was a sense that something might still go wrong, and I didn't want to big up Chelsea – or, by extension, myself – until I knew the frocks had been delivered, quality-checked and dispatched (via Nathan on his moped, to save on courier costs) to their new owners.

Daria might well not care – she might just view it as a minor achievement and send me back a two-line email saying she was pleased things were going well. But, on the other hand, she might tell Barri. And right now I wanted to stay as far below his radar as I could, especially as I was spending my lunchtimes searching for a new job.

I hadn't been sacked, and I hoped I wasn't going to be, but I sensed that my days at Luxeforless were numbered, and I wanted to jump before I was pushed.

I stared at my spreadsheet, making a few minor, pointless tweaks to prices and volumes to try and make my margins better, then closed the file without saving my changes.

At last, at half past six, I gave up, shut my computer down and left the office. The rest of the buying team had already called it a day and only the late-night customer care women were still there, their screens in sleep mode as they played Causality on their phones. It was still brilliantly sunny outside, and I was too hot in the long-sleeved blouse I'd worn to work because the air conditioning in the office was always turned to arctic. The pavements on Regent Street were thronged with tourists and commuters, all wilting in the heat as they hurried towards the even hotter Tube. It hadn't rained for weeks; London was sweltering and Josh had been leaving Tupperware bowls of water out for the foxes at night. I'd have to remember to do that before I went to bed, I thought – his concern for the little family, a vixen and three cubs, was contagious.

It was too early, when I alighted at our stop, to go and meet Adam, so I decided to go home and change after all. Even though I was only meeting a mate for a drink, it was still my birthday, and I was conscious that all my make-up had melted off in the heat and I felt sticky and uncomfortable in my work clothes.

The house was empty and silent. Freezer was perched on the fence, watching to see whether Adam or Hannah would arrive home first. He glanced in my direction, then looked away again, deciding I was of no interest to him.

'You and the rest of the world, Freezer,' I muttered darkly, heading upstairs for a deliciously cool shower. I got ready quickly, keeping my make-up minimal and not bothering to do anything with my hair except bundle it into a messy up-do. I put on a white cotton sundress from a couple of seasons ago and slipped my feet into jewelled flip-flops, and then I hurried out again into the warm evening.

In my haste to get home and freshen up, I hadn't noticed that there was a sign on the door of the Daily Grind: *Closed for a private function. See you again soon. Bollocks.* I was turning the other way, towards the Prince George, cursing other people and their rich and full social lives as I fished in my bag for my phone, when I thought I heard someone call my name.

I stopped and turned again towards the closed glass door of the Daily Grind, taking a proper look inside this time. The bar wasn't crowded, but there must have been at least forty people in there. There were candles burning on the tables and bunting strung from the rafters. Looking more closely, I could see there were letters on the individual triangular flags, and they spelled out a message that said, HAPPY BIRTHDAY TANSY.

My heart was hammering and my legs were shaking a bit as I pushed open the door, and I was greeted by a shout of, 'Surprise!'

'We thought you were going to fuck off in a huff,' Sally laughed, hurrying over and hugging me. 'Kris was about to chase after you down the street.'

'Happy birthday, beautiful.' Kris hugged me. He was wearing a rose-pink satin slip dress and high-heeled silver mules.

'Beautiful yourself,' I said, and he grinned in delight. 'But I can't… How did this even…?'

I gazed around the room. There were Lisa and Lucy and their husbands, Lucy's tiny baby in a sling on her chest. There were Maddy and Henry, Charlotte's friends who'd spent New Year's Eve with us. There were Fawzia and Faaruq, my old friends from school. There was Odeta with her boyfriend, chatting away to Yelena the waitress. A little group of my former colleagues from my previous job were chatting in a corner and my old housemates, who I sporadically kept in touch with on social media, were standing at the bar. Chelsea was drinking beer with Jed and Boyd, the couple from across the street, whose housewarming party we'd been to. Luke was serving pints and Hannah was circulating with glasses of sparkling wine on a tray.

On a table at the back of the room I could see a big bouquet of flowers, a pile of presents and a cake, and next to it…

'Perdita!' I dashed over and hugged my sister. 'What the hell? How are you even here?'

'I left the baby with Ryan,' she said. 'I've had two glasses of fizz and I'm already shitfaced. Your lovely housemate says I can sleep in his bed and he'll crash on the sofa, but I should really get the overnight coach home.'

'Which housemate?' I demanded. Then I looked around and saw Josh and Adam standing together, identical smug grins on their faces.

'Okay,' I said. 'Which one of you did this?'

'It was him,' Adam said, at exactly the same time as Josh said, 'He did.'

'You guys. Seriously. I can't believe this.'

Someone put a glass of prosecco in my hand, and I downed it almost in one go, and it was immediately replaced with another. Feeling as if I was in some strange dream, I looked around the room again, trying to figure out how Adam, or Josh, or the two of them together, must have contacted people through my social media, figuring out who I would want to come to my surprise birthday party, inviting them all, booking the venue – organising this whole wonderful thing for me without me knowing a thing about it.

'I can't believe it,' I said again, and hugged them both tight, even though it made Adam squirm a bit. Then I took my glass – which seemed to have had some kind of magic spell cast on it, because every time I emptied it it was either refilled or a fresh one appeared in my hand – and I mingled.

It was wonderful. Everyone seemed so excited to be there, so thrilled that I hadn't found out and spoiled the surprise. I felt like brides must feel on their wedding day, basking in attention and affection. I was too happy to care that I hadn't dressed up, too happy to worry about eating the samosas and pakoras and bhajis that had been ordered in from the Queen of Kashmir next door, too happy even to mind when I saw Felicity and Renzo together, talking intently.

'Hello.' Felicity enveloped me in a fragrant hug. 'I'm so sorry I had to fib to you at work today. You looked so gutted, it was awful.'

I laughed. 'I was having a bit of a pity party. But now I'm having an actual party, so it's all good.'

'Your bloke is quite the mastermind,' she said. 'He got me to send emails to everyone who I thought you'd want to come, and kept track of the numbers, and your other housemate did a Doodle poll with everyone's dietary requirements. They ought to go into business together.'

Renzo kissed me on both cheeks and wished me a happy birthday, and I thanked him, the smile on my face feeling quite natural, before turning away and mingling some more. But I found myself gravitating back to the main table, where Josh was on his phone, turning up the volume on a Spotify playlist that seemed to have all my favourite music on it.

'This was the most amazing thing you and Adam did,' I said. 'Seriously, thank you so much.'

'It was nothing. Seeing your face when you walked in was so totally worth it.'

I looked up at him. My cheeks were hurting a bit, and I realised I hadn't stopped smiling for what felt like hours. Lots of people had hugged me that evening, of course, but it felt like more than the sum of all the arms in the room was around me – like I was caught up in some lovely, massive group hug, buoyed up by kindness and friendship and love.

I realised, quite suddenly, that I didn't hate Josh any more. What he'd done, and why he'd done it, was a question I'd ask him another day; now, I was too happy for there to be room for any bad feelings in my heart.

And this time, I didn't even think about whether Renzo was watching when I put my arms around Josh and pulled him close against me into a kiss. Like the last time he kissed me, it felt good – great, even. His body was strong and warm against mine. His hands caressed my back gently, then moved up and stroked my hair back from my face. This time I didn't break away from him, because I didn't want it to end.

But he said, 'I mustn't monopolise the birthday girl. Let me get you another drink. Have you had enough to eat? Do you want me to turn up the music so people can dance? Or cut your cake first?'

'Let me go and chat to Perdita for a bit. I haven't seen her in so long, and I must introduce you and Adam to her properly. And then cake and then dancing, I think.'

So that's what we did. I noticed my sister size Josh up appraisingly, telling him he hadn't changed a bit since school, although I knew perfectly well she must be thinking that he had, in all the ways that mattered. Then he made some excuse about going to pop next door for some more samosas, and she and I sat down and had a good old catch-up, but when I tried to quiz her about how Mum and Dad were managing – really, not just 'okay' like Mum told me when we talked – she insisted that everything was just ticking over and I wasn't to worry.

And then I did cut the cake, which was a ridiculously rich chocolate one with real chocolate truffles cut in half and stuck all over the outside and a layer of marzipan underneath the buttercream.

'Where the hell did you get this?' I asked Adam, who was hovering over it, glowing with anxious pride like a *MasterChef* contestant waiting for Jon and Gregg to deliver their verdict – although of course he hadn't made it himself. No way. 'It's insane. It's a total cake-gasm.'

'I designed it,' Adam said. 'And Hannah and I made it together. Well, Hannah mostly.'

And then of course I had to give him and Hannah huge hugs and thank them both all over again.

After everyone had eaten as much as they could hold, and there was still a huge slab left on the cake stand, which I noticed Adam loitering over, Josh picked up his phone again and tapped the screen. But instead of turning the music up, he turned it off.

Kris shouted, 'Speech!'

'What?' I said. 'I can't.'

'Of course you can,' Josh said. 'Look, all these people here love you. You can do it.'

'But I…' And then I stopped and looked around at all the expectant, happy faces. Fawzia, who'd travelled down from Manchester where she ran an anti-FGM charity, and Faaruq, who, as a junior doctor, must be both run off his feet and permanently knackered. Lucy, breastfeeding her little daughter on a chair, a plate of cake next to her. Perdita, who was going to make the eight-hour journey home overnight, having already made it in the other direction earlier. Adam, holding his phone in his hand but not retreating into the screen as I knew he must be longing to do. Chelsea, who must have sacked off a shift at her part-time job or a precious opportunity to work on her collection to be here. And Josh, looking so proud of the surprise he'd helped plan for me, yet so chilled about hosting this gathering of people he'd never met before.

So, unaccustomed as I was, I said a few words. 'This is the most amazing birthday I've ever had. If this is what being twenty-seven is like, bring it on. Thank you all so much for coming. Thank you, Luke and Hannah, for having us all. And thank you especially to Adam and Josh, for being such amazing people. I love you both.'

Then, because I'd drunk so much fizz I was practically floating up to the ceiling on a cloud of bubbles, I added, 'I love you all.'

And, because I realised it was true, I had to sniff and wipe away a tear or several before Josh finally pumped up the volume and "Feel the Love" blasted out, and I could stop feeling self-conscious and go back to having fun.

We kept the Daily Grind properly banging until almost one in the morning, when Luke tactfully approached Josh and reminded him of their 'We're a local coffee shop first and foremost, so please be considerate of our neighbours and friends during late opening' policy, and Josh turned the music right down.

By then only a few of us were left. Felicity had said good night some time before, perhaps to go on with Renzo to somewhere far more fashionable and fabulous – although there was no way it would have been more fun. Adam had slipped away almost immediately after my speech, and I knew that the excruciatingly awkward conversation I'd have to have with him about how he couldn't possibly pay for all of this himself would have to wait. Lucy had got an Uber back to Finsbury Park with her baby. Perdita was hopefully having a good old nap on the coach back home.

So it was only Kris, Chelsea, Sally, Yelena and a hard core of others who spilled out into the night with Josh and me, exchanging yet more hugs and swearing eternal friendship before people hurried to get the Tube or lit fags while they waited for their taxis to arrive.

And then, quite suddenly, I found myself walking down the familiar road towards home with Josh. His arm was loosely around my waist, and that felt like the most natural thing ever, so much so that when we passed either side of a lamp post, my arm slipped around his afterwards.

And then, when he unlocked the front door because my key didn't seem to want to function in my fumbling fingers, I took his hand in mine and we walked up the stairs together. And instead of him going one way into his bedroom and me going the other into mine, I kept hold of him until we were sitting next to each other on my bed. And even after that, I didn't let it go. Our fingers were still intertwined when we kissed again, with no chance of an audience this time.

I only let go when the intensity of the kiss became too much for me and I flopped down on my back on the duvet, feeling absolutely sober and in control all of a sudden, and smiled at him, my hands reaching up for his face.

Chapter Twenty-Two

The thing I remember most clearly about that night is thinking, at the moment when Josh and I had fumblingly removed all our clothes and our bodies were lying together, skin against skin, for the first time, *I want to remember this moment, and what happens next, always.*

And the funny thing was that, afterwards, when I was desperate to forget what had happened that night, the memories kept intruding, pushing themselves into my brain even when I squeezed my eyes shut and pressed my hands over my face to try and keep them out. I remembered the moment when he lay down next to me and we carried on kissing and I knew that this was going to go further and further, up to the point of no return and beyond it. I remembered wondering if I ought to ask him to stop, whether this was the wrong thing to be doing – but how could I, when it felt so very right?

I remembered how, even though no lights were on in the house, the glow from the street lamp outside illuminated his face, and how he looked down at me with tender concentration as he touched me, and how he smiled when he heard me gasp with pleasure. And there was the thrill of touching him for the first time, the hot hardness of him, that made me want to taste him and have him deep inside me and at the same time never take my hands off him.

I remembered him saying, 'Oh my God, I'm going to… Is it okay?' and thinking that if he stopped I would literally die, and how I wrapped my arms and legs around him as tightly as I could, his back slick with sweat underneath my thighs, pulling him closer and closer until it felt like our bodies would melt into each other like butter in a microwave, and feeling him tense and shudder and then suddenly go still again, at exactly the time I did. At the time, all I felt was bliss, and I wanted to hold onto that feeling forever. The night was still warm, and we lay next to each other, sweat sheening our bodies as our breathing gradually slowed. I didn't care how hot we were, I just wanted to be close to him. So I turned over and rested my head on his shoulder, and he wrapped his arm around me and we kissed again, and soon I felt desire surging in me once more as he ran his fingers lightly down my arm, up again over my ribs and around to my breast. He leaned up on one elbow and smiled at me in the near darkness, still touching me, and he said, 'You're so beautiful, Tansy. You always were the most beautiful girl I've ever seen.'

And I felt too shy to accept the compliment, but just giggled and said, 'You're not so bad yourself.'

And then we started to kiss each other again, and hardly said anything at all, apart from, 'Do you like it when I…' and 'Please, more.'

I'd thought, just a few months before, that I could never bear to have sex again with anyone who wasn't Renzo, but in those moments I didn't think of him at all, not once. It was as if he'd never even existed – as if no one else in the whole world did, apart from me and Josh. It was like everything outside my bed and our bodies had disappeared and there was only him and me and the pleasure and happiness that flooded over me.

I suppose at some point we must have fallen asleep, because the next memory I have is of the sun streaming in through the window, far brighter than the street lamp and warm already, even though it was only six in the morning. We'd pulled the duvet halfway over ourselves at some point, and our legs underneath it were nested together, fitting perfectly.

I turned over as carefully as I could so as not to wake him, and felt my face break out in a huge smile as I looked at him lying there, one long arm folded under the pillow, the other reaching out to pull me close. I kissed the hard swell of his shoulder, then tickled his cheek with my eyelashes until I saw his lips twitch in the beginnings of a smile and his eyes open, blurrily close to my own.

'Good morning,' I said.

'Hello.' He pulled me over on top of him, and I loved how strong his arms were, how his hair looked all messy and tousled on my pillow, how his cock sprang instantly erect when he touched me.

'How are you feeling?' he asked.

It hadn't occurred to me that by rights I ought to have the mother of all hangovers.

'I feel great,' I said, surprised.

'Me too. We dodged a bullet there.'

'Maybe we've found the secret to hangover prevention, which has eluded medical science for generations.'

'Maybe we have,' he said. 'It was certainly loads more fun than taking two paracetamol with a pint of water.'

'Much more fun.' I pushed the duvet back and looked at him. 'Shame one of us isn't feeling rough, or we could test whether it works as a cure, too.'

'But maybe the preventative effect will wear off,' he speculated. 'Perhaps we should have an extra dose, just in case.'

'That sounds like a sensible strategy,' I agreed, and then we didn't say anything more for a long time, because after we'd had sex we drifted off to sleep again, the sunshine warming our bodies like we were lying on a beach somewhere.

The sound of the door knocker woke me a couple of hours later, and Josh sat up next to me.

'Want me to get that?'

'Nah,' I said. 'It'll be the postie. If Adam isn't up he'll leave it next door. I should get up anyway, though.'

I needed to wee and clean my teeth, but I didn't say that to him. Daft as it sounds, even though we'd shared a house for the past two months, now that things between us were different I wanted him to perceive me as some sort of permanently fragrant sex goddess.

'I'll stick the kettle on,' Josh said. 'And I'm starving. Fancy a fry-up?'

I swung my legs over the edge of the bed and sat up. Suddenly, this gloriously sunny Saturday seemed replete with possibility. Josh and I would have breakfast together. Then we might have a shower together, and see where that led. And after that we could hang out in the park, where there would be baby geese and ducks and maybe even cygnets swimming on the lake. And I'd be able to enjoy it all with him, and maybe we'd talk about what had happened; maybe I'd explain to him that the way I felt about him, and about Renzo, had changed. Or maybe that was a conversation to have another day, and for now we could just bask in the newness and excitement of being together.

I imagined lying with him under a tree, my head in his lap while he stroked my hair, the leaves casting dappled shadows over our faces. I imagined walking with him hand in hand, stopping for ice creams somewhere, whiling the day away together until we drifted home and back to bed. At some point, we'd need to pop into the Daily Grind and pick up the pile of presents that were waiting there for me, and I'd open them slowly, one by one, saving his for last.

Maybe later on, I supposed, we'd have to talk about what had happened – not just in the past few weeks, but all those years before. But for now, I longed for the little happy bubble we were in to stay just how it was.

'That sounds…' I began, and then I paused. 'That sounds like Adam.'

We could hear feet pounding up the stairs, and Adam calling, 'Hey, Tans, you won't believe this.'

'Shit.' Josh and I looked at each other, starting to laugh. We were both stark naked, sat next to each other on my bed. There would be no hiding from Adam what we'd been up to. Together, quick as we could, we lay back down and pulled the duvet up to our chins, just as Adam burst into the room.

His arms were full of flowers.

'Look what came for you! Roses and… pink things.'

Then he stopped. His face froze with embarrassment and surprise, and then he grinned.

'Am I interrupting something?' he asked.

'Er, no, not at all,' I said.

'We were just getting up,' Josh said easily, with no trace of awkwardness. 'Want some breakfast?'

'Yes, sure, thanks.' Adam put the flowers down on the floor just inside the door and stepped away like they might bite him. Then he smiled again and said, 'So much for the fake boyfriend.'

As the door closed behind Adam, Josh and I turned to look at each other. I didn't know what to do with my face; my features felt all stiff and strange, like I'd put on one of my peel-off masks and left it too long. He'd gone all still, too; it was weird to see him not smiling.

'Fake boyfriend?'

'I… it was just a stupid thing. Because I wanted to… I thought I could…'

'I see where this is going.' Josh hadn't raised his voice, but it still felt like he was shouting at me. I pulled the duvet higher and shrank away to the very edge of the bed. 'You thought you could make your ex jealous. You used me to try and get him back. Even though he's dating your mate.'

'It's not like that,' I protested. 'Well, okay, it kind of was. But not any more. Not after last night. And even before that. I…'

'You led me on,' he said. 'You let me think there was something between us, that you had feelings for me. And last night – you let that happen, knowing none of it was real?'

'It was real,' I said in a small voice. 'It is real. It is now.'

Josh looked hard at me. 'I don't think so. Don't get me wrong, I've got nothing against casual sex, but I don't appreciate being lied to.'

I felt anger flare inside me, overwhelming the shame and panic. 'So, what I did isn't okay, but you watching those girls bully me at school, and that prank you played on me with them, and that vile text you sent, and then trying to trick me into going to the dance with you so you could make a fool of me somehow, in front of everyone, or have sex with me because you thought I was the town bike like everyone else did, that was absolutely fine, was it?'

He looked bemused. 'What the fuck are you even talking about?'

'You remember,' I said. 'Stop pretending you don't.'

'I remember I liked you. I had the most massive crush on you. I wanted to ask you out for ages, but you were seeing that creep Connor. And then when I found out me and Mum were moving to Australia, I thought I'd have one last chance to tell you how I felt. But you didn't feel the same.'

'But the things Anoushka and Kylie said about me, the way everyone treated me – you knew. And you did nothing.'

'So that's what this was all about, was it? Something some stupid, spiteful girls did to you back in high school years ago makes it okay to play mind games with me to try and take someone else's bloke off her? I don't even know what text you're on about. What prank? I never texted you. I didn't even have your number. I wished I'd had the guts to ask you for it but I never did. If that's the way your mind works, I feel sorry for you.' He pushed back the duvet and stood up. 'Guess a hangover wasn't the only bullet I dodged. I'm going for a run, and tonight I'm flying to Belfast for work.'

He picked up his clothes and walked out, closing the door hard behind him. I pulled my knees up to my chest and hugged them, my whole body feeling numb with shock. Looking at what had happened through his eyes made it all seem different. Maybe he hadn't been aware of what had gone on back then. Maybe he'd forgotten, or maybe he just hadn't known. Maybe he had liked me, and I'd been too isolated, scared and ashamed to realise it.

I waited until I heard the front door crash behind him and then I went to the bathroom. It felt like all my thoughts, the version of reality I'd held onto for so long, had been wiped away, and there was nothing new to replace it: my mind was completely blank.

On my way back to my room, I almost tripped over the flowers. Even though less than half an hour had passed since Adam brought them to me, I'd forgotten they were there.

A huge bunch of pale pink rosebuds and peonies, blowsy and delicate as a wedding dress. And a note with them that said, *I'm sorry. Can we talk? Love Renzo.*

They were the words I'd waited months and months for – words that I'd imagined reading, or hearing him say, and my heart soaring with hope and joy. So why wasn't it?

Chapter Twenty-Three

That Monday morning at work, Felicity completely blanked me. She didn't mention the party, or Renzo, or Josh, or anything at all. She just sat, staring at her screen, and occasionally she blew her nose.

'Are you okay?' I murmured at last, when the silence became too oppressive to endure any longer.

'I've got a cold,' she said.

To be totally honest, it didn't look like a cold to me. But there was nothing else I could say, and it wasn't like I didn't have my own problems to preoccupy me, so I worked on in silence. Well, when I say worked – I was mostly polishing my CV, getting it ready to send to the shortlist of potential new jobs I'd identified.

With Chelsea's dresses nearly finished and another order on its way to the lovely ladies at Stitch Together, Chelsea's business looked like it was getting on an even keel. Soon, she wouldn't need my mentorship any more – and if she did, I could offer it as a friend.

At lunchtime, desperate to escape the atmosphere in the office, which was almost as toxic as the time Kris came in wearing Poison Girl perfume, I got up and reached for my bag. Felicity asked if I was going out, and I was tempted to reply sarcastically that I was just going to do a spot of mindful meditation under my desk, but I refrained.

'Yes,' I said. 'It's lovely out. No point festering in here.'

'Mind if I join you?'

I was torn between relief that she had apparently thawed, and annoyance that my chance to get some longed-for time alone to clear my head had been snatched away.

'Of course not.'

'Shall we grab some food somewhere?'

'Sure,' I said, although I was mentally rolling my eyes at the prospect of her demanding to know how many grams of carbs there were in everything and texting photos of her food to Fidel on her phone.

But she said, 'Let's go to Patty and Bun.'

'Patty and Bun?' I parroted, stopping in my tracks. But she was already striding off towards the lift, so I followed obediently. It was just as well I was close on her heels, because even though said heels were five-inch platforms, Felicity power-walked all the way to Old Compton Street like she'd been told the Selfridges sale was about to start and she was going to be first in line if it killed her, apparently not noticing the blazing heat. Even if I'd known what to say to her, I wouldn't have been able to speak; I just panted along in her wake, sweat snaking down my back.

'Table for two, please,' she said, fixing the waiter with a stare that quite clearly conveyed that if one wasn't provided immediately, there would be hell to pay.

'Let me just check what we have available.'

'That one right there will do,' Felicity said, gesturing towards a booth for four. Magically, like a conjuring trick, a twenty-pound note appeared and passed with amazing sleight of hand from her to him. She smiled dazzlingly.

'Of course, madam.'

Seconds later, a waitress appeared, presumably alerted by her colleague to the prospect of untold riches – or at least a larger than usual tip – if she did what the slightly demented woman in the lilac suede dungarees wanted.

'What can I get for you ladies?'

'I'll have a cheeseburger, please,' I said. 'And a Diet Coke.'

'Same, with a double patty and extra bacon,' Felicity said. 'And we'll share pickle fries and cheese balls, and I'll have a triple chocolate malt. And a carafe of tap water, please.'

She smiled again at the waitress, who scurried away, notepad in hand.

Then she looked at me and said, 'So.'

'I take it you and Fidel are on a break,' I said cautiously.

'Break, shmeak. I dumped the fucker.'

'Really? But you were so committed.'

'Yeah, I was committed to Renzo, too. But I dumped him as well, this morning, right after I told Fidel where he could shove his ketogenic omelettes and power burpees.'

I had absolutely no idea how to respond to this, but I was momentarily saved by the arrival of my Diet Coke and Felicity's milkshake. She stuck the straw deep into the glass – with some difficulty, triple-thick being exactly what it said on the tin – and sucked hard, her cheeks hollowing.

'He's still in love with you, you know.'

Just a few days before, that revelation would have made me feel giddy with ecstasy. Now, the knowledge of what I'd done to Josh and what I'd been prepared to do to Felicity herself meant that my relief was soured, tainted by guilt.

'What makes you think that?'

'He never stopped being,' Felicity said. 'It was pretty fucking obvious from the start, if only I'd been able to see past my own nose. When he first asked me out, I should have realised that he was doing it to keep tabs on you.'

'To keep…?'

'Sure.' The waitress brought greaseproof-paper-lined baskets of deep-fried things to our table and Felicity sprinkled salt liberally over everything without asking me if I minded. 'And he kept talking about you. Tansy this, Tansy that. "When I was in Paris with Tansy…" Made me feel just fabulous, that did.'

'I'm sorry,' I said, picking up a deep-fried cheese ball and biting into it. Felicity hadn't been wrong about the salt.

'Yeah, well, it serves me right, I suppose. I should never have gone after your bloke, even if he was your ex. It was a vile thing to do.'

I ate the rest of my cheese ball.

'It wasn't, though, because I wasn't straight with you about how things ended between us,' I said. 'I told you it was mutual, but it wasn't really.'

'No, I figured that out,' Felicity said. 'And I should have kicked him to the kerb when I did. But, you know, Renzo is Renzo. Hard to resist, even when he's calling you someone else's name right when he shoots his load.'

'Oh, no.' I put a pickle fry back in the basket, untasted. 'He didn't.'

'He did,' Felicity confirmed, dipping a cheese ball in mayonnaise and eating it. 'And then there were the other things he said, that weren't in the heat of passion. "Tansy had a dress a bit like that, but it looked different on her." "Going out to restaurants with you is different. Tansy never enjoyed her food so much." "Sorry, I forgot to put milk in your coffee. Tansy has hers black."'

The waitress brought our burgers. Cheese was oozing out of the sides of them both, but Felicity's was twice the height of mine and had shards of crispy bacon sticking out of its edges. I cut mine in half and then cut one bit in half again, took a bite and put it back down. Felicity picked hers up with both hands and started to devour it with relish – or with extra mayo and ketchup, at any rate.

'And then he mentioned Fidel to me,' she went on, swallowing. 'He said all the women at work use him, and they've had "amazing results".'

'Charlotte didn't,' I said, remembering how comfortable my ex-housemate had been in her own skin, how casually she'd suggested ordering a pizza or a curry, because that was what you did when you were hungry. How ashamed I'd felt when she walked in on me eating Pringles out of the tin, as if she'd caught me having a wank or something. 'She just got on with it. Ate what she wanted, and looked fabulous. Like you.'

Felicity put her half-eaten burger down, sucked a bit more of her milkshake and ate a pickle fry.

'You know what?' she said. 'I'm no feminist. I wax my minge and everything. But I've always said there's no fucking way I'm buying into body fascism, and starving myself to be a shape that's not the way I naturally am.'

'But why would you, anyway?' I asked. 'You're stunning. You're totally knock-out gorgeous just the way you are. No wonder Renzo fancied you.'

She took another bite of her burger, and I picked up one of the bits of mine and finished it.

'That's what I thought,' she said. 'I mean, I don't want to sound vain or anything, but I know I scrub up okay. And when Pru and I go out, neither of us cares that she's a size eight and I'm a size fourteen – it's just how we are. But dating Renzo changed that. I felt like I was heading somewhere I didn't want to be. He made me feel differently about myself.'

'If that was because of me, I'm genuinely sorry,' I said. 'But I didn't know. I thought he hated me, even though I'm – I was – still in love with him.'

'I could feel it creeping up on me,' she said thoughtfully, almost as if I wasn't there at all. 'It was horrible. Sending my weight every day to Fidel, and feeling as if he was judging me. Well, of course he fucking was, that's what I was paying him to do. But suddenly I wasn't feeling okay about myself any more. I was feeling downright shitty. And it wasn't Fidel making me feel that way. It was Renzo. So, even if he wasn't still hung up on you, he'd have had to go. No man is worth that. If things don't work out with your musician fellow, who I have to say is extremely tasty, you're welcome to Renzo. Assuming you still want him.'

I sipped my Diet Coke. *I've wanted him for months! Of course I still do! I do, right?*

'You're each other's type,' Felicity carried on calmly. 'Or at least, you've got what each other wants. You're arm candy, Tans. I know there's so much more to you, but if you want a bloke like him – not *him*, necessarily, there are loads of them out there – basically all you have to do is be there. I mean, come on.'

Feeling pathetically needy, I asked, 'What do you mean?'

'Tansy! For God's sake. Have you looked in a mirror lately? You're tall. You're blonde. You're slim as fuck. You've got blue eyes and perfect skin and legs up to here and you do it all without even trying. You've got the currency, honey. You can use it to get Renzo. Or a Renzo.'

I looked down at my burger, and suddenly it went all blurry. Two massive tears splashed down onto it, soaking into the glossy surface of the bun.

'What? What did I say?'

'I do try,' I said, looking up at her and mopping my eyes on a wad of paper napkins. 'Seriously. I get on the scales every fucking day, and every day, no matter what it says, I feel rubbish. If I've gained a pound, I panic about getting fat. If I lose a pound, I panic that I'm getting obsessive about restricting again, like I did when I was at school. I'm kind of okay now. I guess I've got used to it so it's just background noise. But it's there in my head, all the time. How many calories I'm eating – whether it's Pringles or sliced fucking cucumber, I count them just the same – how many inches around my waist measures, how my bones feel. It's bloody knackering. And I look at someone like you and I feel so jealous that you don't have to care and think about it all the time. I lie awake at night, worrying about my body. It's stupid, but I do. Some people worry about Brexit, or the war in Syria, or climate change or whatever. Big things that are actually important. I worry about whether the woman at the till in Sainsbury's judged me because I bought a packet of biscuits.'

Felicity had listened intently to my whole speech – or rant, more like – while she finished her lunch. When I stopped talking, she wiped her lips and put her knife and fork carefully together on her plate, although she hadn't used them.

'I'm sorry,' she said. 'I had no idea. I should have guessed – I was at boarding school, after all. Half the girls practically did GCSEs in how to have an eating disorder. I don't know why I never thought that you were struggling.'

'I guess I hide it well.' I shrugged. 'I've had lots of practice. And anyway, like I said, it's not nearly so bad now.'

'Still, though. That's not cool, Tansy.'

'I know,' I said. 'It's not cool at all. And it's time I did something about it.'

We paid the bill – actually, I did, although Felicity tried to insist that she should – and we walked together back to the office, not hurrying and not talking, just elbow to elbow, companionably silent, thinking our own thoughts.

Chapter Twenty-Four

The next week, I took Monday and Tuesday off work. I had two job interviews, which I didn't want Barri to get even a hint of; my financial situation was still so delicate that being pushed out of Luxeforless before I could jump in somewhere new would have been a disaster. And Barri, I knew, would have no qualms about sacking me if he got so much as a hint of disloyalty.

When I was leaving the house on Monday morning, dressed for the first of my interviews in my one and only suit, my hair in what I hoped was a professional-looking up-do, I almost literally bumped into Josh. Just as I was raising my hand to open the front door, I heard a key in the lock and stepped back, narrowly avoiding being smacked in the face by two inches of solid hardwood.

What was it about him, I thought, that he couldn't go from place to place like a normal person, but had to crash about everywhere? Underneath my grumpiness, though, was a pang of sadness – almost a sense of loss. A feeling that all those things about Josh I'd got used to, come to know and like, I somehow had no business liking any more. He wasn't wearing his shorts and trainers, to my surprise, but was in jeans and a checked shirt. His hair was sticking out at odd angles and he looked knackered, like he'd been up all night.

We stood facing each other in the doorway for a second, then I said, 'Sorry,' and stepped back into the hallway.

'Excuse me,' he said, and we edged past each other, leaving as much space as possible between us. There was none of the easy friendship that had begun to develop between us; none of the mild flirtation there'd been in the lead-up to our night together that had been so blissful and had ended so horribly. There was only awkwardness and coldness, and it made the distance between me and him feel much, much greater than the width of our narrow hallway.

He dumped his bag – a large-ish one, although not the enormous backpack I'd seen when he arrived – at the foot of the stairs, then went into the kitchen, and I heard the hum of the coffee machine.

I waited a moment, torn between going back inside and trying to talk to him, and the knowledge that, if I did, I'd be late for my interview. The interview won – if we were going to talk, it should be when we didn't have to rush, when we had all the time we needed to explain and hear each other out.

But then, when I got home that afternoon, he was out again, and when I didn't see him at all the next day, I realised he must be avoiding me. So I began to avoid him, too.

In the evenings, I went round to Chelsea's mum's place with my laptop and perched in the sewing room while Chelsea worked, admiring the ingenuity with which she adjusted the design of her dresses as she went along so every scrap of precious fabric was used. The sewing machine was mostly silent now; she was spending less time sewing and more time designing, planning and thinking, which was exactly as it should be.

I, meanwhile, was fleshing out the business plan I'd started for her, developing projections for her autumn/winter collection and the following spring/summer. If – and it was a massive if – the dresses continued to sell as they had been, she had the beginnings of something that could be a medium-term success, and perhaps even more than that.

Nathan had volunteered to act as courier on his moped, ferrying the pieces of fabric and the finished garments between Hackney and Canning Town, where Stitch Together was based, and was spending less time hanging around with his dodgy mates as a result. Optimistically, I factored a wage for him into my calculations of Chelsea's overheads. I couldn't carry on paying him in pizza and fried chicken indefinitely, anyway – Nathan, like Josh, ate like a horse and it was costing me a fortune.

Josh.

I hadn't had a chance to even sit down and have a coffee with him, and try to explain why I'd behaved the way I did. My explanation was a valid one, I thought, even though I wasn't proud of what I'd done. The way he treated me back at school – well, everyone knows it's petty to bear a grudge, but who can honestly say they've never borne one? I wanted to ask him that question, and others, too. He said he hadn't sent that text, but he must surely have known about it. Had he imagined me waiting there, all alone, outside the cinema for more than half an hour (or half an eternity, it had felt like)? Had he wondered how I was feeling: how foolish and friendless? Did he know that I'd run straight up the stairs to my bedroom in floods of tears when I got home, and stayed there for the rest of the weekend? Did he know how much courage it had taken for me to show my face at school the following Monday?

I was sure that the Josh I knew would hear me out, would realise that emotional wounds so deep don't heal quickly or easily. He'd understand that, in my desperation to get Renzo back, he had seemed like a convenient solution, and that, when my feelings for him began to change, it was too late to change the plan I'd put into action – because, after all, if he didn't know he'd been my fake boyfriend, how could I have told him when it suddenly started to feel real?

And then there was Renzo. The biggest barrier to our getting back together – that he refused to entertain the idea – had apparently been removed. He'd said he was sorry. And the other barrier – Felicity – was gone too. I turned all the different puzzle pieces of my life and my feelings over and over in my head, trying to get them to fit together in a way that made sense. But I couldn't. I knew I needed to speak to Renzo, and part of me longed for the moment when I'd see his face and hear him say in person the words he'd written to me: *I'm sorry.*

I'd thought about texting him to thank him for the flowers, then realised I couldn't – I'd deleted his number from my phone back in January to stop myself sending desperate late-night messages to him. So instead I'd emailed, and immediately received an out-of-office reply saying that he was working away for two weeks, travelling between Hong Kong, Singapore and Tokyo, and might therefore be delayed in responding to my message.

He hadn't been delayed responding to me, though. A few minutes after I sent it, he replied.

I'm glad you liked them. Let's meet up as soon as I'm back in London. Love, R.

shoeboxes and piles of sealed plastic-wrapped parcels threatening
to slide to the floor at the slightest touch were everywhere.

But I didn't need to rummage through it all. I saw straight away
what I was looking for, right at the front of one of the garment
rails, and unwrapped.

There were three dresses, each in a different colourway: one
charcoal, grey and silver; one peacock blue, cerise and lilac; one
saffron, tangerine and peridot green. They were all the same
design, though: pieces of mismatched fabric sewn together to form
a harmonious pattern, cut on the bias with shoestring straps that
laced down the back.

They were gorgeous. But I hadn't ordered them. And, more to
the point, they were blatant, near-exact copies of the dress Chelsea
had made me, which I'd worn out to Home House with Felicity
and Pru. That dress was unique, of course, made just for me. These
were the prototypes of what would be a production run, presumably
identical. Instead of recycled fabric, they'd be made from bolts of
polyester, designed, ordered and dyed to our specification.

But whose specification, exactly? Who the hell had done this?

I heard the ping of the lift behind me and flinched, feeling as
guilty as I had back in March, when I'd sneaked into the office to
pick up those other dresses, the unwanted, delayed ones made by
Guillermo Hernandez, to send to Mum to sell. Then, I'd known
deep down I was doing something… not immoral, exactly, but
certainly dubious. Now, though, I was just doing my job.

Only someone else appeared to have been doing it, too.

I heard the ring of heels on the marble tiles outside and turned
around. Felicity stood in the doorway. She was wearing a tailored,

sand-coloured shorts suit over a neon-green crop top and nude shoe boots with heels so high I knew she must have got a cab to work. Actually, the suit itself told me that – if I'd worn a lined jacket on the Tube that morning, it would have been a soggy, limp rag by now.

She still had her sunglasses on, but I could see her looking at the dresses on the rail, and then at me.

'Shit,' she said. 'They're here.'

'You knew about this?'

She hesitated, then nodded.

'Felicity, was this your idea? Ripping off the designs of a young girl who's just starting out, who's got nothing – literally fuck all – going for her except talent and people who believe in her? Because if it was… Well, I think that's a crappy thing to do.'

I'd meant to sound all assertive – aggressive, even – but somehow I couldn't manage it. Suddenly, I just felt tired and defeated, thinking of all the work Chelsea, her mum and brother – not to mention the lovely refugee women who'd worked so hard, fuelled by chatter and endless cups of tea – had done to try and make her fledgling business succeed. And now, thanks to buying power and marketing clout and a manufacturer who, while he treated his workers well and paid them fairly, was able to undercut just about anyone, it was all for nothing.

I reached out and rubbed the polyester fabric between my fingers.

'How much are these things retailing for, anyway?'

'A hundred and fifty quid,' Felicity said.

About half what Chelsea charged for one of her original creations, and they'd have cost about five per cent as much to produce. Suddenly, the business plan I'd laboured over looked like a silly work of fiction. If you abandoned the whole idea – the whole *point* – of Chelsea's work, that she made unique garments from repurposed material, all one-offs, all special and sustainable, then of course there were generous profits to be made. But it was nothing to do with her vision, her passion or her purpose – it was just a tacky, mass-produced knock-off of her designs.

Looking at that dress, a cheap parody of the one I'd been given, and loved, and worn when I kissed Josh, I suddenly felt sick with shame and disillusionment about the job I thought I loved.

'Right. As soon as Lisa gets in, I'm handing in my notice. I've been looking for another job anyway, but I'm done here.'

Felicity pushed her shades up onto her head. Her eyes were wide and alarmed, even more so than her fluttery lash extensions made them look anyway.

'Don't do that, Tansy.'

'Why not? I've been ignoring my morals and my instincts for too long in this place. The sweatshop thing back in January, the way Barri treats us – it's too much. It's toxic. I'm out.'

'Seriously,' Felicity said. 'Don't do it. Not yet, anyway. Please? Just wait a week.'

I took a deep breath, biting back the surge of anger and hurt that threatened to overwhelm me. In a week's time, I might have heard back from the two companies who'd interviewed me: the Kensington boutique that sold utterly adorable, ridiculously expensive designer clothes for kids, or the online fast-fashion retailer that was looking for a workwear buyer. Both looked like good options on paper, although realistically they'd come with problems of their own. I realised that I'd secretly been hoping to find a way to work with

Chelsea longer-term, building her business up into the major label I'd believed it could become. But now, that ship had sailed.

And then something else occurred to me.

'Wait, you knew this was happening. Why didn't you say anything to me?'

'I'm sorry,' Felicity said. 'Honestly, I am. But I couldn't. I'm not supposed to know about it myself. I had nothing to do with it, I promise. I just found out.'

'You found out? How?'

'It doesn't matter.'

She was looking shifty, I thought, no longer meeting my eyes. And I remembered again the time I'd come into the office that Sunday evening, and how I'd seen Felicity there. I'd never asked her about it, because it would have meant telling her that I'd been there myself, and why.

'Felicity! Of course it matters. Look, I saw you here. On a Sunday night, back in February. I'd come into the office for... something, and I saw you coming out of Barri's office. What were you doing here?'

'What were *you* doing here?' she shot back.

We stood there, glaring at each other. For a second, I thought about demanding that she tell me first. But that seemed childish and petty. Then I thought of making something up – *I was picking up some samples for a shoot*, I could say. Or, *I thought I left my phone in the office*.

'I asked you first,' I insisted.

Felicity looked shifty for a second, and then she said, 'I left my phone in the office.'

I didn't believe her for a second, especially as she'd told me the very same lie I'd been planning to tell her. But I was done with that. I was done with lying, and with a load of other things too. I'd already made up my mind about that. I'd already booked a train ticket, to have a face-to-face conversation that was going to cause me more pain than anything Felicity could say or think about me.

So I told her the truth.

But a fat lot of good it did me. She said, 'Oh, Tansy. You poor love. That must be so hard. And Barri was shitty about it? You mustn't feel bad. Samples walk all the bloody time in this business. It wasn't just you, anyway. I happen to know that Barri had that exact same conversation with at least five other people. He's not going to sack everyone, is he?'

'How do you know? How do you know all this stuff?'

'I can't tell you,' she said. 'I really can't. But you'll find out really soon. Please just trust me?'

I wasn't sure whether I did. But, for now, I had no alternative.

*

This time, when I got off the train at Truro, Mum wasn't there to meet me. Her message had said only how lovely it would be to see me, and did I mind getting a bus from the station. But I'd just missed one and there wasn't another for half an hour, so I walked instead, along the high street where Debbie's shop used to be, past my old school, past the park where Josh and his friends used to hang out and the fields beyond it where I'd gone with Connor, past Mr Nabi's shop, where I stopped to buy a bottle of wine for Mum.

It all looked familiar, but different too: smaller, the way places you remember from childhood always do. It hadn't really changed – even the displays of chewing gum, sweets and newspapers in front of Mr Nabi's counter were the same, although his handsome son, who I remembered as a teenage boy, was a positively fanciable young man now, and told me he was married with two kids. I supposed, like him, I'd changed, grown up a bit.

The street where Mum and Dad lived was slightly shabbier than I remembered, the paint peeling off the fronts of the houses, an old washing machine dumped in a front yard, grubby net curtains draped in an equally grubby window. Weeds were growing through cracks in the pavement outside their house, and I remembered how Mum always used to take pride in how tidy her house looked, inside and out. I guessed she didn't have much time for weeding now, with all the extra shifts she was working, and I felt the weight of guilt I was carrying grow even heavier.

I fitted my key into the lock and pushed open the door, calling out a greeting. The house was spotless inside, at least, and the smell of roasting chicken filled the air.

'Hello, love.' Mum hurried through to meet me, her familiar zebra-striped apron tied over her jeans. She'd changed her hair, I noticed with a jolt of shock: it had always been mahogany brown, sometimes with plum or aubergine-coloured lowlights in it when she was feeling daring, but now it was dusty blonde, the roots showing, undyed.

'New hair,' I said, hugging her.

'It's meant to hide the grey better,' she sighed. 'But it doesn't really, does it? I'm thinking I might just have to embrace my age and let it grow out. Come on through.'

I followed her and sat in my familiar place at the kitchen table, resting my elbows on the familiar oilcloth, its pattern of bright jungle leaves faded where the sunlight from the window fell on it. The seascape Mum had painted when we first moved to Cornwall hung above the table as it always had, and I remembered sadly how confident she'd been that she'd paint more like it, and sell them, and eventually maybe open a little gallery. But of course she never had.

'It's just you and me for lunch,' she said. 'But I roasted a chicken, anyway. It'll do for sandwiches for your dad's supper, and I can make soup tomorrow.'

'I brought a bottle of Sancerre,' I said. 'And some of that coffee you like from the Daily Grind.'

I didn't ask where Dad was; there was no point.

'I didn't see your car outside. Has it gone in to have the gearbox fixed again?' I asked.

Mum shook her head, and I knew what she was going to say before she said it.

'I've been managing all right walking to work. It's only four miles, and when the weather gets worse there's always the bus. For now I'm telling myself the exercise will do me good. Sandy at work gave me her old Fitbit and I'm averaging seventeen thousand steps a day – it's really addictive! And that old banger was costing more in repairs each time, it just wasn't sustainable any more. Besides, think how much lower my carbon emissions are now.'

Mum's carbon emissions had never exactly been astronomical, I thought, imagining with a pang how her ten-hour working days would now increase to twelve or more, and what it would be like for her walking home at three in the morning after a late shift.

'Can I give you a hand with that?' I asked, as Mum took a head of broccoli out of the fridge and started chopping.

'You could check the spuds,' she said, and I opened the oven door and shook the pan of perfect, crisp roast potatoes. Mum would never dream of using Aunt Bessie's.

'It's too hot for gravy, really,' she said. 'But I thought, why the hell not? Since you were coming all this way just for Sunday lunch.'

She glanced at me sideways, past the curtain of her hair, which looked as parched as straw. I wondered if she thought I'd come with exciting, happy news – I'd been promoted, I'd met A Man, I'd won the lottery and none of us would have to worry about money ever again – and I wished that was the case.

'I've been so busy,' I said feebly. 'I just had a free day, and I haven't seen you for ages, and I thought I'd go for it. I wish I could stay longer, but work's so frantic at the moment.'

And Barri's narky as hell, and if I don't jump soon I'm likely to get pushed, so any time off I take needs to be time spent going to job interviews, otherwise you won't be the only one trying to work out how the hell to pay the rent, I thought.

Mum didn't interrogate me; that wasn't her way. She'd wait until I said what I'd come to say, I knew, dreading having to say it more with every moment that passed.

'We won't waste your nice wine on the gravy,' she said. 'There's an ancient bottle of vermouth in the cupboard under the telly that'll do, with some of the broccoli water and a bit of stock powder.'

I fetched the things she'd asked for without actually asking, tipped the potatoes into a serving dish and poured wine for us both.

While she carved the chicken, I drained the broccoli and took the tray of garlicky butternut squash out of the oven.

'This all looks amazing, Mum,' I said. 'You didn't have to make such an effort. I'd have been happy with toast and jam.'

'Toast and jam and Sancerre,' she said, smiling. 'Is that a thing now, in fancy London restaurants? Is jam the new avocado?'

'According to BuzzFeed, pineapple's the new avocado,' I said, as we sat down and Mum pushed the platter of chicken across the table to me. 'Not sure it would work on toast, though.'

While we ate, she asked me about things that didn't really matter: whether it was worth buying the bargain leopard-print coat she'd spotted in the Oxfam shop, or whether leopard was going to be a single-season trend. (I assured her it was a classic in neutral colours, but in pink or turquoise would look totally 2018 in six months' time.) How Debbie's boy was enjoying London. (I swerved that question by saying that Josh was back in Belfast for a few days, cringing at the memory of him storming out of my bedroom after we'd spent the night together, and how he'd totally blanked me since on the couple of occasions we'd happened to be in the kitchen at the same time.) How Perdita's little Calum was having a growth spurt and keeping the whole house up at night, and Ryan had taken them all off to soft play today so my sister could catch up on sleep, which was why she hadn't joined us.

'I've got some ice cream,' Mum said. 'And there's chocolate sauce in the pan on the hob. Will you heat it up while I clear this away?'

I nodded. It felt like I had run out of things to talk about, apart from the really important thing I'd made the four-hour train journey from London to say, and was going to return home having said.

I sparked up the gas under the pan and stirred the thick brown gunk – the recipe Mum had got from her own granny, with margarine, cocoa powder, golden syrup and brown sugar, which by rights should be properly minging but totally worked – until it became runny and hot.

And then, still stirring, I said, 'Mum, you know how I've been sending you money? And the clothes and stuff I sent for you to sell?'

'Sure, love,' she said. 'And you know how grateful I am that you do it.'

I thought, *I'd rather tip this whole pan of boiling sugar over my head than say this*. But I said it anyway.

'I can't any more.'

Mum took a tub of ice cream out of the freezer and put it on the table with two bowls and two spoons. I kept stirring.

'That's all right, love. We'll manage.'

I turned away from the cooker and looked at her. It felt like we were looking at each other properly for the first time that day – maybe for the first time in a long while.

'Mum,' I said. 'Please just listen to me for a second. I got into massive shit at work about the samples. I didn't know it wasn't allowed, but if I'd actually asked if it was okay to send them to you to sell, I know what they'd have said. So I never asked. I just did it. And I've maxed out all my credit cards on just living – okay, I've been stupid and extravagant, but anyone my age should be able to be a bit stupid and extravagant without having to worry about paying their parents' rent. I've ended up doing things I regret, to help you and Dad. And I've always wanted to help, you know that, but I can't any more. I'd lose my job. And really, was I even helping?'

Mum nodded again, quite calmly, and she said, 'It's okay, Tansy. You don't have to do anything you don't want to do.'

She'd scooped ice cream into our bowls, and I poured the chocolate sauce into the jug and put it on the table.

'It's not that I don't want to. Of course I want to. I'd do anything at all if I thought it would really help. But come on. Let's say I married Renzo. Let's say I could give you thousands of pounds a month and not notice. Would that really help? Would it?'

Mum poured chocolate sauce onto her ice cream. It hardened immediately into the consistency of toffee, and I knew I'd boiled it too long. I added some to my own bowl anyway.

'Mum,' I said. 'Whatever you do, and whatever I do, Dad's just going to carry on pissing money away. I don't mind giving every spare penny I have to you, but I do mind giving it to Ladbrokes, or Paddy Power, or Jack Fortune round the corner. I can't go on like this. It's not making me happy, and I don't think you're happy either. I know you're not.'

Mum picked up her spoon, but a huge sheet of chocolate gloop came with it, so she put it down again. I didn't even bother trying to eat anything more.

'Okay, Tansy,' she replied. 'I won't expect anything more from you again. I understand. I appreciate everything you've done, and I love you.'

'I love you too, Mum.' I knew it was true, and I knew she believed me. But really, what use was my love to her? Love wasn't going to pay the rent, or make Dad change his ways. I felt like I'd come to the end of a long, difficult road, but the destination I'd reached was a horrible place where I realised I didn't want to be after all.

The sunny kitchen, full of the smells of cooking and silent except for a blackbird singing his head off outside the window, felt suddenly stifling and oppressive, and all I wanted to do was leave. I glanced at my phone and saw that the last train to London left in half an hour. I picked up my bag, gave Mum a quick hug and said goodbye, and hurried back past all the familiar places to the station. All the way back home, I kept crying and thinking about how I'd ruined the special chocolate sauce.

The Third Last Date

'But what am I going to wear?' I sat bolt upright in Renzo's bed, pushing my tangled hair away from my face.

'I don't know,' he said. 'Something. A dress. The one you had on yesterday was fine.'

I didn't point out that what I'd had on yesterday hadn't been a dress at all, but the midi-skirt and jumper I'd worn to the office, and that even if it had been, the jumper was cashmere and would have to be dry-cleaned before I could wear it again.

Renzo looked at his phone. 'Tommy says we're meeting at twelve. It's nine now, you've got plenty of time. Go to the shops and buy something if you need to.'

I swung my feet reluctantly onto the floor and stood up. I'd kind of been looking forward to a quiet day in the flat, just the two of us. But Renzo had come back from an early-morning session at the gym and casually told me that we were off to Ascot to see his friend's horse run its first race over hurdles.

Horse racing? Gambling? The idea made a whole host of doubts spring up in my mind, but I had no chance to voice them.

'It pulled a ligament, or something,' Renzo had said. 'The trainer wasn't sure it would be fit, so Tommy didn't arrange anything, but now it's all going ahead. There'll be about twenty of us and he's booked a box. He got a great deal at such short notice.'

I'd met friends of Renzo's before, on nights out, shouting over cocktails or dancing in nightclubs. But this felt different – kind of formal. It was like I'd been told I was going to be a guest at a wedding with only four hours' notice. Okay, maybe you're the kind of person who'd react to an invitation like that casually and happily, slapping on some make-up and finding an outfit in your wardrobe that would do – because, after all, it was about the happy couple, not you, and no one would remember or care what you looked like.

If that sounds like you, I envy you from the bottom of my heart. Because I'm not like that. This would be the first time I'd meet a group of Renzo's friends – and their other halves – en masse. Even more than not wanting to show myself up, I didn't want to let him down. If I asked him what the other women would be wearing, he'd shrug and say he didn't know. But I knew. I knew that all his mates' girlfriends or wives would have only to glance in their wardrobes, rifle through a few things and go, 'This is my November race day outfit. I'll wear this.'

That's if they hadn't had enough advance notice to get their personal shopper to do the job for them, who knew exactly what was expected. I didn't. I could tell Maje from Marc Jacobs at a glance, but that was no help to me now, when I needed to fit in rather than stand out.

'Here you go, *fragolina*,' he flicked a credit card at me. Not the black Amex one, one of the others. 'I think you look beautiful whatever you wear, but what do I know about fashion? There are loads of shops on the high street. Treat yourself to something nice. The PIN's seven-three-nine-six.'

'Thank you,' I said, thinking for the millionth time how lucky I was to have a boyfriend who was so generous and so kind. Half an hour later I was dashing out of Zara with a wine-coloured jumper dress that looked like it had cost far more than forty pounds and, more to the point, would go with the taupe boots and camel-coloured coat I'd worn the day before.

I dressed quickly, did my face at top speed and put my hair up, because there was no time to wash it, and I was ready only a few minutes after Renzo had started to pace up and down the living room looking at his watch.

In the end, of course, we weren't late at all, because as soon as we hit the motorway Renzo put his foot down and his lime-green Lamborghini shot forward like it, too, was a horse in its maiden race. I spent the journey with my toes pressed hard against the footwell, trying not to close my eyes as he weaved through the traffic, occasionally swearing at drivers who were inconsiderate enough to stay within the speed limit.

By twelve o'clock we were all assembled in the plush private box, and waitresses with trays of champagne and canapés were circulating. I'd been introduced to everyone and promptly forgotten all their names. The men had gravitated together on one side of the room and were talking about work; I gathered that Tommy, the host, had been Renzo's boss in his previous job, and the others were all connected through the same world. I longed to stick close to Renzo's side, but the conversation so obviously excluded me that I drifted away to the group of women, collecting a fresh glass of fizz on my way.

They were all slim, all beautiful and all wearing the kind of expensively tailored dresses you see Kate Middleton in when she's going to a wedding and there's a nip in the air. On the rack where we'd left our coats, there were at least two that I was sure were real fur.

Shyly, I hovered on the outskirts of the group.

'So Georgie started at Dulwich in September,' one of them was saying. 'He's thriving there. Honestly, it's not just strong academically – which is so important because Andrew's set his heart on Eton for him – but the pastoral care is wonderful, too, and of course it's that bit more diverse than many prep schools.'

'How lovely to be able to have him at home, too,' one of the other women sighed. 'With Martin and I dividing our time between London and Hong Kong we more or less had to send Cressida to boarding school. But she's always been such a sociable child – honestly, the life and soul of the party – that she's settled in so well I swear she was begging to go back this summer, even though we were staying at our place in Cap d'Antibes, which she adores.'

'And how's your new nanny getting on, Emma? When you came for supper last time she'd just started with you, I think?'

'Lucia's great. We love her and so do the kids. But we found she just wasn't able to give them quite the level of enrichment we'd hoped for, so we've engaged a tutor three evenings a week and on Saturdays, a lovely boy who's doing his PhD at King's. They're all off to the Science Museum today. Benedict's an astrophysicist, and he's taught them so much. Perry was explaining the theory of bouncing cosmology to me the other day and, I have to admit, he completely lost me.'

'Very impressive for a six-year-old,' laughed one of the other women. 'And how do you know Renzo?'

Since I'd been entirely ignored until that point, it took me a moment to realise she was talking to me. I muttered something about how we'd met through my housemate, but then one of the other women cut in.

'We simply can't make up our minds about Tonbridge versus Benenden for Miranda and we literally have to make a decision within a month or two, because we're relocating to Kent anyway to make Paul's commute to the Paris office easier. I wonder what you girls all think?'

I felt myself blushing like an idiot, feeling hideously out of place among these women, none of whom looked old enough to have had children but clearly were, and was relieved when people started to drift towards the table. I prayed that Renzo hadn't seen me standing there like a lemon with nothing to say for myself, instead of being all witty and charming, at the centre of an intelligent conversation, the way I wanted him to think of me.

Maybe I could sit next to him at lunch, I thought. At least he'd talk to me. But I was directed to a seat between a man called Matthew, who immediately turned to the woman on his right and started talking about whether it was sensible to buy property in France now or wait until after Brexit, and a man called Martin.

I gulped some of the white wine that had been poured into my glass, expecting him to ignore me, too. But he didn't.

'So what do you fancy for the third race, Tansy?' he asked kindly, picking up a printed, cream-coloured booklet from next to his plate. 'Tommy's horse is number four, Wingman, see? There he is, with the pink and yellow colours.'

'Yes,' I said, picking up my knife and fork to eat my smoked salmon as I cast my eye down the list of names. Bagatelle, Shirley's Lost, Charming Cousin, Finchcock – all with their jockeys' colours printed next to them and the data explaining their form below.

'A fiver on Charming Cousin, maybe?' Martin twinkled at me. 'It's at five to one on. That means if he won you'd get your original stake back plus another pound.'

Thanks to Dad, I'd never bet on anything in my life, ever. I'd never even bought a Lotto ticket. It felt like putting my foot on a slope down which I might too easily slip. But also thanks to Dad, I'd acquired a knowledge of horse-racing form, and handicapping, and how the whole rigged system worked, almost by osmosis and certainly against my will. Now, the little rows of numbers and statistics felt as familiar and understandable as one of my spreadsheets at work.

And besides, emboldened by wine, I was suddenly resentful at being ignored by the women and now mansplained to by Martin.

I leaned over his racecard and said, 'Number three's carrying more weight than she's used to, and the going's heavy. Charming Cousin's the favourite but he's got an outside draw and will struggle to make up ground over the distance. Number nine is having her first run over fences, too, so she's at long odds and the handicapper's been kind to her. But look at her breeding, and her trainer, and her record on the flat. She's a stayer, and likes the wet. I'd go for her to win, and Tommy's horse each way.'

Martin barked with surprised laughter. 'You talk a good game. Let's see if you deliver.'

And he squeezed my knee under the tablecloth, put his knife and fork together and went off to put his bet in.

We ate roast beef with mashed potatoes and green beans, and I drank more wine, and then Tommy strutted self-importantly down to watch his horse being saddled up, accompanied by his wife and a few others. I stayed where I was, not wanting to risk the heady atmosphere that was building up getting to me and sending me scurrying over to bet everything that remained in my bank account on a horse.

But when Martin appeared by my side again and said, 'They're off! Come and watch,' I couldn't help but follow him.

There was number nine, Surfer Chick, a rangy chestnut, her jockey in black and white, coming easily up to the first fence and sailing over, gaining a good length in the process. The sense of mounting excitement, the thrill of watching the beautiful animals doing what they'd been bred and trained for, even the smell of the wet, crushed grass being churned into mud under the galloping hooves, was just the same as it had been when Dad used to take Perdita and me with him to the races, before Mum refused to let us go any more.

I only hoped that the sick feeling of disappointment and regret wouldn't be the same, too.

It wasn't. Number nine did her thing, winning comfortably with Tommy's horse just scraping into third and the favourite nowhere.

Martin was elated. 'We've got a prodigy here, chaps! I won two grand! Come on, Tansy, give us your tips for the rest of the afternoon.'

I sat back down at the table and drank more wine and studied the racecard some more. Suddenly, I was having fun. The women had drifted off again and were discussing which Harley Street surgeons did the best anti-ageing treatments while they drank their coffee, but I didn't feel left out any more, even though Renzo was deep in conversation out on the balcony, apparently oblivious to my new-found stardom. But it was okay: I was laughing, sparkling, being admired. If he looked over in my direction, that was what he'd see.

My tip for the next race came in second; for the one after, it won. Martin, Tommy and their friends tried to persuade me to accept a share of their winnings, but I refused. I didn't want their money, especially not money they'd come by like this. I knew I was getting lucky, that my knowledge was rudimentary at best, but for the moment I seemed to be having a charmed afternoon.

I was studying the runners for the final race, the numbers blurring slightly from all the wine I'd drunk, when Renzo came over.

'I'm sorry to deprive you of your tipster, gentlemen,' he said, 'but we must go. Thanks for the hospitality, Tommy.'

I stood up, startled, while he shook hands and clapped backs, and then said goodbye and thanked everyone too, and put on my coat.

It was almost dark now, and a thin drizzle was falling as I hurried behind Renzo through the car park. He didn't slow down for me, even though I was unsteady on my high heels and he had our only umbrella.

When I got to the car, he'd opened the door for me but already got in himself, and started the engine. Before I'd fastened my seatbelt, he pulled away, tyres screaming on the wet tarmac.

'Is everything okay?' I asked. 'Thanks for today, I had a great time.'

But he said nothing, putting some Italian pop music playlist on the stereo and turning the volume up loud.

I hunched in my seat, knowing I'd annoyed him but not knowing why. I did know, though, that there was no point trying to talk to him about it now, not while he was driving, anyway. The rain was thundering on the windscreen, the wipers flailing against it, the car's fat tyres swishing great waves of water up around us. The lights on the motorway flashed by. I pressed my feet forward again, hard, but this time I let my eyes close, and quite soon, in spite of my fear, I fell asleep.

The squeal of tyres coming to a stop and the jerk of the seatbelt against my shoulder woke me. Blearily, I straightened up and looked around. We weren't in the white stucco-lined street where Renzo's flat was; we were in Hackney, outside my house.

'Get out,' Renzo said.

'But what…?'

'I don't want to talk about this now. I'll call you in the morning. And don't ever make me look a tit in front of work people again. Okay?'

I stumbled out of the car, rummaging for my keys as he pulled away with another scream of rubber. Besides the cold, the rain and my parched, sour-tasting mouth, I was conscious of one overwhelming thing: the fear that he wouldn't ring the next day like he'd said.

But it was okay. He did.

Chapter Twenty-Five

I stood in front of the mirror in my bedroom, as I'd done so many times before, getting ready. I applied primer, foundation and concealer. I highlighted and contoured and stroked blusher over my cheekbones. I dusted coral-coloured eyeshadow over my eyelids, then carefully drew liquid liner over the base of my lashes. I put on two coats of mascara and powdered and waxed my eyebrows. I considered a couple of false eyelashes, but my hands were shaking so much I knew that would end badly.

I plugged in my curling wand and, while I waited for it to heat, surveyed my wardrobe, pulling out one summer dress after another, looking at them and putting them back again. Nothing felt right. I didn't feel right. This wasn't how it was supposed to be.

So many times over the past months, I'd imagined what this meeting with Renzo would be like. I'd be at home and hear a knock on the door, and when I opened it he'd be standing there, his arms full of flowers and his eyes full of tears.

Or, as I'd hoped would happen back in February when I first started hanging out with Felicity and Pru, our eyes would meet across a crowded room. I'd be wearing something fabulous, my hair loose and glossy down my back, my nails perfectly manicured, which they never were in real life. He'd cross the floor towards me, our lips curving into identical smiles as we realised we were feeling exactly the same feels, and he would take me in his arms and lead me onto the dance floor to the sound of soaring violin music.

Or maybe our encounter would be more random. I'd be walking along a rain-slicked street somewhere at twilight, wearing knee-high boots, a cream trench coat and a beret to keep the drizzle off my hair. This version of events must have been heavily influenced by art-house French films, because when I pictured it I was always carrying a baguette in a paper bag (which I had to edit out of the picture, knowing the rain would make it go all soggy). I'd hear feet hurrying up behind me and Renzo would appear, putting up a huge red umbrella to shield us both, taking my arm and saying, 'I've been looking everywhere for you.'

But now it was happening, and it wasn't like any of the pictures I'd painted in my mind. It was Saturday evening, and we'd arranged to meet for a drink in a pub near Renzo's flat. Just an ordinary pub: the sort of place where tourists go when their feet are aching from walking and their arms are burning from carrying bags from John Lewis and Primark, and they need a bit of a sit-down while they work out how to get back to their hotel. I'd suggested it in desperation, when he'd called me to say he was back from his work trip, and was I free to meet up, because none of the flash places where we'd usually been together felt right.

I turned back to the mirror, remembering Felicity's words: *You're arm candy, Tans.*

That was what I'd wanted: to be a girlfriend Renzo could show off, a woman who was always perfectly dressed, perfectly made-up, with perfect hair and a perfect figure. However far I felt the reality of my appearance was from that ideal, it was what I'd aimed for. I'd wanted him to see that, and I hadn't cared if it wasn't the real me.

In fact, I'd actively tried to conceal the real me from him: the Tansy who worried about not being good enough, about being found out. The Tansy who paid for each and every one of our posh meals out not with money, but with punishing workouts in the gym next day and barely any food. The Tansy who'd decided that the only future that would work for her was to marry a rich man to escape the shameful poverty of her past and the grinding skintness of her present.

I turned away from the mirror again, and then I went to the bathroom, soaked two cotton pads in make-up remover and cleaned every scrap of the cosmetics I'd so painstakingly applied off my face. I unplugged my curling wand and tied my hair back into a ponytail. I put on an old yellow-and-white-striped T-shirt dress and battered white Converse.

And then, avoiding my reflection altogether, I went downstairs. I wasn't sure whether this was the real me, or whether the Tansy who'd spent three hours getting ready for a date was. Somewhere along the line, I realised, I'd lost her – or maybe I'd never found her in the first place.

But my navel-gazing musings were interrupted. Josh was in the kitchen, Freezer winding around his legs and mewing as he unpacked groceries from a reusable nylon carrier bag.

For the past couple of weeks, I'd done a pretty excellent job of avoiding him. I'd spent a lot of time in my bedroom, listening for his footsteps on the landing, waiting to hear the front door close before I emerged. When I came home from work or from Chelsea's mum's flat in the evening, I'd gone straight up to my room if I saw lights on downstairs.

'Going out?' he asked, unnecessarily.

I nodded. 'So you don't have to,' I said, a bit sarkily.

'I wasn't going to,' he replied. 'I do live here. For now, at least.'

I considered giving a *Do what you want, it's all the same to me* shrug and swishing out of the door. Then I realised how ridiculous it was to carry on like this. Josh and I had been friends. We'd been a lot more than friends, too, for that one night. And my duplicity and dishonesty had spoiled it. My desire for Renzo, and my hang-ups about my past, had made me treat him appallingly, and I regretted it more than I could say.

I tried, anyway. I said, 'You're not planning to move out, are you?'

'I've been thinking about it,' he said. 'This was only ever going to be a temporary thing, anyway, while I found my feet.'

'Please don't,' I blurted out. 'Not unless you want to, anyway. I mean, not on my account. Look, I behaved horribly, and I owe you an apology.'

He grinned, and for a second I saw the old Josh. 'I was going to say the same thing.'

I walked towards him, the wooden floor feeling a bit unsteady under my feet – or maybe it was my legs themselves. Josh was unwrapping a piece of steak and putting it on a plate, and Freezer's mews increased in intensity.

'You did nothing wrong. It was me. I...'

Josh shook his head. 'I overreacted.'

We looked at each other for a long moment. There was something between us still, an awkwardness that I supposed would always be there; an awareness of what had happened between us, that we could never make un-happen.

I said, 'I guess I'll see you later.'

'Sure. Going anywhere special? You look nice.'

My stomach lurched violently as I remembered where I was going. For the past few moments, I'd all but forgotten Renzo.

'Just into town. I'm meeting someone.'

'I see,' he said, and I knew that he did see.

*

Half an hour later, I was in the pub, a glass of white wine sweating on a coaster in front of me. I was trying not to gulp it too fast, which was hard because my mouth was as dry as if I'd been eating mattifying face powder. Every time the door opened, my heart hammered. But when at last I saw him, hesitating outside, his eyes glancing down at his phone and then up at the sign, doubtful that this could possibly be the right place, I felt a strange calm descend over me – a stillness, a sense that everything, after all, was going to be all right.

He saw me and opened the door, his face lighting up with one of his megawatt smiles.

'Renzo.'

'Tansy. Babe. It's good to see you.'

'It's good to see you, too.'

We stood and looked at each other as if we'd never get tired of it.

I said, 'Can I get you a—'

He said, 'I'll just go to the—'

And we both laughed, the awkwardness dissipating a bit. He went to the bar, came back with a bottle of Peroni and sat down opposite me.

For a few minutes, we talked about nothing much. I asked him how work was going and he said it was tough out there, the markets were so volatile. He asked me the same question and I shrugged and said things were the same as always, really. This wasn't strictly true – Barri and the Luxeforless management team had been closeted in a meeting room for most of the past week, rumours were flying about what was going on and there seemed to be a strangely tense, feverish atmosphere in the office, although I'd put that down to my own anxiety about seeing Renzo.

Then I said, 'I'm sorry things didn't work out with you and Felicity.'

'I'm not,' he replied. '*Sono cose che capitano*. These things happen. I mean, she's a lovely girl, but I knew for a long time that things weren't right. You know, when you're seeing someone and it just doesn't feel authentic? Maybe you don't. You're so genuine, Tansy, it's one of the things I always – anyway, it didn't feel like a real relationship, somehow. Does that make sense?'

I took a gulp of wine, hoping I wasn't blushing. *Genuine, me?* I prayed he would never find out that I'd been having a fake relationship all of my own.

Until it wasn't fake any more, niggled my mind.

'I guess so,' I said. 'Anyway, I'm sorry. I hope you're okay.'

'Never been better,' he said, although there were lines of tiredness around his eyes that suggested otherwise. 'What about you? How's it working out with Bruce, or whatever his name is?'

'Josh.' I ignored the implication that because he was from Australia, he must be called Bruce. 'Not so good. We're not together any more. It was never really a serious thing.'

Saying it out loud felt like a betrayal, whether of myself or of Josh I wasn't sure.

'Well,' Renzo said. 'So here we are.'

'Here we are,' I echoed, and we smiled at each other again.

Then Renzo's face went all serious and still again.

'I need to say a few things to you,' he said. 'Will you listen? Hear me out?'

I nodded.

'I know I don't deserve it. After how I treated you, I wasn't expecting you to agree to see me at all.'

As if, I thought. But I didn't say anything.

'You see, it came as a shock to me, what you told me. All the time we were seeing each other, I thought – I knew – you were different from the other girls I've been out with. You don't care about material stuff, or about money.'

I flinched, knowing exactly how wrong he was about that.

He carried on, 'You took me bowling on our second date, for God's sake. Do you remember that?'

I nodded silently. I remembered every detail of that evening – of course I did. How the muscles in Renzo's back had bunched and flexed as he sent the ball hurtling down the wooden lane; how, when it had veered off into the gutter, he'd turned to me, briefly furious, and then laughed. How he'd shouted encouragement when I got a strike, even though it meant I'd beaten him. How we'd eaten greasy burgers afterwards and I'd wiped a smear of ketchup off his chin with my finger.

'It was just a small thing, but it made me see what being with you could be like. You were so funny, so fresh, so natural.'

I sipped some more wine, finding it hard to meet his eyes. If only he knew how long I'd spent that evening perfecting the 'no make-up make-up' look, or that the ripped jeans I'd scrounged from the sample cupboard to wear retailed for four hundred pounds. If only he knew I'd had to flog them on eBay afterwards.

'And so when you told me... When you told me what you'd been doing, it was like you were talking about another person,' he went on. 'Someone cynical and cold. Someone who used men for money. And I'd never thought of you as being like that.'

Because I'm not like that, I wanted to protest. But then I remembered what it had been like, when I'd first started doing the work that had later come to feel so demeaning and, later, so frightening. In the beginning I'd felt a kind of triumph: *They're paying me to sit here and talk to them! They're paying me because they want to look at me! If I can make money being looked at, I must look okay. If I can make more, I must look* great!

It was only later that I'd come to realise that wasn't what it was about. Not at all. It wasn't about me, or even about what I looked like. It was about something different – some kind of weird power dynamic that I wasn't sure I fully understood yet. And some deep need of my own – a need for validation as much as for money – which I understood even less.

I remembered Travis, who'd become first a regular in my webcam room, then later frighteningly obsessed with me, and a knot of shame curled tighter inside me, reminding me that it had always been there. Almost always.

But I'd promised Renzo that I'd hear him out, and anyway, I had no words to articulate the thoughts that were whirling frenziedly through my head, so I just nodded again.

'Whenever I saw you, after that night – and it felt like I saw you all the fucking time – it hurt me so much,' he said. 'I felt like I'd lost something so precious to me. I missed you, Tansy.'

He reached his hand across the sticky varnished table and I hesitated for a second, then reached mine over to meet it.

'I missed you, too.'

'I was seeing Felicity, but I couldn't stop thinking about you.' He pressed his hand to his eyes. 'Was it the same for you with Br— with Josh?'

I shook my head, because of course it hadn't been the same at all. But I said, 'Kind of.'

He went on as if I hadn't spoken.

'At your birthday party, and even before, at that gig where I saw you, it was like you were the centre of everything. *Così bella*, so happy, so confident. You didn't need me. God, that hurt.'

Not as much as you calling me a whore hurt. The thought surprised me with its vicious intensity, but again I said nothing.

'I talked to your sister that night,' he said.

'What?' I couldn't help blurting out.

'Perdita. She's lovely, so like you. I asked about your family, what it was like growing up in Cornwall by the sea.'

The knot in my stomach twisted again, growing so tight I thought I might be sick. When the hell had Renzo and Perdita even spoken that night? It must have been when I was dancing with Josh, oblivious to everything else. I remembered the text she'd sent me the next day: *Oh my God, I was so pissed! Fear I made an utter tit of myself.* And how I'd replied, far later than I should have, assuring her that it was all fine, because by then I hadn't the headspace to think about anything except Josh and how cruelly and unfairly I'd treated him.

'What did she say?' I asked, dry-mouthed.

'She was a little bit drunk, bless her.' Renzo smiled. 'She said it was the first time she'd been away from her baby for so long, and she talked about him a lot, and his father. And she told me how you help, how you send money all the time to keep your mamma and papa's little ship afloat.'

Keeping a little ship afloat sounded a lot more wholesome than the reality. Maybe Perdita hadn't revealed too much about Dad and the chaos he'd reduced our family to. I waited, almost holding my breath, for what he would say next.

'It made me see you differently again. Made me think of my own sisters, especially the littlest one, Chiara, my favourite sister. What if she had to support my parents, and my older sisters and their kids? What would she have done? Not the same as you, I hope. But if she had, I would have forgiven her. And I forgive you. We can put this all behind us and move on, if you want.'

'Yes. That's exactly what I want.' With a surge of relief, I knew it was absolutely true.

His face broke into a dazzling smile. His teeth were perfect, white and even, and there was a deep dimple in his left cheek. The lines of tiredness seemed to smooth away from around his eyes, replaced with creases of laughter.

'*Fragolina*,' he said. 'You remember that night, when I told you I loved you? I really meant it.'

He couldn't possibly know just how clearly I remembered it. How I'd turned the memory over in my mind again and again, like a precious trinket that I'd take out of its tissue-paper wrapping and admire, turning it around in my hands until every contour, every colour, even its smell, was familiar, before carefully tucking it away again in its place.

I remembered it again now, but I remembered something new: I hadn't said I loved him, too. At the time, the only thing I'd been able to tell him was the secret I'd been hiding – and once that had been revealed, it was all over. And I remembered the words he said, the contempt on his face.

I said, 'Thank you for saying that. I think you did mean it. The problem is, I think you meant the other things you said, too.'

'Tansy! No, honestly, I—'

I held up my hand to stop him. My fingers were trembling slightly.

'I think you did. It's not your fault. Lots of people would feel the way you did – the way you do – about it. Hell, I even do. I'm fucking ashamed of myself, to be honest. And I think that if we were together, that would always be there between us. What I did, and what it makes you feel about me.'

The smile had vanished from his face. He looked shocked, almost angry. 'But you said you wanted—'

'To put what happened behind us, and move on,' I said. 'And that is what I want. To put it all behind me. You, our relationship, that night – all of it. I don't think you're a bad person, I just don't think we're right for each other.'

There was hurt in his eyes now, and wounded pride, and they expressed themselves just as I'd expected.

'You don't know a good thing when it's right in your face,' he spat. 'I can get another girl tomorrow, you know.'

'I know you can. And I hope you do. I hope you'll be happy. But I've been single for a long time, and I'm fine with it. I thought I needed a man, but I don't. If someone comes along, great – but if they don't, that's fine too. I need to leave now.'

I really did need to, I thought. If I hesitated for even a minute – if he touched me again – I feared I might weaken. If I stayed there for even another minute, looking into the eyes that had filled my dreams for so many months, I might forget what I'd come here to do, and the absolute rightness of the decision I'd made. So I finished my drink, put my glass carefully back down on the table so it didn't rattle at all, and I left. But, as the door closed behind me, it felt like it wasn't just Renzo I was leaving behind. It was a dream I'd cherished for almost a year, which had vanished now, like it had never been there at all. And it was a piece of myself that I realised I didn't regret turning my back on one bit.

Chapter Twenty-Six

At work, the sense of weird unease persisted into the next week. I received three emails from Kuan-Yu asking if the dress samples were okay. The first two I ignored – although I felt bad about it, it hadn't been me who'd ordered them in the first place, and he'd obviously sent them to me in error. If Barri had ordered them – and I was pretty sure it must have been him – he'd eventually get back to Kuan-Yu, and I'd have to discuss with Chelsea what the impact might be on her and her business – a conversation I wasn't looking forward to even slightly.

But, for now, Barri wasn't in the office. He'd been signed off work with a virus, Lisa told us. So, eventually, I replied to Kuan-Yu saying that the dresses were great, but we weren't ready to place the bulk order just yet, and would he mind bearing with me for another week or so.

Everyone seemed on edge. Felicity dropped a full cup of latte all over her keyboard when her phone rang. Lisa and the other managers spent lots of time in the meeting room with the door closed. Kris bit his nails so badly he had to go and get a full set of acrylics put on.

I heard back from the two companies who'd interviewed me. One was a polite 'We regret that on this occasion...' knock-back, and the other was an offer. It was a good offer, too – a few thousand pounds a year more than I earned at Luxeforless, a move from online into bricks-and-mortar retail and the chance to work with kids' clothes, which would be a new challenge.

But I didn't accept it. I dithered for a long time, and then replied thanking them very much and asking for a few days to consider. It was a risky move – they might well withdraw the offer, or, if they really liked me, they might come back proposing a higher salary, which would make my decision even harder.

The problem was, until I knew whether Chelsea's business was viable – until I knew whether a flood of mass-produced, knock-off versions of her designs was going to become available on Luxeforless – I didn't feel ready to commit to anything. Felicity refused to say anything more about the hints she'd dropped the previous week; every time I tried to quiz her about what was going on, she just pleaded with me to wait a few more days, and see.

'It'll all become clear, I promise,' she said with infuriating vagueness. At last, on Thursday, it did.

'Guys, could you all please come through to the boardroom.' Lisa collected a notebook and pen from her desk, and we all followed her obediently to the end of the office. Marketing, Design, Customer Services and Accounts were all in there already, crowded into the available seats, so we squeezed through to the back of the room and stood against the wall, and soon the digital team arrived and joined us.

Everyone was quiet, waiting for Barri to come in and break whatever news he had. Of course, rumours had been flying round the office, each more unlikely than the last. We'd been bought out by Net-a-Porter. Luxeforless was relocating to New York, and we'd all be out of work. Barri himself hadn't been off ill, but had undergone gender reassignment surgery and would be returning as Bernice.

When the door finally opened, for a second I thought that that last and most improbable theory might be true.

A woman came into the room, closed the door behind her and walked over to the wall-mounted screen, where she stood in silence for a moment.

That was all it took for me to realise that, of course, she wasn't Barri in a new, feminine incarnation. She was taller than he was, and older – probably in her mid-fifties. Her hair was dark, glossy and bouncy. Her skin was smooth and perfect. She was wearing a slim-cut optic-white trouser suit and pointed taupe stilettos.

'Holy shit, it's Catherine Zeta-Jones,' whispered one of the digital guys.

There was a burst of nervous giggles, and then an absolute hush fell again.

It was impossible to know if the woman had heard him, but her calm half-smile didn't waver.

'Good afternoon, ladies and gentlemen,' she said, glancing around the room. Then her eyes fell on Kris, who that day was wearing matte violet lipstick and a Pucci kaftan that showed off his long, unshaven legs, teamed with purple Doc Martens. 'Colleagues and, er, friends,' she added hastily. 'My name is Jessica Croft-Gallagher. Thank you for taking the time to be here today; I know you're all extremely busy.'

Felicity reached over and squeezed my hand. Hers was ice-cold and clammy, but I squeezed back anyway. I couldn't speak for her, but I felt like a school kid in assembly when the new head teacher has just walked in and is about to say that things are going to be shaken up around here, make no mistake.

'You may be aware that there have been changes afoot here at Luxeforless,' Jessica went on, her composure apparently recovered. 'In a high-growth business such at this, founders are always on the lookout for new opportunities to enhance their existing offering and expand into new areas. It's been my pleasure and my privilege to be part of the success of many such businesses, enabling their growth through venture capital funding.'

I knew what that was, thanks to Renzo, who'd once spent most of a bottle of Cristal champagne explaining to me the difference between VC – as he'd casually called it – private equity, angel investors, crowdfunding and something called an IPO. I was pretty sure I should know what that stood for, but right now I hadn't the foggiest.

In spite of myself, my mind wandered back to that night, how thrilled I had felt to be drinking champagne in an exclusive club with a man I was convinced was impossibly out of my league, yet appeared to be as keen on me as I was on him. Now, almost a year later, I knew I'd never see him again. I felt a pang of something almost like regret – not for Renzo, exactly, but for the person I'd been then, so convinced that her life was finally starting out on the path she felt she was destined for. Felicity must have noticed that my mind was wandering, because she elbowed me gently in the ribs, and I focused once again on Jessica, who had flicked a slide up onto the screen, showing a sleek orange and teal logo.

'Don't worry,' she said. 'This isn't going to be death by Power-Point. But by way of introduction, I wanted to give you a little insight into who I am and what I'm doing here. I founded Croft Partners fifteen years ago, with the aim of supporting entrepreneurs financially and through my own experience building brands in the fashion industry. I started out looking for businesses that were exciting, inspiring and ready to gear up to the next level.'

She touched the screen of her tablet and the slide changed, showing a range of logos. I was impressed – I'd heard of all of them, and many were household names.

'So, naturally,' she went on, smiling, 'when I came across Luxeforless and learned that Barri, its founder, was seeking investment to help the business grow, I pricked up my ears. The more I learned about this business, the more excited I became about its potential, its disruptive energy and the fantastic, talented team of people working here.'

Everyone in the room was listening carefully, but I could sense them relaxing slightly when they heard her describe us as fantastic and talented. At least that meant we weren't all about to be sacked. Hopefully, anyway.

'So, over the past few months, my team and I have been carrying out due diligence, and I was sufficiently impressed with what we found to make the decision to acquire a stake in the business.'

'Oh my God, it's like we were on *Dragons' Den* and we didn't even know!' someone said, and someone else said, 'Sssh!'

But Jessica laughed. 'Sadly, the process isn't nearly as exciting as *Dragons' Den*. But I'd like to talk about my vision for Luxeforless, and what Croft Partners envisages the next phase of the company's growth looking like.'

She flicked through a few more slides, talking about her vision. As she spoke, the atmosphere in the room changed again. There was a new air of excitement – a kind of happy optimism that I hadn't felt in the office for the longest time.

When she finished, everyone applauded – and I was pretty sure it wasn't just because there were no more slides to be sat through.

'Exciting stuff, I hope you'll all agree,' Jessica said. 'However, there is a problem. As I and my team worked through the process of analysing the business, we came across some areas of concern that I simply wasn't able to overlook.'

I glanced around the room again. Felicity was listening intently, her face guarded and still. One of the customer care women whispered something to her colleague, who shrugged and whispered back. Kris started gnawing on one of his lemon-yellow acrylic nails, then stopped himself and tried to put his hands in his pockets before realising his silk kaftan didn't have any.

'Serious issues,' Jessica went on. 'From questionable labour practices by some of this organisation's suppliers, to infringement of what I believe to be certain designers' intellectual property.'

'Chelsea!' I whispered to Felicity, and she nodded almost imperceptibly.

'But most concerning of all,' Jessica said, 'it became apparent to me that this organisation operates at an unacceptably low level of colleague motivation and morale. It has always been a maxim of mine that a Croft Partners business is a happy business. And within these four walls, I did not see a happy business.'

Shit, I thought. *She's changed her mind. She's not going to invest after all.* If this was the news for which Felicity had persuaded me to delay handing in my notice, I wasn't delaying it any longer. As soon as we were out of there, I was going to send an email accepting the job I'd been offered, and pray that they still wanted me.

'It's the nature of venture capital investment,' Jessica said, 'that founders have to accept a certain slackening of the reins, a sharing of responsibility. Over the years, we've worked with many start-up owners to develop a healthy management structure and bring an integrated leadership team on board. However, in this instance, I do not believe that will be possible.'

The silence in the room was total. Everyone seemed to be holding their breath, waiting for Jessica to say, 'And therefore, I'm out.'

'And therefore,' she said, 'I made our investment conditional upon the CEO of this organisation stepping down.'

All at the same time, everyone gasped. Sally did a discreet fist-pump. Lisa looked like she might be about to faint. One of the marketing women actually burst into tears of relief, and had to be ushered out to the ladies' by her line manager.

'I shall be taking over for an interim period,' Jessica carried on, unruffled, 'until a new leadership team is in place. And I hope that by the time it is, we will have eradicated the toxic culture that has prevailed here, which I firmly believe came from the very top of the organisation.

'Now, that's all from me. We have a delivery of champagne and cake arriving shortly, and I hope you'll come and say hello, and ask me any questions you may have. If we don't have the opportunity to talk this afternoon, I'll be arranging one-to-one chats with each and every one of you over the coming days. And remember, my door is always open.'

She placed a not-so-subtle emphasis on the word 'my'.

And with that, we all flooded out and a team of caterers flooded in and arranged bottles, glasses, piles of napkins and trays of food on the table. At first, everyone approached the cupcakes and canapés warily, as if Barri might leap out from behind the door and shout, 'Caught you! Moment on the lips, lifetime on the hips!'

But he didn't, and Jessica herself picked up a miniature burger and tucked in, wiping ketchup off her chin before it could drip down onto her immaculate white collar.

'Oh my God,' I said to Felicity, 'she's absolutely awesome. Don't you just love her?'

'I should bloody well hope I do,' Felicity said, her face alight with pride. 'She's my mum.'

*

It was a couple of hours before I left the office, tipsy after several glasses of fizz and stuffed full of food. I hadn't spoken to Jessica – I'd mostly been making Felicity fill me in on events from her perspective and, naturally, she hadn't wanted to look like a suck-up by joining the small, shifting crowd around her mother.

As Jessica worked the room, Felicity told me that her mum, when she was first considering investing in Luxeforless, had persuaded her to apply for Lucy's maternity cover, and do a bit of discreet digging into the organisation at the same time.

'I mean, Barri's got quite the reputation in the industry,' she said. 'Everyone knows he's not the easiest of people to work with. But this is fashion – it's full of divas, right? And the competition for jobs is so fierce, people will put up with all kinds of shit. I worked for a designer in Paris for a while who didn't even pay his stylists – they worked for free, and occasionally they'd get pieces from his collection, except they were all tiny size zeros, so no one could even eat so they'd fit into the clothes. Which was okay, in a way, because no one had any money to buy food even if they'd wanted to.'

She'd explained how, with a bit of persuasion from Jessica, she'd sneaked into Barri's office after hours and dug through his files, finding evidence that he had authorised the use of factories employing underage workers.

'And worse,' she said. 'You know those faux-fur-trimmed boots Kris ordered? It's not faux fur at all, it's real rabbit fur from China. Barri knew about it and ordered them anyway, because the real stuff is cheaper. I found all kinds of dodgy stuff.'

'And what about the dress designs he copied from Chelsea? Well, pretty much stole from her?'

'He emailed Kuan-Yu a link to her Instagram page,' Felicity explained, 'and basically said, "Make me these."' And Kuan-Yu did, obviously. I knew about it, but I couldn't tell you that the order was going to be cancelled, because that would have meant telling you Mum was buying into the business, and the other investors wanted everything kept absolutely secret until the deal was signed. And it almost wasn't – Barri didn't go without a fight.'

'I bet he didn't,' I said. 'But I suppose he's got loads of money now.'

'Loads,' she confirmed. 'But, to be fair, he did build the business up from nothing. It's only right that he should be compensated for that.'

'I suppose. But what will he do? There's nothing to stop him starting up again, is there?'

'Well, there kind of is.' Felicity talked for a bit about the restraint of trade clause in the final contract, which meant that Barri was legally prevented from launching another start-up in the same field for five years. It was something, I guessed. Maybe he'd take himself off to a Caribbean island and retire. Maybe he'd get a lucrative consultancy role somewhere. It was a shame he wouldn't live out his days in poverty and disgrace, but you couldn't have everything, I supposed.

At least I didn't have to work for him any more – none of us did. At least the threat to Chelsea's business was negated – unless she became successful enough that knock-offs of her designs were appearing all over the place, in which case she'd be so successful that it wouldn't really matter any more.

'We're off to the pub to carry on the party,' Kris said, when half past five came and people began picking up their bags and moving towards the lift. 'Coming?'

'For sure,' Felicity replied. 'Tansy?'

'Good plan, I'll just get my stuff, and…'

I picked up my bag, and was about to tuck my phone in it without bothering to check it – no one was likely to have tried to call me. But then it vibrated in my hand with an incoming call, and I saw that I'd missed three others, all from Adam.

Chapter Twenty-Seven

Ten minutes later, I was standing on a packed Tube, my head spinning not only from the champagne I'd drunk but from what Adam had said. Not that he'd been particularly clear about what was going on; Adam hardly ever sounded flustered, but he had then.

'Tansy, there's a problem. You need to leave work now.'

'What's the matter? Are you okay? Is it Freezer?'

'No! I mean, not as far as I know. He's fine. At least, he was when I left this morning.'

'So what…?' I was already hurrying towards the lift.

'It's Renzo. Tans, you need to get to his flat. Quick as you can.'

I stopped. I didn't want to go to Renzo's flat. I didn't want to see him again. My dream of being able to have him back had come true, only I'd said no to him and to our relationship, and I wanted to keep it that way.

'But, Adam, I—'

'Tansy, just go. Please?'

'But why? You can't just ask me to go and not say what's happening.'

'He called in sick this morning. He's got flu. Apparently he sounded awful.'

'So? I'm not a doctor. And if I was, I'd tell him to stay in bed, take paracetamol and drink plenty of fluids.'

'No, but Tansy,' Adam carried on, sounding almost frantic. 'He just rang me on my mobile. He sounded delirious. He was asking for you.'

'Adam! Come on. I don't want to see him. It's over between us. If he sounded so ill, why don't you phone for an ambulance?'

'Come on, Tans. The poor bloke. He said he needs you. Have you no compassion?'

I opened my mouth to say that if Renzo was that ill, he needed medical help and not compassion, and then remembered that my battery was on its last ten per cent. With Adam in this mood, there was no point trying to argue with him – he could go on for hours. And besides, what if Renzo really was ill, and maybe too weak to make another call? If he ended up in hospital or something, and it was my fault, I'd feel terrible.

Adam had no reason to exaggerate or invent a cry for help from Renzo. He didn't like him – he didn't want us to be together. He'd only gone along with all my elaborate schemes on sufferance; there was no way he'd want to manufacture some touching sickbed reunion. And he had sounded genuinely concerned. Even though he and Renzo weren't close, perhaps someone in HR had made the connection between Adam sharing a house with me, and me being Renzo's ex, and given Renzo Adam's mobile number because they were worried… and to do something so random, flying in the face of all I knew about data protection, they must have been very worried indeed.

So, reluctantly at first and then increasingly hastily as my mind conjured up horrible scenarios of Renzo passing out in the bath, or trying to get to A&E and not making it, I got the Tube the three stops from work to his flat.

It was only when I emerged from the station that I realised the long dry spell was over. The drought had broken and rain was coming down in sheets, soaking the pavement and rushing into the gutters. All around me, commuters and tourists, taken by surprise without umbrellas, like me, were dashing blindly through the deluge, holding newspapers or carrier bags over their heads in an unsuccessful attempt to stay dry.

But I didn't mind if I got soaked. I walked as quickly as I could, barely noticing that my shoes were squelching and my thin summer dress was sticking to me and had gone almost see-through. Mascara stung my eyes as the rain washed my make-up off, and my hair hung wringing wet down my back.

I was almost blinded by the water in my eyes, and almost deafened by the sound of it drumming on the pavement, when at last I arrived at the block of flats where Renzo lived, where I'd spent so many hours, believing that I'd found happiness at last.

I sheltered under the porch and took a deep breath before I pressed the buzzer for number thirty-one. I'd never had my own key – him giving me one was one of the things I'd longed for, one of the signs I hoped would mean our relationship was moving to the next level. But he'd never suggested it, and I'd never asked.

I waited for an answer, but there wasn't one. I buzzed again; still nothing.

Shit. What do I do now? I could call Adam again and tell him Renzo wasn't in – or if he was, he wouldn't or couldn't answer. I could wait for a neighbour to come and see if I could persuade

them to let me in. I could call the emergency services. I could…
But when I took my phone out of my bag, I saw the red battery
icon for just a second before it died.

This time, I swore out loud. There was nothing I could do – I
was completely helpless. I dithered for a second, then made up my
mind: I'd have to go back to the office, let myself in and then call
for help. I'd turned and was starting to hurry through the pelting
rain back towards the station, when I heard a familiar sound:
the roar of a car engine being revved to its powerful maximum.
Seconds later, Renzo's green Lamborghini swooshed past me, its
tyres sending up a wave of water that would have soaked me if I
wasn't already soaking.

I turned around again and started back towards the building, but
he was driving fast and I was well behind him. I wouldn't be able
to catch him up before he'd driven into the underground parking,
and from there I knew he would get the lift straight up to his flat.
I'd have to wait, and then buzz again.

But he didn't turn into the car park. He swung the car right
up to the entrance where I'd been waiting, sprang out, leaving the
engine running, hurried round and opened the passenger door.

Even in those few seconds, I noticed something. This wasn't a
man flattened by a bad case of flu. He was practically luminous
with health and vigour. He was laughing as the rain beat down on
his dark hair and dark-suited shoulders. He almost skipped around
the back of the car. He opened the door with a flourish and a grin.

And a tall, red-haired woman in a bright yellow summer dress
stepped out, kissed him briefly on the mouth and let herself into
the building with her key.

I stood there, staring, the rain forgotten. Renzo was fine. There was nothing the matter with him. He had a new girlfriend. Already. I'd process my feelings about that as soon as I was capable of processing any sensible thought, but I hadn't experienced any of the hollow sense of loss I'd felt when I learned he and Felicity were an item.

All I felt was relief – relief and confusion. How had Adam made such a massive mistake? Why had he told me to come here? What the hell was going on?

I'd got so used to the water pouring down over me that I jumped with alarm when it suddenly stopped, and then let out a little yelp of fright when a warm, dry hand touched my shoulder.

'Tansy? Are you okay?'

It was Josh. Josh, carrying a massive umbrella, its segments each a different colour of the rainbow. He was holding it over us both, and I noticed that he was quite dry.

'I'm fine. What the hell are you doing here?'

'Adam told me you'd be here. He told me I needed to get here and find you.'

'What?'

We looked at each other, both equally perplexed.

'Look, you're soaked. You must be freezing. Come on, I'll call an Uber and get us home.'

In the cab, I bewilderedly told Josh how Adam had sent me to Renzo's flat, claiming to be concerned about his health. Josh told me how Adam had sent him there on the pretext that I'd told him I was going to make one last-ditch attempt to persuade Renzo to take me back, and that he was already seeing someone else and it was bound to end in disaster.

And, for both of us at once, just as the car pulled up outside our house, everything clicked into place. We were both laughing helplessly as we let ourselves in.

'Go and get into some dry clothes,' Josh said. 'I don't think our resident Cupid is in right now, but when he gets back I'm going to tell him what I think about him pissing us around like that. In the meantime, I'll put the kettle on.'

When I came downstairs ten minutes later, he was sitting at the kitchen table, a pot of tea and a plate of flapjacks in front of him.

'I got these at the farmers' market,' he said. 'Dig in.'

Suddenly, the miniature burgers and smoked salmon blinis I'd eaten at the office seemed like a very long time ago. I had the beginnings of a headache from all the champagne, and a mug of hot tea and some biscuits sounded like an even better idea than getting into dry clothes had been.

I sat down, and Josh poured me some tea.

'I suppose I should explain,' I said. 'About me and Renzo, and what happened.'

'You don't have to,' Josh replied calmly. 'I already know. Adam told me.'

'Adam did?' I felt a flash of annoyance, then remembered the elaborate plan Adam had just concocted to try to reconcile me and Josh, and my anger melted away.

'Maybe he shouldn't have,' Josh said. 'But to be fair, he was trying to help. I was basically crying into my beer about how badly you'd treated me, and he felt bad because he'd been part of it, and he felt I was owed an explanation. So he told me what happened with you and Renzo, how you were in a fix financially because you'd been sending money to your folks, and what you'd done in order to be able to help them.'

'Oh.' I looked down into my mug, feeling the hot steam on my face, but there was no accompanying flush of embarrassment. If Josh was going to judge me and tell me he thought less of me, so be it. It wouldn't be anything I hadn't heard before.

But he didn't. He said, 'To be totally honest, I think Adam thought that if I understood, there was more of a chance of us getting together for real. But I guess that isn't going to happen, because I know how you feel about your ex.'

'But I don't feel that way about him any more,' I said. 'I met him for a drink and he said he wanted to try again, and I told him I didn't. Tonight just reinforced that. I was worried about him, I wanted to help if I could, but I didn't feel – you know. There are some things you just can't get past. I'd had a chance to think about them, and I realised… I realised I'd been making a massive mistake. Not just because of how he reacted when he found out about the…'

I stopped. Even though Josh knew, I found it hard to say. But I forced myself to carry on.

'When he found out I'd done webcam work. But other things, too. I think he doesn't like women very much. I don't think he'd ever have truly respected me, or treated me as his equal, or even really seen me as a person. And I'm worth more than that.'

'Yes, you are,' Josh said. 'I mean, everyone is, obviously. But you're amazing. You're worth a whole lot more than that.'

'Thank you.' I looked up now, and met his eyes. He was smiling, but only slightly, not the broad grin I was used to seeing, that was like the sun coming out.

'I just wanted you to know,' he said, 'you have nothing to be ashamed of. I don't know what exactly that kind of work involves – I'm not some sleaze who gets off on paying women to do stuff they wouldn't do of their own free will. But I know for sure that you did it because it's what you felt you needed to do at the time. It can't have been easy.'

I remembered how I'd felt that first night, sitting in my bedroom with the camera pointing at me, the three glasses of wine I'd had to down before I could bring myself to switch it on, the sick, churning shame I'd felt at the end of the night, mingled with dizzy relief that it was over, I'd made some money to send to Mum, and next time would surely be easier. Newsflash: it wasn't.

'It was fucking brave of you,' Josh went on. 'You've no need to feel embarrassed about a single thing.'

'Thanks,' I said. 'But I guess I won't be putting it on my LinkedIn profile just yet.'

Josh laughed, and the familiar smile was back.

'Friends?' he asked.

'Friends,' I agreed.

And I supposed that was as good as it was going to get.

Chapter Twenty-Eight

I slept horribly that night. Actually, I don't think I slept at all. I lay awake, too hot underneath my duvet but too cold if I moved it, feeling like the weight of the night was pressing down onto my eyes whether they were open or closed, every noise making me jump. I heard Adam come home, unusually late for him, and the murmur of his and Josh's voices before they both came upstairs and went into their rooms. Even later, I heard Luke open and close the neighbouring house's front door.

I heard the bloody birds starting up their cheery dawn chorus at half past three in the morning.

The day dragged horribly. The sense of giddy optimism in the office should have rubbed off on me, but it didn't. Felicity asked if I was okay, and when I told her I had a hangover from her mum's champagne, she tutted sympathetically and went out and bought me an Egg McMuffin and a full-fat Coke, which was so kind it almost made me cry. When Kris came back from lunch and gave me a pale pink Essie nail varnish he'd got as a gift-with-purchase at Boots, saying the colour didn't suit him, I actually did cry. And when Sally came into the ladies' as I was wiping my eyes and asked me what was wrong, I had to say I just had PMS. I should be feeling elated, I knew, that my job was safe and so was Chelsea's collection. But I wasn't. I was feeling a flat sense of anticlimax, that even though I didn't have to worry about those things any more, there was so much else in my life that wasn't going right. I might not need to worry about finding money to send to Mum any longer, but I did worry. I worried all the time about how she would manage, and whether she'd ever talk to me again. The goal of getting Renzo back, which had carried me through the past months, was gone now, and I could see how foolish it had been. The *thing*, whatever it had been, that I'd had with Josh was well and truly over before it had even properly begun, and I blamed myself for it.

I'd been single before – single for ages. And I didn't think it mattered. I could go on Tinder dates, I could see friends – and, after the outpouring of warmth I'd felt at my birthday party, I resolved to do that much more than I had. I could have fun. Life would go on.

So why did I feel so hollow and lost?

*

All in all, not the most productive day ever. At five thirty on the dot, I picked up my bag and left, praying that my motivation would return after a decent night's rest, but at the same time wondering if I'd ever sleep again.

The Tube – especially the Tube at rush hour in summer – isn't exactly the best place for thinking. Around me, people were determinedly staring at their phones, reading newspapers with their elbows pressed tight against their sides so as not to encroach on the space of the person next to them and get passive-aggressively tutted at, or gazing blankly into space, lost in whatever was playing on their headphones.

Everyone was carefully ignoring the man at the end of the carriage who was tunelessly warbling "Let It Go" from *Frozen*. I could feel the thoughts of my fellow commuters rippling through the carriage: *I don't know if you're drunk, or high, or just like singing, but please, please don't talk to me.*

Still, even in the pressure cooker of that train, I managed to think. In fact, I couldn't *not* think. I thought about the determination with which I'd pursued Renzo, the daft scheme I'd come up with to get him back. It hadn't worked – in the end, it was he who'd decided that I could have him if I wanted, but I hadn't any more.

I'd changed my mind. *I'd* changed – not much, but enough to know that he wasn't the answer for me. But what if I could take that determination, that willingness to pursue happiness, whatever it took, and use it in a way that really would make me happy?

When I got home, Josh was sitting out in the garden with a bottle of cold rosé. Freezer was perched up on the fence, where he had a view of both Josh and his owners, so he could hop down on whichever side looked more likely to provide treats.

Josh had kicked off his flip-flops and stretched out his long legs, resting his feet on the edge of the brick planter where once, Charlotte had told me, Maddy and Henry had started a herb garden. Now, it was choked with weeds, but maybe there would be herbs again there some day, or even roses.

'Mind if I join you?' I asked.

'Funnily enough,' Josh said, 'I brought two glasses out. Just, you know, in case.'

I stepped out and sat next to him on the wooden bench, which was faded to a silvery grey by years of sun and rain. He splashed pink wine into both our glasses.

'I really am sorry, you know,' I said, even though I'd said it before. 'Parading you around under Renzo's nose like that, and not telling you what I was up to. It was pretty shitty of me.'

'We all do shitty things.' Then, looking sideways at me, he added, 'Just, some of us grow out of doing them when we're, like, sixteen.'

'What? You mean, the school leavers' dance thing? I'm sorry I knocked you back. I was so insecure, and I thought everyone hated me and I...'

'And I told you, the morning after your party, that I'd asked you because I liked you,' he said. 'That was true, but it wasn't the whole truth.'

'Go on,' I said.

He sighed. 'School – you know what it's like, right? All those dumb petty hierarchies, and one minute people are best friends, or going out, even, and then the next they're not talking and slagging each other off. I hated that, but I couldn't help getting sucked in. I'd seen what the alternative was – when kids got cast out.'

'Like I did.'

'Well, yeah. And I liked you, but I could never let on, first because you were seeing Connor and then because you were... you know.'

'One of the untouchables.'

'Right. And I was pathetic and stupid and sixteen, too, and I just didn't have the guts to go against the grain and risk that happening to me. I had it so easy, you see. I was just kind of coasting along. But then I started looking at you more and more, and imagining what it would be like to tell them all to get stuffed, and have the courage to just go for it.'

'So you did.'

'No,' he looked down at his hands. They were kind of twitching in his lap, like he was strumming a guitar that wasn't there. 'I didn't. I didn't have the balls.'

'But you…'

'Not me,' he said. 'Kylie dared me to ask you. Her and Anoushka. I knew they were planning something, but I didn't know what. And I thought that if I did, and you said yes, I could somehow find a way to make it look like I was playing their game, but also protect you from whatever they were going to do, on the night. And find some way of emerging looking like an all-round hero.'

'And I didn't play along?'

'Nope. I don't blame you, of course. I caught a whole load of flak for it – for being turned down by you. But I deserved it.'

'I really wanted to say yes, you know,' I said. 'But that thing with the movie, and the text you sent me…'

'That text,' he said. 'You mentioned it before. I don't know what you're talking about. Honest. I know I behaved badly, but I never sent you any text. I didn't even have your number.'

'Then who…?'

I thought about it. I remembered Danielle holding out her phone to me, showing me the words I believed Josh had written, saying he fancied me. At the time, I'd been so desperate to believe it was true, I hadn't questioned it at all. And I hadn't questioned the other message, either, the cruel words I'd seen after waiting and waiting alone outside the Plaza cinema. *You really think I'd go out with the town bike? Haha – you're not just a slag, you're stupid, too.*

It was pretty obvious, now, how easily I'd been manipulated.

'It was them all along,' I said. 'It wasn't even your number, was it? I was so desperate for them – and you – to like me. It seems pretty pathetic, looking back.'

There was a brief pause, and then he said, 'You're not pathetic. Not now, and you weren't then.'

He reached over and put his arm around me, and I kind of snuggled into his shoulder.

It was only a hug – but at the same time, it wasn't. With his strong, warm arm wrapped tight around me, it felt like everything had stopped. Suddenly, I was safe, calm, able to just be without worrying about a single other thing. What had happened all those years before didn't matter any more.

It was like the woman had said on that mindfulness app about being in the moment. Except I found myself yearning for this particular moment to last forever – and it felt as if it could. I leaned my face against his chest, and I could hear his heart beating. I could smell the lovely scent of him: shower gel and deodorant and man, so different from Renzo's smell of expensive cologne. I could feel his breath ruffling my hair, steadily, in and out.

We looked at each other in the fading light. The dandelion clocks were all blown away, and the air smelled a bit of barbecues and a bit of rubbish, because it was bin collection the next day. There was a thin crescent moon just appearing over the chimneys of the house behind, and I could hear rap music playing loudly somewhere.

It wasn't the most romantic setting I can think of, but I guessed I had to work with what I had.

'Josh,' I said. 'Come to bed.'

He didn't hesitate. 'Your bed or mine?'

'Yours is bigger.'

'But your room's tidier.' In the end, though, we didn't make it past the sitting room sofa until much, much later that night.

Chapter Twenty-Nine

The Spice Goals might not have been the worst netball team in London, but we were pretty bad. On the fourth Tuesday night in September, we'd been trounced by the Net Benefits by twelve goals to three, and my outstanding contribution to the match had been scoring one of the opposition's goals for them.

But no one cared – we always came off the court laughing and congratulating each other, and I was relishing rediscovering the sport I'd loved as a child, making friends with my team-mates and even baking a cake when my name was pulled out of the hat to provide treats for Carla's birthday.

It had kind of crept up on me, the realisation that things had changed – not just in my life, but in me. I noticed it one evening, when Adam brought home a massive box of doughnuts that a supplier had sent to his work, which no one would touch because they all thought carbs were far worse for you than cocaine. I'd eaten one, and enjoyed it, and realised with surprise that afterwards I felt no guilt – and no compulsion to punish myself by hoovering the rest. So we regifted the remaining ones to Hannah, who said they went down a storm in the school staffroom.

I noticed it when I looked at myself in the mirror and didn't automatically turn sideways and hold my arm above my head to check that I could still see all of my ribs. Instead, I noticed that the heatwave had left a dusting of freckles on my nose and cheeks, which I kind of liked. Very on-trend, very Meghan Markle, I told my reflection approvingly.

I noticed it when I saw a pair of giant footprints in the film of dust that had built up on the bathroom scale, and realised that Josh had hopped on it to weigh himself more recently than I had. And when I was able to turn away from it, because I didn't need a number to feel okay about myself.

Part of it was the counsellor I'd been seeing, who specialised in eating disorders. Talking to her about my feelings in such raw detail was excruciating, but in a good way. It felt productive, somehow, like the enormous clear-out Jessica had made us do of the sample room, which had ended up in a sale that raised tens of thousands of pounds for charity.

Part of it was netball, and the twice-weekly runs I'd been doing with Josh. Realising what my body was capable of – that it could *do* stuff, rather than just look a certain way – was so thrilling I didn't care that I was even worse at running than I was at netball.

And part of it was Josh himself. Josh, and how cheerfully, easily happy he made me feel. How I could have sex with him without worrying that my breasts were too small or my thighs too big, because he just utterly adored every inch of me, as he kept saying until I got all shy and told him to shut up. How, for the first time in ages, I felt secure.

That night, as usual, everyone in the netball team was preparing to decamp to the pub for a commiseration drink, but this time I declined. Adam had texted earlier with exciting news – he'd been promoted, and was now Chief Technology Officer at Colton Capital, and he felt a few beers and a pizza at the Daily Grind were called for to mark the occasion. So I was heading straight home to shower and change before meeting him and Josh there.

The Daily Grind would be just the same as always, I knew – the stacks of vinyl records, the crowds of people chatting and drinking together, Luke smiling behind the bar and Yelena whisking around delivering orders and clearing tables.

But there was so much else that had changed.

Pru and Phil weren't together any more, which was sad news for poor Phil, who I liked, but meant that Pru had been featured in *Tatler* as one of London's fifty most eligible twenty-somethings, and had insisted on wearing one of Chelsea's dresses for the shoot. Chelsea's sales were going from strength to strength, and she was giving the Stitch Together ladies as much work as they could handle. Thanks to Luxeforless's new flexible working policy, now that Lucy was back from maternity leave she and I were job-sharing, and I was able to devote half my time to Chelsea's business. Chelsea had been nominated for a Young Designer of the Year award, and even if she didn't win, it was a massive coup for someone just starting out. Nathan, too, appeared to be a reformed character – not least because, Harriet had told me, he was absolutely smitten with Malia, a Syrian girl he'd met when he dropped off some fabric at Stitch Together. Luxeforless was on the hunt for a new lingerie buyer, because, as Felicity put it, 'I love Mummy to smithereens. But could I work for her? Could I fuck.' And she'd decamped back to New York to stay with her father for a bit while she worked out what to do next.

Josh and I were planning to visit her soon. It still felt weird saying it – 'Josh and I', 'me and Josh'. But we were a couple, an item, a team. When we FaceTimed Debbie to tell her, she said, 'I knew all along you two were made for each other!' and Josh and I rolled our eyes and said that if only she'd told us a decade earlier, she could have saved everyone a load of grief.

*

I was hurrying down our road, my mind on my shower and then hurrying back up again to the Daily Grind, when I heard footsteps pounding behind me.

'Tansy! Wait up!' It was Adam. 'There's been a change of plan. Josh and I are cooking. He packed me off to the supermarket to buy ingredients. There wasn't any crème fraîche so I got normal cream instead and I bet he's going to moan at me.'

'You're cooking? Why?'

'Unexpected guest.'

'Unexpected what? Who?' We hardly ever had guests – and never unexpected ones – and when we did, we catered for them with a single trip to the off-licence (and, in the interests of full disclosure, occasionally a second trip later in the evening to resupply).

'Wait and see,' Adam said.

'Adam! Tell me! Is it Charlotte? Charlotte and Xander?'

Adam shook his head mysteriously, and there was no point in trying to interrogate him further, because we'd arrived at our front door and he was fitting his key into the lock. The house was spotless – fortunately, Odeta had been and worked her magic that day – and I could see that Josh had lit candles and put them on the kitchen table. He gave an excited little wave when he saw me, and half stood up, then beckoned me over.

There was a woman sitting opposite him at the table, her back to me. At first all I noticed was her hair – it was a pixie crop, dyed bright pink with violet flashes.

Then she stood and turned to me, and of course I recognised her straight away.

'Mum! What's with the hair? You look amazing!'

'Hello, my love. Sorry to burst in on you like this. I thought I should come and see you in person rather than ringing up.'

'Why don't you two take the bottle and go through to the front room?' Josh filled a glass for me and handed it over, accidentally-on-purpose brushing the inside of my wrist with his fingertips.

I smiled gratefully at him – not only was he absolutely miraculous in bed, but he was turning out to be the hostess with the mostest, too.

Mum and I sat down on the sofa, babbling away non-stop. She told me how Perdita, Ryan and the children were doing – although I already knew, because Perdita, unlike Mum herself, hadn't been ignoring my calls and messages. I updated her on work, and on Josh, who she approvingly described as 'absolutely charming'.

And then, as I was filling up our glasses, she said, 'I suppose you're wondering why I've turned up here.'

'Of course not,' I lied. 'It's amazing to see you. Can you stay the night? Josh's room is free.'

And I caught myself blushing and doing a little squirm of embarrassed pleasure.

'That's very kind, but actually, I'll head off after dinner. They've booked us all into a hotel for the night.'

'What? Who's they? Who's us?'

'Oh, love, it's been too long since we had a proper catch-up! "They" is work, and "us" is a group of us who've been selected for fast-track management training. We're in London this week for a course.'

'Management training? But you…'

'I'm only fifty years old, missy,' she said, with a hint of spirit I hadn't heard in her voice for years. 'I could be working for another twenty, and I don't see why I should be stacking shelves when I could be making something of my life after all this time.'

'That's great, Mum.' But I didn't sound convinced – and I knew why. Mum had always insisted that her job at Tesco was just a temporary thing – just until Dad 'got back on his feet', as she put it, and her life resumed the path she'd intended it to have: him making artisan furniture, her painting and maybe eventually opening a little gallery by the seaside, where local artists could exhibit and sell their work.

But the temporary arrangement had dragged on now for almost fifteen years, and Mum's conviction that things would change soon, get back on course, had become less and less believable as time went by.

Tentatively, wary of reopening the wound I'd created the last time I saw her, I said, 'Does this mean Dad has…'

'He hasn't changed, Tansy.' She sighed. 'God knows if he ever will. But I can't let his problems take over my life any more. And I can't let myself get sucked into it any longer, either. I've been going to a group, not a formal thing, just a meeting for partners of problem gamblers. It's been a bit of an eye-opener. Enabling, that's what they call it – what I did for all those years. Well, I'm not doing it any more.'

She sighed again, but this time it sounded like a sigh of relief. I splashed more wine into our glasses and waited for her to carry on.

'I've left him,' she said. 'I've rented a flat on my own. It's only small, but it's lovely. It's close enough to Perdy and Ryan that I can still help out with the kids, and there's enough space and light in the front room for me to paint. Perdy's friend Marcus did my hair for me – he's only an apprentice, and he said he needed models, so I volunteered. People are so kind, if you let them be.'

'Mum.' I felt a massive lump in my throat, and swallowed it away. I should be feeling joy for her, embarking on this new chapter in her life, but all I could think of was the years she'd wasted.

'It was down to you, you know,' she said. 'Not the money, although that was part of it. I know how much you sacrificed to try and help out.'

I thought of Travis, and Renzo, and Barri, and I realised she didn't know, not really, and that I'd do everything in my power to make sure she never found out. 'It was nothing.'

She shook her head. 'It wasn't nothing. It was a lot. And I ought never to have accepted it from you. But I thought I was doing the right thing, keeping things afloat until he changed. Maybe now I'm not there, he'll find it in himself to stop. But if he doesn't, it won't be my problem any more. Or yours, or Perdy and Ryan's.'

'So are you…' I began. I wanted to ask, *Are you getting divorced?* Not that it ought to matter, not at my age, whether my parents were together or separated, or if everything was all formal, with lawyers and stuff involved. But I worried that Dad, and his debts, could come back and haunt Mum, destroying her new-found freedom.

'We're formalising everything,' she said with a sigh. 'It's all too legal and dull and complicated for words. But I'm in touch with a lovely solicitor who specialises in cases like mine – financial abuse, it's called, apparently. I had no idea it even had a name – and she's on the case. So you mustn't worry.'

We sat in silence for a minute. I could hear Josh and Adam in the kitchen, clattering pan lids and Josh saying, 'No, Freezer, get off the counter,' and Adam arguing that as it was a celebration, surely he could have just a tiny bit of ham.

The rich, savoury smell of mushrooms frying drifted through to us, and I heard my stomach rumble. Mum's did, too. I knew we'd enjoy the pasta the boys were making just as much as I'd enjoyed meals with Renzo that had cost hundreds of pounds – more, even, because it was made with love, by people I loved. I knew I'd share it as a whole person, not as a decorative prize to be paraded around, acceptable and desirable only as long as I had no skills or opinions of my own.

'I tried for so long to change him, you know,' Mum said, in a way that was both sad and matter-of-fact.

'I know. But you can't change other people. You can only change yourself.'

A Letter from Sophie

Thanks so much for reading *It's Not You, It's Him*. If you enjoyed it, and would like to stay up to date with all my latest releases, just sign up at the following link. Your email will never be shared and you can unsubscribe at any time.

www.bookouture.com/sophie-ranald

My story of writing *It's Not You, It's Him* is also the story of a little cat with a loud voice and a cross face.

In June 2018, when I'd just begun work on the novel, my partner Hopi and I went for one of our regular walks around the neighbourhood and came across an elderly cat, thin and dirty with matted fur, in a front garden. Neighbours told us that the cat had been living outside for some time, even during the snow earlier in the year.

Of course, once we knew this, we couldn't turn our backs, so we spoke to her owner and offered to help look after the cat. Twice every day, throughout that long, hot summer, we visited to give her food and water. We took her to the vet (a mission that took several attempts and a lot of patience and chicken). After the drought broke and we found the cat soaking wet, we bought a shelter for her to use.

All this meant that writing the book took a great deal longer than it should have done – and I'm quite sure is part of the reason why Freezer plays such a significant role in the story! But it was worth it, because eventually, just before Christmas, once her owner acknowledged that she wasn't able to cope with having a cat, we brought Hither home to live with us. Shortly afterwards, I finally submitted my book to my editor – meeting my deadline by the skin of my teeth – and, as I write this, Hither is snoozing on the duvet with her tummy full of chicken.

Writing – even when you're not devoting a couple of hours a day to cat-wrangling – can be an arduous process. And launching a novel isn't much easier: it's a bit like walking into a room full of thousands of strangers and having to ask each one, individually, if they'll be your friend. So it's absolutely amazing when my readers reach out to me, either on social media (where you can see pictures of Hither and Purrs!) or by leaving a review.

I respond to every message I receive, and I read every single review, even if they sometimes smart a bit!

A huge thank you for reading *It's Not You, It's Him.*

Love, Sophie

 @SophieRanald

 SophieRanald

 @SophieRanald

Acknowledgments

When I wrote my previous novel, *Sorry Not Sorry*, in which Tansy first appeared, I decided that being a buyer for an online fashion boutique was a sufficiently glamorous-sounding career for my beautiful – but minor – character to have. But over the course of the narrative, I became increasingly fascinated by Tansy and felt that she deserved to have her own story told. Oops – I was going to have to do some serious research to find out what being a fashion buyer actually involves!

Fortunately, my gorgeous and glamorous sister Juliet was on hand to help. Over the past ten years, Juliet's biannual work trips from Auckland have been an absolute highlight of every spring and autumn for me, even though they left her knackered from traipsing round high streets and shopping malls in Hong Kong, London, LA and Frankfurt. On a wonderful holiday in South Africa to celebrate my late father's ninetieth birthday, I was able to pick Juliet's brains about what she got up to in her job. With patience and generosity, she shared the low-down on budgets, forecasts, samples and suppliers, and I have shamelessly used her knowledge in *It's Not You, It's Him*. Thank you, my darling sister.

Huge thanks also – as always – go to everyone at The Soho Agency, who have represented me for the past seven years. Araminta Whitley, Alice Saunders, Niamh O'Grady and Marina De Pass have provided unstinting support and excellent advice throughout the first year of my journey as a published author. You're all amazing, and I am so grateful.

It's been a delight and a privilege to work with the brilliant team at Bookouture. My editor, Christina Demosthenous, is a total book-whisperer. When I submitted this manuscript to her, I was deep in the Fear, thinking that it was all wrong and would never be right. But Christina's absolutely rigorous attention to every detail of plot, character and structure turned *It's Not You, It's Him* into a novel I'm hugely proud of – and her passion, energy and humour make her enormous fun to work with. Thank you, Christina, you're ace!

Also at Bookouture, the wonderful Peta Nightingale, who's been involved in my writing career right from the beginning, has provided support, encouragement and advice. Alex Holmes keeps everything running like a well-oiled machine during the production process, while Alex Crow's marketing genius made *Sorry Not Sorry* succeed beyond my wildest dreams. And the utterly lovely Noelle Holten is not only a cheerleader and a shoulder to cry on for the authors she looks after, but a seriously tough cookie, too. Huge thanks to you all.

At home, my darling Hopi and our precious Purrs and Hither have kept me going with cuddles, laughs and afternoon naps. I love you all, and I couldn't have done it without you. Just a bit less hissing, please, cats.

Made in United States
North Haven, CT
08 July 2022